TERMINUS

ADAM BAKER

HODDER &
STOUGHTON

First published in Great Britain in 2013 by Hodder & Stoughton
An Hachette UK company

A CIP catalogue record for this title is
available from the British Library.

Trade Paperback ISBN 978 1 444 75585 5
Ebook ISBN 978 1 444 75586 2

Typeset in Plantin Light by Palimpsest Book Production Limited,
Falkirk, Stirlingshire
Printed and bound by Clays Ltd, St Ives plc

Hodder & Stoughton policy is to use papers that are natural,
renewable and recyclable products and made from wood
grown in sustainable forests. The logging and manufacturing
processes are expected to conform to the environmental
regulations of the country of origin.

Hodder & Stoughton Ltd
338 Euston Road
London NW1 3BH

www.hodder.co.uk

For Oliver

I

Northrop Grumman
B2 bomber Fatal Beauty.

BASE OF OPERATION:
509th Bomb Wing, Whiteman AFB, Missouri.

FLIGHT CREW:
Mission Commander Maj. R.G. DeWinter
Pilot Capt. T. Weiss
Co-Pilot First Lt. O. Gary

PAYLOAD:
Five kiloton B84 Sandman variable yield nuclear
device.

DESIGNATED TARGET:
New York City.

CURRENT SPEED:
200 knots.

CURRENT ALTITUDE:
15,000 feet.

POSITION:
Holding pattern over Kinzua Dam,
Allegheny, Pennsylvania.
Weapon armed.
Waiting for executive authorisation to
commence bomb run.

2

A subway plant room deep beneath the streets of lower Manhattan.

A single, bare bulb furred with dust and webs.

Shadow and dereliction. Baroque electro-conductive iron-work. *Westinghouse*. Ampere/volt gauges. Ropes of cable sheathed in tar. Porcelain insulators, the milky glass bulbs of mercury-vapour rectifiers, a corroded rack of lead-acid batteries. Dormant, web-draped apparatus that hinted bygone years of high voltage crackle and dancing Tesla arcs.

Three prisoners cuffed to a water pipe. They each wore red NY Corrections state-issue.

'Hear that?' said Lupe. She nodded towards the plant room door. Rapid footsteps and shouting from the subway ticket hall outside. 'They're coming for me.'

'Maybe the army guys are pulling out. Listen. Something's got them spooked.'

Lupe shook her head.

'No. I'm next on the kill list. They're prepping the table, getting ready to dissect my ass.'

She gripped the pipe and tried to rip it from the wall.

'Forget it,' said Wade. 'It's anchored in concrete.'

'Pull together. Come on. All three of us.'

She turned to Sicknote. The man was slumped against the wall in a drugged stupor. She kicked him alert.

'Hey. Come on. We got to wrench this thing out the wall. Count of three, all right?'

They gripped the pipe.

'One. Two. Three.'

They strained. Knuckles clenched white. Tendons in their arms and necks stood taut, distorting knife scars and gang tatts.

'Told you,' panted Wade. 'It's not going to shift.'

Lupe hung her head.

'Go down defiant,' he said. 'Kick. Spit. Don't make it easy for them.'

The door handle turned. Light shafted into the room.

Moxon stood in the doorway. His guard uniform was mottled with sweat. He cradled a Remington pump.

He stepped into the room and closed the door.

'You here for me?' asked Lupe.

Moxon shook his head.

'What's going on out there?' asked Wade. 'Why all the shouting?'

'A presidential address on the emergency network. They're going to bomb New York. Last chanced to halt the contagion. Couple of hours from now this city will be an inferno. The team are heading down into the tunnels.'

'Oh my fucking God,' said Wade.

'So what about us?' asked Lupe. She gestured to the shotgun. 'Going to shoot us like rabid dogs, is that the plan?'

'I got orders. Sorry.'

'So how about it? You got what it takes to pull the trigger?'

He shook his head.

'There's been enough killing.'

He engaged the safety and hitched the gun strap over his shoulder. He unhooked keys from his belt. He released the cuffs.

The prisoners flexed their arms and massaged cuff-welts.

'Thanks, dude,' said Wade.

Moxon gave him a canvas satchel. An MRE food pack and a couple of bottles of water.

'You got to run for it. Sprint across the ticket hall, down the steps to the platform and into the tunnel. Do it quick before anyone has a chance to draw down and waste your sorry asses. Don't stop for anything or anyone. Element of surprise. That's all you've got.'

'All right.'

'Two hours until detonation. Get deep as you can and ride out the blast.'

'Thanks, man,' said Lupe. 'Thanks for giving us a chance.'

'Get going. The plane is already in the air. Run. Run as fast as you can.'

They sprinted through the tunnel darkness.

Distant shouts. Gunshots. Bullets blew craters in concrete.

They threw themselves against the wall, took shelter behind a buttress.

'They won't follow,' said Lupe. 'Too busy saving themselves.'

Wade examined the wall.

'This section of tunnel is pretty new, pretty strong. Maybe we'll be okay.'

'I'm not staying here,' said Lupe. 'I'm heading up top. I'm going to try and get across the bridge.'

'You're nuts. You've got less than two hours. You'll never make it.'

'I'll make it.'

'What about the streets? Infected. Hundreds of them.'

'I'm fast. They're slow.'

'Madness.'

'Come with me.'

'No.' He gestured to Sicknote sitting slumped and narcotised by the wall. 'I can't leave him.'

Lupe stood. She gripped Wade's hand.

'Take it easy, bro.'

'*Via con dios.*'

She turned and ran into deep tunnel darkness.

3

Manhattan.

Cold dawn light. No people, no traffic. Avenues lifeless and still.

Looted stores. Abandoned yellow cabs. Dollar bills blew across Fifth like autumn leaves.

The city-wide silence was broken by engine noise reflected and amplified by Midtown mega-structures. Thin jet-roar reverberated through glass canyons, a shriek like dragging nails.

A high-altitude contrail bisected a cloudless sky. A thin ribbon of vapour. Something big, something vulpine. A B2: delta silhouette, wide span, heavy airframe.

Times Square.

Empty streets. Dead neon.

Theatres chained shut, yellow quarantine tape strung across the doors.

A stack of bodies outside Foot Locker, each corpse wrapped in carpet and tied with string.

All Uptown routes blocked by sawhorse barriers.

THIS AREA IS UNDER QUARANTINE
FEMA 846-9279

A wrecked limo at the centre of the intersection. Fender bowed and roof flattened by a toppled light pole. A chauffeur lay dead in the street. He wore a gas mask. Rats tore flesh from his hands.

The distant turbine shriek echoed around the empty junction. Crows shocked into the air. Shrill caws and a flurry of beating wings.

Central Park.

Barren trees. Tiered penthouse balconies, deserted terraces and sky gardens.

A white, cylindrical object slowly drifted to earth, twirling like a sycamore seed. A bomb suspended beneath a canopy of silk.

Detonation flash. A sudden, terrible radiance. The park engulfed in stellar light. The buildings surrounding the park instantly shattered to stone chips.

The shockwave dilated at a thousand miles an hour. Midtown spires encompassed by a fast-expanding bubble of overpressure. A tornado of flame and debris swept down the avenues.

The Empire State collapsed in a cascade of rubble, Zeppelin docking tower liquefied by the furnace blast.

The Chrysler Building's deco pinnacle crushed like foil, limestone cladding pulverised to dust.

The pearlescent curtain walls of modern office buildings were ripped away in a blizzard of glittering shards. Girder frames wilted in supernova heat.

The firestorm washed down avenues like raging flood water, blowing out storefronts, flipping cars, melting asphalt to bubbling tar.

Then the inferno abruptly reversed and receded, snatching street debris and vehicles up into the conflagration as the nuclear heatcore rose and blossomed into a thunderous column of fire.

Liberty watched, impassive, as the roiling blast plume towered above the city, flame and hell-roar ringed by heat strata and an incandescent halo of ionised air.

4

Three days later.

The Empire Cinema: '*Brooklyn's Finest Viewing Experience!*'
A sign taped to door glass:

THIS BUILDING CLOSED UNTIL FURTHER NOTICE
QUARANTINE ORDER 846-9246

A derelict foyer lit by weak sunlight.

Torn posters.

Scattered popcorn.

Motes of dust drifted through weak sunbeams.

Lupe dived through the main door in an explosion of glass
and rain. She brought down an old guy in blue striped pyjamas
and a bathrobe. A rotted, skeletal thing, frame barely held
together by sinew and cartilage. His eyes were jet black. His
skin was threaded with metallic tumours.

They hit the floor and rolled.

Lupe sat on his chest. He snarled. He spat. Hands clawed
her face, tore at her coat.

She pulled a tin of beans from her coat pocket and pounded
his head. Skull-splintering blows. Brain spilt on blue carpet.

She caught her breath. She wiped sweat from her brow
with the back of her hand.

A yellow ribbon of quarantine tape had caught round her
neck like a scarf. She tore it free.

She ripped the hem of the pyjama jacket. She towelled rain from her hair. She wiped her hands. She cleaned blood and matted hair from the bean tin and put it back in her pocket.

She searched the bathrobe. Coins. Candy wrappers. A lighter.

Distant engine noise. A gruff rumble. Something big, something powerful heading down the street. Sound of an automobile shunted aside: deep revs, shattering glass and metal shriek.

Lupe tried to stand. She fell to the floor. Glass embedded in bare feet. The soles of each foot were studded with granules of safety glass. Heavy blood drips.

She clenched her teeth and prized chunks of glass from her skin. She tweezed each little sliver-blade with ragged fingernails and cast them aside. She tore pyjama fabric and bandaged each foot.

The engine got louder.

A cop siren whooped a single rise-and-fall.

Feedback whine. An amplified voice echoed from the street outside, reverberated down the row of smashed storefronts:

'This is the New York Police Department hailing any survivors. Please come out of your homes. We are here to help. We have food and water. We can provide you with shelter and medical assistance. This borough is no longer safe for human habitation. If you can hear me, if you are able to respond, please come out into the street so that we can convey you to safety.'

Engine noise getting closer.

'This is the New York Police Department. Leave your homes. This is your last chance to evacuate the exclusion zone. Please come out into the street.'

Lupe tried to get to her feet. Stabbing pain. She fell to her knees.

Engine noise reached a crescendo. She lay prone and

pulled the body of the old man on top of herself. She played dead.

Diesel roar.

An eight-ton armoured NYPD Emergency Service Vehicle slowly rolled past the cinema entrance. It mounted the sidewalk. The winch fender bulldozed a Lexus aside.

Lupe opened one eye. The vehicle slowly passed in front of the cinema doors. Daylight blocked by a wall of matt black ballistic steel.

The vehicle stopped and idled. A blue haze of exhaust fumes filled the atrium.

White light. She lay still and held her breath as the searchlight washed the foyer walls.

Scattered dollars.

A dead escalator.

A bloody palm print on the ticket booth glass.

The beam scanned the floor. Carpet dusted with scintillating granules of safety glass. Two bodies entwined.

Lupe tried to remain relaxed and impassive, tried not to screw her eyes tight shut as the harsh beam passed over her face.

Maybe they can tell I'm not infected. If I hear a door slam, if I hear boots on the ground, I'll have to get up, try to run.

The vehicle revved and moved on.

Lupe pushed the body aside. She crawled across the atrium carpet on her hands and knees.

She crawled behind the concession stand.

A corpse. A girl in an Empire Cinemas shirt. She was curled on the floor, surrounded by crushed popcorn buckets like she made a cardboard nest in which to die.

Lupe hauled herself through a doorway into a store room. Darkness. She sat with her back to the wall. She flicked the lighter and held up the flame.

Freezers. Steel food preparation counters. CO_2 cylinders and soda syrup. A big metal tub for popping corn.

She took the bean tin from her pocket and hammered it against the door frame, trying to split it open. She gave up and threw the dented tin aside.

A green first aid box and fire blanket on the wall above her head.

She picked up a mop and used the handle to prod the box from its hook. It fell in her lap. She cleaned her wounds with antiseptic wipes and dressed her feet.

Distant, ponderous boot steps. Someone pacing the sidewalk outside the cinema.

Lupe knelt on the mop and snapped the shaft. Muffled, splintering crack. She crawled out the door and crouched behind the concession stand, clutching the jagged spear.

A cop with a shotgun. SWAT body armour. Kevlar helmet, respirator. He wore a prairie coat with the collar turned up. Rainwater dripped from the barrel of his gun.

The cop approached the cinema entrance. He shone a flashlight inside. Lupe ducked behind the counter.

Faint rustle. Lupe turned. The dead girl curled behind the counter slowly came to life. She lifted her head. Half her face was a mess of metallic spines.

Lupe hurriedly backed away. She crawled into the darkness of the storeroom. The putrefied revenant followed.

The girl crouched in darkness, sniffed and looked around.

Lupe pushed the door closed. Weak light through an inch gap.

She kicked the creature in the head, then winced and hopped from the pain.

The infected girl rolled on her back, opened her mouth wide like she was about to deliver a shrill, animal howl. Lupe knelt on her chest and jammed the mop head in her mouth to stifle the scream. The girl thrashed her head side to side and chewed the wad of mop yarn jammed between her jaws. Lupe speared the infected creature's eye socket with the broken handle shaft, drove it deep into brain. The girl fell limp like someone hit an off switch.

Lupe peered through the door gap.

The cop had gone.

She opened the door. The street was empty. Sodden garbage. Rainwater tainted with ash.

She returned to the storeroom. She took the dead girl's shoes and laced them onto her own feet. She flapped open the fire blanket and wrapped it over her head like a silver shawl.

FIRE ESCAPE

She nudged the release bar with her hip and pushed the door ajar.

A narrow side street. Fading light. Burned out cars. Torrential rain.

Lupe edged into the street. A rat-stripped body hung from a yellow cab fifty yards away. A snub revolver clutched in a rotted hand.

She ran to the body. She paused. She circled the corpse, checked for signs of infection, any sign the dead thing would get up and attack.

Blinding light.

'Freeze. Show me your hands. Show me your fucking hands.'

Lupe shielded her eyes.

'Hands, or I'll shoot you in the face.'

Brief moment of decision. Snatch the pistol, or surrender.

She raised her hands and let the fire blanket fall to the ground.

'On your knees.'

She knelt in pooled rainwater.

An approaching flashlight. Two SWAT cops armed with shotguns.

'Don't fucking move.'

One of the SWAT guys stood over her. Contemptuous eyes behind the Lexan visor of an M40 respirator. He lifted Lupe's chin with the barrel of his gun and checked her out.

Mid-twenties, hair woven in tight cornrows. Gang tatts circled her neck. LOS DIABLOS, in gothic script. Two tears inked beneath her right eye made her look cartoon-sad, like a Pagliacci clown.

Knuckle tatts. Right hand: VIDA. Left hand: LOCA.

The cop pulled the lapel of her leather jacket aside. Stencil letters on the breast pocket of her red smock:

NEW YORK DEPARTMENT OF CORRECTIONS

'Gangbanger. Better take her to see the Chief.'

5

Lupe sat cuffed to a bench seat in the rear of the armoured car.

They drove through forest. They jolted down a rutted track. She could see trees through milky ballistic view slits. A second prisoner chained to the seat beside her. A scrawny guy in a looted suit. Slate grey silk. A couple of sizes too big. He looked like he had been dressed for his coffin.

'I'm David,' said the guy. 'Where did they pick you up?'

'Brooklyn.'

A guard sat on the opposite seat. SWAT body armour. Respirator. Remington. The name tape on his vest said GALLOWAY.

'Where are you taking us?' demanded David.

The guard didn't respond.

They continued down the forest track. Weak sunlight through bare branches.

They drove through a high chain-link gateway topped with razor wire. A rusted sign draped with creepers thick as jungle vine:

Ridgeway
Flying School

A neglected airfield. A wide airstrip slowly reclaimed by woodland. Civilian planes overwhelmed by thick brush and saplings.

A wrecked Huey gunship sat in tall grass. Rotor blades dripped rain. Paint flaked from rust-striped body panels. Nose art: red eyes and snarling teeth. *Hammer Strike*. A tree had grown through a hole in the cockpit floor. Branches protruded from vacant canopy windows.

They kept driving.

A Cessna lay in waist-high bracken, fuselage snapped in two like someone broke it over their knee.

The vehicle stopped.

The engine died.

'So what is this place?' asked David, craning to look out the windows. He could see hangars and a couple of fuel trucks.

The rear doors were pulled open. SWAT with assault rifles. Galloway flicked open a knife, leaned across the aisle and cut the plastic ties that bound Lupe and David to the bench.

'Get out.'

They jumped from the truck.

'Move.'

They walked a few paces.

'Stop. Hands on your heads.'

They stood beside a battered FDNY fire truck. One of the cops slung his rifle and unwound the hose.

'What is this shit?' asked Lupe.

'Decon shower,' said the cop. He threw open a nozzle valve and blasted her with a jet of ice water. She was thrown from her feet. She curled foetal, covered her face and waited for the deluge to stop.

The scavenged hulk of a Fairchild Provider. Faded tail code and insignia of 302 Tactical Airlift. The airframe had been stripped for parts. The Pratt & Whitney turboprops were long gone. No flaps, rudder or undercarriage. The alloy wings and tail torn like ragged sail fabric. NO WALK. PROP DANGER.

The fuselage was mottled with moss and lichen. The carcass sat in weeds, wing-tilt to the left like it was banking hard.

The cavernous cargo bay was ribbed with reinforcement spars. Frayed cable and hydraulic line hung from the roof. No seats.

Lupe sat cuffed to one of the spars. The rear loading ramp was down. Rain drummed on the skin of the plane, beat down grass and bracken.

David sat nearby, shackled to a floor stanchion. He shivered with cold.

'What do you think they will do with us?' he asked.

'Nothing good.'

She looked towards the front of the plane. The cockpit door was open. Galloway sat in the pilot's seat, smoking a cigarette. His feet rested on the flight controls. Reclaimed avionics: sheet metal studded with cookie-cutter holes where dials and fuel gauges used to sit.

David tried to saw the plastic tie against the stanchion.

'Forget it,' said Lupe. 'They make this shit out of special nylon. You need a knife or bolt cutters to slice them.'

'How many cops do you reckon they have here?'

Lupe nodded to the open loading ramp.

'Couple of trucks by the hangar. They're burning pallets inside the building, got themselves a campfire. Less than a hundred guys, at a guess. But they're well armed.'

'Reckon we could make it over the fence?'

'Razor wire would cut you to shit, but you could get through it if you wanted freedom bad enough.'

'Hey,' shouted David. 'Hey, you.'

Galloway turned in the pilot seat.

'What are you guys going to do with us?'

Galloway stood and stretched. He walked the length of the plane. Boots clanked aluminium floor planks. He stood over them. He leaned against a retaining spar and cradled his shotgun. He took a long drag on his cigarette and blew smoke.

'When do we get to speak to your boss?' asked David.

'The Chief ain't got time for a lowlife like you.'

'Bring us some food, at least. A blanket.'

Galloway gestured to a porthole in the wall of the plane. David and Lupe peered through dust-fogged Plexiglas. Silhouette against a stormcloud sky: three lynched bodies swinging from a tree.

Galloway blew the smouldering tip of his cigarette until the embers glowed like a hot coal.

'Don't worry. You'll get what's coming to you.'

Dawn. Ceaseless rain.

David sat sobbing. Lupe tried to chew through her cuffs.

Galloway walked up the aft loading ramp. He carried two lengths of rope. He threw the bundles on the floor. He ruffled rain from his hair and lit a cigarette.

'Why drag it out?' said Lupe. 'Kill us. Get it done.'

'I'm waiting on the results of your appeal.'

'You're kidding me.'

'There was a trial. Someone spoke in your favour. Someone spoke against. Everything was done right.'

'Who was the judge?'

'The Chief.'

'When do I meet this guy?'

'You don't.'

Galloway sat cross-legged on the floor, shotgun in his lap. Lupe watched him smoke.

'You're not SWAT, are you? These other guys. A real take-down crew. Taut. Focused. But you're just a slob in a vest. What did you do before this? Mall cop? Sit in a tollbooth all day?'

Galloway pulled up his sleeve. *Sine Metus. Brotherhood of the Wire.*

17

'Corrections?'

'That's right,' said Galloway. 'Don't expect mercy from me.'

'Which jail? Some place upriver, I bet. Sing Sing. Attica. You look like a sit-on-your-ass union guy.'

Galloway didn't reply.

'Bet you walked out on them, didn't you?' said Lupe. 'All those prisoners. You and your guard buddies. Left them to starve. Poor fuckers. Must have been hell in there. Worse than hell. Tier after tier, hammering the bars, screaming through their tray slots.'

Galloway lit a fresh smoke.

Footsteps. Someone thrashing through tall grass.

A second SWAT climbed the loading ramp into the plane. He handed Galloway two sheets of paper. Galloway read them and smiled.

He handed one of the sheets to David. David held rain-spattered paper with trembling hands and read the terse note.

```
The State of New York hereby provides notice that
the defendant DAVID BLAKE has been found guilty
of common assault, attempting to evade arrest
and multiple counts of theft, and that upon a
finding of guilt at the trial of these matters the
State of New York sentences DAVID BLAKE to death
on the grounds that the defendant will likely
commit further acts of criminality and remain a
continuing serious threat to society, pursuant to
Martial Code 143.
May God have mercy on his soul.
```

An unreadable signature at the foot of the note.

David crumpled the paper in his hand. He hung his head and sobbed.

Galloway handed Lupe a similar death notice. She scrunched it unread and threw it at his face.

18

'I've got pen and paper,' said Galloway. 'If you folks have any last words, I can take them down.'

David continued to sob. Lupe kicked his leg.

'Hey. Suck it up. Don't give him the satisfaction.'

Galloway took a last long drag on his cigarette and stubbed it beneath his boot.

'No final message for the world?'

'Fuck you all,' said Lupe.

6

They marched through tall grass to the hanging tree. Rain beat down. David stumbled and sobbed.

'Keep it together,' said Lupe. 'They want you to beg.'

They reached the tree.

'Stop,' ordered Galloway.

His SWAT buddy checked wrists, made sure they were securely bound.

Lupe looked up. Three corpses hung from a thick branch, necks broken, flesh pecked by crows.

'Pretty, aren't they?' smiled Galloway.

Lupe stared him out.

He wound a noose and threw the rope over a branch. He stood on a rusted chair and tied off. He tugged the rope, made sure it was secure.

He turned to David.

'Anything you want to say?'

David stared at his feet. He stifled sobs, tried to regain composure.

'Want a blindfold?'

No reply.

'All right. Get on the chair.'

David climbed up. Galloway looped the noose over David's head and tightened the coiled knot round his throat.

'Sure you've got nothing to say?'

He didn't reply.

'Hey,' said Lupe. 'David. Look at me. Don't look at him. Look at me.'

David looked at Lupe.

'It's all right,' she said. 'It's a shitty world. You're going to a better place.'

He nodded.

Galloway kicked the chair from under him.

Jerk. Neck-snap.

David hung limp. The rope creaked. He spun and swayed. Piss darkened his pants.

Galloway knotted a second noose. He turned to Lupe.

'Didn't think you were the religious type.'

She ignored him. She closed her eyes, tipped back her head and savoured the rain.

'Get on the chair.'

'Go to hell.'

He punched her in the gut with the butt of his shotgun. She doubled up and fell to her knees.

He hung the noose round her neck and pulled it taut. He threw the rope over a branch. He and the SWAT got ready to pull.

A voice echoed across the airfield. An indistinct shout.

They looked towards the hangar. A figure ran through bracken, waving his arms.

'Wait. Hold on. Just wait.'

7

They led Lupe to a hangar. An old Lockheed Jetstar, minus engine pods. A government plane. UNITED STATES OF AMERICA blurred by mildew and corrosion. Pooled sump-oil on the hangar floor.

Galloway nudged her up the steps. She ducked through the low doorway and entered the executive jet.

Eighties decor: white leather and chrome trim gave the place a coke-snorting, last-days-of-disco vibe.

'Release her hands.'

A small guy wearing the dress uniform and single collar star of a Deputy Chief of Police. He sat in one of the padded flight chairs, papers spread over the table in front of him.

'I said release her hands.'

Galloway reluctantly flicked open a knife and cut the tuff-tie binding her wrists. Lupe massaged deep skin welts.

'Take a seat.'

Lupe looked around. Galloway and his SWAT buddy flanked the door. An army guy and a woman in civilian clothes sat across the aisle from the Chief.

'Please. Sit down.'

Lupe took a seat opposite the Chief. The woman cracked a Coke and set it on the table in front of her.

Lupe massaged the rope burn at her throat.

'My name is Jefferson.' He pointed to the army guy. Fifties, pale blue eyes. 'This gentleman is Lieutenant Cloke. He's with the Institute of Infectious Diseases.' He pointed to the woman. Thirties, lean. 'And this is Captain Nariko. She was, until recent events, with the Fire Department.' He examined a mug shot. Lupe holding her inmate number, mouth twisted in a defiant sneer. 'You are Lucretia Guadalupe Villaseñor, am I right?'

'Where did you get that?'

Jefferson ignored the question.

'You were under observation at Bellevue's secure psychiatric facility, correct? You were under the care of Doctor Conrad Ekks?'

Lupe feigned boredom. She looked out the window. Cops stood in the corner of the hangar, warming their hands over an oil drum fire.

'Your life is in my hands, Ms Villaseñor.'

'Yeah. I've seen your handiwork.'

'I've got sixty men living by candlelight. Rationed food, rationed water. It's a miserable existence. We average two suicides a week. I try to keep the men busy because if they think further than sundown, if they think about all they've lost, they blow their brains out. There is a place here for honest folk, people willing to work, people willing to contribute. But I've got no time for junkies and gangbangers. Can't have them running around.'

Lupe sipped Coke.

'You fled along with Ekks and the Bellevue team when the hospital was overrun, am I right? You took refuge underground.'

'I was held prisoner,' said Lupe.

'At Fenwick Street. The disused subway station.'

'Yes.'

'There is reason to believe Doctor Ekks and his team may still be alive. We have been ordered by the continuity government based at NORAD to send a rescue party.'

Lupe sat back.

23

'Why are you so anxious to find this guy?'

'You need to understand the context of your time below ground. As soon as this disease took hold, medical teams across the country, across the world, started looking for a cure. Every virologist, haematologist, got to work trying to figure out this disease. Ekks and his team at Bellevue were studying the neurology of infection, trying to understand how the virus attacks the central nervous system.'

'We were lab rats,' said Lupe. 'Me and a bunch of other poor fucks. That's the only reason they kept us alive.'

'How did you escape?'

'We broke out. Me and two other guys. We fled into the tunnels. We split up. No idea what happened to them.'

'What was the status of the Bellevue Team when you left?'

Lupe shrugged.

'Scared. Fighting amongst themselves. Who gives a shit? They're dead. Nobody could survive the bomb.'

Jefferson glanced at Nariko; her cue to speak. She sat forwards.

'There was a transmission,' said Nariko. 'Just before detonation. A voice. Very weak.'

She took a digital recorder from her pocket. She pressed Play.

A mournful wind-howl of static and feedback. A faint ghost-voice carried on the ether.

'. . . *Mayday, mayday. Can anyone hear me, over? Hello? Is anyone out there? This is Bellevue Research Team broadcasting on emergency frequency one-two-one point five megahertz. We have a solution. We have a cure. If anyone can hear me, please respond . . .*'

'Is that him?' asked Jefferson. 'Ekks. You met the man. Is that him?'

'No,' said Lupe. 'That's Ivanek. A young guy. A radio operator.'

'You're sure?'

'Ekks has a southern accent. Very distinct.'

Nariko gestured to a dossier in her lap.

'The file says he is from Ukraine.'

'Not any more,' said Lupe. 'When he opens his mouth, it's pure Tennessee. Hypnotic son of a bitch.'

More static. Churning electromagnetic interference. The desperate voice battled fast-dying signal strength, shouted to be heard over a desolate static-storm.

'. . . *The virus. We have a solution. We have an antidote. Hello? Anyone? If you can hear me, if you can hear my voice, please respond . . .*'

Nariko shut off the recording.

'We tried to reply to their Mayday. We got no response.'

'Like I said. The bomb dropped. They're all dead.'

'A few months ago there were ten billion people on this planet, give or take. Now there are a handful of us left. If Ekks and his boys achieved some kind of breakthrough, some kind of antidote or vaccine to this virus, then we have to retrieve it. Yes, the Bellevue team were probably killed by the bomb. If they survived the blast, they are fatally irradiated. But they might live long enough to tell us what they know. And if not we can, at the very least, secure their research.'

'Only a fool would make the journey.'

'We have our orders,' said Jefferson.

'So what do you want from me?'

'Like I said. You were down there, in the tunnels, with Ekks and his team. The only surviving witness. You know the layout, the environment.'

'Are you coming along on this joyride?'

'Nariko and her rescue squad will escort you to Fenwick Street Station. My men will provide fire support.'

'And why should I help?'

'Freedom.'

'I get to join your happy band?'

'No. You're a liability. In fact, you make me want to puke. We use a rope because scum like you aren't worth a bullet. Only silver lining to this situation: we get to start the world over, wipe it clean, make it fit for decent folk. But help us, and we'll spare your life. We'll put you out the front gate. Give you a little food and water, send you on your way. My advice? Go out of state. If our paths cross again, there will be no second chance.'

'Do I have a choice?'

'No. No, you don't.'

8

Grey dawn light. Rain dripped through holes in the corrugated hangar roof and formed splash-pools on the floor.

Two Bell JetRangers. One brown, one blue. SWAT loaded weapons and ammo. Nariko and her crew loaded rescue gear.

Lieutenant Cloke flipped open a couple of equipment trunks. NBC gear and respirators.

They stepped into overboots and squirmed into canary yellow C-BURN radiological suits. Heavy fabric. Nylon ripstop over a layer of Demron gamma shield.

'Hold out your hands,' said Nariko. Lupe held out hands sheathed in heavy gauntlets. Nariko wrapped sealer tape round each wrist.

Lupe checked her out. 'Fire department, huh?' said Lupe.

'Yeah.'

'A captain.'

'Yeah.'

'You don't look the type.'

'Rescue Four. Extraction crew.'

'Three man team. Seems pretty light.'

'There used to be six of us.'

'This is messed up,' said Lupe. 'The whole thing.'

'We're packing plenty of firepower. You'll be okay.'

'Think I'm worried about prowlers? Least of my problems.'

'I'll make sure the Chief keeps his word. Help us find Ekks, and I'll get you out of here in one piece.'

Cloke taped a map of Manhattan to the hangar wall. He uncapped a Sharpie and drew concentric rings. Each pen squeak delineated pond ripples of destruction.

He clapped hands for attention and began the mission brief.

'Airburst over the refugee camp in Central Park. A five kiloton Sandman dropped from a B2 at dawn. Detonated at fifteen hundred feet.

The entire Red Cross tent city vaporised in the blink of an eye. The park itself is gone. Trees, topsoil and ornamental lakes seared down to bedrock. No one has surveyed the centre of the blast, no one has performed an overflight, but I guarantee Uptown Manhattan is now a crater a quarter of a mile wide throwing out lethal gamma radiation.

Surrounding buildings will have been crushed flat. MetLife, Citicorp, UN Secretariat. Everything in a two-mile radius of Central Park scythed by the blast wave. Nothing left but burning rubble.'

Cloke pointed at the tip of the island.

'Our objective: the subway terminus at Fenwick Street. The station has been mothballed for decades. It is situated beneath the old Federal Building; headquarters of the Federal Union Bank. Built in the nineteenth century, six storeys high, limestone, steel frame. The site is about five miles from the detonation point. The structure will have suffered major damage, almost certainly burned out, but I'm hopeful it will be sufficiently intact to allow us to access the sub-level station.'

'Where do we set down?' asked Nariko.

'The junction of Lafayette and Canal. Closer, if we can. The choppers won't be able to hang around. They will both be operating at the limits of their weight capacity. Full cabins and a sling load of equipment. They'll be flying on fumes by the time they get back to Ridgeway.'

'We'll be wading ankle-deep in fallout.'

'Exactly. We will have to get below ground as quick as we can.' He looked around. 'Any more questions?' None. 'All right. Wheels up in five.'

Nariko made a final inspection of Lupe's wrist seals. Galloway took the opportunity to slap steel cuffs in place and bind her hands.

'What the hell?'

'I see through you like an X-ray, bitch. You're planning to bolt on touchdown. Well, you can forget that shit. Put it from your mind. I'm going to be riding you for the duration.' He prodded her in the belly with the Remington. 'Give me any crap, I'll knee-cap your sorry ass and feed you to the prowlers. Itching to do it. So go ahead. Give me an excuse.'

9

Chopper roar. Rain lashed the cockpit glass. The pilot flew by instruments.

Lupe looked out the window.

The adjacent chopper suspended in grey nothing.

Fleeting glimpse of a highway, two hundred feet below. The Brooklyn-Queens Expressway jammed with incinerated cars.

She looked around the cabin.

Galloway sat beside her, shotgun laid across his lap, barrel pointing at her belly.

Nariko sat on the opposite bench seat, flanked by the remaining members of her FDNY rescue squad. Donahue: blonde, thirties. Tombes: heavyset, forties.

Lieutenant Cloke sat up front with the pilot.

Galloway unzipped the side pocket of his backpack and pulled out a Glock. He offered the pistol to Nariko. She shook her head.

'Take it,' he shouted. 'Seriously. Take it.'

She took the weapon. She turned it in her hand, inspected the safety switch and magazine eject.

'Headshot. Don't waste bullets on the torso.'

She nodded.

Galloway kept talking, bellowing over the rotor roar, anxious to demonstrate some hard-ass wisdom.

'Saw a couple of prowlers cut down by an M16. Took a full clip to the chest, kicked clean off their feet. Jumped right back up and kept coming, tripping over their own entrails. Relentless motherfuckers. They don't get tired, don't feel pain. Once they catch your scent, they'll chase you down, night and day. They never quit.'

Byrne, the pilot, turned in his seat.

'Check it out,' he shouted.

They craned to look out of the starboard window.

'Holy shit,' said Tombes.

A gargantuan ghost-shape glimpsed through a curtain of rain.

The Brooklyn Bridge. A cyclopean ruin. The central span collapsed and sunk to the silted darkness of the tidal strait. Six lanes of fissured asphalt terminated just beyond the granite caissons of the east-side cable tower. A stump of snarled girders and splintered stone jutting into space. Catenary suspension wires hung limp and swayed in the wind.

Lupe looked across the river. An ebb tide. Refuse heading for the bay. A steady stream of detritus that would, in time, form garbage archipelagos off the Florida shoreline.

The ruins of Manhattan were hidden behind a veil of rain.

Nariko put on a headset.

'Give me an open channel.'

The pilot adjusted radio frequency.

'This is Fire Department Rescue Four, can anyone hear me, over?'

No response.

'This is Rescue Four calling Manhattan on maritime one-two-one, anyone out there, over?'

No response.

'Rescue Four calling Manhattan, is anyone alive?'

She took off the headset.

Cloke turned in his seat.

'Time to mask up.'

★

Lower Manhattan.

They looked out the cabin window. Glimpses of the shattered metropolis beneath them. Rubble-clogged avenues. Flame-seared ruins. Exposed rooms and stairwells.

Byrne had a night vision monocular clipped to the rim of his helmet. Nariko tapped him on the shoulder.

'What can you see?'

'I can see the whole damned city.'

He gestured to a storage niche beneath Nariko's seat. She found night vision goggles. She powered up and held them to her visor.

Mile after mile of luminescent ruins.

She looked north to the detonation site. A beam of ionised radiation projecting into the night sky. A pale column of light.

'Jesus. It's beyond words.'

Galloway nudged Lupe with the shotgun.

'GPS is out. Find the Fed. Do your damned job.'

Nariko passed the night vision headset to Lupe.

Lupe looked out the side window and scanned the ruins.

Wrecked automobiles. Bomb-shattered office buildings.

'Wall Street, right? Head for the Broadway intersection, then head north towards City Hall.'

'Yeah?'

'The Fed is on east Liberty.'

Lupe adjusted magnification. Streets lit ghost-green by UV. Grotesque, shambling figures turned and looked towards the sky.

'Prowlers,' she said. 'They can hear us. They can hear the chopper.'

'Hoped radiation would have sterilised the whole damn island,' said Nariko.

'They're in bad shape, as far as I can tell. But alive.'

Lupe lowered the night vision goggles and sat back. She glanced round the cabin. She suddenly tore her mask off with cuffed hands.

'Watch it,' she yelled, pointing out the starboard window. 'Watch out.'

The two helicopters were drifting together.

The pilot wrenched the joystick. Too late. Rotor strike. A blade struck the canopy. The cockpit window shattered. The cabin filled with typhoon wind and broken glass.

The chopper banked hard left. The pilot fought to keep control.

Lupe fought G-force and pulled the mask back over her head.

The chopper levelled out.

Nariko grabbed Byrne by the shoulder and shouted to be heard over wind roar and motor howl.

'Are we going down?'

He checked instrumentation. Green lights.

'We're still Go.'

'Get us to the drop site.'

'Where's the other chopper?' shouted Lupe.

The pilot pointed down.

Lupe leaned forwards and looked down. She adjusted the ENVG focus.

A baleful glow in the mist below. A raging fuel fire.

'Can we get close?' demanded Nariko. 'Ditch our gear, bring them aboard?'

'The street is too tight,' said Lupe. 'Nowhere to land.'

A couple of crew pulled themselves from the burning wreckage. Shuffling figures converged from doorways and alleys. The crew were quickly overwhelmed and torn apart.

'Survivors?' asked Nariko.

'No. None.'

'You're sure?'

'Yeah, I'm sure.'

'Then guide us in, dammit. Do your job. Find the damned Fed.'

IO

The storm-lashed roof of the Federal Building. Cracked bitumen. Pooled rainwater. Rotary air con vents. A shattered water tower.

Hurricane down-wash. The chopper nose light projected a shaft of brilliant white light through spray as the chopper began its descent.

The sling-load: rescue gear and trauma bags suspended in a rope net. Byrne tripped the hook release. The load dropped four feet and hit the roof, sending up a geyser plume of rainwater.

The chopper jinked left. Skids settled on the roof.

'Sure you want to do this?' shouted Byrne.

Nariko threw open the side-door and jumped clear. Donahue and Tombes followed her lead.

Lieutenant Cloke climbed from the co-pilot seat. He sprinted across the roof to the stairwell door.

Padlock and chain.

'Fetch bolt cutters.'

Galloway pulled Lupe from the chopper cabin. Her feet were bound by ankle shackles. She slid from the bench and fell to her knees on the roof surface.

Escalating rotor roar. The helicopter rose, banked, and was lost behind a curtain of rain. They watched the nose light head east and dwindle to nothing.

Dancing flashlights near the equipment sling. Nariko and her crew retrieved rescue gear.

Galloway pulled Lupe to her feet.

'Come on. Let's get under cover.'

A sixth floor hallway. Shadows and dereliction.

> ## ROOF
> ## No Unauthorised Access

Nariko kicked open the stairwell door. She dumped a heavy backpack on the floor.

Tombes and Donahue wrestled an equipment trunk down the stairs and set it down. They ran back up the stairs to fetch more gear.

Lupe descended the stairs. Tight ankle shackles forced her to bunny-hop each step. She reached the hall. Galloway kicked her legs. She dropped to her knees.

'Stay down. Don't move.'

'Could you see much from the roof?' asked Nariko.

'Fire to the south,' said Cloke. 'Miles of it. Must be the petrochemical terminal on Staten Island. The storage tanks, separators and fractioning towers. The entire installation up in flames. Probably burn for months.'

'We ought to call Ridgeway. Tell them we lost a chopper.'

'Byrne will check in, tell them what they need to know.'

'We just lost fire support. And if that second bird drops out the sky, we're marooned.'

'Nothing I can do about it,' said Cloke. He turned to Lupe. 'So how do we reach the subway station?'

'How should I know?' said Lupe. 'We went below ground at 23rd Street. We reached Fenwick by tunnel.'

Cloke surveyed the hallway. Elevator doors. He pushed his

flashlight through an inch gap and looked down. The brick shaft descended into deep darkness.

'There's an elevator. But no power.'

A door marked:

STAIRS

Cloke shouldered the door and leaned over the balustrade. He trained his flashlight. Jumbled rubble six flights below.

Nariko joined him.

'You got three flights of stairs. After that, thin air.'

'Let me see how far I can get.'

She pulled on a backpack and shouldered a coil of kernmantle rope.

'Watch yourself.'

She descended the stairs. Three flights of concrete steps and an iron balustrade. The steps led nowhere. The stairs ended abruptly. A black chasm. She leaned over the edge and shone her flashlight downwards into darkness. The lower prefabricated sections of stairwell had detached from the wall and lay in a jumble of rubble far below.

Nariko tested the balustrade railing beside her. Firm. Anchored.

She buckled a harness and clipped a carabiner to the balustrade. She walked to the edge of the chasm and rappelled into black nothing.

She passed numbered doors in the wall.

3 . . . 2 . . . 1 . . .

She switched on the flashlight hanging from her belt. The beam lit the pile of masonry beneath her.

She touched down, booted feet coming to rest on splintered concrete. She unclipped the harness.

She wiped condensation from the visor of her respirator. She blinked sweat from her eyes.

She scanned the walls of the wrecked shaft.

She unhooked her radio.

'I'm at the sub-level.'

'*Is there a route below ground?*'

'Hold on.'

A wood lintel. She crouched and pulled rubble aside. Top of a blocked doorway. She hauled chunks of concrete until she exposed a narrow cavity.

She shone her flashlight through the gap.

Darkness.

'I think I've found a way through.'

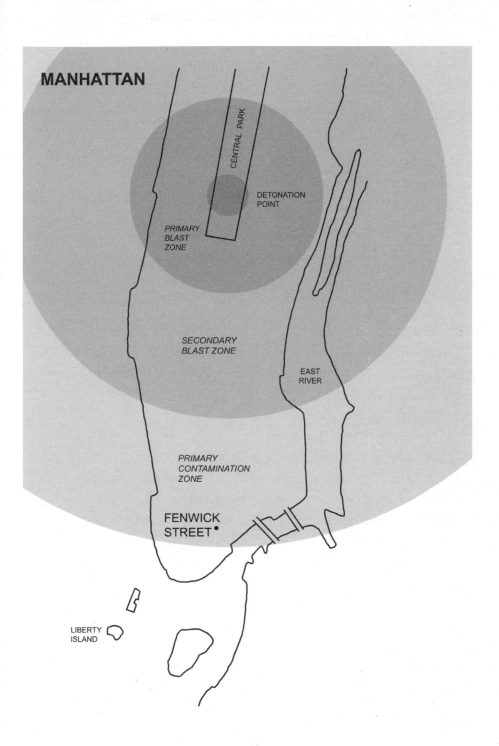

11

Nariko explored the darkness.

The beam of her flashlight washed across pillars and archways.

Silence and shadows.

An abandoned subway station built long before MetroCards, steel turnstiles and Helvetica signage. One of the derelict crypt-spaces of the city.

She crept through the sepulchral gloom of the ticket hall. Mausoleum hush. No sound but the grit-crunch of her boots, the rasp of her respirator and the rustling fabric of her NBC suit.

Her flashlight pierced the shadows.

A rusted Coke machine.

A smashed clock, hands hanging at half-six.

A phone booth. Screw holes and frayed cable where a trumpet earpiece would once have hung.

She examined a couple of panel ads. Faded paper curling from the station wall.

A cartoon bikini babe rode an eagle, coy wink like B17 nose art. '*Driving is like flying, with Burd piston rings!*'

A debonair guy reclined on a Riviera yacht. '*Camel Cigarettes – Pleasure Ahoy!*'

Nariko caressed the sunset with a gloved hand.

She wiped grime from wall tiles, revealed the mosaic letters of the station sign:

Fenwick Street

She crouched and examined a deep fissure at the foot of the wall. She probed split tiles, held a nugget of concrete in a gloved hand, and crumbled it to sand between her fingers. She traced the jagged crack with the beam of her flashlight, followed it up the wall and across the ceiling.

Radio crackle:

'*How's it looking, Captain?*' Cloke's voice echoed through the vaulted shadows, abrupt and metallic.

She fumbled for the yellow Motorola handset hanging from a belt loop.

'Structural damage. Strong chance of subsidence.' Her voice was muffled by the heavy respirator. 'Give me a minute. Let me check the place out.'

She unhitched her backpack and dumped it on the bench. She pulled the Glock from a side pocket, slapped a magazine into the butt and chambered a round.

She wiped condensation fog from the Lexan visor of her mask.

She walked deep into subterranean darkness, Maglite projecting a cone of brilliant white radiance ahead of her.

Tickets

An oak-panelled ticket kiosk. Smashed teller glass crackled underfoot. She leaned through the window. Scattered tokens. A cobwebbed bar-stool chair, seat leather cracked like dried mud. A brass till with ornate lever keys.

The deep recesses of the station hall. The beam of her flashlight ranged across bone-white tiles.

IRT Superintendent Office

She checked the Glock. She fumbled the safety and adjusted her grip.

She kicked open the door, the impact of her boot gunshot-loud in the oppressive chapel-hush of the deserted station.

The door swung wide. Assault entry. A swift sweep of the room, braced to fire.

A windowless office. A desk and a couple of toppled chairs. A wooden filing cabinet with no drawers. A gramophone next to a stack of 78s sheathed in paper sleeves.

She lowered the weapon.

She checked out the desk. She stroked a finger through dust. Rotary phone, inkwell, blotter. She turned the phone dial and watched it slowly grind back to zero.

She left the office and crossed the ticket hall.

Steps sloped downward.

A brass arrow:

To All Trains

Nariko cautiously descended the steps. Skin-crawl blackness. The long stairway lured her further from the surface world, took her further from help. She fought claustrophobia, the sudden, gut conviction that she was climbing into her own grave.

She reached the bottom of the stairs. Dark water lapped the foot of the steps. She stood at the water's edge and shone her flashlight into the cavernous tunnel space.

ALL PERSONS ARE FORBIDDEN
TO ENTER UPON OR CROSS THE TRACKS.

The track-trench and platform were submerged. Drifting detritus. A milky skim of rock dust. Street garbage swept down through the drains: soda bottles, chip bags, clamshell burger cartons, leaves.

The south entrance was blocked with crooked planks. The north tunnel mouth framed impenetrable darkness.

Something white in the water. Nariko trained the beam. A naked body, floating face down, hand locked round an empty whiskey bottle. Hard to tell gender. Bloated bruise-flesh marbled with livid veins.

She raised the pistol and fired a shot into the cadaver's flank. Crack. Puff of muzzle smoke. Meat-smack as the bullet punctured inert flesh.

She watched the corpse, waited for movement. A couple of air bubbles broke water. She steadied her aim and fired a second shot. The round blew out the back of the cadaver's cranium. The impact sent the carcass drifting in a slow and stately pirouette into deep shadow.

She unhooked her radio.

'The place is deserted. The subway tunnel is flooded. It was a wasted journey.'

'*No sign of Ekks?*'

'No sign of anyone.'

'*We've got to get below ground, Captain.*'

'The emergency stairs are choked with rubble. Give me two minutes. I'll crank up the elevator.'

43

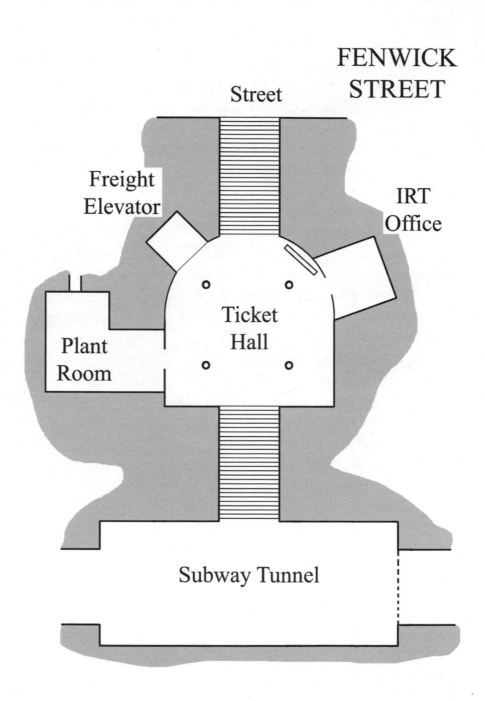

FENWICK
STREET

Street

Freight
Elevator

IRT
Office

Plant
Room

Ticket
Hall

Subway Tunnel

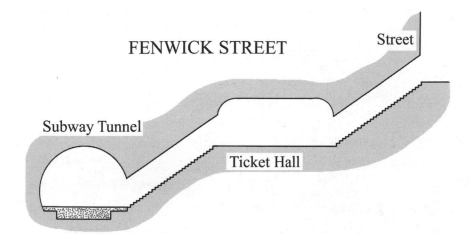

FENWICK STREET

Street

Subway Tunnel

Ticket Hall

12

Nariko struck a flare. It burned fierce red. She held it above her head and peered into the shifting shadows of the plant room.

She put the flare on a brick ledge, let it fizz and smoke.

She crouched next to a big traction motor bolted to the concrete floor. Dust-furred hoist gear. *Murphy Elevator Company, Louisville.* Cracked rubber belts and interlocking gears. A cable drum controlled counterweights in an adjacent shaft.

She unhitched her backpack. She set it on the floor, unbuckled the straps and pulled out a compact Schneider two-stroke generator. She wrenched the starter cord. The motor sputtered and whined like a lawnmower. Puff of exhaust fumes. She attached bulldog leads to corroded copper terminals and threw a web laced, wall-mounted knife switch. Pop and spark. 120 volts AC. Steady hum.

She returned to the ticket hall, struck a second flare and threw it down.

A cage elevator:

Freight
IRT Staff Only
No Passengers Allowed

Nariko unhooked her radio.
'Okay. You got power. Take her up.'

Clank and shudder as the elevator began to ascend.

Nariko peered upwards into the brick-lined shaft. She watched the wooden platform rise out of sight. She watched the counterweights descend on rails.

The filigree clock hand of the floor indicator gradually swung from *Sub* to *6*. Brief pause, then the elevator began its descent.

Cloke.

He stepped from the elevator. He looked around the flare-lit ticket hall. Flickering shadows. Porphyry columns. Mosaic tiles. Tannoy horns. A leaded glass light dome.

'Place is a tomb,' he said, voice muffled by his respirator. 'The old Federal Building. Walked past the place a bunch of times. No idea they had a derelict subway terminal hidden in the basement.'

Nariko helped drag a Peli trunk from the elevator. Lid stencil:

UNITED STATES ARMY
MEDICAL RESEARCH INSTITUTE
OF INFECTIOUS DISEASES

She slammed the gate and spoke into her radio.

'Clear. Sending her back up.'

'*Ten-four.*'

'Where's the street entrance?' asked Cloke.

'This way.'

A brass arrow pointed upwards to street level.

Exit

They climbed the steps. A cage gate sealed the entrance like a portcullis. Nariko shone her flashlight through the lattice grille.

Darkness. Merciless rain.

A garbage-strewn side street. Toppled dumpsters. An abandoned motorcycle on its side.

Flakes of ash drifted to earth: fallout blown from ledges, parapets and rooftops. Burned paper. Melted textile fibres. Carbonised people.

A warning notice spray-stencilled on brickwork next to a fire escape:

IT IS FORBIDDEN TO DUMP BODIES VIOLATORS WILL BE SUBJECT TO ARREST PURSUANT TO FEMA 373-8729

A lightning flash lit a broken, skeletal figure as it feebly dragged itself through rainwater. Ratty overcoat and a watch cap. Advanced infection: metallic sarcomas erupted from flesh.

A homeless guy. Probably didn't have the resources to flee the city when the outbreak began. Hid in a shitty basement somewhere, ate from cans and sucked a crack stem while loudspeaker trucks cruised street-to-street broadcasting martial law.

The creature hauled shattered, useless legs. Terrible blistered burns down the left side of its body. An empty eye socket wept pus. The remaining jet-black eye fixed on Nariko.

'Jesus,' said Nariko. 'That guy really caught the crispy.'

'Must have been out in the open when the bomb dropped,' said Cloke. 'Seared by the thermal flash. Classic gamma burn.'

'They were people once. The infected. Easy to forget.'

Nariko raised the pistol and took aim. The slow-dying

creature turned towards her and struggled to raise an arm. It reached towards the light.

'Don't waste your ammunition,' said Cloke. 'It stopped being human a long time ago. It's beyond your help.'

She lowered the Glock.

'How many prowlers are left, do you think?' she asked.

'Most died in the initial blast, I suppose. Those inside the detonation zone would have been vaporised in a millisecond. Those outside the heat-core would have been ripped apart by a hurricane of high velocity glass and metal. The rest, those that were far enough from the hypocentre to survive the initial explosion, are fatally irradiated. They won't last long. Accelerated cellular breakdown. Couple of weeks from now Manhattan will be truly lifeless. No birds, no grass. Nothing but scorched rubble.'

'When do you think New York will be safe for human habitation?'

'Some of the isotopes will decay over the next few months, but plenty of contaminants will seep into the soil, the water. This region will be lingering death for the next quarter of a million years.'

Cloke jerked the gate.

'I don't trust this latch. Do we have any chain?'

'I'll look around, see what I can find.'

'Help me curtain the entrance. We'll decontaminate as best we can.'

They lashed polythene sheet across the lattice gate, then returned to the ticket hall.

Cloke strapped a water tank to his back. A steam cleaner for blasting graffiti from brickwork. He hosed walls and pillars with 0.5% hypochlorite solution.

'Now you.'

Nariko stood cruciform, enveloped in a jet of broiling vapour.

'Do me.'

She shouldered the cleaner and scoured Cloke front and back. Condensed water pooled on the floor. She blasted run-off towards the platform steps.

Cloke flipped latches and opened the crate. Radiological equipment set in foam. He selected a Geiger counter. A yellow handset with an LCD screen. He tested for power. He took a reading.

'It's okay. You can take off your mask.'

Nariko pulled the respirator from her face. She massaged strap welts.

She unzipped, and stepped out of her C-BURN radiological suit. She kicked off heavy butyl overboots and stripped down to Fire Department fatigues. A blue T-shirt with an embroidered breast patch: a snarling rodentine face.

RESCUE 4
FDNY
TUNNEL RATS

She lifted the hem of the shirt and towelled sweat from her face.

Cloke shrugged off his suit.

'Stinks in here. Damp and rot.'

Nariko sniffed.

The acrid stink of melted synthetics and seared flesh filtered from the streets above.

'Burned plastic. The whole city.'

Cloke checked the Geiger unit. He held it towards the station entrance, watched numerals flicker.

'How bad?' asked Nariko.

'Hard to tell without proper dosimeters. Those minutes we spent outside were the worst. Fully exposed, transferring gear from the chopper to the roof. Got to be eighty, ninety roentgens, out in the open. Maybe more. How long were we up there? Six, seven minutes before we got under cover? The suits gave us some protection, but we still took a heavy hit. Not so bad down here. Concrete and bedrock protect us from the worst. Every hour probably the equivalent of a chest X-ray.'

'Twenty-four hours until the chopper picks us up.'

'We should be okay if we stay below ground.'

'*We're on our way down.*'

'Ten-four,' said Nariko.

The elevator hummed and rattled. The floor indicator counted down from *6* to *Sub*.

Lupe and Galloway slowly descended into view.

Nariko pulled back the rusted gate. Metal shriek.

Jab with the shotgun barrel.

'Move.'

Lupe shuffled out into the ticket hall. Her ankle shackle forced baby steps.

'Stand still, both of you,' said Cloke.

He hosed them head to toe.

'All right,' said Nariko. 'You can take off your masks.'

Galloway pulled back his rubber hood and peeled off his respirator.

Nariko loosened head harness straps and removed Lupe's mask.

'How you doing?' asked Nariko.

Lupe held out her hands.

'You folks going to uncuff me, or what? I got nowhere to run.'

Galloway unzipped his NBC suit. His armpits were

blotched dark with sweat. He unclipped cuff keys from a belt ring. He threw them to Nariko.

Nariko released Lupe's shackles. Galloway stood back, shotgun raised.

'Pull any shit, I'll blow your fucking legs off.'

Lupe stretched, slow and defiant. She looked around.

'Take off your gear,' said Galloway.

'Freezing in here.'

'Take it off.'

Lupe unzipped the heavy rubber suit and stepped out of the overboots.

'Hold out your hands.'

'What the fuck, dude?' protested Lupe.

'I said hold out your hands.'

Nariko re-cuffed Lupe's wrists. She looped a chain round a pillar and padlocked Lupe's ankle.

'Down,' said Galloway. He prodded her shoulder with the shotgun barrel. 'Down on the ground.'

Lupe sat cross-legged on the floor.

'There'll be no warning shot, all right? If you mess with me, I'll waste you.'

The freight platform juddered back into view. Donahue and Tombes. Quick decon drill. They stripped off their suits.

They both wore RESCUE 4 – TUNNEL RATS shirts.

They struck a fresh flare and unloaded the elevator. A pallet of holdalls and equipment trunks. Rescue gear, trauma bags, coils of polypropylene rope. They threw them skidding across the floor.

Lupe sat with her back to the pillar and watched them work.

'Anyone got a smoke?'

They ignored her.

'Give me a drink, at least.'

Nariko crouched beside Lupe. She held bottled water to her lips. Lupe swigged.

'So how about it?' asked Nariko, gesturing to the cavernous shadows of the ticket hall. 'Where is he? Where's Doctor Ekks?'

13

Radio crackle. Cloke's voice:

'*Anything?*'

A light-dome on the ceiling flickered and glowed weak orange. A cluster of sodium bulbs behind an opaque bowl of leaded glass.

'Yeah,' said Nariko. 'We've got light.'

She looked around the ticket hall. Palatial dereliction. Cracked tiles. Scuffed dirt. Broken glass. Arch spans draped with a delicate lacework of dust and webs. Ghosts of the jazz age. Plutocrats at the height of their reign. Astors, Morgans, Vanderbilts.

The superintendent's office.

Nariko shook open a five borough street map and smoothed it over the table.

She blew to warm her hands. Steam breath. She was wearing her Nomex turnout coat, black with hi-viz trim, collar raised against the cold.

'So where the hell is Ekks?' asked Nariko. 'He should be right here. We made brief contact just before the bomb dropped. There wasn't time to organise an airlift. So we told them to stay below ground, get as deep as they could. Ride out the blast and wait for the rescue party.'

'Doesn't make sense,' agreed Cloke. 'There's no way off the island.'

'How about the Battery Tunnel?' asked Nariko.

'Battery. Holland. Almost certainly ruptured and flooded.'

'The Marina?'

'Forget it. Anyone with a yacht or sports fisher took off months ago. Packed a couple of suitcases and sailed south, soon as the outbreak began. Must have looked like a big-ass regatta, all those rich fucks heading for the Bahamas.'

'What are their chances at street level?' asked Nariko.

'Nil,' said Cloke. 'Ekks and his team weren't radiologists, but any fool would know time above ground without an NBC suit would be fatal. The streets are dusted with fallout. Strontium, caesium, all kinds of nasty shit. A steady ash-fall, settling on the rubble. If anyone walked north up 5th or Broadway towards the epicentre of the blast, they would be dead in minutes.

Ekks and his boys would know, instinctively, their only shot at survival would be to stay below ground, conserve food and water, and hope Mayday calls summoned a rescue party.

He should be right here. He's got nowhere else to go.'

Lupe sat chained to the ticket hall pillar.

Galloway sprawled on the bench. He took a state correctional baseball cap from his pocket, flapped it open and set it on his head.

'Wearing your old uniform. Aim to show me who's boss, is that it?'

He didn't reply. He took a soft pack of Marlboros from his pocket. He broke the seal, tore foil and shook out a smoke.

Lupe craned and examined the brand burned into the wooden stock of the Remington twelve–gauge.

PROPERTY OF SS

'Sing Sing. Yeah. I figured you were up river. Gun tower, or did you work the galleries?'

Galloway ignored her. He took a matchbook from his breast pocket and scratched a flame.

'Like your moustache. Got that gay porn star thing going on.'

No response. He brushed ash from his uniform. Grey polyester. Pin holes for collar brass and a name badge. His stars and stripes shoulder patch was a fleck of brilliant primary colour among the shadows and dust of the ticket hall.

He wore a thick leather belt. Loops for chemical spray, radio and latex gloves. An empty holster that looked like it used to sheath a .38 revolver. A baton ring. A cuff pouch. Keys hung from a clip.

His boots were polished to a high gleam. He had rolled the short sleeves of his shirt to emphasise his biceps.

'Bet you're a big hit in the leather clubs. I can picture you, standing at the bar in your boots and chest harness, scoping the crowd. Picture it real easy.'

'Bitch, you got a big mouth.'

Galloway stood. He kicked her in the side. He aimed for a low rib. Lupe grunted and twisted in pain.

'You live with your mother, don't you?' said Lupe. 'Shitty, train-rattle apartment somewhere. Bet you've still got a box of G.I. Joes under the bed. Bet you line them up and have little battles when no one else is around.'

Galloway shook a fresh cigarette from the pack. He lit it, and tossed the burning match in Lupe's lap. She slapped out the flame with cuffed hands.

'Don't think you've quite grasped the new reality,' he said. 'No laws. Think about it. No Miranda, no recourse to appeal. Just you and me. Shit, I'm not even sure why we keep your tweaker ass alive. You're a liability. A waste of food. Better off without you. Start the world over. Burn it clean. Let decent folk run the place for a change. You better hope no one puts it to a vote. Plenty of guys back at Ridgeway happy to pull the trigger. They'd draw lots for the privilege.'

Nariko emerged from the office. She sat on the bench beside Galloway.

She thumbed through the dossier. A thick bundle of mismatched documents pinned by brass brads. A picture of Ekks on the inside cover. A smudged scan of his driver's license. An older guy. Fifties, sixties. Lean, silver hair. His face reduced to a pixel blur. Slavic bone structure. Thin lips. Eyes masked by shadow and printer grain.

She closed the dossier and threw it on the bench beside her.

'Hey. Galloway. Give me your cuffs.'

'What?'

'The spare set on your belt.'

'Why?'

'For the gate.'

Nariko held out her hand.

Galloway reluctantly popped a belt pouch and slapped steel cuffs in her palm.

'I got to talk to Lupe,' said Nariko. 'Give us five, all right?'

Galloway stared her down. Nariko met his gaze.

'Yeah,' said Lupe. 'Let the grown-ups talk.'

The guard reluctantly stubbed his smoke, crossed the ticket hall and crouched by a distant wall. He sipped bottled water.

'Maybe we better take it easy on the guy,' said Lupe. 'A correctional officer with nobody to correct. He's got nothing and no one.'

She picked Galloway's crushed cigarette from the floor. She examined the stub to see if it could be relit and smoked.

'Where's Ekks?' asked Nariko.

'Guess he took a walk.'

Nariko retuned her Motorola, checked for signal and held it up. The radio emitted a faint tocking sound, regular and metallic.

'Hear that? That's a live transmission. It's coming from somewhere nearby, right now. Their comms equipment isn't broadcasting a voice any more, but it's still emitting a weak VHF signal on maritime one-two-one. It's like someone is sat at the microphone with their finger on Transmit. The radio is down here, somewhere. It's still active, still powered up, still singing in the dark.'

'Who gives a shit?' said Lupe. 'Complete waste of time. Listen: Ekks might have been some big-shot brain surgeon, back in the day. He might have had his own parking space, set of golf clubs in the trunk, but I know a stone-cold psychopath when I see one. The look in his eye. I was down here for weeks. Me and three cons from Bellevue. We were guinea pigs. A tissue farm. Don't let anyone tell you different. He dissected one guy. Kept his brain in a jar. I was next on the list. I'd be dead by now if I hadn't escaped. Ekks was a sadist. He wasn't engaged in research. He was torturing the shit out of people because there was no one left alive to stop him, because actions no longer had consequences. End of the world, see. A serial killer's paradise. Cure? The guy was bullshitting you. Trying to stay alive, trying to get rescued. There is no antidote. This expedition is a bad joke.'

'I'm here to do a job. I'm going to see it through.'

'This place is killing us,' said Lupe. 'We're dying by degrees. Every minute we sit here shooting the shit a little more radiation seeps into our bones. Admit it. The mission is a bust. Send for the chopper and get the hell out of here.'

'No.'

'You guys volunteered for this kamikaze deal. Jumped at the chance to pull on your boots and run into the flames. But I wasn't given a choice. I was dragged here in chains. What gives you the right to throw my life away? Answer me that.'

'Do you understand what's at stake?' asked Nariko.

'Humanity reduced to a few pockets of survivors. Little outposts. Humans are an endangered species. We're on the edge of extinction, about to join the fossil record, our time on earth reduced to a geologic layer, a vein of compacted garbage. We're ready to bequeath the world to rats, roaches and scorpions. Get the picture? Maybe Ekks was full of shit. But research teams around the world studied this virus for months, with no sign of a vaccine or cure. If Ekks made progress, if he came close to understanding this fucking disease, then we have to roll the dice. We have to find his documents, his research, whatever the cost. It's our last chance.'

'And why should I give a shit?'

'Flesh and blood, aren't you?' said Nariko. 'Not exactly immune. You might be a hard-ass in the prison yard, but right now you are nothing on your own.'

'And when we are done here?'

'We'll take you back to Ridgeway. That was the deal.'

'And then what? Think your Chief will shake my hand and send me on my way? His guys will keep me as some kind of pet. A slave. Someone to mop the floors, empty out the latrine bucket. Tie me to a bed and set up some kind of fuck rota.'

'Not everyone is as sick as you. Some people try to do the right thing.'

'Unchain me. Let me go. I'll take my chances outside.'

'There's no way off this island. No bridges, no tunnels, no boats.'

'I'll swim, if that's what it takes.'

Nariko stood and began to walk away.

'I can help you find Ekks,' said Lupe.

'You know where he is?'

'I know exactly where he is.'

'You can take us to him?'

'I'll show you on a map. If you want to chase after the guy, it's up to you.'

'He's close by?'

'Yeah. He's real close.'

'Tell me where he is.'

Lupe held up her ankle chain.

'Uncuff me. I'll give you Ekks if you set me free.'

'Fuck you.'

Lupe shrugged. She leaned back, head against the pillar and closed her eyes.

'Come on,' demanded Nariko. She kicked Lupe's foot. 'Enough games. Where the hell is Ekks?'

Lupe smiled. A gold incisor.

'Can't say I know much about radiation. But you guys are on a clock. All of you. You've taken on a shitload of rads already. Few hours from now, you'll feel the first effects. Few hours after that, the sickness will take hold for real. The longer you stay, the worse it will get. How long before the damage becomes irreversible? How long before you shit yourself blind? Puke your entire digestive system over your shoes?'

'You'll get sick too.'

'Then I guess we've got ourselves a standoff.'

'Want me to talk to Galloway?' asked Nariko. 'Maybe I could arrange some time alone, just you and him. Pretty sure he could engineer a little attitude adjustment.'

Lupe smiled and shook her head.

'You won't do shit. Haven't got the cojones. Face it, girl. I'm holding all the cards.'

14

Cloke's watch beeped.

'Meds,' he shouted.

He distributed potassium iodide and anti-nausea capsules. They passed round a bottle of mineral water and knocked back pills.

He reset his watch and started a four-hour countdown.

Nariko unzipped a backpack and shook out the contents. Toiletries, fresh underwear, fresh T-shirt. Each member of the team had brought personal possessions, stuff they might need for the duration of the mission.

She took out a battered leather fire hat. She polished the captain's badge with her sleeve and set the helmet on her head.

'Nice hat,' said Cloke.

'Belonged to my stepdad.'

'They'll burn it, once we get back to Ridgeway. You know that, right? They'll have us strip naked for a decon shower. Probably shave our heads. And while we get hosed down, they'll scrub down the chopper and incinerate our clothes. Torch everything. Your watch, your earrings. They won't let you keep a thing.'

'I'm going to wear this hat into the shower. If they give me any shit, I'll break their arms.'

Cloke crossed the hall. He shouldered the fire exit door. Jammed.

He kicked until he forced a six-inch aperture, then shone

his flashlight into the stairway. Steps and door blocked by massive chunks of concrete.

'How the hell did you make it through?' he asked.

'Whole lot of squirming.'

'Got to be six, seven tons of debris.'

'This whole place is a death trap.'

Donahue climbed the steps to street level. She unzipped a backpack. She unfolded a tripod antenna and set it facing the curtained entrance. A mesh dish supported by a skeletal rod frame.

'Hey, babe.'

Tombes watched her work.

'Bitch to get a signal down here,' said Donahue. 'Schist bedrock capped with reinforced concrete. Smothers any transmission stone dead.'

'How did Ekks and his team get coverage?'

'I heard they used steel cable. Ran it out the gate into the alley. Tethered it to a fire escape, turned the ladders and balconies to a big antenna. Ingenious.'

'Maybe we should pull the same trick,' said Tombes.

'You want to go out there? Take a plutonium shower? Be my guest.'

Rain crackled against the opaque polythene sheet lashed across the entrance gate. They could hear ragged fingernails rake the plastic.

'Check it out,' said Tombes. 'It's got our scent. Trying to force its way inside. Tough motherfucker. Must have absorbed a dose strong enough to kill ten men. Just won't quit.'

'A few of these infected fucks might crawl from the rubble,' said Donahue, 'but they won't last long. They might be tough, but nothing can survive that level of radiation. Anything out there in the street will slowly dissolve in the toxic rain. Fallout will burn away their skin, strip muscle from bone. The bomb is doing its job. It might take a while, but a few weeks from now, there will be nothing left. A dead city. Jumbled bones lying in the street. Ribs. Skulls. Tufts of hair.'

'Fine by me.'

'I don't know how these things communicate,' said Donahue. 'I can't figure it out. They seem dumb as rocks. They don't talk. They don't gesture. Ever looked one in the eye? Nothing there. Not a glimmer of awareness. No thought, no memory. Maybe they're telepathic. Maybe they release some kind of pheromone. Soon as one of these bastards senses fresh meat, every infected shithead for miles around perks up and joins the hunt.'

Tombes inspected the gate, checked the bolts that anchored the iron frame to cement.

'Is this one of Galloway's handcuffs?'

'Cadmium steel. It'll hold.'

'Not sure about the frame. The ironwork is pretty corroded. If enough prowlers show up and try to force their way inside, it might give way. Better keep watch. We might need to cull a few, keep the numbers down.'

'Wish we had those SWAT guys.'

'No use wishing.'

Donahue spooled flex down the steps, across the tiled floor of the ticket hall, to the IRT office.

She sat on a metal folding chair and unboxed the radio. A military transmitter with a resin case. *US ARMY SIGNAL CORPS*. She flicked an on switch. Green light. Intermittent power-up hum. She turned a heavy black dial. She tapped glass. A signal-strength needle twitched and rose.

The stars and stripes lay bundled on the floor. Part of the old office decor, along with a framed Ten Commandments in gothic script: a reminder to any IRT employees summoned to the Super's office that his brass-buttoned, chest-puffing authority was backed by God and state.

Tombes picked up the pole. The flag had faded pale pink and lavender, like a winter sunset. He slapped webs from the braid fringe. Thick dust swirl. He straightened the brass staff over his knee and twisted it into the floor stand.

'They bombed Washington too, you know,' said Donahue. 'The Constitution. The Declaration. The First Lady and her damned Chihuahua. All that history up in smoke.'

Tombes shrugged.

'Politicians. No one will miss them. If we beat this disease, maybe the world can start over. A second chance. Maybe we can do it right.'

'Is that the daydream? A ranch? A nice little farmstead?'

'Always wanted to be a blacksmith. I'll pound horseshoes on an anvil.'

'What the hell do you know about horses?' asked Donahue. 'You're from Bensonhurst.'

'There'll be a book on a shelf, somewhere. Old knowledge, waiting to be found.'

Tombes pulled up a chair and rested his boots on the table. He turned his Zippo over in his muscled hand, knuckle-skin melted tight by an old burn. He clicked the lid, an instinctive ex-smoker fidget. Shamrock insignia. *No Irish need apply.* He gazed at the flame, then snapped the lid closed.

He shivered.

'Jesus. Freezing down here.' He huddled deeper into his turnout coat. 'Maybe we should break a couple of chairs, start a fire.'

'Never thought I'd be reduced to rubbing sticks together.'

'Where the hell did you get that trash?' he said, pointing at the radio. 'Dug it out of landfill? Bunch of GI junk. Looks like someone stormed the beaches at Normandy with that thing strapped to his back. Liberated fucking Paris.'

'Yeah. Well, every communication satellite is drifting dead in orbit, so cell phones aren't much use right now. Got to make do with scavenged crap. It's like someone stopped human history and hit rewind.'

'Better believe it. Fucked up roads, sour gasoline. Couple of years from now you'll be riding place to place with a six-shooter strapped to your hip.'

Donahue pulled on headphones and gripped a metal microphone big as a showerhead. She scanned wavebands.

'Extraction to Ridgeway, do you copy, over? Come in Ridgeway.'

Washes of interference rose and fell like breaking waves.

'Anything?' asked Tombes.

Donahue slid the headphones across the table. He held them to his ear.

'. . . *This is a test of the Emergency Broadcast System. The broadcasters of your area in voluntary cooperation with federal, state and local authorities have developed this system to keep you informed in the event of an emergency. If this had been an actual emergency the Attention Signal you just heard would have been followed by official information, news or instructions. This concludes the test of the Emergency Broadcast System . . .'*

'Plenty of channels still on air,' said Donahue. 'All of them automated.'

Tombes slid the headphones back across the table.

'People used to believe the final image a person saw before they died was retained in the eye. I guess America ends with a bunch of test signals and channel idents.'

She retuned.

'Ridgeway, this is extraction, do you copy, over?'

It took ten minutes to raise a reply.

'*Ridgeway to extraction, go ahead, over.*'

The Chief. Clipped intonation.

'*What's your status?*'

'We are in position. The site is secure.'

'*Have you located the Bellevue team?*'

65

'There's nothing down here, Chief. The station is empty. No sign of Ekks or his team. Not a trace. We're not sure how to proceed.'

'*Twenty men. A lab. A camp. All of it located at Fenwick Street Station. Multiple eyewitness reports. No ambiguity.*'

'They're gone, sir. They cleared out.'

'*What's left of the city?*'

'Pretty much every building sustained major structural damage. Secondary fires put a ton of fallout in the air. The place is a wasteland, utterly hostile to life. It's like someone lifted Manhattan Island and put it down on Venus. If Ekks and his boys headed outside, they're already dead.'

'*What's your current exposure?*'

'Tolerable, as long as we stay below ground, but we'll need immediate evac once we have completed our sweep.'

'*What about the prisoner? What does she say?*'

'She's holding back, sir.'

'*Make her talk. You have my authority to use any method you see fit to secure her cooperation, understand? Extreme measures. Ethics are a luxury. Do whatever is necessary. You are to locate Ekks. You are not to return without him.*'

'What's the situation at base, Chief?'

'*We have a crowd of infected massing at the fence. They showed up at first light. More every hour. There must have been a refugee camp somewhere in the forest. A steady stream stumbling out the treeline. Too many to shoot. I've set men to patrol the perimeter with searchlights, checking for a breach. We can hold out for a couple more days, but sooner or later they'll break through the wire and we'll be overwhelmed. It's hard to understand. We kept quiet, kept out of sight. But they sniffed us out. Maybe they heard the choppers.*'

'Damn.'

'*We may be forced to abandon Ridgeway. We're making urgent preparations to hit the road and find somewhere more remote.*'

'Understood.'

'And I'm worried about the fallout plume. Madness to stay this close to Manhattan. If the wind changes direction it could bring a blizzard of radioactive ash our way. We need to reach a safe distance, and ultimately head out of state.'

'Where do you have in mind, Chief?'

'I've checked the maps. There's a lodge in the Adirondacks, near Avalanche Lake. It's deep in the forest, easy to defend. A good staging base. Somewhere to regroup and figure out our next move. We'll patch up the remaining helicopter and send it out. They'll overfly the place, take a look around. Night, but that could work to our advantage. Infrared will let us know if anything is moving around in those woods. If the place seems inviting, we'll box our equipment. Airlift our gear and personnel in stages.'

'Well, don't forget about us, sir. You folks are our lifeline. If that chopper clips a pylon or runs out of gas, we're stranded. We've got no way off this damned rock.'

'The plan still holds. Stay below ground. Complete your mission. Exfil in twenty-two hours.'

Donahue shut off the radio and sat back.

'You caught all that?'

'Some,' said Tombes.

'They're sending the chopper upstate. They're scouting for a new base, trying to find somewhere more secure.'

'About time. We can't beat these bastards. Best to put some distance.'

'Just got to find Ekks.'

'And what if we don't?' said Tombes. 'Reckon they'll still come get us? Sounds like they've got a battle on their hands. What if they can't spare the manpower? The Chief might decide we aren't worth the time. Expendable assets. We're not shooters. We're no use in a combat situation. He might leave us to die.'

67

'He wouldn't abandon us.'

'Hope you're right,' said Tombes. 'Looks like we're stuck here for the duration. No chance of an early ride home. Shit. Should have brought a deck of cards.'

15

Nariko and Cloke descended the steps to the platform.

Nariko struck a flare and held it above her head. The cavernous rail tunnel was lit by red, sputtering flame light.

A mildewed sign pasted to the wall:

> No Smoking
> No Spitting
> Thank You

'The water is rising,' said Nariko. 'A couple of inches in the last hour.'

'Inevitable. The subway system lies beneath the water table. Constantly pumped to keep it dry. Millions of gallons every day. The moment the city lost power, it began to flood.'

Cloke crouched by the water's edge. He held his Geiger counter an inch from the surface. Warning beep. The LCD screen flashed a threshold alert.

'Jesus. Off the scale.' He powered down the handset. 'This stuff is a mix of groundwater bubbling from bedrock and run-off from the street. Fallout settled over the city and got washed into the drains. Rain tainted with radioactive ash, lethal isotopes cooked up in the blast. My equipment isn't military spec. It's from a power plant. It's built to measure minor leaks, fractional deviations from background. But these are the kind of heavy contaminants found near a ruptured reactor core. The counter isn't calibrated to measure this level of pollution.'

They listened to the hiss of the burning flare, the distant trickle of water and the whisper of the tunnels.

'Awful stench,' said Cloke.

Nariko pointed to the corpse floating in far shadows.

'Rot gas.'

She inspected the tunnel brickwork.

'When was this place abandoned?'

'Nineteen fifty-four,' said Cloke. 'The platform was too short to accommodate the new ten-car trains. They mothballed Fenwick when they built more capacity at Wall Street. Simply shut the station at the end of a working day. Waited until the last train left the platform, killed the lights, chained the doors. The place has been deserted ever since. Frozen in time.'

Nariko pictured trilbied businessmen waiting for a trolley car. Flannel suits, umbrellas, attaché cases, rolled copies of the *Times* and *Post*. America at the height of empire.

A deep, thunderous rumble. A groan of shifting masonry. The flood waters shivered and rippled. A trickle of dust from a fissure in the tunnel roof settled on the water, forming a white crust.

'What the hell was that?' murmured Nariko.

'A nearby building must have toppled,' said Cloke. 'You can bet every tower and tenement on the island took major damage during the blast.'

'As long as the Federal Bank doesn't come down on our heads,' said Nariko.

'Hard to judge. Six storeys. Heavy stone. Built to last. It was shielded by surrounding office towers. They took the brunt of the shockwave. Citigroup Plaza and the AmCo Building. All those glass curtain walls. They took the impact like an airbag. But the ground shock must have split the foundations, subtly thrown the centre of gravity. Slow subsidence. The building is starting to tilt. She won't last long.'

Cloke turned up the collar of his jacket. He blew his hands for warmth.

'So what do you know about Lupe?' he asked.

'Lucretia Guadalupe Villaseñor. Born in Honduras. Raised in the Bronx. She's done plenty of time, for sure.'

'The tattoos?'

'The stillness,' said Nariko. 'Prison zen. Watch her. The way she sits back and closes her eyes, puts herself into hibernation. She's spent a long time in solitary. Weeks locked in holding cells, punishment blocks, no window, no daylight. Nothing to do but work out, stare at cinder walls and count the minutes until the next meal gets pushed through the tray slot. She knows how to retreat into her head.'

'Think she's dangerous?' asked Cloke.

'Shit, yeah. Look at her. Hardcore gangster. A rattlesnake. Youth correction, one jail after another. Why else would she end up at Bellevue?'

'She said she was getting her kidneys checked out.'

'All supermax penitentiaries like Bedford Hills or Taconic have basic medical facilities. Sick prisoners get transferred to the infirmary. No need to take them outside the walls. Only reason a convict gets brought to Manhattan, sent to a neurological clinic like Bellevue, is for brain scans and court-ordered psychiatric evaluation. Violent recidivists trying to parley their way out of a life sentence. Lawyered-up third-strikers trying to blame their crimes on frontal lobe damage or childhood trauma. Bet that barcode stencilled to the front of her tunic would tell her whole life story if only we had a scanner. Bet it would make grim reading.'

'She wants to cut a deal,' said Cloke. 'She'll give us Ekks if we cut her loose.'

'She'll say anything to buy her freedom. I rest a lot easier knowing she is in chains.'

'You understand the gravity of the situation, right?' said

Cloke. 'One way or another, we have to persuade her to talk.'

'What have you got in mind?' asked Nariko. 'We can't let her go. If she gets her hands on a knife or a gun, we'll have real problems.'

'There are other means.'

'Chop her fingers? Burn her feet? She won't break. She'll laugh in our faces.'

'I know. But we have to try.'

Nariko crouched next to Lupe.

'I figured it out,' she said.

'Oh yeah?'

'Ran the whole scenario in my head.'

'Hope you had fun,' said Lupe.

'Ekks and his team had the third floor at Bellevue. 101st Cav guarded the main entrance. Sandbags and machine guns. They were okay for a while. A good place to hold out. But the city turned to hell. It looked like the hospital would be overrun. A fast contracting pocket of safety. So they gathered up their shit and fled to the 23rd Street Station. They took to the tunnels and headed south. They headed here. Fenwick Street. Because this station is hidden, sealed from the public, entrance padlocked for decades. A perfect refuge.

It was a two-mile journey. But they didn't schlep their shit through the tunnels. They rode a subway train. They loaded their gear on to an MTA locomotive they found at 23rd Street, didn't they? The third rail was still active. So they threw their shit aboard, broke into the motorman's compartment, found a brake handle and figured how to get the locomotive moving. Smart thinking. As long as the power held, they could take that train anywhere they liked, move around the subway network at will. Hundreds of miles of

72

tunnel. If their location got overrun they could simply jump in the cab and relocate. That's the little detail you held back during your debrief, isn't it? Ekks and his crew camped here, on the Fenwick platform. But they had a loco standing by, in case they had to haul-ass.'

Lupe didn't reply.

Nariko sat cross-legged beside her.

'They were here for weeks, conserving food, conserving water, trying not to go batshit insane,' continued Nariko. 'They kept their receiver tuned to the emergency frequency day and night. They were desperate for rescue, hoping the continuity government at NORAD finally got their shit together and the cavalry were on their way.

'Word comes through. The new president will address the nation at midnight.

'They crowd round the radio, anxious, excited. They want to hear that the army has regrouped. Tanks and troops are massed outside each major metropolitan area, infantry ready to take back the streets. Help is coming.

'But instead, the president declares the battle lost. The cities cannot be saved. The son of a bitch announces an airstrike. Planes are on their way, carrying a cleansing fire. The countdown has begun.

'The Bellevue team panic. Minutes to detonation. They throw their gear aboard the train.

'They couldn't move further south. Fenwick Street is the end of the line.

'They couldn't go north. That would take them into the blast zone.

'So they hid in the tunnel. They pulled away from the Fenwick platform. Not far. Just clear of the station entrance and street grates. They wanted to get deep as they could, put a little distance between themselves and the shockwave. They sat aboard the train as the last seconds ticked away, plugged their ears, huddled in the crash position, and hoped the tunnel roof wouldn't come down on their heads.

'That's your big secret, isn't it? Your ace in the hole. You knew exactly where Ekks and his boys would hide when the bomb dropped. The team are still here, aren't they? They're inside the tunnel, just out of sight.'

Lupe leaned and spat between Nariko's boots.

'And so what? So what if they are down in the dark? The bomb dropped. They're dead a dozen times over. Burned, drowned, irradiated, buried under rubble. And even if a couple of them made it, ate their buddies, drank their own piss, whatever it took to survive, you can't reach the train. The tunnel is fucked. Radioactive flood water, rising higher by the minute. And this is an old section of line. Some old-timer with a trowel put it together brick by brick. That passage was a serious subsidence risk even before the bomb. Face it. You're wasting your time here, girl. You're on a fool's errand. There's nothing to find. No cure. No salvation. Just lingering death. Sooner we all get out of here the better.'

16

The IRT office.

Nariko pushed the radio aside and spread charts on the table. Cloke helped shake scrolled maps from chart-tubes and unravel them. They pegged the curled sheets open with bottled water and an old rotary phone.

Multiple street plans. Port Authority. Department of Transport. Utility schematics. The veins and capillaries of sub-surface Manhattan. The city spread open like a biopsy, marbled with sewer pipes, gas mains, copper-core Con Edison trunk lines and Verizon fibre optic cable clusters.

Nariko examined an MTA map. She circled a section of tunnel.

'Fenwick Street is part of the Downtown Liberty Line, the oldest and deepest section of track.' She pointed to a dendritic junction. 'If Ekks and his boys headed north a little ways towards Canal they should be here: the tunnel beneath Broadway.'

'That's a half-mile hike. In these conditions? Might as well be on Mars.'

'It would be a tough extraction. But it could be done. They aren't beyond reach.'

'The flood water is already waist-deep,' said Cloke. 'The suits will offer some protection, but we'd still get a steady gamma dose just by being in proximity to such a strong radiation source. And if that residue splashes bare skin, the beta burns would be horrific. Essentially, we'd be navigating a river of acid.'

'My boys trained for this kind of deal.'

'I don't like it. It's a hell of a risk.'

'You pushed for this shit. You brought us here. Can't pussy out now.'

'I guess.'

'It's down to you. This is a military assignment. Stay or go. You decide.'

Cloke thought it over.

'Bottom line: we've got orders. We've got a job to do.' He spoke like he was lecturing himself, psyching for the mission. 'Ekks is probably dead. But if he left a scribble on a note pad, a string of code on a hard drive, it could be the only thing standing between the human race and extinction. We can't walk away. Not while there is a flicker of hope.'

'So who goes?' asked Nariko.

'Me. You. Ideally, we need a third person for backup. Donahue or Tombes. But we can't force them to go. A mission like this has to be volunteers only.'

Nariko hefted a big blue vinyl kitbag from the equipment pile. FDNY MARINE RESCUE stencilled on the side. She unlaced drawstrings and shook out the bag. A tight PVC roll hit the tiled floor with a thump, whipping a dust-plume.

She flipped strap-buckles. She kicked the PVC roll. A grey, inflatable raft unravelled.

'You're not seriously going into the tunnels, are you?' asked Lupe. 'You're actually going to paddle around in that shit?'

'Yeah.'

'You're insane. You heard the guy. If that thing pops a hole while you're down there, you'll burn while you drown.'

'Bet if I come back with some kind of inoculation, you'll be the first to hold out your arm.'

Nariko screwed a battery pump to the Boston valve embedded in the flaccid prow of the raft. She set the pump running. The compressor hummed and hissed. The air hose bulged and unkinked. Slow inflation. Chambers within the boat's rubber hull began to plump and expand.

A four-man raft. No outboard.

Nariko unzipped a vinyl case and pulled out two fibreglass oars. She threw the oars to Cloke and Tombes.

'Ready to break a sweat?'

They propped the oars against the wall and climbed into NBC suits. They pulled on butyl overboots. They pulled on gauntlets.

The crackle of heavy rubber, and the burr of zipper teeth, reminded Nariko of the countless occasions her attendance at a house fire or auto wreck had concluded with a body bag loaded onto an EMT gurney.

She buckled a leather utility belt.

'Assholes,' said Lupe. 'All of you.'

Nariko glanced at Galloway.

'Feel free to tape her mouth.'

Nariko picked up the Glock. She re-checked the safety, re-checked the chamber. She tucked the gun into her belt.

'Reckon you'll need it?' asked Cloke.

'No idea what reception we will get. What if the Bellevue team got infected? What if one of them got bitten and turned on his friends? You'll need something in your hand. There's a bundle of heavy tools over there by the equipment pile.'

Nariko tucked a hatchet into a hip-ring on her thick leather belt.

'Pick something heavy, something with a spike. Just don't sink the boat, all right?'

Cloke stood at the head of the platform steps and looked down into darkness. He held a respirator over his face and tested for visibility.

'Masks will be useless down there,' he said. 'No peripheral vision. Wouldn't see a damned thing.'

'You're sure?'

'Just seal your suits and stay out of the water. Like I said, it's nasty shit. If you go over the side, you'll get more than wet.'

Nariko and Tombes stood face to face. They tore strips of duct tape and wrapped them round each wrist and ankle joint. A well-drilled haz-mat protocol.

Fist bump.

'Good to go.'

'You folks done this before?' asked Cloke, trying to break the tension.

'Suit up?' said Nariko. 'Before today? Big chem spill out on the FDR last year. Rush hour. A truck blew a tyre, jackknifed, spilled a bunch of drums across the lower deck. Some kind of noxious, carcinogenic shit. Put the whole city in gridlock. Had to foam down the freeway and mop it up. Closest we ever got to this kind of duty.'

She twisted at the waist and wheeled her arms to make sure the suit was sitting right.

'This is your mission, but I manage the turn-around, okay?' said Nariko. 'We'll take it as far as we can. But if it goes bad, I'm pulling the plug. I don't want to hear any argument. My word is final.'

'Understood.'

She re-checked glove seals. She paused for a moment, distracted by the mildewed Camel poster on the wall beside her. Rich red amid grey dereliction.

'Do you think we'll ever see the sun again?' she asked.

They listened to the steady, white-noise roar of torrential rain, the rumble of thunder and the faint rasp of ragged nails dragged down polythene.

'Maybe we are better off down here, below ground,' said Tombes, and crossed himself.

17

The tunnels beneath Manhattan.

Eight hundred miles of darkness and silence. Dripping water. Mournful wind-whisper. Passageways and caverns sealed for ever. A necropolis that would endure long after surface structures collapsed and were subsumed by forest.

A subterranean realm ruled by rats.

Rodents navigated the tunnels in packs. They sought out survivors, the handful of New Yorkers that fled into subterranean darkness to escape ground-level horror. Bewildered refugees stumbling through unlit passageways slowly succumbing to dehydration. Weak. Injured. Maimed by the concussive detonation: the crushing shockwave which burst eardrums, ruptured capillaries, made blood fizz with liberated nitrogen. Victims convulsed, dripped frothing blood from ears and nose as they were subject to massive decompression trauma, like a diver dragged from the depths.

One by one the helpless survivors were overwhelmed by a swarming, seething tide of vermin. Screams echoed through the tunnels as countless yellow incisors sank into flesh.

Rats burrowed into eye sockets, gnawed soft extremities, chewed deep into muscle and viscera.

Bodies quickly reduced to scattered, skeletonised remains.

Rushing water. A rumble like an oncoming train.

Rats scattered and ran. They fled the tidal rush. A rippling stream of dirt-streaked fur. They scurried across rail beds. They scampered along pipe work and ropes of high-voltage cable, looking to reach high ground, looking for air-locked tunnels and chambers that would escape the flood.

Grand Central Terminal. A flame-seared ruin. A cascade of roof rubble had buried each concourse, pulverised the ticket booths and destination board, crushed the information stand and four-faced clock. The 9/11 memorial flag had burned and shrivelled to black melt-drips.

The netherworld beneath the station, the labyrinth of stairways, passageways and ducts, still intact.

Substation Four. A deep-level generator house beneath the ruins of the terminal. A vast dynamo hall. Five hulking rotary DC converters in a row.

Rats infiltrated sub-levels beneath the terminal, but instinctively avoided the generator room. They turned tail rather than explore the long corridor leading to the power house. They reared and shrieked when they glimpsed the rivet-studded entrance at the end of the passageway, the high-voltage zags and danger signs.

The substation doors hung ajar. Impenetrable darkness.

A powerful sentience evolving in shadow deep inside the monumental chamber. A sleepless alien intelligence that pervaded the entire subterranean network, reaching out through the structural fabric of the flooded tunnels.

It sensed an intrusion.

Fresh meat had entered the subsurface system far south at Fenwick Street.

18

The subway tunnel, lit crimson by flickering flare-light.

Nariko, Cloke and Tombes waded knee-deep across the submerged platform. They kicked through drifts of floating garbage.

'Walk slow,' advised Cloke. 'Don't splash.'

Nariko held the grab line for stability as they climbed into the boat. She crouched at the prow. She held a floodlight.

Cloke and Tombes sat behind, each with an oar. Tombes wore his battered leather fire hat with a brass RESCUE 4 insignia.

The boat sat low in the water. They pushed away from the platform and began to paddle. Slow, deliberate oar strokes.

Donahue stood at the platform steps, flare held high. She watched them depart.

'Catch you later,' shouted Tombes. His voice echoed in the cavernous space.

'Watch your ass,' replied Donahue.

The boat headed into the tunnel mouth.

Donahue tossed the flare into the water. It floated, spitting fire for a couple of seconds, then dimmed and died.

Galloway inspected the rusted Coke machine. He pounded the side of the cabinet and checked the return slot for nickels.

Lupe shifted position. She stretched. She rubbed her wrists, massaged cuff abrasions.

'Sooner or later, you'll cut me loose,' she said. 'How will

that feel? When the chains are off and you have to look me in the eye? Whole different ball game.'

'Think I'm scared? I've straightened out a few hard-asses in my time. I know how to deal with street trash like you.'

'Bronx accent, right? Must have been tough. How many ex-cons lived in your neighbourhood? Bet you spent a lot of time looking over your shoulder, worrying some ex-jailbird with a grudge is going to spot you in a bar and turn his mind to payback. What did you tell people? Did you say you were a plumber or some shit? Did you chain the door each night? Keep a .38 under the pillow?'

'None of your damned business.'

'Corrections. Only law enforcement job you can get without an education. The police department turned you down, didn't they? *Thank you for your resume, but due to the high volume of applicants . . .*'

'Fuck you.'

'Should have worked at the airport, man. Could have sat on your ass and watched a luggage scanner all day. Easy money.'

'Think you can get under my skin? I get shit from you lowlives every working day. Scumbags shouting through the bars. Lifelong losers.'

'Most COs just punch the clock. Do their shift, drive home, pop a cold one. But you love it. I can tell. You're the type. Tuck your pants into your boots like you're SWAT. Does it make up for being a short guy?'

'You're nothing but noise.'

'Live for it, don't you? Pulling on your pads and helmet for a cell extraction. Choke-holds. Beatings. Some juicy pain compliance. You're nothing without your nightstick, nothing without your keys. The moment they unlock these cuffs, the moment you got no one to push around, you'll cease to exist.'

Galloway stood over Lupe. He racked the slide of his

Remington and jammed the snout against her temple. He twisted the barrel, tried to brand a ring-bruise into her flesh.

'Keep pushing, bitch. Nobody here but us. Can't seem to get that into your skull, can you? No cops, no CCTV. Easy equation: you, me, this twelve-gauge. The old law. Simplest thing in the world.'

A sudden, metallic rattle from the entrance gate. Heavy impacts. The groan of stressed metal.

Galloway lowered the shotgun and backed off. He ran across the ticket hall and stood at the foot of the street exit stairs.

'What's going on, man?' shouted Lupe. 'Are they in? Did they break in?'

Galloway watched hands scrabble at the opaque plastic sheet that curtained the lattice gate.

'Uncuff me, man. Undo the cuffs. Come on. You can't leave me chained to a fucking pillar.'

Fingers raked plastic. Blood smears and snagging nails.

'Shit,' murmured Galloway.

He ran to the platform stairwell.

'Donahue.' His voice echoed back at him. 'Donahue. Where the hell are you?'

She ran up the steps to meet him.

'I think we're starting to draw a crowd.'

The station entrance. Galloway and Donahue in respirators.

'Four or five of the bastards,' said Donahue. 'Guess the gate will hold, for now.'

She pulled back the curtain with a gloved hand.

Galloway took casual aim with his shotgun. He squinted down the barrel at a jawless priest pressed against the gate, reaching, snarling, air escaping a ruptured throat in a series of guttural pig-snorts.

'Want me to thin them out? At this range I could take two with each shot.'

'Gunfire would bring more down on us,' said Donahue. 'Might as well ring a dinner bell. These creatures are dumb as rocks, but if they hear noise associated with living, breathing humans they'll crawl through the rubble from miles around.'

'Always adults,' said Galloway, contemplating the jostling revenants. 'Never kids.'

'I like to think parents took care of their children, as a mercy.'

Donahue rehung the curtain.

'The chopper isn't due for hours. Better play smart until then. We need to reinforce this entrance. I'll look around, see what I can find.'

'I need a piss,' shouted Lupe.

'Shut up.'

'Seriously. I need a piss.'

'So wet your pants,' said Galloway.

'You want me to urinate on the floor? We're stuck down here for the rest of the day. You want to splash around in a puddle of piss?'

'I honestly don't give a damn.'

'Yeah. I guess you don't. Smelt yourself lately?'

Galloway shook his head. Weary, don't-have-time-for-this-crap.

'And what about you?' asked Lupe. 'We could be stuck here a while. What if you need a shit? Want to burn your dick off crouching over that radioactive cesspool? Find a bucket. That's the least you can do.'

Galloway pushed open the plant room door. He hesitated to cross the threshold. Deep gloom. Nariko's two-stroke generator supplied power to a fluttering ceiling bulb. Racks of dust-furred electrical apparatus threw grotesque shadows. Rows of porcelain insulators draped with webs. Asbestos-lagged steam pipes.

He crouched beside the generator and tapped the fuel gauge. A gallon tank. Juice to keep the station lights burning four hours, then a refill.

He switched on his flashlight and explored deep darkness at the back of the room. He found a fire bucket. He picked it up. A fist-sized rust hole in the base.

A rusted gum machine. *Chiclets. Dentyne.*

Stacked boxes. Cardboard turned to mulch. He lifted a box flap. Rusted tins of paint. Mildewed labels. Cans of Nu-Enamel for the radiators. Boxes of Navajo white and crimson red: the two-tone wall scheme of the office and stairwells.

Documentation piled in a heap. Curled, autumnal pages. IRT admin: staff rotas, payroll, customer complaints. If any of the team felt the need to defecate, they would have to squat over spread paper, wipe, and toss a shit-parcel into the tunnel water.

A can full of nails and screws. He shook it out. *Gulf Auto Grease.* Big as a cookie jar. Large enough for a piss pot.

Something caught his eye. He crouched. A bare footprint in the dust.

He looked around. He shone his flashlight into the corner of the room. Some kind of hobo camp. Scrunched paper, like the inhabitants bedded down under garbage.

He kicked the detritus aside. Beige MRE wrappers. Empty vacuum seal bags and a couple of plastic spoons. Remains of an army ration pack.

He examined the wrappers under light. Ready-to-eat spaghetti bolognese. Tongue smears: someone had eaten the meal, then ripped open the bag and licked the liner.

More sachets. They'd eaten sugar. They'd eaten coffee granules. They'd eaten pudding powder with a spoon.

An empty water bottle. He shook a drip into his palm.

He brushed aside papers heaped against the wall. Some kind of pattern etched into the brickwork. He crouched and trained his flashlight. A screaming face scratched into the mortar with a nail.

He turned and shouted towards the plant room door.

'Hey. Hey, Donahue. I don't think we're alone down here.'

'Need a drink?' asked Donahue.

Lupe nodded.

Donahue fetched water from a bag of bottles and energy bars. She tossed the bottle to Lupe. She caught it with cuffed hands, uncapped and swigged.

'Personally, I'd let you go,' said Donahue. 'Doesn't seem much percentage keeping you chained.'

Lupe held out her hands.

'So do it.'

'Not my call.'

The plant room door kicked open. Galloway stood in the doorway. His nose was broken. He drooled snot and blood. He had a shotgun barrel pressed to the back of his neck.

'All right,' shouted a husky voice from inside the plant room. 'Nobody move.'

'Wade?' replied Lupe. 'Damn, is that you?'

19

The flooded tunnel.

Ancient brickwork. Arched buttresses. Calcite leeched from mortar in petrified drips like candle wax.

Corroded brace girders. Load-bearing I-beams bowed under the weight of slow subsidence.

The boat headed north. Paddle strokes and laboured breathing.

'Where does this lead?' asked Tombes.

'According to the map, this passageway connects with a modern MTA tunnel about three quarters of a mile north, somewhere close to Canal Street.'

'Doesn't look too stable.'

'Nobody set foot down here for years. Nobody official.'

'What's above our heads?'

'Broadway.'

'The flood water is pretty deep in this section. Must be a downward gradient.'

Nariko sat at the prow. The surface of the water gleamed iridescent gasoline rainbows.

'Something floating up ahead.'

A body.

'Get closer. I want to take a look.'

The corpse was floating face down. Combat fatigues. Army boots.

Cloke prodded the carcass with an oar. He flipped the body. The corpse rolled and bobbed.

'Christ,' muttered Tombes. He covered his nose and mouth to mask the stink.

The corpse was shrivelled by long immersion in water.

Nariko focused the beam, and inspected the cadaver head to toe. Face mottled purple. Fat tongue furred with fine needles. The side of the soldier's face was knotted with metallic sarcomas. Fine splinters protruded from his scalp and ears.

The chest and abdominal cavity were empty, intestines and internal organs stripped by rats. Rib cage held to the spine by shreds of cartilage.

'Give me the oar.'

Nariko turned the corpse and examined the cadaver's shoulder patch. Black horse head on a yellow shield.

'101st Cav. This guy was part of the platoon guarding Ekks.'

She leaned close over the rotted corpse, squinted to read dog tags.

'His name was Donovan. Sergeant Donavan.'

'So the mission is a bust,' said Tombes. 'The team got wiped out.'

'Maybe,' said Cloke. 'But we have to know for sure.'

Nariko drew the pistol from her belt, disengaged the safety and took aim.

'The guy looks pretty dead,' said Tombes.

'I've seen these bastards fragged with grenades. Three of them. Spun twenty feet, legs gone, but they kept coming, hand over hand.'

She fired through the soldier's eye socket. The gunshot echoed from the tunnel walls.

'Bullet to the brain. Only way to be sure.'

She tucked the pistol back in her belt.

A clump of papers floating in the water. Nariko scooped wet pages with an oar and examined smeared ink.

'What does it say?' asked Cloke.

'Nothing. Requisition forms.'

'Show me.'

Nariko held out the oar. Cloke examined the mulched pages.

'Army mindset. End of the world, and still filling out paperwork.'

'Maybe it kept them sane,' said Nariko.

They paddled deeper into the tunnel.

They passed an old IRT coach laid up on a siding. Water lapped the bodywork. Flakes of paint suggested the carriage might once have been Tuscan red.

Nariko trained her flashlight on the decaying hulk as they drifted past. Warped panels. Rusted girder frame. Side doors hung from their hinges.

'Been here a long while.'

Faint gold letters:

INT OUGH APID TRANSI

The beam of the searchlight shafted through vacant windows. It lit the flooded carriage interior, projecting a shimmering ripple-glow across the ceiling.

Rotted leather hanger straps. Split and buckled coachwork. Rattan upholstery peeling from corroded spring-frame seats.

Relic of a gilded age.

They paddled past and continued down the tunnel.

'How far have we travelled?' asked Tombes.

'About a quarter of a mile, at a guess,' said Cloke.

'Hello?' shouted Nariko. Her voice echoed down the dark passageway and died slowly. 'Hello? Anyone hear me? Anyone out there?'

No reply.

Tombes cleared his throat and cupped his hands.

'Hey,' he bellowed. 'Hey. Anyone. Sound off.'

Silence.

'The roof is getting low.'

'Ten minute cut-off,' said Nariko. 'Ten minutes, then we turn back.'

'We should keep going,' said Cloke. 'That soldier was guarding Ekks and his boys. Part of the team. His body drifted south on the current until he snagged on something beneath the water. Proves the rest of the Bellevue Team must still be up ahead.'

'Probably dead.'

'Doesn't change a thing.'

She pointed to the G-Shock strapped round the wrist of her gauntlet.

'Ten minutes. Then we're done.'

They paddled further down the brick tunnel.

An arched passageway to their left. The entrance was blocked by prop-beams and planks. An old work notice nailed to the wood:

DANGER
DO NOT ENTER
UNSTABLE
KEEP OUT

Nariko trained her flashlight on the tunnel entrance. The beam shafted through crooked planks. Absolute darkness beyond.

'You didn't say anything about a junction,' said Tombes. 'You said it would be a straight run.'

'It isn't on the map,' said Nariko. 'It shouldn't be here.'

'There are bound to be uncharted passageways,' said Cloke. 'The city has been overbuilt so many times no one knows exactly what's beneath the surface. Records were lost when City Hall burned to the ground in the nineteenth century.'

He looked around at crumbling brickwork. 'There are hundreds of miles of subway tunnel, a warren of speakeasy cellars and opium hideouts, sewer channels dating back beyond the revolution. A vast subterranean realm. No wonder homeless guys took refuge down here. They could siphon water from the pipes, splice power cables. Create their own world.'

'Place gives me the damned creeps,' said Tombes. Involuntary shiver.

'Ionised air,' said Cloke. 'Moving water. Prickles your skin like a static charge.'

They kept rowing. Nariko's flashlight lit nothing but crumbling brickwork and rafts of floating garbage.

'We must be approaching Canal,' said Cloke. 'Doesn't make sense. Why would they travel this far north?'

'Something up ahead,' said Nariko. 'Some kind of obstruction.'

The tunnel choked by a wall of debris. The flashlight lit tumbled cinder blocks, deformed girders, massive slabs of reinforced concrete bristling rebar. A BROADWAY street sign protruded from the rubble.

Nariko leaned from the boat. She lashed the tether to the Broadway sign.

She shone her flashlight over the jumbled blocks. Marble. Travertine. Polished granite.

'Guess a building collapsed. Compacted the tunnel.'

She leaned over the side of the boat and shone her flashlight into the depths. The beam shafted through black water.

'Something yellow down there. Something big. A school bus? A Ryder?'

Tombes surveyed the rockfall.

'We've got a few demo charges,' he said. 'Nowhere near enough to shift this masonry. Maybe we ought to head overground to Canal.'

Nariko shook her head.

'Forget it. Heavy rads. Street fires. Buildings collapsing left and right. Down here, we have a chance. Up top, we'd get ripped apart.'

She unhooked the Motorola and fumbled with gloved fingers. She retuned and held up the handset until she got signal bars. Hiss of static. A faint, rhythmic tocking sound.

'Hear that? Their radio is still live, still transmitting, beyond that wall of rubble.'

'Doesn't mean a whole lot,' said Tombes. 'Might be a dead man with his hand resting on Transmit.'

'Hold on,' said Nariko. She mimed hush. 'Listen.'

A young man's voice whispering through waves of static. She held the radio to her ear and strained to make out words.

'. . . *Help us. If anyone can hear this transmission, please, send help* . . .'

She upped the volume and switched the speaker to vox. The ghost-voice echoed from the tunnel walls.

'. . . *Can anyone hear me? Is anyone out there? Can anyone hear my voice?.* . .'

'Jesus,' murmured Cloke. 'They made it. The Bellevue guys. Some of them are still alive.'

'Who is this?' asked Nariko, addressing the radio. 'What's your name?'

'*I don't know.*'

'Get a grip, kid. Come on. Get it together.'

'*Ivanek. Casper Ivanek.*'

'What's the situation? Where are you?'

'*I'm not sure.*'

'Describe what you see.'

'*It's dark. It's cold.*'

'Is anyone with you? The Bellevue team? Is anyone else left alive?'

The voice faded to a whisper.

'*I'm alone. They were here, with me. But now they are gone.*'

'All right. Sit tight. This is Rescue Four. We're coming for you, kid. We're coming for you.'

20

Galloway stood in the plant room doorway, hands on his head, shotgun barrel jammed against the back of his neck. Blood dripped from his shattered nose.

Donahue snatched a heavy crash axe from the equipment pile.

'Who's back there? How many guys?'

'Keep your fucking mouth shut.'

'How's it going, Wade?' shouted Lupe.

'You all right, babe?' said the voice.

'Yeah. I'm good.'

Donahue fumbled at her belt for her radio. The clip hung loose. She had left the radio in the office.

She adjusted her grip on the axe shaft, shifted foot to foot, tried to figure her next move.

'Walk.' Another barrel-prod to the back of Galloway's head.

Galloway stumbled to the centre of the ticket hall.

A man stood behind him. A tall guy. He had a bandana tied round his forehead. A blonde mullet and goatee. He wore the same red state-issue as Lupe. *NY CORRECTIONS* streaked with dust and dirt. His right hand kept the shotgun pressed to the back of Galloway's head. His left hand gripped Galloway's collar, steering him forwards, keeping him upright.

'Stop,' he ordered. 'Stand there. Don't move.'

Galloway came to a halt. He was white with shock. He started to tremble.

The convict stood in a half crouch, using Galloway's body for cover.

'Drop the axe, girl,' said Lupe. 'Scissors beats paper. He's packing a shotgun.'

Donahue shifted left. The convict reacted to the crunch of her boot falls. He pulled Galloway to the right, keeping cover. They circled.

'Seriously. Better drop the axe.'

Donahue readjusted her grip on the shaft. White knuckles.

The convict nudged Galloway forwards.

'Kneel.'

Galloway slowly sank to his knees.

'Please. Don't. Don't shoot.'

The convict kicked him in the back. Galloway sprawled face down. The gun barrel pressed to the nape of his neck. He stared at the floor, wide-eyed, like dust and chequered tiles were the last thing he would ever see.

The convict crouched. He fumbled at Galloway's belt. He slapped and groped the leather. He unclipped the key fob.

'Where are you, babe?' He shouted like he was trapped at the bottom of a deep well calling upwards to distant daylight.

'Here, you dumb fuck,' said Lupe. 'What the hell is the matter with you?'

The convict threw the keys towards the sound of her voice. They skittered across floor tiles. Lupe snagged them with her foot. She released her hands. She reached down and unshackled her ankles. She got to her feet.

'Stop,' shouted Donahue. She raised the axe, ready to swing. 'Both of you. Keep still, all right? Just stay where you are.' She circled, to keep both convicts in view.

'*Nadie se mueve*, all right?' said Lupe, hands raised in a placating gesture. 'Relax. Let's all just cool the hell out. We don't want to hurt you. We don't want to hurt anybody.'

She took a step forwards.

'Back up,' shouted Donahue, hefting the axe, tensed to strike. 'Back the fuck up.'

'Chill,' said Lupe. 'We all want the same thing: a route out of this shithole. No point fighting. Just put down the axe.'

'Screw that. We throw down together, all right? Count of three. We sit tight until Nariko and the rest of the team get back.'

The convict shook his head.

'I don't think so,' he said, smiling a sour, crooked smile. He stared through and beyond her.

Galloway lifted his head. Blood dripped from his shattered nose and splashed on the tiles in front of him. He looked at Donahue. His lips moved. His eyes flickered like he was trying to indicate something behind her.

Donahue turned, and caught a fist to the side of her head.

Donahue and Galloway sat with their backs to the ticket hall wall. They sat cross-legged, hands on their heads.

The side of Donahue's face had started to swell and bruise black, pinching her left eye closed. She tongued her gums, made sure she hadn't lost teeth.

Galloway's nose dripped blood. He licked drips from his upper lip and spat.

Lupe stood over them. She had taken off her state-issue smock and tied the arms round her waist. She wore a white vest. Crude illustrations etched down both arms. Skulls. Devils. A snake coiled round a dripping hypodermic. The tattoos had already faded pale, like they had been in place since early childhood.

She held the shotgun. She had Donahue's radio clipped to her waistband.

She stroked the Remington, relished the weight, the ergonomic comfort of the grip-stock.

'Wipe your nose,' she commanded.

Galloway looked up at her, eyes full of hate.

'I haven't got a tissue.' Lupe stepped back to avoid blood-spray as he spoke.

'Give him a tissue.'

Donahue pulled a pack of tissues from the pocket of her jacket and handed them to Galloway. He dabbed blood from his nostrils. He wiped his lip and chin.

'So who are your friends?' asked Donahue.

Lupe pointed to the tall convict.

'That's Wade.'

'Why was he in jail?'

'Biker stuff.'

Wade stood at the equipment boxes. He found an open carton of water by touch, uncapped a bottle and chugged it straight down. He fumbled for a fresh bottle, twisted the cap and emptied it over his head.

'What's up with his eyes?' asked Donahue.

'Damned if I know.'

Donahue gestured to a second convict. He was short and fat, with thick, black-rimmed glasses.

'And him?'

'Sicknote. One sandwich short of a picnic. Mother dropped him on his head, or something. He's all right most of the time. But he has seizures. You can see it in his eyes. One minute he's talking, making perfect sense. Next minute his face freezes and his eyes go cold. That's when you got to steer clear.'

'Dangerous?'

'Don't worry. We got him on a short leash.'

Sicknote searched through the rescue pile. He tore open

boxes. He emptied bags. Trauma gear. He threw sterile dress-ings over his shoulder. A bag of clothes. He held up firehouse pants and jackets, checked pockets and threw them aside.

He found energy bars.

'I got eats, brother.'

He and Wade tore foil wrappers with their teeth. They gorged like they hadn't eaten in days.

'Give me another.'

Sicknote unwrapped a second bar and slapped it in Wade's hand. Wade folded it into his mouth.

'Fuck is this crap?'

'Forest Fruit.'

'Give me a bunch.'

Sicknote gave him the box.

'What about weapons? Can you see any weapons?'

Sicknote glanced over the pile.

'Axes and hammers. Couple of folding knives. Shitload of flashlights.'

'Guns?'

'No.'

'They got plenty of first aid stuff, right?' asked Wade. 'Pills and shit?'

'Yeah.'

'See what they got. Check for Valium, Vicodin, any kind of ride.'

Sicknote rattled pill boxes and bottles. He wiped grime from his glasses and squinted at labels. He mouthed words as he struggled to decipher text.

'Hey,' said Wade. 'Lupe.'

'What?'

'So who are these dicks? What do they want?'

'Fire department,' explained Lupe. 'Some kind of rescue squad. They came for Ekks.'

'Fucker is dead.'

'You saw him die?' asked Donahue.

'He was down in that tunnel when the bomb dropped. Him and the rest of his crew. Place probably caved on their heads.'

'You can't be sure.'

'We've been camped in this shithole for days,' said Wade. 'Me and Sick. If those Bellevue bastards survived, they would have shown their faces by now. They went into that tunnel and they haven't come out. No sight, no sound.'

'So this is where you came? After we broke loose?'

'Yeah. Decided to hide in the plant room. Last place anyone would look, right? They'd expect us to run. They wouldn't expect us to double back to Fenwick. How about you?'

'Got picked up by a patrol. Bastards tried to lynch my ass.'

Sicknote gagged. He bent double and convulsed. Thick vomit splattered on the floor. Half-chewed energy bar. He wiped his mouth with the back of his hand.

'Someone clean that shit up,' said Wade, turning his head from the stench. 'I don't want to smell that stink.'

'Hey,' said Lupe. 'You. Galloway.'

Galloway shook his head.

She lowered the shotgun to his chest, nudged his breast bone with the barrel.

'Come on. Down on your knees. Get scrubbing, fucknuts.'

'With what?'

'Your hands. Your shirt. Whatever. Get it done.'

Galloway laid tissues over lumps of regurgitated energy bar. He tried to scoop them up. Vomit dripped through his fingers.

Radio beep. Lupe unhooked the Motorola from her waist-band. Nariko's voice:

'*Donahue. Come in, over?*'

Lupe held the radio beside Donahue's head.

'Say "Go ahead".'

'Go ahead.'

'*We've made contact with at least one survivor. Heading back.*'

'Sign off,' ordered Lupe.

'Ten-thirteen. Roger and out.'

'Well done, girl,' said Lupe. She patted Donahue on the shoulder. 'Let me get some painkillers for your face, all right? Take the edge off the hurt.'

Lupe crossed to the equipment pallet. She led Wade away from the group. They stood at the foot of the entrance stairwell.

She switched on a flashlight. Wade's face lit harsh white. She trained the beam eye-to-eye. No reaction. Dilated pupils.

'What's wrong with your eyes?'

'Night blind. Been down here too long. I'll be okay once we reach daylight.'

'I guess,' said Lupe, unconvinced.

'So. Some kind of rescue team, yeah?'

'Yeah. Three, travelling by boat. One nine milli between them.'

'An army guy?'

'Some kind of boffin. Institute of Infectious Diseases. He's not a shooter. The other two are fire department EMTs.'

'We can take them.'

'We?'

'Jump the fuckers soon as they get off the boat. Take them out. Do it quick, do it right.'

'No. We rope them. Keep them compliant and intact.'

'When did you grow a conscience?' asked Wade.

'They got a helicopter scheduled to pick them up in a few hours. If they go off air, the guys back at base won't send the chopper. Think you're going to walk home? Go tapping your way through the streets with a white stick? It's hell out there.'

'So what's the plan?'

'Tell Sicknote. Make sure he understands. These folks are our ticket out. We need them, bro. We need them alive.'

21

The boat drifted through the tunnel darkness.

Nariko unhooked her radio.

'Donahue. Come in, over?'

'*Go ahead.*'

'We've made contact with at least one survivor. Heading back.'

'*Ten-thirteen. Roger and out.*'

Nariko pulled the Glock from her belt and press-checked for brass.

'What's up?' asked Cloke.

'Ten-thirteen. Urgent assistance required.'

'Lupe?'

'Who else?'

Fenwick Street. They waded across the submerged platform to the steps. They stood in the stairwell.

Nariko drew the Glock.

'Get me out of this suit.'

Nariko kept the pistol trained on the ticket hall above them. Cloke and Tombes flanked her. They pulled back duct tape and zippers, helped her squirm from cumbersome NBC gear.

'You guys hang back.'

She crept up the ticket hall steps, pistol gripped in both hands. She was stripped down to T-shirt and pants. Her skin prickled in the cold. Her breath fogged the air.

Cloke and Tombes followed behind her.

A face appeared at the top of the stairwell. A chubby guy with black-frame glasses.

'Hey,' shouted Nariko.

Shotgun roar. Smack of impact. The wall beside Nariko erupted. She shielded her eyes from whirling tile splinters and stone chips.

She fired back. 9mm rounds blew craters in the ticket hall roof.

Gunfire died slow like thunder. Silence and dust-haze.

Nariko heard a distant shout. Lupe's voice. She couldn't make out words. Angry, like she was calling some kind of ceasefire.

Nariko crept upwards.

The ticket hall.

Wade, sitting on the bench. He sat, legs crossed, arms stretched over the back of the seat like he was sitting in a park, enjoying the sun.

Nariko took aim at his chest.

'Where's Donahue?' demanded Nariko, glancing round the empty hall. 'Where's the other guy? The guy with glasses? The guy with the shotgun?'

Wade didn't reply.

Tombes grabbed a crowbar from the equipment pile. Cloke grabbed a hammer.

'Donahue?' shouted Nariko. Her voice echoed through the vaulted ticket hall.

'Donnie?' yelled Tombes. 'You okay?'

Muffled shout from the office:

'Yeah. I'm all right.'

Nariko turned back to Wade.

'Come on. Talk. Who the hell are you?'

'Just a guy waiting for a ride.'

'Who's the other creep?'

'My spiritual advisor.'

Something weird and unfocused about the convict's expression. Nariko leaned sideways. His gaze didn't shift as she moved from his field of vision. He continued to stare straight ahead.

'Cut the crap. What do you want?' she asked.

'Like I said. I'm looking for a way off this island.'

Nariko crept closer. She waved her hand in front of his face. No reaction.

'Okay,' she said. 'Maybe I can get you a ride.'

Wade twitched, startled to hear her standing so close.

'That easy?'

'You were down here with Ekks, is that right? You were one of his lab rats?'

'Yeah,' said Wade.

'Listen. I honestly don't give a damn who you are, or what you want. But I don't have time to waste on some lame-ass Mexican stand-off. Just stay out the way until we're done. That's all I ask. Call off your friend. I'll get you home.'

Nariko engaged the safety and tucked the Glock into her belt. She sat beside Wade.

'You're blind.'

'Yeah.'

'Totally blind?'

'Yeah.'

'How long?'

'Couple of days. Vision went blurry. Thought my eyes were tired. Tried to sleep it off. Woke the next day and couldn't see a damn thing. Nothing. Not even black. It's got to be a temporary thing, right? Eye strain. Down in the dark too long. Be fine, once I'm out of here and get some sun.'

Nariko checked out Wade's shin. Red on red: a deep

crimson streak below the knee of his scarlet state-issue pants.

'What's up with your leg?'

'Cut it shaving.'

'Let me take a look.'

Tombes picked a trauma bag from the equipment pile and threw it skidding across the floor to Nariko.

'Roll your leg.'

Wade rolled his pant leg. Black, crusted blood.

'That's a pretty bad sore.' She double-gloved and cleaned the wound. She probed the lesion. Wade winced.

'Doesn't look infected.'

She packed the wound with gauze and wrapped bandage round his shin.

Cloke discreetly unhooked the Geiger counter. He set it to silent. He took a background count, then swung the handset towards Wade. Flickering digits. The LCD readout flashed a threshold warning.

'You folks here for Ekks?' asked Wade.

'Yeah,' said Nariko. 'Any member of his team left alive. Failing that, his research.'

'The guy is long gone.'

'We know where he is. Just got to figure how to reach him.'

'You've got a chopper set to pick you up?'

'Yeah. A JetRanger. It's fucked up, but it flies.'

'And go where?' asked Wade.

'Ridgeway. An old airfield upstate. It's a temporary base. A few cops, reservists and civilians. Handful of folks trying to stay alive. You can join us, maybe find a role. Or we can dump you by the side of a highway somewhere, if you want. Try and make it on your own. Your choice.'

Wade cocked his head, tried to gauge if she was lying.

'Yeah?'

'It's Year Zero,' said Nariko. 'I don't give a damn who you

are, or what you did. Doesn't matter much any more. I'm happy to give you a ride out of here. I'm happy to blow your brains out. Honestly don't care either way. I came here to do a job.'

'On the level?'

'A straight deal. Stay out of our way, and you get a ride.'

'What's waiting for us at this airbase?'

'It's safe. Safer than here.'

'Have they got doctors? Can they fix my sight?'

'Let me take a look.'

Nariko shone a pen torch into Wade's eyes. No dilation.

'They're okay, yeah? My eyes. No actual damage?'

'Where were you when the device exploded?'

'Hiding in the plant room. Me and my buddy. Waiting for the bomb. Felt it before we heard it. I was about to drink some water. Had the bottle raised to my lips when there was a sudden weird change of air pressure. My ears popped like I was dropping in an elevator. Then the ground shook. A massive jolt. Half a second later, we heard the blast. The loudest thunderclap you can imagine. We covered our heads. Thought the roof was coming down. Thought we were dead for sure.'

'We have to tell him,' said Cloke.

'Tell me what?' demanded Wade.

'The bomb,' said Cloke. 'It was a Sandman. A tactical nuke. Small. Probably fit in the trunk of a car.'

'And?'

'The Sandman is an enhanced radiation warhead: a fissile core jacketed with cobalt. At the moment of detonation the device pulsed a wave of fierce neutron energy strong enough to pass through bedrock. Everyone for miles around caught a lethal dose. Wouldn't matter if you were sheltered within a building or hidden in a basement. Wouldn't matter if you were shielded by lead, steel, or concrete. The wave would pass right through you like an X-ray.'

'We were forty feet below ground.'

'Not deep enough.'

'But I feel good. Apart from my eyes. I feel fine.'

'Open your mouth.'

Wade opened his mouth. Cloke peered inside.

'Ulcers. Bleeding gums.'

'Yeah.'

'You've got a sweet taste in your mouth right now, don't you?' said Cloke. 'Kind of like honey.'

Wade nodded.

'You're exhibiting the typical symptoms of acute radiation poisoning. The prodromal stage lasts a couple of days. Nausea and vomiting. Dry throat, hacking cough. Burns, blisters. Random neurological effects, like blindness. Then there is a latent phase, the illusion of recovery. The initial symptoms abate for a while, but remission doesn't last long. Day or two at the most. You'll go downhill fast. It'll be bad. Brain swelling. Congested lungs, internal bleeding. You may shit your guts out, literally excrete your own stomach lining. That's the reality of the situation. So if you've got any thoughts about hijacking the chopper and heading south to the Caribbean, put them from your mind. You'd never make it.'

'Can we beat this thing? Me and Sicknote? Do we have a chance?'

'The dose you took? No. Nobody has received that kind of exposure and lived. You're going to die. You should be dead already.'

'Take us back to Ridgeway. Send for the chopper.'

'If the world were still intact, if there were hospitals and surgeons, then we might have options. We could put up an oxygen tent, isolate you from infection. We could transfuse blood, maybe find a marrow donor. But we don't have much equipment back at base. A few bandages. A few antibiotics. Enough to fix a broken arm, maybe pull a tooth. Basic first aid. But we've got morphine. We can manage the pain. That might not matter much right now. But in a day or so you'll be screaming for a shot. At that moment you'll need us more than you've needed anyone in your life.'

'Fuck.'

'There's an alternative.'

Cloke unzipped the trauma bag. He took out a cardboard box. The box looked like it had sat on a shelf for a couple of decades. Faded serial number. Faded radiation emblem.

He opened the box. Little brass cylinders in rows, like a pack of rifle bullets. He put a cylinder in Wade's hand. Wade held it to his ear and shook it. Faint rattle.

'What's this? Lipstick?'

He uncapped the cylinder and shook a glass ampoule into his palm. He rolled it between his fingers.

'Cyanide,' said Cloke. 'We all carry one. My advice? Keep that capsule in your pocket. Hold out as long as you can, then use it.'

'You're kidding.'

'Like I said. Forget about fleeing south. You got bigger problems.'

Wade stroked cold glass.

'Does it hurt?'

'Cyanide? I hear it's a pretty quick way to go. Takes effect within seconds. Shuts down respiration. You might convulse a little, fight for breath, but not for long. Your world will be over in less than a minute.'

'Christ.'

'Better than the alternative.'

'You should have just put it on my tongue,' he said quietly. 'Told me it was a painkiller or some shit.'

'If I were dying, if I had hours to live, I would want to know. I would want to choose my moment, make my peace.'

'Sorry man,' said Nariko. 'Guess you reached the end of the line.'

22

Wade turned the cyanide cylinder between his fingers.

'Do you think he's lying?'

'About the radiation?' said Lupe. 'About the bomb? I doubt it.'

'You trust him?' asked Wade.

'Yeah, I guess. Broom up his ass, but he's on the level.'

'We were below ground. Me and Sicknote. Miles from the blast site. We didn't set foot outside. We didn't breathe fallout. Maybe we'll be all right.'

'Yeah,' said Lupe. '*Asi es, asi será.* Some people beat the odds. It's like cancer. Someone has a big-ass tumour. Melanoma the size of an apple lodged in their lung. Next time they take an X-ray it's gone. It happens. Don't bite that capsule just yet.'

She looked towards Sicknote. He sat on the street exit steps, staring into space, lost in waking nightmares. His lips moved. He whispered to himself. He pulled strands of hair out of his scalp and watched them drift to the floor.

'Is he cool with this truce?'

'He'll do whatever I say.'

'So what do we tell him?' asked Lupe.

'Nothing. When the time comes, I'll feed him the capsule myself. Say it's vitamins or some shit. Let him bite down and fall asleep.'

Nariko and Cloke stood in the IRT supervisor's office. They leaned over schematics spread on the table.

Cloke uncapped a Sharpie and scribbled a break in a Liberty Line tunnel.

'One of the buildings flanking Broadway must have pancaked, crushed the tunnel flat. And I'm guessing there was another collapse, further north.' He scribbled a second break. 'It's created an air pocket. That's how this Ivanek guy, the young man you heard on the radio, survived. The subway train must be sitting in a sealed section of tunnel, cut off from rising flood water.'

'We haven't got equipment to shift that much concrete aside,' said Nariko.

'We brought scuba gear,' said Cloke. 'We could check beneath the waterline. There might be a gap between some of those big slabs. Some way to worm our way to the other side.'

'The flood water is tainted with fallout,' said Nariko. 'You said it yourself: if anyone dives in that water, they will get seriously irradiated. It's potential suicide.'

'I'll go,' said Cloke. 'This is a military mission. I brought you here. It's my responsibility.'

Nariko wearily shook her head.

'How long since you pulled basic? Twenty years? Thirty? You're a lab tech. You spend your time behind a microscope. I trained for this shit. Confined space operations. I do it every day.'

'This is a little bit worse than a neighbourhood house fire. A whole different league. If you get in that water you'll pay for it. Maybe not right away, but somewhere down the line.'

'Comes with the job.'

'You need to keep your exposure to the absolute minimum. Make a brief survey. Be thorough. But don't hang around.'

'Yeah.'

'If there's a route through the rubble, some kind of crawl-space to the other side, we'll send a team.'

'Okay.'

'Like I say. Do it quick, but get it done. We can fail but we can't quit, understand?'

'Yeah. I know the score.'

Lupe and Donahue pushed the Coke machine across the tiled floor of the ticket hall, inch at a time. Metal shriek. Flaking rust. They hauled the Coke machine up the stairwell. Donahue called a breathless three-count each time they hefted the heavy cabinet a step higher.

'Hold on.'

Donahue wiped sweat from her forehead. She winced as she touched her bruised and swollen cheek.

'Sorry about your face,' said Lupe.

'Sorry about yours.'

They reached the top of the stairs and paused for breath. Donahue bent double, like she was about to vomit.

'You all right?' asked Lupe.

'Yeah,' she said, straightening up. 'Yeah, I'm fine.'

'Is it the sickness?'

Donahue clapped a hand over her mouth and fought back rising bile. She waited for nausea to subside.

'I'll be all right.'

Clawed fingernails raked polythene. The plastic bulged as hands tried to pull it aside and reach fresh meat.

'Got to admire their persistence,' said Lupe. 'This virus, this parasite, whatever the hell it is pulling their strings. A single driving purpose.'

'You prefer it to humans?' asked Donahue.

'Darwinism in action, baby. This bug wants the world more than us. You can't win against that kind of enemy. Trust me. I've seen it. On the street, in the yard. Some guys have their own dark purpose. Spooky fuckers with a weird, Charles Manson charisma. They've got an aura, like they've seen

112

further, deeper than anyone else. They're driving headlong to hell, and nothing better get in their way. You can't beat that intensity. All you can do is back off.'

'Come on,' said Donahue. 'Give me a hand.'

They put their shoulders to the Coke cabinet and shunted it against the curtained entrance gate.

They stood back. The vending machine gently creaked and rocked as hands clawed it from behind.

Donahue leaned against the tiled wall for support. She held her head like she was waiting for pain to pass.

'Sure you're okay?'

'Stop asking.'

Lupe unslung the Remington and handed it to Donahue. 'You better take this.'

'Thought you'd want to hang on to it,' said Donahue.

'Galloway is itching to start a war.'

'You think?'

'The guy is totally transparent. He wants to snatch Nariko's nine milli and provoke another stand-off. Me against him. Not what we need right now. You look after that thing, okay? Keep it close.'

Donahue took the gun. She checked the safety. She checked the chamber.

'Don't be pointing that thing at me, though,' said Lupe. 'I'm done being a prisoner.'

Nariko flipped latches and threw open the lid of an equipment trunk stamped MARINE DIVISION. Folded drysuits and three full-face diving helmets. She lifted a heavy steel helmet, pulled away its protective polythene sleeve and examined the neck ring.

'Used this stuff before?' asked Cloke.

'Fished plenty of bodies out the river. Jumpers. Flew upstate and helped a mine rescue one time.'

'A mine?'

'Half-assed coal operation. Seven guys trapped in a flooded tunnel. Local cops thought they might have found an air pocket.'

'Find any of them alive?'

'No.'

Cloke snapped open a lock knife. He sliced through nylon rope and pulled tarp from a wooden pallet. A stack of fibre-glass air tanks.

Nariko kicked off her boots and dropped her pants. She stripped to underwear, tied loose hair in a ponytail and pulled on a heavy trilaminate drysuit. Tight neck seal, tight cuffs. Cloke helped check the chest zipper. He hefted a weight belt and buckled it round her waist.

'Give me the gun.'

Cloke handed her the Glock.

'Will that thing fire underwater?'

'No idea,' said Nariko. 'Hope I don't find out.'

She tucked the pistol into her weight belt.

Cloke popped two tabs of IOSAT potassium iodide from a foil strip.

'Open your mouth.'

'I've had my dose,' said Nariko.

'Have some more.'

He put the pills on her tongue and held a bottle of water to her lips. She swigged.

'Don't hang around down there. Ten minutes, at the very most. Make a swift survey of the site, then get out the water and back in the boat quick as you can.'

She nodded.

'But don't rush. Poor visibility and a lot of snarled metal. Don't get caught up.'

Cloke laid the aluminium rebreather frame on the floor. A snarling rat sprayed on yellow fibreglass. He unclipped the cowling. Two AL80 diluent tanks strapped to the back. Black marker on duct tape: NITROGEN and HELIUM. A small green liquid oxygen cylinder between them, alongside a lithium hydroxide CO_2 scrubber cartridge.

Final check of the breathing loop. He checked psi gauges. He checked valves. He clipped the protective cowling back in place.

He helped Nariko shoulder the heavy trimix pack and adjust nylon harness straps.

Gauntlets secured by lock rings. She held out her arm while Cloke buckled an LCD depth gauge to her wrist.

Nariko bent forwards as Cloke lowered a steel helmet over her head. A pig-snout manifold. Halogen lamps at each temple, visor secured by heavy hex bolts. He clamped the helmet to the neck ring and span lock nuts. He equalised pressure and adjusted oxygen. Faint hiss and rubber-crackle as the suit filled with air. Nariko's ears popped.

Cloke gave a good-to-go fist knock on the helmet.

Nariko checked her wrist screen. Green. Gas mix and tank pressure flashed nominal. Five hours of breathable air.

She gestured A-OK.

Cloke clipped a Motorola radio to her weight belt. He ran the jack cable up her back to a socket in the helmet.

He stepped back and spoke into his radio.

'Can you hear me?'

'*Five by five.*'

'Ready?'

'*Yeah.*'

She lumbered across the ticket hall and headed for the stairs. She walked hunchbacked, centre of gravity thrown by the tanks strapped to her back. Cloke walked beside her, holding flippers, offering a guiding arm.

She walked past Donahue. She walked past Lupe, Wade and Sicknote. They watched her pass, silent and solemn like she was a shackled death row inmate making their final journey to the execution chamber.

Tombes spoke into his radio.

'God bless, Cap. Stay safe.'

Cloke took Nariko's arm and helped her descend the steps. She gripped the handrail and leaned forwards so she could see her feet over the visor rim. Her breathing rasped loud inside the helmet.

She reached up and triggered the headlamps. The twin halogen beams lit the dark stairwell noonday bright. Grime-streaked tiles, chipped concrete steps.

She was spooked by black water waiting to receive and engulf her. She rolled her shoulders, told herself to shape up.

Cloke knelt and helped her step into flippers. He tightened ankle straps.

He spoke into his radio.

'You set?'

Thumbs up.

'*Let's get this done.*'

23

Lazy flipper strokes. Nariko enveloped in amniotic silence, as if she were drifting at the furthest edge of the solar system, the point where the light of a pinprick sun yielded to inter-stellar darkness.

She was sheathed in a deep-water drysuit, but could still feel an insidious chill, the gentle squeeze of water pressure.

She spooled a white paracord guideline.

She reached behind and adjusted the knurled knob of the buoyancy dump valve. Urethane bladders tethered to her back-mount bled shimmering bubbles like globules of mercury.

Her breath roared loud and hot inside the helmet. A steady Vader-rasp of exertion. She heard the reassuring solenoid click of the rebreather apparatus inject fresh oxygen into her suit.

Helmet lights lit the tunnel floor. Quartz-halogen beams shafted through the sediment haze. The lamps illuminated a vista of concrete dusted with ochre rail silt, the sleeper-sill of the track bed, the inert third rail that used to hum with a death-dealing six hundred volts.

Scattered garbage. Crack pipes. Pennies. A dead rat.

She checked her wrist gauge. VR3: a crude dive computer strapped to her left wrist. An LCD screen encased in pressure-proof acrylic and steel. A depth/oxygen/psi readout. The screen winked green. Three bars charting gas levels within the suit:

FHe 17%
FN₂ 57%
FO₂ 26%

A soothing computer voice gave a thirty second update.

'*Depth: three metres. Atmosphere: good. Four hours, fifty three minutes remaining.*'

The green light and voice alert were a redundancy designed to cut through the stupor of hypoxia or nitrogen narcosis. A warning for a diver succumbing to the lethal euphoria of a failing nitrox mix. Even if they could no longer read gauge numbers, even if their vision narrowed and they headed for blackout, a flashing screen and urgent voice would urge them to act on instinct and head for the surface.

'*What's my time?*'

'*Coming up on eight minutes,*' said Cloke. '*How's it going down there?*'

'*I'm doing okay.*'

Nariko's voice, tight and intimate within the confines of her helmet.

The rockfall. Tumbled slabs of ferro-concrete bristling with rebar. Twisted girders. The splintered stump of an ailanthus tree.

Yellow metal near the tunnel floor. Nariko ducked beneath a girder to get a closer look. A school bus, half crushed beneath a titanic block of masonry.

She gripped the twisted fender. She pulled herself over the hood and shone her flashlight into the buckled cab.

A bus driver. He was still lashed in position by his safety belt. Eyeless and mummified, like he died at the wheel and sat parked in the street for weeks before the bomb brought an office building down on his head.

She looked past the driver. She peered into the dark interior of the bus. Silt and shadow. Rows of empty seats. The roof had crumpled and bowed.

She trained her flashlight down the centre aisle and focused the beam on rubble beyond the rear window. Tumbled masonry seemed to form a crooked tunnel, a tight passageway that snaked into darkness.

'*I think I've found a way through.*'

The IRT supervisor's office.

Nariko towelled her hair with a bandana. She had a foil blanket draped round her shoulders.

'This crevice. This worm hole. It is passable?' asked Cloke.

'Yeah. Pretty gnarly. A narrow sump. Doesn't look too stable, but I reckon we could make it to the other side.'

'A three-man team?'

'Ideally.'

'What about survivors, Captain?' asked Tombes. 'We have three diving suits and a limited supply of oxygen. How do we bring them back?'

'We'll find a way,' said Nariko.

Cloke shook his head.

'We're here to retrieve research. Papers, disks, hard drives. That's the priority. We scour the site, harvest whatever information we find, then leave. That kid we heard on the radio? Offer whatever help you can. But, ultimately, our job is to locate and rescue Ekks. We need him alive, long enough to tell us what he knows. Anyone else is a secondary concern.'

'We're a rescue squad,' said Tombes. 'We save lives. That's what we do.'

'We didn't come here to save one life,' said Cloke. 'We came to save thousands. That's the bottom line.'

'Maybe I'm old school,' said Tombes. 'But there are people on the other side of that rock pile and they need help. Count me in.'

'Damn right,' said Nariko. 'We help anyone we can.'

Cloke picked the Geiger counter from the table. Steady background crackle. He slowly swung the handset to point at Nariko's chest. He switched the counter to silent so she wouldn't have to hear Geiger clicks rise to a sputtering hiss, like frying bacon. He watched LCD digits. Escalation blur as the handset approached a hot source.

'How are you feeling?'

'I'll be okay for the next few hours, right? Long enough to complete the mission?'

'At your current level of exposure, you'll get sick, but you'll probably recover.'

'You're sure?'

'I wouldn't lie to you.'

Donahue stood with Wade and Lupe at the foot of the entrance stairwell. She cradled the shotgun.

'What time is it?' asked Wade.

Donahue checked her watch.

'Ten.'

'In the morning?'

'Yeah.'

'Can't tell day from night down here,' said Lupe. She cocked her head and listened to the torrential roar. She held out her arm. 'See? Goosebumps. Beautiful. I spent so long in segregation, cold is a luxury. Locked up all day. One hour of exercise on an indoor basketball court. They kept the heat way up. Reckoned it would keep the inmates placid or some shit. Make them dozy. Fuck Ridgeway. Soon as we get off this island, I'm heading north. Alaska. Canada. Some place with snow.'

Donahue looked up the stairwell to the street entrance. The Coke machine shook and rocked.

'We should keep watch,' she said. 'If those bastards get down here, into the ticket hall, we're in real trouble.'

Lupe shook out a Marlboro. She lit and passed it around. Donahue took a drag.

'Fire department, huh?' said Wade.

'Yeah,' said Donahue.

'Running into the flames. You and your buddies.'

'We've been down a few hallways.'

'Bet you've seen some gnarly shit.'

Donahue took another drag on the cigarette. She coughed.

Lupe held up the matchbook. *Juggs XXX Bar.* She gestured to Galloway. He sat on the bench, dabbed his broken nose with tissue.

'Classy son of a bitch.'

She blew rings.

'You better keep a close watch on that guy,' said Donahue. 'Seriously. Better not turn your back. You broke his nose, took his gun, took his smokes. You folks all but cut off his dick. He won't forget. Somewhere along the line, he'll want payback.'

The lights flickered. They looked up at the fluted glass dome above their heads.

'How long will the generator keep running?' asked Lupe.

'A gallon of gas gives us four hours' light. A couple of refills should give us power for the duration.'

Donahue gestured towards Sicknote.

'What's the deal with that guy? Can we trust him?'

Sicknote crouched barefoot on the tiled floor, scratching patterns with a nugget of concrete. Fierce concentration.

Lupe shook her head.

'Batshit crazy. He doesn't belong in jail. He belongs in an asylum. Category J. In an honest world, if the prison system actually gave a shit, he'd be making macaroni art in the TV room of a sanatorium somewhere, drooling on psych meds. Look at him. Look at his eyes. Skull full of madness. Someone should shoot the poor bastard as a mercy.'

'Maybe we should tie him up.'

'Seems pretty placid right now. I'll keep watch. We can lash him to a pillar if he starts to weird out.'

'What was he doing at Bellevue?'

'Ekks kept him in his Special Management Unit. Had him dosed on Haldol, Largactil, all kinds of shit. See that pink thing behind his right ear? Beneath his hair? An implant. It's supposed to zap his brain each time he goes manic.'

'Does it work?'

'No.'

Lupe took a last drag on the cigarette and flicked it into shadows. The dying butt glowed like a hot coal.

Sicknote pricked blood from his thumb with a sliver of glass. He squeezed droplets, and smeared them across floor tiles. Broad strokes. He painted swirling astral bodies. He sat back once in a while, contemplated his work and composed his next addition. Orbital rings, moons and comet tails. And behind it all, the outline of a massive sun, a flaming aurora at the centre of the planetary alignment.

'So what the hell is that supposed to be?' asked Galloway.

'The chasm between stars.'

'The stars?'

Sicknote glanced around, made sure no one could overhear. He leaned close to Galloway like he was imparting a secret.

'Did you know that atoms are basically an electrical charge? They aren't made of anything. They are nothing. The basic building block of the universe, the primal substance, is Nothing.' He pointed at blank tiles. 'See? There are things, and there are spaces between things. That's what I'm painting. The Howling Absence. The Terminal Truth. It speaks through me.'

Galloway shifted along the bench. 'I'm not your nursemaid, all right? I'm not listening to your garbage all damn night.'

Sicknote pointed to the darkness of the platform stairwell.

'There's something in the tunnels. Can't you feel it?'

'Prowlers? The passageways are flooded. Nothing alive down there.'

'No. There's something else. Something blacker than black, colder than cold.'

'Like what?'

'This virus is smart. Probably shouldn't call it a virus at all. People only use the term because it makes them feel better. Kid themselves they are up against a dumb germ, something they can beat with a pill. Those poor shambling folk out in the street? You think they're the final stage? Think that's the sum of its ambition? It wants more. A lot more. It's going to tear down this world and build something new.'

'You're nuts.'

'It knows we are here. It's been watching since the very first moment we arrived. It's reaching out.'

'Keep away from me, all right? Just stay the fuck away.'

Nariko stripped to underwear. She stepped into her drysuit and zipped it to the neck.

She crouched beside her backpack. She checked cylinder pressure, adjusted valves, and shouldered the tanks.

She buckled a weight belt and pulled on gloves.

'I can't force you guys to come with me. If either of you want to stay behind and sit this one out, that's cool. I'll go on my own.'

Cloke shook his head.

'That would be chickenshit beyond words. I'm coming with you.'

'Yeah,' said Tombes. 'Fuck that. Rescue Four. The Rats. Sooner we get it done, sooner we can all get the hell out of here.'

Nariko watched Cloke and Tombes suit up. She stretched

and paced, adjusted her tank harness straps and weight belt.

Her eyes were once again drawn by the cigarette sunset pasted to the wall.

Cloke stood by her side. He checked his gauntlet seals.

'We'll make it. We'll be okay.'

'Maybe.'

'You were the first to raise your hand.'

'It's my job.'

'You must have known the others would come too. Donahue. Tombes. They'd follow you anywhere.'

'Don't lay that crap on me. They're adults. They made their own choice.'

'You're strong. You'll be all right.'

'This place is killing us. I can feel it. Closing round us like a fist. But I'll be damned if I am going to go out snivelling like a bitch, you know? If I check out, I want it to mean something.'

She headed for the platform steps, helmet in one hand, flippers in the other. Cloke picked up his helmet and followed her.

Tombes turned to Donahue.

'See you later, babe.'

'Don't do anything stupid, all right?' said Donahue. 'The Captain wants to be a hero. Screw her. No offence, but screw her. Stay safe, you hear?'

'Back before you know it.'

He crossed himself, then he headed for the stairs.

Donahue sat in the office. She pulled up a chair.

Maps and subway schematics scattered on the table.

She shuffled papers. She picked up a five borough pocket atlas and contemplated the cover. *Easy-Read, Large Scale*. The Midtown skyline lit by the summer sun. Brooklyn Bridge and, beyond it, the ethereal spire of the Empire State. Life before the pandemic. Life before the bomb. A lost paradise.

She pushed the maps aside, clamped headphones and powered up the radio.

'Rescue team to Ridgeway. Come in, Ridgeway.'

No response.

'Rescue party to Ridgeway, over. Come in.'

No response.

She dropped the mike and rubbed tired eyes.

'Get your shit together, guys,' she murmured. 'You're supposed to man the damned radio.'

She picked up the antiquated mike. She adjusted frequency.

'Ridgeway, can you hear me? Rescue team calling Ridgeway, where the hell are you, over.'

She sat back and listened to electromagnetic interference. The hiss of empty wavebands rose and fell like a desolate night wind.

She closed her eyes and pictured the raging surface of the sun: vast solar flame-licks ejecting coronal mass into the void.

She turned up the volume and listened to the crackle of stellar tides washing across the ionosphere: song of an indifferent universe.

24

The Federal Building. Six floors of derelict office space. Windows shattered as the atomic firestorm ripped through decades of cobwebbed silence in a moment of concussive violence.

A nurse lay slumped in a stationery cupboard among scattered index cards and manila envelopes, as if animal instinct compelled her to find a secluded niche, a womb-like space to curl and die. Her name badge said NGUYEN. Her uniform was streaked with blood and soot. Grotesque metallic sarcomas burst through fabric. She sprawled like a puppet waiting for someone to pull strings.

The nurse shocked awake. Jet black eyes stared into darkness. The air was tainted with the ferric scent of blood. New flesh, somewhere within the building.

She crawled into the hallway. The linoleum floor was wet with rain blown through vacant windows.

No moonlight. Transformed vision cut through shadow and picked out detail bright as day.

She sniffed the air, tried to locate the blood-taint, track it to source.

She crawled across the hall. She reached the elevator doors. She sniffed the inch gap. Blood. Rich and strong.

She gripped the twin slide doors and shouldered them apart.

The elevator shaft. A dust-furred cable. Six-storey drop to the plank roof of the freight elevator.

She climbed to her feet and stepped into the shaft. She fell in a rigid sentry stance. She hit the wall and hit the cable. She hit the cross beam on the roof of the elevator and shattered her shoulder.

She pawed the roof, broke fingernails as she tried to pull the planks aside.

Murmur of voices.

An air vent in the wall of the shaft. A grille veiled by webs. She tugged until screws popped from concrete and the duct cover came loose.

A narrow brick conduit. Darkness. Strange music. Ghost-jazz echoed faintly from within.

25

The IRT office.

Wade found the gramophone by touch. He groped the shelf until he located the leatherette box. He carried it across the office, walked until his thighs bumped the desk. He shunted the telephone and inkpot aside, and set the phonograph down.

He returned to the shelf and fumbled a handful of 78s.

He sat at the desk. He found the lid latch, unsleeved a disk and positioned it on the felt turntable.

He found the crank handle, set the disk spinning, then dropped the arm. Big band jazz. Duke Ellington.

He sat back, lulled by the music, and rubbed useless eyes.

He scratched his goatee. Hair pulled loose in clumps.

He took the brass cylinder from his pocket. He unscrewed the cap, shook the glass ampoule into his palm, and turned it between his fingers.

Donahue unzipped a red trauma pack and searched among pill boxes, sterile-sealed hypodermics and ziplocked dressings. She upturned the bag and shook it empty. She found a strip of Vicodin. She popped capsules from the foil and dry-swallowed. Bitter taste. She threw the pills to Lupe.

'You look washed out,' said Lupe.

'Good job I never wanted kids,' said Donahue. 'Plenty to look forward to, after this fucking trip. Thyroid cancer. Leukaemia. Quite a prospect.'

'Well, we all got to die of something, right?'

Lupe popped a couple of tablets into her palm and swallowed. She examined the foil strip.

'This shit expires in three years. A world without pharmaceuticals. Better brush your teeth. Dentistry is about to get seriously medieval.'

Shriek and rattle from the entrance gate.

They ran to the foot of the stairwell.

The ancient Coke machine blocking the street entrance shook with repeated blows.

'We're starting to draw a Super Bowl crowd,' said Donahue. 'Might have to thin them out.'

'No shooting,' said Lupe. 'Better conserve ammo.' She gestured to the equipment pile. 'We've got plenty of gear. Let's get to work.'

They zipped NBC suits.

A bundle of heavy rescue tools lashed with canvas straps. Lupe released buckles. Clank and clatter. She picked up a heavy metal rod, tipped with a barbed spike. She took a practice spear thrust.

'Ventilation tool,' explained Donahue. 'First thing you do at an apartment fire. Send a guy on the roof to punch a hole. Acts as an artificial flue. Vents heat and smoke. Makes it easier for the hose team to get in there and work.'

'Thought you were a noobie.'

'New to Rescue. I've been riding a truck eight years.'

Donahue hefted an axe. She contemplated the chipped blade, relished the heavy wooden shaft.

'Personally, I like to be first through the door. Look the devil in the eye. Fire is a beautiful thing. Liquid gold.'

They climbed steps to the street entrance. They hauled the Coke machine aside. Hands pawed the opaque curtain draped across the gate.

They pulled on respirators.

Donahue gave the nod.

Lupe flipped open a knife and slit plastic ties. Crackle of polythene as she tugged the heavy sheet aside.

'Jesus Christ.'

Donahue took an instinctive step back. Emaciated arms thrust between the bars. Talons grasped and clawed inches from her mask.

Cadaverous creatures. Hotel service staff. Maids, pot washers, laundrymen. Tumours knotted through burn-blackened flesh. They jammed their faces against the rusted iron lattice. They hissed. They spat.

'How many do you reckon?' asked Lupe.

'Five or six.'

'If they hammer the gate long enough, they'll bring it down.'

'Let's start with this guy.'

Donahue braced her legs and hefted the axe. She took aim at one of the arms thrust through the bars. A chef. Dark spatter on his sleeve. Either blood or bolognese.

Donahue brought down the axe. The first blow cut deep and splintered bone. The second blow sheered the limb at the elbow. Blood-spurt. A severed forearm fell at her feet. Fingers grasped and clenched.

She crouched and picked up the limb.

'Watch yourself.'

She slotted the hand through the grate and threw it into the street.

The chef continued to butt against the gate. The stump of his arm raked the bars.

Lupe thrust the pike through the iron lattice. She speared the chef's eye socket. He toppled backwards into the street, feet dancing as he lay in the rain.

More emaciated prowlers crowded the gate, hungry for fresh meat.

Donahue hacked grasping hands.

Lupe held the pike shoulder-high like a javelin. Each thrust burst eyeballs and dug deep into brain.

A skeletal thing with no legs. Body armour and a Kevlar helmet. Some kind of cash truck guard. It crawled on its belly, thrust an arm through the grate and snatched at Lupe's legs with a gloved hand. Lupe stabbed downwards with the steel pike and speared the creature in the back of the neck. It squealed and frothed as she pressed down with her body weight, twisted the tip of the pike deep into its cortex.

A fat guy in chalk-stripe suit slammed against the gate. He drooled. He snarled. Donahue reached through the lattice and gripped blood-matted hair. She pulled his pudgy face up against the bars. She drove a knife into his eye socket and rotated the blade.

'Nice suit,' said Lupe, gesturing to the body slumped in front of the gate. 'Look at the lapels. Fine tailoring.'

'Yeah?'

'And check out his wrist. Guy is wearing a Breitling.'

'Financial district,' said Donahue. 'Wall Street.'

'You'd think they would be long gone. Hamptons. Connecticut. Wherever the hell rich bastards spend the weekend. Push their antique furniture up against the door and stand guard with a polo mallet.'

'This place used to be central to their lives, I guess. So they came back. An instinct. A faint memory. They feel compelled to return, to mill around the sushi bars and coffee shops, but they don't know why.'

'We're only a couple of blocks from The Federal Reserve,' said Lupe. 'Picture it. Fifty tons of bullion. Stacks of it. All those bars sitting in an unguarded vault. Want to fill your pockets?'

'Hard to think of anything more pointless.'

'We've got a thermal lance. We could cut through the vault door in a couple of hours.'

'Come on. That's a street-trash mindset. Look beyond it.'

'Friend of mine got his throat cut over a pair of K-Swiss.'

'Yeah?'

'I'd like one of those gold bars. I'd like to hold it in my hand just to say I made it, just to say I won.'

They looked down at the misshapen bodies.

'Stinking fucks,' said Lupe.

They re-hung the polythene curtain and shunted the Coke machine back in position.

They pulled off their respirators.

Donahue wiped sweat from her face.

'There will be more,' she said.

'And we'll kill them too.'

They headed down the stairs.

'Can you hear that?' asked Lupe.

'What?'

'Sounds like music.'

'There's something in the walls,' said Wade.

'Where?' asked Lupe.

'Over there somewhere. To my left.'

'Must have been the gramophone.'

Wade shook his head.

'I killed the music.'

The turntable still spun with a rhythmic metallic rasp. Donahue found the brake lever and brought it to a standstill. She closed the lid.

They stood in silence.

'See? Nothing.'

'It wasn't the record player,' said Wade. 'There was a scratching sound, like dragging nails. I definitely heard it.'

'Where exactly did it come from?'

'Over there. The corner of the room. Or thereabouts.'

'There's nothing,' said Donahue. 'Seriously. It had to be the phonograph. The mechanism must be rusted to shit.'

'No. It was the sound of a living thing. You know what I'm saying. Scratching. Clawing. It had purpose.'

Lupe looked high on the wall. She ran her hand across the whitewashed surface.

'Couple of planks screwed to the wall. See that? Beneath the paint? Wooden slats. Something blocked off.'

'Could be rats,' said Donahue. 'Got to be millions of them, skulking around.'

'Sure as hell didn't sound like rats.'

'Don't let your imagination run wild,' said Donahue. 'Chill. We've got axes, knives and a big-ass gun. Anything breaks in, it will rue the day.'

26

Galloway paced the ticket hall.

'Anyone got a smoke? Come on. One of you bastards must have a cigarette.'

'Sorry, brother,' said Wade.

Lupe and Donahue ignored him.

'Assholes. The lot of you.'

Galloway stood over Sicknote and watched him paint. He cocked his head, tried to make sense of the image.

Sicknote pricked his thumb with a sliver of glass. He squeezed a fresh bead of blood and smeared it on the tiles. Bold, broad strokes. Blood and dust mixed charcoal black. He painted a swirling vortex. Screaming faces sucked downwards into the singularity.

Galloway repositioned himself to get a better view.

'What's that? Sinners dragged to hell or some shit?'

'The Great Absence. It's calling us, drawing us in.'

'Calling? You can hear an actual voice?'

'I can hear the smothering silence. It's reaching out to us, reaching through the tunnels. It's almost here.'

'Has it got a name?'

'It can't have a name. It's like antimatter. The opposite of existence. A creeping, expanding null. It's new to this planet. Nothing like it has ever walked the earth before. But it is here now, singing in the dark.'

'Whatever, man.'

Galloway took a Sharpie from the breast pocket of his shirt. He dropped it on the tiles.

'Stop cutting yourself, for God's sake.'

Sicknote uncapped the pen and started to draw.

Galloway sat on the bench next to Wade.

Wade held out his hand.

'Guess we got off on the wrong foot.'

'Fuck you,' said Galloway.

'We'll be down here a while, bro. No point throwing punches all damn night.'

Galloway reluctantly shook his hand.

'Does he always do that? Your friend. Sicknote. Does he always daub mad shit over everything?'

'Yeah. He draws pretty much every waking minute. They had him in a holding cell at Bellevue. He decorated the walls with his own faeces. So they gave him crayons. More hygienic.'

'Screaming faces.'

'Yeah,' said Wade. 'A detailed delusional system, according to the docs. Obsessive motifs. Fills his head, night and day. Soon as he wakes up each morning he gets to work. Swings his legs from the bunk, yawns, scratches his ass, then picks up a pencil. Never stops.'

'But always the same thing? Faces?'

'Always. You know who he is, right? Real name is Marcus Means.'

'Am I supposed to recognise the name?' asked Galloway.

'Albany, ten years ago. Any other state he'd be on death row. Personally, I'd tie him to a chair, but Lupe seems to have a soft spot for the guy.'

'The Chief will order him killed,' said Galloway. 'You too.'

'He's that kind of guy, huh?'

'His boys spent a couple of months bulldozing bodies into

mass graves, and shovelling lime. They were pretty strung out by the end. He's kind of protective.'

Wade took the cyanide cylinder from his pocket and turned it over in his hand.

'According to Cloke, neither of us will be making the trip.'

'How are you feeling?' asked Galloway.

'All right, I guess. One minute I'm hotter than hell, next minute I'm freezing cold.'

Wade pulled off his do-rag and dabbed sweat from his face and neck. Wisps of blond hair shook loose and drifted to the floor.

'Well, hang in there, man,' said Galloway, without conviction. 'Maybe you'll be all right.'

Donahue descended the platform steps and stood at the water's edge. She listened to the deathlike silence of the tunnels. Strangely peaceful.

An unwelcome recollection. A woman retrieved from water, far out in the Hudson bay. A winter suicide. She jumped from the Brooklyn Bridge. An office worker. CCTV showed her strolling along a traffic lane, calm, relaxed, ignoring horns and flashing headlamps. She stopped and patted her pockets like she forgot keys. Then she set down her briefcase, squirmed through the lattice bars of the side barrier and dropped into the heart-stopping cold of the East River. Her body was discovered weeks later during a scuba training dive. Saponification: a long-submerged cadaver trapped among weeds, protected from microorganisms by depth and cold. Her flesh turned white like wax. Body fat slowly transforming into soap.

Donahue tried to push away the memory.

She gulped. She coughed. She bent double and puked. A torrent of vomit splashing into the flood water. Each hard retch echoed through the vaulted cavern. She caught her breath, and spat the taste from her mouth.

She pressed another couple of Vicodin from a foil strip and knocked them back.

She closed her eyes and breathed slowly, tried to get her body back under control.

A distant splash.

Donahue trained her flashlight into far shadows. The beam lit dissipating ripples.

She took a step back and unhitched the shotgun from her shoulder.

She scanned floating rafts of garbage. Big Gulp cups and clamshell burger cartons pirouetted in an almost imperceptible slow drift.

Another ripple. Bubbles broke the surface, an unmistakable trail heading from the distant tunnel gloom towards her.

She held the Maglite between her teeth like a cigar and shouldered the shotgun. She squinted and took aim, followed the approaching bubble-trail with the front sight.

The stairwell lights winked out.

She backed up the steps. She stumbled in the gloom. She dropped the flashlight.

She unhooked the Motorola hanging from her belt.

'Guys? What's going on? What's the deal with the lights?'

The ticket hall.

Lupe fumbled the matchbook. She struck a light. The match flared, then burned steady. She peered into shadow.

'Hey,' she shouted. 'Donnie? What's going on?'

'It's all right,' said Galloway. 'The generator stalled. Give me the matches. I'll get her going.'

The plant room.

Galloway struck a match. The weak flame threw sulphurous shadows.

Scattered papers on the floor. He scrunched a few sheets

into a fire bucket and lit them with the match. The yellowed, desiccated sheets burned fast like autumn leaves. He threw more paper onto the pyre. Sheaves crisped, blackened and curled.

He crouched by the inert generator. He tapped the fuel gauge. The level rested at zero. He unscrewed the fuel cap and began to decant kerosene from a plastic jerry can.

Radio crackle. Donahue's voice:

'Guys? What's going on? What's the deal with the lights?'

'Give me a moment,' said Galloway.

Rotted fingers gripped his shoulder. Nails dug into his flesh. Teeth sank into his neck.

He screamed. He twisted away. He dropped the kerosene. The plastic bottle fell on its side. Fuel washed across the floor.

The creature crouched and hissed.

It was dressed in the tattered remnants of a nurse's uniform. White polyester streaked with blood and pus. Name tag: NGUYEN. Skin like leather, stretched taut over tendrillar tumours that snaked and branched down each limb. Arms bristled with metallic spines.

The creature's shoulder was broken. Its right arm hung lose and useless.

Galloway scrambled clear, kicked distance between himself and the crouching, leering thing. He clapped a hand to his neck and checked his palm for blood, desperate to see if teeth had punctured his skin.

The monstrous figure crouched on its haunches, gathered strength and sprang forwards. Galloway scrambled to his feet. It was on him before he could run. He threw up his arms to protect his face. Bodyslam. They hit the floor. The creature sat on his chest, straining to reach his throat with its one good hand.

Galloway jammed his hand beneath its chin and struggled

to push away the snapping, biting face. He groped for a weapon. He snatched a pencil from his breast pocket and punched it into the creature's temple. Blood-spurt. Splintered wood nailed deep into flesh.

The creature twisted its head and gripped Galloway's right forefinger between its teeth. It bit down. He screamed. It gnawed and ground its jaw. Frothing blood. Bone crunch. He roared in pain.

He fumbled for the jerry can. He gripped it and bludgeoned the creature's head. He put all the force he could muster behind the blow. He hammered the skull-face, breaking a cheek bone.

The emaciated thing fell clear and climbed to its feet, dripping kerosene. It leered. It spat Galloway's finger onto the floor.

It stepped towards him, arm outstretched.

Bare feet kicked through burning paper. The hem of the nurse's smock caught alight. Polyester fabric smoked and shrivelled. Burning melt-drips hit the floor.

Galloway rolled, lunged for the kerosene can and threw it into the blaze.

Blue fire washed across the creature's body turning it to a pillar of flame. It held up a burning hand, mesmerised by dancing light. Then it emitted a high, shrill shriek.

Galloway crawled away from the conflagration, shielding his face from the heat.

Lupe and Donahue ran into the room.

The blazing creature grabbed for Donahue. She aimed a high-kick at its belly and pushed it away. It thrashed. It bounced off walls. Donahue shot it in the gut. It struggled to stand. She kicked it in the face. It lay burning, movements slowing to a spastic dance, like a clockwork automaton winding down.

Donahue slapped shreds of burning fabric from her boot.

'Look at that,' she said. 'Brain cooking in its skull. Poaching like an egg.'

Lupe ran to the ticket hall and fetched a hand extinguisher from the equipment bags.

'Stand back.'

She broke the ring-tab and trained a stuttering burst of carbon smoke. She doused the burning figure, then turned the carbon jet on smouldering wall cables.

Shut off. Darkness. Silence.

Lupe set down the extinguisher and switched on a flashlight. The beam shafted through thick smoke. She trained the light on Galloway. He crouched by the wall, trembling with shock, hugging his injured hand to his chest. He shielded his eyes from the glare.

'You all right?'

He didn't reply.

She checked the generator for fire damage.

She crouched next to the carbonised body. She inspected contorted arms, skin blackened to a crust, fabric fused to bubbling, steaming flesh.

'Damn,' murmured Donahue.

Lupe examined the creature's face. Black eyes. Mouth locked in a silent scream. Taut, carbonised lips. Brilliant white teeth.

The rib cage rose and fell, weak respirations, medulla retaining a last spark of will-to-life, like the dimming embers of a discarded cigarette.

A final, shuddering breath.

Lupe examined a half-melted name badge.

'She worked for Ekks. One of his disciples. Vietnamese chick. Total bitch. A privilege to incinerate her ass.'

'How the hell did she get in here? Where the hell was she hiding?'

Lupe stood up. She contemplated the shadows at the back of the room.

'The Bellevue crew. About fifteen, twenty guys in total. Medics and soldiers. If they got infected, if they are sniffing around in the tunnels, then we've got a serious problem.'

27

Donahue and Lupe searched the recesses of the plant room. They crept between racks of chemical batteries.

Hand signals: go forwards, check left.

Donahue held the shotgun. Lupe held the flashlight. Blue haze. They shielded their mouths to mask the sour barbecue stink of cooked flesh. They blinked smoke-tears from their eyes.

An air-con turbine at the back of the room. Lupe's flashlight lit blades furred with dust and webs. Huge, like someone detached the engine nacelle of a passenger jet and put it in storage.

'Wouldn't want to be standing here when that thing is switched on.'

The blades faced a duct mouth. The grille was ripped open. The torn mesh was tipped with flesh and tufts of white fabric.

Lupe shone her flashlight into the brick pipe. A ribbed, intestinal conduit receded to darkness. She held up her hand. A gentle air current. A fetid exhalation of tunnel breath.

Donahue crouched and examined the floor.

'Give me more light.'

Blood drips.

'Maybe that thing was already down here, with us,' said Donahue. 'Crawling round the ventilation pipes the whole time.'

'Tight squeeze,' said Lupe, contemplating the duct. 'Hands and knees.'

Donahue gestured to a pile of boxes and cable drums.

'We should stack some stuff in front of the grille. Do our best to plug it closed.'

'But why now?' asked Lupe, still mesmerised by the tunnel dark. 'I don't get it. Wade and Sicknote were camped in this room for days. They weren't attacked. So what changed? How did the bitch sniff us out?'

Galloway sat on the ticket hall bench. He hugged his injured hand, face grey with shock.

Lupe sat beside him.

'It'll be all right, yeah?' he pleaded. 'Just got to clean the wound. Disinfect.'

'You're a dead man walking.'

Lupe thrust her hand inside his trouser pocket.

'What are you doing?' he said, drawing away.

She pulled out a fistful of shotgun cartridges.

'This all you got? Five shells?'

'Yeah.'

'Did you bring a bag? A backpack? Sure you don't have a spare box of ammo somewhere?'

'No.'

'Five. And four in the gun. That's not a whole lot of firepower.'

She paced the ticket hall. She blew her hands and clapped her arms to get warm.

She crossed to the equipment pile. She pulled clothes from a canvas duffle. She pulled on an over-sized fire coat and turned up the cuffs.

'Did I hear right?' asked Wade. 'Nine shells?'

Lupe picked up a fire axe and took a couple of practice swings.

'We'll be okay,' she said. 'Any of those bastards make it inside, we'll take care of them.'

'What about me?' said Wade. 'I want a knife.'

'You're blind.'

'I can fight.'

She upturned a tool bag. She found a lock-knife and put it in his hand.

'Thanks.'

He flipped it open and tested the blade with his thumb.

'Hey, Lupe.'

'What?'

'I heard there's a bike out there, in the street.'

'Yeah. Other side of the alley.'

'What kind?'

'No idea.'

'Messed up?'

'Looked in one piece.'

'A Harley?'

'Maybe.'

'Describe it.'

'Chromed out. High handlebars, ape hangers. Extended forks. Someone spent a lot of money on that bike. Lavished a whole lot of love. She was somebody's baby.'

'How old?'

'God knows.'

'What did the cylinder look like? Was it a panhead?'

'Dude, I don't know shit about bikes.'

'Man. If only I had my eyes.'

'You wouldn't last long out there, brother.'

'Fuck it. I just want a ride. I want to be under the sky. I don't want to die down here, in this sewer like a roach, you know? Anywhere but here.'

'Yeah,' said Lupe. 'Yeah, I hear what you're saying.'

★

Donahue and Lupe dragged a table from the IRT office. They hauled it across the ticket hall, kicked it over and blocked the platform stairwell.

'So what exactly did you see?' asked Lupe.

'I'm not sure. Something in the water, below the surface. Bubbles. Ripples. Reckon they could survive under water? Infected? How long can they last without air?'

'Might have been rats,' said Lupe. 'You can bet the flood water drove a swarm of rats from the tunnels. Bet there are plenty swimming around down here.'

'No more surprises. We stick together. No wandering off alone, all right? Line-of-sight, at all times.'

'Relax. You got the gun.'

'I got nine rounds. Won't go far. You guys stay sharp, all right?'

Galloway sat on the bench, sweating and rocking, teeth clenched in pain.

Donahue knelt in front of him. She loaded a hypodermic, jabbed into his bicep and shot Galloway 20mg of Demerol.

He relaxed as opiate bliss washed over him.

'Let me see your neck,' said Donahue.

He pulled his collar aside. Bruised. No blood.

'Quite a hickey. Show me your hand.'

Galloway held out his right hand, sticky with blood. The forefinger was bitten through at the knuckle.

Donahue wriggled on two pairs of Nitrile gloves.

'Hold still.'

She rinsed the injured hand with mineral water and began to swab it clean with cotton wool. She didn't look him in the eye.

'Doesn't look like you lost too much blood. Vasoconstriction. The cold worked in your favour.'

'It'll be okay, right?' he asked. 'Few stitches. It'll be fine, yeah?'

'Relax,' she said. Calming voice. 'Let me do my thing.'

She knelt beside plenty of injured folk during her time as an EMT. Pedestrians who ignored DONT WALK and got their legs crushed by a truck. Balcony jumpers impaled on railings, broke-backed but with a weird look of acceptance as if this horror were an average day in a lifetime of bad luck and failure. Disoriented stab victims lying on a sidewalk, trying to plug a wound with their hands, trying to tell her, as they slid into unconsciousness, they had looked into the dumb, dull eyes of the kid demanding their wallet and seen the true face of evil.

She had a personal code. Soothe, but don't lie. Say: *Help is on its way.* Don't say: *You'll be fine.*

'There,' she said, dabbing the wound clean. 'Looks a bit better.'

She felt icy detachment steal over her. A familiar mindset. The willed callousness she adopted each time she faced catastrophic injuries, certain her patient could not be saved, nothing to be done but supervise a painless death.

Galloway was infected. A talking corpse.

She stitched the stump with suture, and lashed bandage in place with micropore tape.

'We'll give you regular shots,' she said. 'Should dull the pain.'

She gathered up bloody swabs and scraps of suture, balled them ready to be hurled into the flood water.

'You have to amputate my arm,' said Galloway. 'You guys are trained EMTs. You have medical gear. Drugs. Scalpels. You've got to cut my arm at the elbow. Before the disease spreads.'

Donahue shook her head.

'Sorry, bro. You know the score. One bite. That's all it takes. You're infected. No antidote. No cure.'

He looked up at her like a frightened child.

146

'There must be something you can do.'

Lupe joined them. She stood over Galloway. She held out an axe.

'Tie a tourniquet, if you want, and bring down the blade. But we both know you're done. Best decide how you want to spend your last hours.'

'Congratulations,' said Wade with a grim smile. 'You just joined the cyanide club.'

'It'll be all right,' said Sicknote, looking up from the elaborate artwork slowly metastasising across the ticket hall floor. 'It's a blessing, in a way. No more thought. No more you. It'll be beautiful.'

Galloway scuffed the mural with his boot.

'Fuck the lot of you. Talking like I'm already dead. Fuck you all.'

He crossed the ticket hall and sat on the platform stairwell steps. He contemplated the subterranean blackness below.

28

Trinity Church. A sombre gothic-revival structure built from massive blocks of limestone. The spire had toppled. The nave was open to the sky. Rain dripped from shattered arch spans, danced on pews and marble tiles.

Lightning flash.

The dead sat in rows. A succession of suicides. Scattered pill pots. Skulls vaporised by shotguns. Throats gouged by strop razors.

The dead faced a rubble-strewn altar and toppled cross. Congregants at a macabre Eucharist.

Thunder crack.

A priest lay sprawled on the altar steps. He slowly climbed to his feet. Cassock streaked with pus. One arm gone.

He looked up, mesmerised by roiling cloud and forked lightning. Rain splashed his rotted skull-face.

Movement among the congregation. Infected among the dead. Those that were too sick to die; already infected when they opened their veins.

They climbed to their feet and stumbled along the pews, kicked cadavers aside, until they reached the aisle.

Some kind of unspoken command jerked revenants to their feet and propelled them towards the doorway at the back of the nave.

The priest hobbled down the centre aisle, dragging a useless leg behind him. Other infected fell in line.

The great bronze doors hung off their hinges. The rotted horde filed out of the church and stumbled down stone steps into the street.

Lightning flash.

A garbage truck lay on its side, driver still buckled in his seat. He vomited maggots.

The crowd shuffled through the rain-lashed street, squeezed between the hulks of burned out cars.

They filed past Zuccotti Park and headed east down Liberty towards Fenwick Station.

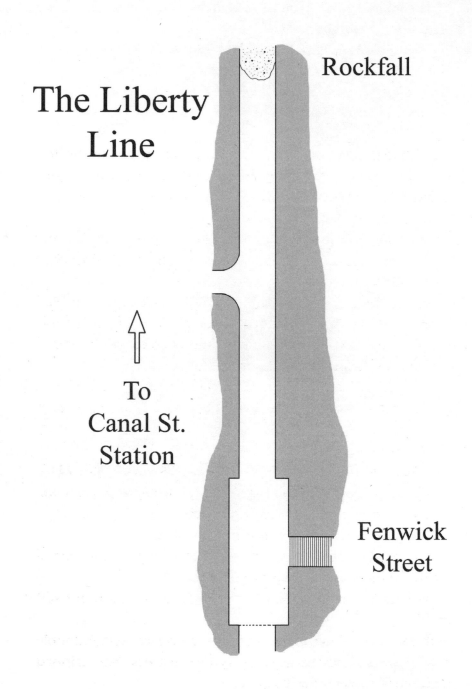

The Liberty Line

Rockfall

To
Canal St.
Station

Fenwick
Street

29

Nariko drifted in black silence. Twin helmet lights shafted through swirling sediment. Bone-chilling cold. She kicked against the velvet dark with a series of muscular leg strokes.

Cloke and Tombes swam behind her. Lights danced in the dark. They carried a stretcher between them. A fibreglass backboard loaded with equipment.

She reached a wall of rubble. She gripped the tumbled blocks and manoeuvred hand over hand. She clipped a karabiner to the rivet hole of a girder and spooled safety line.

She sank to the tunnel floor.

Her helmet lamps lit the buckled yellow hull of the school bus sitting on the track-bed, part-buried beneath masonry.

She inspected the bus.

'*The rubble has shifted. I think the roof is starting to fold.*'

'*We can't abort, Captain,*' said Cloke. '*We have to press on.*'

'*I'm heading inside. You guys stay here.*'

She pulled herself through the windshield

The driver. Hands fused to the wheel. The corpse leaned right, like he was taking a hard corner.

She used the dash and driver's seat to haul herself inside.

She touched down in the passenger compartment. A double row of seats. The bus listed forty-five degrees. She gripped a seatback to keep her balance.

'*Tombes? You got the breaching gear?*'

'*Right behind you, Cap.*'

Nariko glanced around at buckled window pillars, the bulging, ridged metal of the roof.

'*Let's hurry it up, guys. This thing could implode any moment.*'

Light shafting through the vacant windshield. Twin helmet beams. Tombes floated into view.

'*Here.*'

He leaned into the bus. He shouldered the dead driver further aside, and passed Nariko a black cylinder lashed with webbing.

Nariko hugged the cylinder under her arm and manoeuvred down the centre aisle in a series of slow lunar strides. She spooled braided paracord tether behind her. She tied the line to the rear seat frame.

'*Need a hand, boss?*'

'*Hang back. Place is a death trap. Less time we spend in here, the better.*'

She rested the steel cylinder on the back seat of the bus. She unwound hose, checked regulator pressure and unsheathed the cutting head: a red pistol grip tipped with an exothermic heat rod.

She positioned herself in front of the rear door, braced her legs, and pulled the trigger. The unit vented a jet of high-pressure oxygen/hydrogen, and simultaneously popped an igniter spark.

An incandescent flame, hot as the sun. Water surrounding the exothermic head fizzed and boiled. Nariko felt spreading convection warmth through the trilaminate of her suit.

She pressed the cutting head to the door panel. Steel turned angry red and began to sweat. The burn hole widened and dripped metal. Steel tears fell and scattered like ball bearings.

'*How's it going?*' asked Cloke.

'*Good. An easy cut.*'

'*We've been submerged nine minutes.*'

'*Just shut up and let me work, all right?*'

The cutting head burned at ten thousand Fahrenheit. She could feel the steel of her helmet radiate heat like a hot plate. She cooked in her suit. She shook her head, blinked to clear perspiration from her eyes. She licked sweat from her upper lip.

She completed the cut. She shut off the plasma torch and took a step back into cooler waters.

A vein of super-hot metal glowed red like neon. She kicked the door. It fell open.

'*That's it. I'm through.*'

She stood in the rear doorway and surveyed the debris beyond.

A crevice between two massive chunks of concrete.

'*It's a tight traverse, but we can make it to the other side.*'

She returned to the front of the bus. Tombes fed her the spinal injury backboard piled with equipment. She laid the plasma cylinder alongside EMT kit and lashed it down with nylon rope.

They wrestled the stretcher down the aisle towards the rear door.

Cloke crouched on the hood of the bus. He looked through the windshield into the dark interior. He watched the dancing helmet lights of Nariko and Tombes as they struggled to manoeuvre the bier to the rear door.

He looked up. Rubble and girders. A precarious Jenga-stack. A massive tonnage of stone piled above the bus roof.

'*This stuff could collapse on our heads any moment,*' said Nariko, wind-rush of exertion captured by the helmet mike. '*If this were a standard street rescue, I would tell my guys to hold back. At least until we got proper structural support.*'

Cloke psyched himself to enter the buckled hull of the bus. He gripped the tether line and pulled himself past the dead driver. His helmet lights briefly illuminated empty sockets and a yellow-tooth grin.

He called to Tombes at the rear of the bus:

'*How's it looking? A clear route?*'

'*Looks that way.*'

Cloke's left foot snagged. He squirmed. He tried to shake free. He was stuck fast.

He turned and looked back. The bus driver had twisted in his seat and sunk teeth into the fabric of his drysuit. He could feel the tight vice-pressure of teeth grinding into his suit lining, trying to break flesh.

Cloke screamed.

'*What's up?*' shouted Nariko. '*What's going on?*' She grabbed seat backs and hauled herself towards the front of the bus. '*Cloke. What's going on?*'

Cloke kicked at the cadaver's eyeless face. He balled a fist and pounded the creature's skull. Water pressure slowed his arm, softened every movement like he was battling monsters in a helpless fever-dream.

Rising panic. He thrashed and flailed. He lost a flipper. His helmet and gas pack slammed into the roof as he tried to wrench lose.

'*Keep still.*'

Nariko pushed past him. She gripped the back of the driver's seat for support. She pulled the Glock from her weight belt.

She clubbed the creature with the butt, hammered its forehead and temple until the driver's teeth reflexively parted and released the fabric of Cloke's suit.

Nariko deactivated the safety with a gloved thumb.

The skeletal driver strained against the seat belt, snapped and lunged.

Nariko jammed the gun between gaping jaws, twisted the barrel deep into the creature's throat and pulled the trigger. Muffled thump. A slow-blossoming burst of brain tissue and skull fragments. The bullet streaked out the windshield into darkness, fast-decelerating trajectory delineated by a plume of gas bubbles shimmering like globules of mercury.

The dead thing slumped, head flung back, and was still.

'*Are you all right?*' asked Nariko. '*Are you bitten? Did it puncture your suit?*'

She turned Cloke's helmet to face her. He was sweating, eyes wide with fear.

'*Get it together. Control your breathing.*'

He nodded.

'*Focus. Be calm and focus.*'

'*I'm okay,*' he said. Each panting exhalation roared over the open radio channel.

She checked the leg of his dive suit. Deep gouges in the trilaminate fabric, but no tears.

She gripped his arm and checked his wrist screen. An amber oxygen depletion warning.

'*Hey. Breathe slow. You're burning too much air.*'

'*How the hell was that thing still alive? How long had it been submerged?*'

'*The virus never quits. Come on. Get it together. We have to get out of here.*'

Cloke replaced his right flipper and tightened straps. He swam towards the back of the bus using seatbacks for guidance, gas tanks scraping the roof.

He helped Tombes lift the equipment bier and manoeuvre it towards the jagged burn hole in the rear bulkhead.

Lupe took a last look at the dead driver. She leaned close. Her helmet lamps lit his shattered face. His head was thrown back, mouth open in a grotesque yawn. Wisps of blood curled from between his teeth and out his nostrils like cigarette fumes. Eye sockets bristled with metallic splinters.

The roof began to collapse.

The rasp of shifting concrete, the grind of abrading cement. Roof panels creased and bulged. Torsion and metal shriek.

The cab began to crumple and cave. Pillars started to bend and fold. The remaining side windows frosted and shattered with a muffled crunch. Serpentine clouds of silt curled through the vacant frames and began to fill the passenger compartment. Visibility dropped like the bus was filling with smoke.

'*Fucking move,*' shouted Nariko, voice deafening loud inside her helmet.

She lunged for the guide line. Her gauntlets scrabbled at the fine, nylon rope. Too insubstantial. Too smooth. The cord danced between her fingers, like a wisp of gossamer.

She caught the line, twisted for grip, and began to haul herself hand-over-hand.

The three divers scrambled down the centre aisle, grabbed seatbacks, kicked up a silt-storm. The buckling hull closed around them like the piston-walls of a compactor. The roof kinked and crumpled, pressed lower as the steel frame of the bus folded in a series of sudden capitulations. They could hear the torque of stressed metal, deep howls and moans, like whale song.

Cloke and Tombes struggled to haul equipment from the rear of the bus. A narrow crevice. Their headlamps danced as they shifted and contorted, tried to wrestle equipment in the confined space.

Crack and grind. Titanic blocks of masonry shifted and settled. The water around them began to fill with a swirling blizzard of stone dust.

'*Go,*' yelled Cloke, shouting to be heard over the rubble-roar that filled their helmets. Tombes continued to tug at the stretcher. '*Forget the gear. Just go.*'

'*We need this shit.*'

Cloke seized the grab-handle on the back of his tank frame and pulled.

'*Move. Just fucking move.*'

They abandoned the equipment and struggled to kick clear of cascading debris.

Cloke alone, disoriented, spinning in sub-aquatic darkness.

He tumbled through space, no sense of up or down. His wrist screen flashed an amber warning: elevated oxygen consumption.

Stop struggling, he told himself. Be still. Be calm.

He slowly spun to a halt. He sank and gently hit bottom, kicking up a silt-plume.

Occluded vision. He reached up and tried to clear his visor. A jagged crack running the width of the Lexan. A blot of blood on the glass. Ear-whine concussion.

His helmet lights lit a tennis shoe lying on the tunnel floor. Grey with dirt, been there years. He stared at the shoe, tried to regain his balance, willed his head to stop spinning.

He fumbled the radio clipped to his weight belt. He checked the jack was still plugged to his helmet.

'*Nariko. Captain. Come in, over.*'

No reply.

'*Captain. Captain, can you hear me? Sound off, if you can hear my voice.*'

Nothing.

'*Tombes. What is your status, over?*'

No response.

'*Tombes. Captain. Guys. Speak to me. Sound off.*'

Something tendrillar coiling round his feet. He grabbed it. A loose length of safety line. He pulled hand over hand. The end was frayed and torn.

He peered into a fog of swirling rock dust. He slowly turned around, tried to figure north from south, tried to locate the rockfall.

'*Captain. Tombes. Come on, guys. Where are you? Talk to me. Tell me you're alive.*'

30

Cloke surfaced. He broke through a crust of floating garbage. He gripped a ledge in the tunnel wall for support.

He wiped water droplets from his visor with a gloved hand. He studied the cracked Lexan, anxious to see if irradiated flood water were leaking into his helmet.

Twin lamps lit the tunnel walls. He looked around. Crumbling brickwork arched overhead. Old gang graffiti. DEF CON MUTHAFUKAS. A flaking portrait of Malcolm X.

Tombes surfaced beside him.

'*Where the hell is the Captain? Did she get out?*'

'*She was right behind us,*' said Cloke. '*Right at my back.*'

They looked around at the bobbing scrim of garbage, expecting Nariko to break surface any moment.

Tombes:

'*Captain, do you copy, over?*'

No reply.

'*Captain, can you hear me?*'

No response.

'*Shit.*'

Tombes resubmerged.

Cloke checked his wrist gauge. They had been in the water twenty-nine minutes.

He ducked beneath the surface and followed Tombes as he kicked for the rockfall.

Sediment broiled like smoke. Their headlamps lit curling vortices of stone dust.

They floated side by side. Particulates settled. The water around them slowly cleared.

The bus had been buried by an avalanche of rubble.

'*Captain?*' called Cloke. '*Cap? Can you hear me?*'

Tombes settled flippered feet on the tunnel floor and began to dig. He clawed at the rubble, grabbed fist-sized lumps of cement and hurled them aside. Cloke joined him. Grind of stone on stone.

'*Did her suit have some kind of locator? Some kind of beacon?*'

'*Look for bubbles,*' said Tombes. '*She may have a ruptured tank.*'

Cloke lifted a paving slab aside and exposed a coil of rope.

'*I've found the gear.*'

They excavated their equipment. Trauma packs. Clothes and boots sealed in polythene. The plasma arc. They dragged the stretcher clear.

They kept digging.

'*Nariko? Captain? Are you alive? Can you hear my voice?*'

'*Sound off, Cap,*' called Tombes. '*Where the hell are you?*'

Nariko lay in darkness. A minute of slow-spinning who-am-I/where-am-I. Then she remembered Fenwick Street, the dive, the bus.

She lazily raised a hand. She touched stone. A wall of concrete close on every side.

No sound but her own irregular breath, and the click of the oxygen solenoid injecting fresh gas into the micro-environment of her suit.

She coughed. She shook her head, tried to clear her thoughts. One of her dead helmet lights blinked to life and glowed weak orange. The beam lit concrete inches from her face.

She tried to move. She was pinned tight. She lay on her back, entombed in rubble, trapped in a pocket little bigger than a coffin.

She was numb below the waist.

For a brief moment she succumbed to claustrophobia. She clawed at her helmet. Head encased in a steel bubble, held rigid by foam pads, vision restricted by the hex-bolt porthole inches from her face.

'*Fuck, fuck, fuck . . .*'

She thrashed. She punched ferro-concrete boulders hemming her on all sides. She struggled to lift her head. The helmet butted cement. Harsh abrasion; metal on stone.

'*Hey.*' Deafened by her own cry for help. Hot, stale breath filled the helmet. '*Hey, I'm here. I'm right here.*' A tone of shrill hysteria creeping into her voice. '*Someone. Hey. Help.*'

Feedback from her earpiece. Cloke's voice:

'*. . . ome on . . . me . . . your head . . . alive . . . hear my voi . . .*'

She reached down to the Motorola clipped to her weight belt. She checked the jack and upped volume.

'*Hey. I'm here. I'm right here.*'

Nariko fumbled the shoulder harness of her back-tanks and flipped the release latches. She struggled to lift her head and look down at her feet.

The bus had been crushed by subsiding rubble. Nariko was halfway out of the rear door when the vehicle compacted flat. She was pinned in an envelope of yellow metal. Her lower body, her groin and legs, compressed into a space eight inches high. Wisps of blood in the water.

'*Tombes? You out there? Cloke? Can you hear me?*'

'*Yeah. Yeah, we hear you. Are you all right?*'

'*I'm stuck. I'm trapped.*'

'*Have you got any room for manoeuvre? Any room to crawl?*'

'*No.*'

'*Are you injured?*'

'*Think I broke my back.*'

'*Lie still, all right?*'

'I hurt my head. I don't feel so good.'

'Keep talking. Recite a poem or something.'

'I can't think. My head is fuzzy.'

'Do the alphabet. Count backwards from a hundred. Just stay awake, okay? Stay with me. Don't close your eyes. We're coming for you.'

Cloke and Tombes hauled rubble aside. They hefted chunks of cement. They levered a NO THRU TRAFFIC sign loose and threw it clear. They rolled a Con Edison manhole lid. They extracted a baby stroller, did it quick, did it with the periphery of their vision so they wouldn't have to see if it were occupied.

They burrowed beneath a massive slab bristling with rebar.

A cacophony of cracks and grinds as debris shifted around them. A steady cascade of stone dust and trickling grit.

Cloke held back. Tombes kept digging.

'Jesus,' said Cloke, surveying the mountainous rubble pile. 'We need major lifting gear. Some kind of Hurst tool. A bunch of them. We'll never shift this stuff.'

Tombes pointed to the radio clipped to his belt and made a zip-mouth gesture. Open channel. Nariko listening to every word.

Tombes dug towards Nariko's helmet lights. He wormed between slabs. His helmet and air tank scraped rock.

'Don't rip your suit,' said Cloke.

Tombes ignored him.

'How you doing, Boss?'

'Not so great,' said Nariko.

'You need an air line?'

'I can't feel my legs. I think they might be gone.'

'They're probably broken. You'll feel them big time once the shock wears off.'

'I honestly think they're gone.'

162

'We're almost there, all right? I'm a couple of feet away. So just relax. I'm going to unfuck this, okay? The torch will rip that bus apart like paper. You'll be out of there in a couple of minutes.'

A thick girder blocked his path.

'I can see you, Captain. I can almost reach you. But there's a bar, some kind of steel beam. Got to cut the damned thing. This could take a few minutes. Can you hold on?'

'There's blood in the water.'

'How much?'

'I don't know. Some. Don't think it's arterial.'

'Are you in pain? Do you need a shot? If we passed you a hypodermic, taped it to a pole or something, could you use it? Self-administer?'

She didn't reply.

He squirmed deeper into the narrow space. He turned to Cloke.

'Give me the plasma gear.'

Cloke passed the webbed cylinder.

Tombes struggled to manoeuvre in the confined space.

Stone-crack. Grinding concrete. Tumbling debris. Swirling rock dust fogged the water.

Tombes froze, waited for the tremor to pass.

'Work fast,' said Cloke.

'I am.'

'Work faster.'

Boulders shifted and settled. The hull of the bus groaned and compressed an inch further. White pain shot through Nariko's spine. She screamed. She gripped the slab above her head and strained to lift the impossible tonnage from her body.

'Hold on, Boss. Just rest easy. Almost there.'

Nariko lay still. She tried to breathe steady. Muffled roar of the cutting flame. The water around her began to cook. The tight sarcophagus space was lit fluttering white.

'I think I'm pretty messed up.'

'Just chill, boss. Cutting through this thing like butter.'

'Whole lower body seems pretty trashed. I think this bus is the only thing holding my guts together. I'll bleed out the moment you lift me.'

'One thing at a time. We've got to reach you first.'

Another gunshot crack. A fresh puff of rock dust fogged the water.

'Get out of here, guys.'

'Relax, Captain. You're hurt. You're not thinking straight. Let me make the calls.'

'Seriously. Command decision. This debris pile could subside any minute. I'm ordering you to pull back.'

'Rescue Four. We don't pussy out, am I right? Shut the hell up and let me do my thing.'

'Listen. Just listen. People are counting on us, understand? We are the last frigging hope. Forget about me. I don't matter. Neither do you. Find Ekks, whatever the cost.'

'Just rest easy, Cap. You know how this works. I'm the responder, okay? You're the pin-job.'

'I got water in my helmet.'

'Can you reach your tanks? Can you increase suit pressure, force the water out?'

'Go. Just go.'

Nariko clumsily reached behind her back. A sudden jolt of pain stole her breath. She let it subside, then gripped the regulator valve of her gas tanks.

She twisted the demand valve. Her wrist screen flashed brief amber, then glowed red. The depth/time readout was replaced by:

DANGER
EXCESS NO_2

An alarm. Computer voice, calm but insistent:

'. . . danger . . . danger . . . nitrogen toxicity warning . . . danger . . . danger . . . adjust levels now . . .'

'*Captain. What the fuck are you doing?*'

'*Find the cure. Get it to Ridgeway.*'

She twisted the valve full open.

'. . . *danger . . . danger . . . nitrogen level critical . . . danger . . . danger . . . operate manual shut-off now . . .*'

Pounding blood-roar in her ears like crashing waves.

'*Captain. Hang on, you hear me? Don't you dare. Don't you dare fucking code on me.*'

Nariko was back in the womb, enveloped in warmth, surrounded by the reassuring diastole/systole tidal surge.

Drooping eyelids. Drowsy smile.

'. . . *danger . . . danger . . . nitrogen level critical . . .*'

She unplugged her wrist gauge.

She closed her eyes. She took a deep breath. And another. Her body relaxed.

'*You're wasting time,*' she murmured. '*Been in the water too long already. Get going. Go on. Get out of here.*'

'*We'll patch you up, get you back to Ridgeway. It'll be all right.*'

'*Good luck guys.*'

'*Nariko, for God's . . .*'

She reached down to her belt and pulled the jack cable from her radio.

She coughed. A deep, guttural bark. She convulsed, arched her back. A last involuntary struggle. Her gloved hands pawed the walls of her concrete tomb then fell still.

Her breathing settled. Shallow respirations merged with the hiss of the regulator valve. Nitrogen flooded her body. It filled her lungs, infusing arterial blood, saturating every muscle.

Creeping euphoria. A chance to put herself on a tropical beach, or some other endorphin-induced paradise, but she fought it, determined to be present at the moment of her own death.

'*Never enough . . .*'

Her consciousness contracted to a point of light that glimmered like a star. Then the light was gone, and there was nothing but the whisper of tanks bleeding lethal gas, smothering Nariko in cold bliss.

31

'. . . Mayday, Mayday. Can anyone hear me, over? Hello? Is anyone out there? This is Bellevue Research Team broadcasting on emergency frequency one-two-one point five megahertz. If anyone can hear me, please respond . . .'

Ivanek trapped in the dark. No sense of time.

'. . . Please, if anyone can hear me, answer this call . . .'

A voice, right by his ear. Deep, mellow, pure Tennessee:

'How you doing, son?'

'Doctor?'

'Are you feeling okay?'

'I'm cold.'

'Yeah. Me too.'

'I can't see you. Why can't I see you?'

'Don't worry. I'm right here.'

'It's so dark. I can't see anything. I can't see my own hands.'

'It'll be all right. You've just got to hold on.'

'Where are we? I don't understand where we are.'

'It's hard to explain.'

'I'm scared.'

'No reason to be frightened. Think back. What do you remember?'

'I remember the train, the bomb. Are we still in the tunnel? Did the roof collapse?'

'We are in a strange place, you and I. Nothing like it has existed before. Nothing on earth, anyway.'

'Are we dead?'

'No. No, we're not dead.'

'Is this hell?'

'It's too cold for hell.'

'I want to leave. I want to get out of here. How do we get out?'

'We have to be patient.'

'I want to go home.'

'Where is home?'

'Bushwick.'

'It's not there any more.'

'Please.'

'There are men on the way.'

'How do you know?'

'I just know. A rescue party has entered the tunnels. They are coming for us. They will be here soon.'

'How soon?'

'Soon. Hold on, son. They are almost here. It won't be long. All we have to do is wait.'

32

The tunnel followed a gentle upward gradient. Cloke and Tombes swam, then waded, as the water level diminished. Chest high. Waist high. Knee high. They dragged the backboard behind them like a sled.

They trudged clear of the flood water. They were robbed of buoyancy, suddenly burdened by the full weight of their diving gear.

They unbolted lock-rings and removed their helmets. They released their back-tanks, shut off gas valves and lowered them to the dead track.

'We can't abandon the mission,' said Cloke.

Tombes didn't reply. He looked back at the dark waters from which they had emerged. Deep shock.

'We've no choice but to proceed. What would she say if she were here right now? Focus. Keep your shit together. People depend on us. Finish the damned job.'

'Yeah, yeah.'

Cloke switched on his flashlight and surveyed the tunnel walls. Ancient brickwork. Gang tags.

Water splashed his face. He looked up. Seeping groundwater. Calcite hung from the ceiling in petrified drips.

Tombes unclipped his radio. He checked for signal bars.

'Donahue, do you copy, over?'

'*Go ahead.*'

'Nariko is dead.'

'*Say again.*'

'She's dead. The Captain. The Captain is code one.'

'*How?*'

'A rockfall. The rubble shifted. She got trapped.'

'*Oh Jesus.*'

'We did our damnedest to reach her. There was nothing we could do.'

'*You actually saw her die?*'

'She's dead, Donnie.'

'*Are you guys okay?*'

'We're fine.'

'*Where are you?*'

'Other side of the rockfall. We're out of the water, north near Canal.'

'*Any sign of the Bellevue team?*'

'Not yet. Listen. We're trapped in this section of tunnel. Our route back is sealed. Check the charts. Check the schematics. There must be a way out of here. Some kind of utility pipe, sewer tunnel, whatever.'

'*Okay.*'

'Our flashlights are good for a few hours. After that, we'll be stumbling in the dark. We're depending on you. Check every map, every survey you've got. Get us out of here.'

The ticket hall.

'Nariko's dead,' announced Donahue. She listened to the harsh echo of her voice. Wade lay on the bench. He instinctively reached for the cyanide cylinder in his pocket, gripped it like a talisman. His ride. His ticket out of this world. A guarantee he would not be marooned sightless and starving in the tunnels.

Galloway sat on the entrance steps. He stared down at his hands, overwhelmed by the horror of infection and his own imminent death.

Sicknote ignored her. He remained crouched on the floor,

coaxing the last ink from the Sharpie, obsessively mapping the cosmic void, the horrors in his head more real to him than anything taking place at Fenwick Street.

'Guess I'm the only one that gives a shit,' murmured Donahue.

She turned her back on the ticket hall and re-entered the office.

Donahue hurriedly unravelled nicotine-yellow charts and spread them on the table.

Lupe joined her.

'What happened? How did she die?'

'There was a rockfall,' said Donahue. She didn't look up from the charts. 'Some kind of landslide. Cloke and Tombes got clear. The Captain didn't.'

'Christ.'

'The rescue went bad. Could happen to any of us. Comes with the job.'

'What about the guys?'

'Trapped. No way back.'

'So who's in charge of this cluster-fuck?'

'Cloke. The mission was his idea.'

'So I guess that makes you the boss right now.'

'Yeah,' sighed Donahue. 'I guess it does.'

'Sorry,' said Lupe. 'Sorry about your friend.'

They examined a tunnel schematic.

'Can they walk north to Canal Street?' asked Lupe.

'They can try. But I doubt they would get far. If that section of tunnel is dry, it must be sealed both ends. The blast probably collapsed Canal Station. Our guys are trapped in an air pocket. No maintenance exits, no junctions. No way out.'

'Do they know?' said Lupe.

'Of course. They're screwed. They've got no food, or water. Their flashlights are good for a few hours. After that . . .'

'Fuck that shit. Give me the map.'

Lupe grabbed the scrolled chart. She checked the legend.

'Department of Transport. City engineers schematic. This thing is twenty years old. Plenty of underground construction since then. Give me everything you've got.'

Cloke and Tombes kicked off flippers. They unzipped and stripped out of their drysuits. They left their dive gear piled on the tunnel floor next to their tanks and helmets.

They shivered in T-shirts and shorts.

'I wish we had time to say a prayer,' said Tombes.

'Nariko?'

'Yeah.'

'Maybe there'll be time, later.'

Cloke crouched by the stretcher. He cut ropes and opened a holdall. Combat fatigues taped in polythene.

They ripped the bags with their teeth. They dressed. They jumped and swung their arms to get warm.

Cloke unzipped a canvas tool bag. He took out a couple of hammers. He tossed one to Tombes.

'Tuck this in your belt.'

They laced boots, shouldered equipment and headed down the tunnel.

Cloke took a Geiger reading.

'We better watch the numbers. Closer we get to Canal, more chance of a radiation spike. If the tunnel is ruptured, open to the street, we might have to mask-up in a hurry.'

Their breath fogged the air. Their footfalls echoed in darkness.

Distant rustle.

'You hear that?' asked Tombes.

'Relax. It's just rats.'

'Hello?' shouted Cloke. His voice reverberated through the cavernous tunnel space. 'Anyone down here?'

He listened. Silence.

'Hello? Anyone?'

Nothing.

They kept walking.

'What about that kid on the radio?' asked Tombes.

'Maybe he was a recording. Think back. Did he actually talk to Nariko? Answer questions? Did they properly interact?'

'I don't recall.'

Their flashlights lit a track-bed scattered with garbage.

A dead rat.

Cloke crouched and examined the rodent. He prodded the rat with his hammer.

'Strange that this strain, this parasite, never jumped species. Won't attack any other mammal, any other primate. Pops out of nowhere. Super-evolved. Super-lethal. Almost as if it were created with humans in mind.'

'Honestly? I don't give a damn any more. Escaped bio-weapon. Weird-ass flu. Kind of academic at this point. The disease won. Game over. It owns the planet. We should have made for the hills. A damn sight more sense than this hero bullshit. Nariko buried for ever under a pile of rocks back there. For what? Because the Chief gave an order.'

They kept walking. Their flashlights lit ancient brickwork.

'Over there,' said Cloke. 'Human remains.'

A jumble of burned bone by the tunnel wall.

'I count three, four skulls. Army fatigues. Couple of lab coats.'

'Infected?'

'Can't tell.'

'Let me take a look.'

Cloke crouched by the jumble of scorched bone.

'Got a knife?'

Tombes handed him a pocket knife.

Cloke flicked open the blade and probed the ashes. He lifted a wide, metal bangle from the debris. Cyrillic lettering stamped into the ring.

'What's that?' asked Tombes. Cloke ignored him.

A steel box. Cloke scraped ashes from the metal. A weird half-skull symbol embossed on the lid.

'Give me the backpack.'

Tombes passed him the pack. Cloke unzipped a side pocket and pulled out a digital camera. He took pictures of the box. Each flash lit the tunnel like lightning.

Tombes kicked a skull.

'Ekks?'

Cloke shook his head. He lifted a scorched scrap of lab coat with his knife.

'Ekks didn't wear a coat. Insisted his team wore pristine medical whites, even down here in the tunnels, but he always wore a linen jacket like he'd been sipping mint juleps on a Hampton veranda. Kept his hands clean. Gave orders. Let his guys do the work.'

'How will you recognise him?'

'Fifties. Grey hair. People say he wore a silver ouroboros ring. A snake eating its own tail. Never took it off.'

They walked further into the tunnel.

'Check it out,' said Tombes. 'Something big up ahead.'

Glint of silver. Something large blocking the passageway.

The steel hull of a subway train.

Cloke trained his flashlight on the motorman's cab. Cracked windshield glass. A red line designation: *3*.

'Guess we found them.'

Cloke examined the carriage frame. 'Blood all along the front here. Bunch of hair on the nose coupler. Guess she ploughed through a crowd at some point. Ran a bunch of people down.'

'Nice,' muttered Tombes. He checked the tunnel behind

them, jittering sweeps of his flashlight as he scanned buttressed archways, made sure nothing lurked in shadow.

'Wait here,' said Cloke. 'Let me check her out.'

Cloke walked the length of the train. He shuffled the narrow space between the tunnel wall and the cars. His flashlight lit windows blacked out with garbage bags. A route board: BROADWAY.

He crouched and shone his flashlight between the wheel bogies.

'The last coach is buried under rubble. Looks like Canal pretty much imploded.'

'Why did they come this far north? Why not stop in the tunnel?'

'Because the driver screwed up. Panic. Confusion. Darkness. Hard to blame the guy.'

Cloke took a Geiger reading. He scanned the hull of the train. Fierce crackle.

'Heavy gamma. She got pretty cooked. Bedrock didn't give much protection.'

'There are bodies on board,' called Tombes. 'I can smell them.'

'Let's hope they're dead. That Cav officer floating down-stream was infected. Doubt he was the only one to get bitten.'

He cupped his hands.

'Hello?' Heavy echo. 'Anyone down here?' He pounded his hammer on the side of a carriage. 'Anyone home?'

'Might not be such a good idea,' called Tombes, glancing round the tunnel, checking shadows.

'If there are any prowlers down here, let's draw them out, face them head-on.'

'We got problems enough.'

Cloke returned to the front of the train.

'You're right. Doesn't smell too pretty.'

'Let's get these doors open.'

Cloke reached up, pressed his fingers into the rubber door seal and tried to prize it open.

'We could use a crowbar.'

Heavy thud.

They jumped back. They trained their flashlights on the door above them. A bloody, tumourous hand pressed against the window, sliding down the glass leaving bloody finger-smears.

'Fuck,' muttered Tombes.

'Guess we found the Bellevue guys.'

33

Galloway sat on the platform steps. He sought out darkness and seclusion, a chance to examine his hand unobserved.

He flipped open a lock-knife and used the tip to slit the dressing.

Micropore tape slowly tore from skin. He peeled back blood-crusted bandage.

The severed stump of his knuckle bristled with fine metallic splinters. The flesh of his hand was purple and swollen, mottled with spreading rot.

He probed the wound with the tip of the blade. His hand was numb. He pressed the point of the knife into his palm, pressed until he drew a bead of blood. Nothing. No sensation.

'Doesn't smell too fresh,' said Wade. He stood at the head of the steps, hand on the balustrade, sightless eyes staring ahead. 'You should let Donahue take another look.'

'She won't do a damned thing.'

Wade descended the stairs. He kept a tight grip on the balustrade, probed each step with his foot. He sat next to Galloway.

He took the cyanide cylinder from his pocket. 'Maybe you should ask Donahue for one of these.'

'Fuck that.'

'You know the score,' said Wade. 'No vaccine, no antidote. Few hours from now, you'll turn. Is that what you want?'

'If you're so in love with death, why not swallow the damned thing yourself and be done?'

'Let me know if you change your mind.'

'Three, two, one.'

Cloke and Tombes hauled the slide doors apart.

A skeletal figure fell from the train to the tunnel floor. Ripped army fatigues bristled with spines. The thing squinted into the glare of Cloke's flashlight.

It howled.

Tombes delivered three skull-shattering blows with his hammer, and kicked the body aside.

They climbed into the carriage. They stood tensed, keyed for movement.

'Christ,' muttered Tombes.

The beam of his flashlight swept the carriage.

Bodies. Soldiers and civilians. A dozen of them, sat on equipment cases like they were all taking a ride uptown. A hole in the crown of each head. Brain and hair gummed to the melamine of the carriage roof.

Cartridge cases scattered on the floor. Clink and chime.

A Colt pistol hung from a skeletal hand. Cloke prized open fingers. He ejected the mag. Empty. He threw the weapon aside.

'They were trapped. Guess they passed round a pistol.'

Tombes checked insignia.

'Couple of 101st. A nurse. A doctor. This guy is a transit cop.'

Cloke found a battery lamp. He tried the on/off slide-switch. He shook it. Dead. He threw it aside.

'Guess we better check ID,' said Cloke.

'Fifties. Silver hair.'

'That's right.'

Tombes surveyed the rows of bodies. Young guys. Crew cuts.

'He's not here.'

'Double check.'

Cloke shone his flashlight round the carriage. The fibreglass seats had been removed. Boxes and ammo crates stacked on the floor, piled against the carriage wall. The walls had been lagged with opaque polythene: a crude attempt at insulation.

'Must have frozen their asses off down here.'

He kicked through garbage. Empty water bottles. Foil MRE wrappers. He tipped a box. Dozens of shampoo bottles tumbled across the floor.

'They brought some pretty random shit,' said Tombes.

'Looks like they raided a Duane Reade. Snatched whatever they found.'

'Must have been miserable. No daylight. Dwindling rations. Surprised they didn't go nuts.'

'Looks like they did.'

Tombes walked between the bodies. He pulled on gloves.

Tombes plucked a crumpled sheet of paper from a dead hand.

'They wrote suicide notes.'

'Bag them up. That's what we came for. Any written account of their time down here. Anything that might describe their research.'

Tombes took a bandana from his pocket, shook it open and masked his face. He knelt in front of a corpse and tried to push a rigor-stiff arm aside so he could reach a pant pocket. The cadaver toppled forwards, threatened to fall on him. He pushed it back in its seat. He pulled out a leather wallet.

'This guy was a limo driver.'

'Guess they picked up a few civilians along the way. Pretty ragtag bunch.'

Cloke shone his flashlight round the carriage. Grotesque,

gaping mouths. Eyes sunk and rolled back. Some of the corpses leaned, like they were sleeping on each other's shoulders.

He took a Geiger reading. He held the handset in front of an emaciated, shattered face. Fierce crackle.

'They were dying and they knew it.'

'This is how we'll end up, isn't it?' said Tombes. 'Sitting in the dark. For ever.'

'Donahue is checking the charts. Maybe we'll be okay.'

Donahue searched through the trauma bag. She found a box of Codeine. She pressed tablets from a foil strip and dry-swallowed.

Galloway sat on the entrance steps. He watched her and smiled.

'A little something to take the edge?'

'Mind your own damned business.'

'Hey. So you need a little de-stress. I don't blame you. No one would blame you. Nariko got us in this mess. She wanted to die a hero. Dragged us down here and got herself killed. You didn't create this situation.'

'Shut the hell up, all right? You didn't know the Captain. I saw her suit up more times than I can count. One of the best. End of each shift, those hard-ass Irish fucks would save her a seat at the bar. Old-school motherfuckers, twenty-five years on the job. If you work on a fire truck, that's worth more than a Congressional Medal of Honor. You got to eat some serious smoke to impress those bastards.'

'Sure. She was better than me, better than all of us. But right now, we're marooned. Each of us got to deal the best way we can.' He gestured to the pill box. 'Gonna throw me a few of those bad boys?'

Donahue tossed the pill box. Galloway snatched it from the air.

'Could use a cigarette. Shit, I could use a drink.'

He was pale, face coated with a glistening sweat-sheen.

'How's your arm?' asked Donahue.

Galloway looked down at his bandaged hand. He slowly clenched his fist.

'Not so great.'

He pointed to the trauma kit.

'You've got a ton of shit in that bag, right? Got a tourniquet? Scalpels? Sutures? All that stuff?'

Donahue shook her head.

'Forget it. There is nothing anyone can do for you. That's the hard truth. Sorry, dude. Your luck's run out.'

Donahue headed back to the office. She slumped in a chair, head in her hands.

Lupe stood at the table, studying charts.

'Are you going to help, or what?'

'Let me rest,' said Donahue. 'Please. Just for a minute or two.'

'Three cons and a guy on the turn. You're the boss now. You're supposed to take charge, sort shit out.'

Donahue didn't reply. She closed her eyes and breathed deep as the Codeine hit.

'We ought to talk about Galloway. We can't let the disease take hold.'

'So?' asked Donahue. 'What do you want to do? Force a capsule down his throat?'

'We might have to use the shotgun. Could be the kindest thing. Pick our moment. Do it quick and clean. The guy wouldn't have to know a thing about it.'

Donahue held out the gun.

'Be my guest.'

Lupe took the weapon.

'Okay. I'll do what needs to be done. But I don't want to hear any complaints when the time comes.'

Splutter and rev of a petrol engine.

'What the hell is that?'

Lupe and Donahue ran for the door.

Sicknote held a petrol-drive stone-cutter. He shut off the motor. He watched the circular blade slow-spin to a halt. A fine blood spray across his forearms and face.

Galloway sat on the ticket hall floor. He had a leather belt tightly strapped around his forearm. A dripping stump where his hand used to be.

The air around him was tinged purple. A halo of exhaust smoke and blood mist.

He looked euphoric.

'Holy mother of God,' murmured Lupe.

The severed hand lay in a puddle of blood.

Donahue threw a balled T-shirt at Sicknote.

'Wipe that shit off your face. Do it quick. He's infected. And mop the floor, for Christ's sake. We have to clean this mess up.'

'What's going on?' demanded Wade, groping along the wall. 'Someone tell me what the hell is going on.'

'Just stay there, all right? Hang back. There's blood. We've got to glove-up and sterilise this place.'

Donahue double-gloved, crouched and picked up a hypodermic.

'What did you shoot? Dilaudid? How much did you take?'

Galloway shrugged. He held up his stump. Woozy smile.

'Ain't going out without a fight.'

34

Tombes walked among rows of bodies. The beam of his flashlight played over desiccated cadavers.

He plugged his nostrils with tissue. He searched pockets. He uncurled each fist and retrieved crumpled sheets of paper. Suicide notes stained with blood-spray and the mottled leak-grease of decomposition.

Cloke pulled open the door to the adjoining carriage.

Boxed lab equipment. Toppled stacks of high-impact Peli cases, like tumbled building blocks.

He pictured the chaos. The presidential announcement. Planes are in the air. Ten major cities selected for destruction:

Los Angeles.

Chicago.

Houston.

Philadelphia.

Phoenix.

San Antonio.

San Diego.

Dallas.

San Jose.

New York.

Panic. Less than an hour until a B2 reaches Manhattan and releases its payload.

Ivanek screaming at the radio, desperate to reach NORAD,

desperate to tell them the Bellevue team is alive and they should call off the strike.

Soldiers and medics grab gear from the Fenwick Street platform and hurl supplies aboard the train. Their entire bivouac broken down in minutes. Cots, cooking utensils and lab equipment tossed through carriage doorways.

Personnel cower aboard the train, sobbing with fear as Donovan, the commanding officer, makes one last sweep of the station. He sprints across the ticket hall. He kicks open the plant room door and checks the IRT office, makes sure the place is stripped of gear and no one left behind.

He runs down the platform steps three at a time, yells to the motorman hanging out of his cab: *All clear.* He hurls himself aboard the train. The doors slide shut and the locomotive pulls away from the platform.

They sit parked in the tunnel, counting down the minutes, praying and weeping, waiting for the strike.

They knew how detonation would unfold:

EMP would kill the power. A half second of darkness, then they would feel a sudden ear-popping change of tunnel pressure. Half a second later, the blast wave would hit.

Maybe they passed round a pistol and blew their brains out before the bomb exploded. To escape the horror. To escape the fear.

Cloke found a plastic bag. He flapped it open.

He kicked through the wreckage. Thumb drives. A pile of printout. Clipboards loaded with paper. He stuffed them in the bag.

A PC. He threw it on the floor. He kicked the aluminium chassis and tore out the hard drive. He dropped it in the bag.

The next carriage.

Cloke paused in the doorway. He pressed his face to the

184

glass. Darkness within. A couple of winking, emerald LEDs. Something powered up.

He pulled the door aside. Machine hum. Faint white-noise hiss.

He adjusted his grip on the hammer.

'Hey. Anyone home?'

He edged into the carriage.

His foot hit an obstruction. He shone his flashlight at the floor. A desiccated cadaver. Back arched, rigor-stiff, locked in a final death agony. The guy had a bayonet bedded deep in his eye socket, hands wrapped round the handle like he drove the blade into his own head.

No signs of infection. Cloke knelt and patted him down. Empty pockets, empty holster. He plucked the tag from the dead man's neck.

Something grotesque at the back of the carriage. Metallic ropes and tendrils snaked across the floor, the walls, the roof.

Cloke reluctant to focus his flashlight. Sudden, gut conviction that he should turn and leave. Better not to see. Better not to know.

He forced himself to look.

'Mother of God,' he murmured.

Something at the centre of the knotted mess. The radio operator. He sat on a swivel chair, slumped over the receiver, embedded like the radio was eating him head first. He had succumbed to infection. His upper body was a mass of rippled metal. He was fused with the transmitter, fused with the torrent of chrome spilling across the floor, melding with the fabric of the carriage.

Cloke stepped between tendrils rooted in the splintered floorboards.

The young man gripped the edge of the table. His hand seemed healthy, normal. Cloke pulled off a glove, intending to check for warmth, for life, but glanced at the metal-melded head and withdrew.

He examined the radio. A green power light pulsed like a heartbeat. Frequency needles twitched in time to the strange, cardiovascular rhythm.

He checked beneath the table. The power cable hung severed and frayed.

It was as if the radio had become an extension of the kid's nervous system. The chips and circuits were now incorporated into the neural architecture of his brain, responding to fleeting static-bursts of synaptic activity.

Cloke unhooked the Motorola from his belt and retuned.

'Rescue party calling Bellevue, can anyone hear me, over?'

No response.

'Ivanek. Can you hear me? Can you hear my voice?'

Transmission needles twitched and rose.

The young man's voice crackled through the speaker of Cloke's radio. Distant, shouting to be heard over a storm-howl of interference.

'*Who is this? Who is talking?*'

'Cloke. Matthew Cloke. I'm here to help.'

'*Am I dreaming?*'

'No. You're not dreaming.'

'*Am I alive?*'

'Yes, I think so.'

'*Where am I?*'

'You're in Manhattan. You're in a subway tunnel. There was a bomb.'

'*My memory. Things come and go.*'

'Just take it easy.'

'*Why can't I see you?*'

'It's dark.'

'*Where are the others?*'

'The Cav?'

'*We were waiting for the bomb, counting down the minutes.*'
'Don't worry about them.'
'*Where's the woman? I spoke to a woman.*'
'She can't be with us. She had to stay behind.'
'*Please. Come quickly.*'
'What happened? Can you remember?'
'*I don't know how I got here.*'
'Where are you? Can you describe it to me?'
'*I'm alone. It's cold. It's dark. There's no one here but me.*'
'Don't worry kid. We'll be with you soon.'

An ammo trunk stamped 5.56MM PYRO. Tombes lifted the lid. Bean tins.

He sat on the trunk, surrounded by food boxes, bedding rolls and medical gear. Stuff hurled aboard the train in the panic of evacuation.

A Nike holdall on the floor beside him. He lifted the flap. Civilian stuff. Photographs, jewellery, bank documents. Someone fled an apartment, swept their life into a bag as they headed for the door.

He reached into the holdall. A bottle cap protruded from a couple of balled T-shirts. Wild Turkey, quarter full. He uncorked and sniffed. He took a long slug. And a second. He wiped his mouth with the back of his hand.

He looked around. No guns. Each 101st Cav should have been carrying an assault rifle and side arm. Maybe they expended their ammunition during the short journey from the hospital to the 23rd Street Station. Must have been quite a battle. Troops working their way block by block in cover/fire formation. Tossing grenades. Shooting their mags dry, shooting until their weapons smoked hot and jammed, in a desperate race to get underground.

Or maybe most of the soldiers refused to board the train for its final journey into the tunnel. No fight left in them.

Perhaps they rode the freight elevator to the top of the Federal Building and waited for the bomb to drop. Injured, exhausted men electing to die on their own terms. Sat on the roof beside the water tower, sharing a cigarette. They shielded their eyes from the gamma flash, watched the unfurling mushroom cloud, yelled a defiant Fuck You at the oncoming firestorm.

Tombes took another hit of Wild Turkey.

'Rest easy, guys.'

An improvised surgical theatre.

Blacked out windows. Forceps, scalpels and bone saws scattered across the floor.

Tombes inspected rough planks laid across saw-horse trestles. A crude operating table. Blood soaked into the grain, staining it black. Leather buckle straps for wrists and ankles.

A butcher's slab. Unsuitable for surgery, perfect for dividing a side of beef with crude blows of a cleaver.

He took another sip of bourbon.

If Cloke were there he would say:

'Cool it with the booze, all right? Keep a clear head.'

And Tombes would reply:

'A skull full of panic isn't a clear head.'

He surveyed the shelves.

The place was a charnel house.

His flashlight beam washed over jars. Pathological material. Tissue in suspension. Heart, liver, kidneys, pickled in formaldehyde. Organs bristled with tumourous growths.

He picked up a jar.

Sections of lung.

He picked up another jar.

An eye.

'Christ.'

Documents scattered on the floor at the back of the coach.

Tombes corked the bottle, crouched and shuffled papers.

Monochrome photographs. A man lashed to an examination table, naked, head shaved. He was screaming, pleading with his captors. Lab coats and surgical gowns in the corner of each frame, sinister gloved and ministering hands clustered around him.

More pictures. A loaded hypodermic. Desperate, pleading eyes, lips curled in a despairing sob.

Tombes checked his flashlight. The beam dimmed to weak, grey light. He shook it. It flared and died. He shook it again. Stuttering light.

Nightmare glimpses of dissection. A bloody bone saw. A peeled scalp. A brain lifted from a skull. A body, skin peeled back, spine exposed.

Tombes tightened the battery cap until the flashlight shone strong and steady.

'Sick motherfuckers.'

He took another drink.

He tried the door to the adjoining carriage. Locked. He wiped glass, tried to peer inside.

He smashed out the glass with his hammer. He reached through the broken window and unlatched the door. He edged into the carriage, hammer raised.

A camp bed. A desk. A chair.

The coach had clearly been home to a single occupant, the sole member of the Bellevue team privileged to enjoy space and solitude.

A Samsonite suitcase on the floor beside the bed. Tombes lifted the lid with his foot. Toiletries and clothes arranged with fastidious precision. Montaigne, *Essays*. A rosary.

Tombes took the bottle from his pocket, uncorked and raised the neck to his lips.

He glanced at the cot: double-take as he glimpsed silver hair and realised someone lay beneath the rumpled blanket.

'Damn.'

He slapped the stopper back in the bottle.

He slowly pulled back the blanket, hammer raised ready to strike.

A body. An emaciated man. Fifties. Eyes closed, mouth open. Pristine. Uninfected.

Tombes lowered the hammer and knelt by the cot.

The man's hands were folded across his chest. Tombes leaned close. A silver ring. A snake eating its tail.

'Holy fuck,' he murmured.

He sat back. He rubbed his eyes and shook to clear his head.

He unhooked his radio.

'Cloke, you copy? I've found him. Can you hear me? Hey. Switch on, dude. I've found Ekks.'

The man held a notebook clasped in his hands. Tombes prized his fingers apart and took the book. A black Moleskine. Scuffed cover, crumpled pages.

He thumbed through the leaves. Urgent biro scrawl. Letters and symbols, line after line, page after page. Some kind of code.

Gasp. Convulsion. Ekks shook and arched his back.

Tombes dropped the book and gripped the man's shoulders.

'Holy crap. Hold on. Just hold on.'

Tombes grabbed his radio.

'Cloke, can you hear me, over? Get down here. Bring the trauma kit. Ekks is alive. The fucker is alive.'

35

Lupe rubbed her eyes.

More maps and charts. She smoothed schematics over the table. She laid them one over another, let the accumulation of translucent onion-skin sheets plot city infrastructure embedded in the soil surrounding the Liberty Line, aka tunnel 38A.

Gas lines. Fibre-optic conduits. Sewer channels. A dendritic network, layer on layer. Veins and arteries.

'Are you going to help with this shit, or not?'

Donahue sat against the wall. She chewed an energy bar. She was pale with exhaustion.

'It's a sealed tunnel. Not much we can do. If we had more men, if we had boring equipment, maybe we could help. Burrow from the street or parking structure.'

'They're your friends.'

'Tombes is my friend. I don't know Cloke. He's nothing to me. Saw him a couple of times at Ridgeway. Hadn't spoken to him before today.'

'Don't you want to help Tombes?'

'The charts are useless. Lower Manhattan has been dug so many damned times no one knows what lies beneath the surface. Let the guys see what they can find. Tombes knows what he's doing. He's been riding a truck twenty years. He's kicked a lot of doors, sucked a lot of smoke. He'll keep his head. If there's an out, he'll find it.'

'Fuck that crap,' said Lupe. 'We've got the maps. They're relying on us to find a way home.'

'When did you start to give a shit?'

Lupe crossed the room and sat beside Donahue. She uncapped a bottle of water and swigged.

'If we don't find something worthwhile in these tunnels, they won't send the chopper. The Chief doesn't need any of you. He needs shooters, hard-ass trigger men. Civilians are dead weight. They sit around, draining resources. Useless eaters. Waste of food, waste of water. So if you guys strike out, he won't send the chopper. Why risk the remaining machine, the pilot, pulling you guys out of the hot zone? You're all sick. You'll get sicker. You'll need beds, treatment, a shitload of medical supplies. Face it, girl. You're an asset. And you just got expended.'

'Bull.'

'I'd do the same in his position.'

Donahue wiped her forehead. She inspected her sweat-slick palm.

'It's started. The sickness.'

'Fight it.'

'How about you?' asked Donahue. 'Do you feel it yet?'

'Yeah. Worming into my bones.'

Lupe straightened. She stretched.

'Galloway. Idiot is high on Dilaudid, convinced he's going to live for ever. I'll deal with him. Quick and clean. Wade and Sicknote won't give a shit. But you got to take my side when Cloke and Tombes get back. Make them understand. It had to be done.'

Donahue looked away.

'I'm not an executioner. I'm not going to sit here and pronounce a death sentence. You've got a free hand, all right? Do whatever you have to do. But I don't want to be involved.'

Lupe sipped water. She gestured to the scrolled charts spread on the table.

'Is this everything? Are there any other maps?'

'There's a bag under the table. Might be a couple more utility schematics. Power-lines, I think. Con Ed.'

Lupe dragged a holdall from beneath the table. She unzipped, and pulled out a cardboard tube. She popped the cap and unsheathed a couple of charts. She smoothed the translucent sheets over the tunnel map, lined up the surface grid.

'Get over here. Take a look at this.'

They leaned over the maps.

'Fresh city plan. Can't be more than a couple of years old. See? New infrastructure. Some kind of pipeline running the length of Lower Broadway, directly beneath the subway. City Water Channel Number Five. An aqueduct. Big son of a bitch. Wider than the Holland Tunnel. Looks like it drains Lower Manhattan. Must be working overtime right now. All that shit running down from the Catskill watershed. A huge volume of water drained into the harbour.'

'I'll be damned.'

'Maybe there is some kind of inspection shaft, a way of dropping from the subway to the channel beneath.'

'Nothing on the map.'

'Doesn't mean it's not there. They have to scour the floor of that tunnel, hands-and-knees if that's what it takes. Maybe they'll find a manhole lid, a maintenance hatch. But they have to do it before their flashlights fail. Once those lights give out, they're good as dead.'

'I'll tell them to haul ass.'

Tombes crouched by the bed. He stared at Ekks, watched his chest gently rise and fall.

'He's breathing. Shallow. But he's breathing.'

'Hear that?' said Cloke. 'Doesn't sound too good.'

'Yeah. Fluid on his lungs.'

'Want to sink a drain or something?'

'Very last resort.'

Tombes unzipped a clamshell IFAK. Medical gear stuffed in mesh pockets. He leaned over Ekks, snipped his shirtsleeve wrist-to-shoulder, and slapped a vein. He tore open a sterile wrapper, swabbed, and pressed a catheter into the crook of the man's elbow. He hung a bag of saline from a ceiling grab rail.

He checked pulse. He checked blood pressure. He pulled back eyelids, shone a penlight and checked for dilation.

'Well?' asked Cloke.

'Dying, sure enough. Acute radiation poisoning. Coming apart on a cellular level, like Wade and Sicknote. And he's malnourished, severely dehydrated. He's been lying here for days. Should be dead already. Must be a tough son of a bitch.'

'Will he wake?'

Tombes shrugged.

'I treat burns, breaks and bleeding. House fires and car wrecks. Radiological damage? Not part of my working day.'

'Can you keep him alive? Long enough to get him back to Ridgeway?'

'Maybe.'

'He has to talk. Wake up and talk. We have to keep him alive long enough to get him in front of a microphone. We need to hear what he knows.'

Cloke took out his Geiger counter. Harsh crackle. He shook his head.

'Fried.'

'What about us?' asked Tombes. 'What's our current dose?'

Cloke scanned himself. Then he scanned Tombes.

'Bad?'

'Won't kill us outright, but it might bite us on the ass a few years down the line. Cancer. Leukaemia. Not much fun in a world without hospitals.'

Tombes held out the notebook.

'Ekks had this in his hand. Damn near broke his fingers persuading him to let go.'

Cloke examined the book. Letters and symbols, page after unbroken page.

'What the hell is this gibberish?'

'Maybe the guy went nuts.'

He held up a random page.

'This thing is longer than *Lord of the Rings*. See how the ink changes? He burned through three pens.' He flipped more pages. 'See the letters? The handwriting? He took time over this stuff, wanted to get it right. And see here? He struck through a couple of lines, corrected himself.'

'So what?' asked Tombes. 'Seen anything like it before?'

'No. Any other documents lying around? Did he have a laptop?'

'Nothing. Just that notebook.'

'Looks like code. Can't think what else it could be. Might be some kind of weird DNA sequence, I guess.'

'We're going to have a hard time moving this guy. What if we have to re-enter the water? Maybe we could strap him to the backboard, try to keep him rigid.'

'That kind of presupposes there is actually a way out of here,' said Cloke.

'And we only have two suits. That's the hard truth. If Ekks is going to make it back to Fenwick, one of us will have to stay behind.'

Lupe radioed Cloke.

'Come on, man. Pick up. Talk to me.'

No response.

She stood in the office doorway and surveyed the ticket hall.

Sicknote crouched on the floor scribbling his strange phantasmagoria. Swirling vapours. Screaming faces. A black, viscous puddle of madness slowly spreading across the tiles.

Wade sat on the bench, head thrown back, snoring in his sleep. His face was pale, skin glazed with sweat. He mumbled like he was sinking into a fever.

Donahue sat on the platform steps, staring down into subterranean darkness.

Galloway lay unconscious on a pile of equipment bags, bandaged stump spotted with blood.

'Have you all given up?' shouted Lupe. Her voice echoed through the ticket hall. 'Are you all just going to sit here and die?'

They ignored her.

Lupe returned to the IRT office. She stretched, swung her arms, poured water over her face.

She took Donahue's radio from the table.

'Cloke. Switch on your radio, dammit.'

Cloke's voice:

'*We found Ekks.*'

'Is he alive?'

'*Just.*'

'Talking?'

'*Unconscious, but breathing.*'

'Can he be moved?'

'*I didn't come all this way to leave him behind.*'

'Any other survivors?'

'*No. We're going to look around one more time, try and find a way out. Maybe there is some kind of maintenance access, something we missed. Stairs that will take us up to street level.*'

'Check the tunnel floor. Walk the tracks, make a thorough search. Every inch.'

'Did Donnie spot something on the schematics?'

'Maybe. Look for some kind of manhole, some kind of inspection hatch that will take you down to a lower level. Look hard. It could be your only chance.'

Cloke checked beneath each subway car. He ducked between the wheel bogies and inspected the track bed. Rats stared back at him. He made shoo gestures. They stood their ground.

'Give me your lighter.'

Tombes handed over his shamrock Zippo.

Cloke set the lighter to high-flame and wafted fire at the savage-looking rodents. Flame reflected in mean, black eyes. They turned and scurried away.

Tombes stood guard. He scanned tunnel shadows. He shook his flashlight to coax the last power from dying batteries.

'Anything?'

'Yeah. Think I've got something.'

Cloke crouched on hands and knees, flashlight trained beneath a coach. He unhooked his radio.

'There's some sort of grating beneath one of the cars.'

'Get a closer look.'

Cloke squirmed between the wheels of the thirty-ton car. He slid beneath a traction motor and massive suspension springs.

'Bars. Steel bars. Hinges and a big-ass padlock. Any idea what I'm looking at?'

'One of the utility maps shows a large ground-water channel running beneath that section of subway tunnel. You must have found some kind of storm drain.'

Cloke squirmed further beneath the carriage. He leaned

over the grille and shone his flashlight downwards into darkness.

'A narrow pipe. Rungs set in concrete. It goes deep. Way deep.'

'*That's it. That's your route out.*'

36

Galloway leaned against a ticket hall pillar. Drugged stupor. He hugged his mutilated arm to his chest. He was pale with blood loss.

His eyelids drooped. His knees began to buckle. He snapped awake, caught himself as he toppled forwards. A stumbled recovery. He glanced around, wild-eyed, disoriented. He looked down at his stump. The events of the last few hours repopulated his mind like a fast reboot.

Something lying at the base of the pillar. Galloway slowly crouched, picked up the blood-caked belt he had used as a tourniquet, and threw it into corner shadows.

Sicknote held up a Sharpie.

'The pen has run dry.'

'Only one I got,' croaked Galloway. 'Sorry.'

Sicknote scratched his forehead with an inked finger. It left a smear like a soot streak.

'You don't think they'll let you board that chopper and fly out of here, do you?'

'What?' asked Galloway.

'Why are you still here? Hanging round with these guys? They won't offer you a ride home.'

'Fuck are you talking about?'

'You're bitten. Sooner or later, you'll turn.'

'Shut up.'

'How long before the chopper arrives? Twelve hours?

Fourteen? Do you think Lupe will wait that long? Sooner or later, she'll take steps.'

'The others would stop her.'

'Are you sure?'

'Shut up, all right? Just shut your damned mouth.'

Galloway dug an energy bar from a holdall and tore the wrapper with his teeth. He chewed. He looked around.

Wade lay on the bench. He moaned and murmured. His limbs twitched and trembled as he fought monsters in his dreams.

Donahue sat at the head of the platform stairs, antiemetic medication and painkillers scattered on the step beside her. Her shoulders were slumped. She stared down into darkness.

Lupe stood in the office doorway. She was watching him. Backlit. He couldn't read her expression.

She took a swig of water and turned away.

Galloway searched inside the trauma kit. He found a scalpel capped with a rubber stopper. He tested the blade on the fabric of the bag. It sliced through thick Cordura like it was paper. He re-capped the blade and slipped it into his pocket.

Tombes crawled beneath the subway car. He bit a Maglite between his teeth. He squirmed into position over the drain grate. Steel bars. Hinges. Padlock.

He took the flashlight from his mouth and laid it on the track bed.

'Pass me the gear.'

Cloke pushed the plasma cylinder between coach wheels.

Tombes grabbed the webbed cylinder and hugged it to his belly. He unbuckled a strap and unravelled the hose. He pulled on leather gauntlets. He balled a fire coat and pushed it between himself and the grate as a partial heat shield.

'All right. Here we go.'

He twisted the regulator and triggered the handset. The cutting flame burned brilliant white, roared a high, continuous scream.

He shielded his face and held the cutting head at arm's length. He pressed the exothermic flame to the padlock. Thick smoke. Steel began to sweat and drip. The heavy padlock melted like butter and fell away.

He pressed the cutting head to the grate hinges. The underside of the carriage was lit by flickering arc-light. He blinked sweat. He worked by touch, unable to look directly at the incandescent flame.

He cut through the first hinge, then the second. The grille twisted, detached and dropped into the shaft.

Tombes shut off the cutting flame. Sudden silence. He listened to the grate as it tumbled down the pipe, abrading concrete, slamming tunnel rungs, hitting water with a deep and distant splash.

They examined Ekks.

Tombes checked pulse and blood pressure. He checked the saline drip.

'How's his respiration?' asked Cloke. 'Any better?'

'Not great. But better.'

Cloke searched the carriage. He kicked over a couple of boxes. He upturned a suitcase and emptied it over the floor.

'Forget it,' said Tombes. 'I already looked. Nothing in the bags, nothing under the bed.'

Cloke picked up the notebook.

'Just this?'

'Yeah,' said Tombes. 'Just the book.'

Cloke thumbed pages.

'Reckon he found a cure?' asked Tombes. 'These notes. Reckon they amount to some kind of formula?'

Cloke held up a random page. Dense, urgent text.

'He spent hours writing this stuff. Days. It's got to mean something.'

'Reckon you can hack it?'

'Given time.'

Cloke dropped the notebook into the document bag, and lashed the bag with tape.

Tombes watched him work.

'Well, guess I got the short straw,' he said, looking down at his hands. 'Three guys. Two dive suits. I'll cover your back. I'll make sure you and Ekks get safely into the water. But do me a favour, all right? Achieve something. Get that back to Ridgeway. Crack that damned code.'

Cloke shook his head.

'You're not staying behind.'

'How do you figure?'

'Nariko. She's down there, in the water, with a helmet and air supply. We can lash her tanks to an NBC suit. Probably enough residual oxygen to make the journey.'

'You want to strip her body?'

'She would want you to live.'

Galloway climbed the steps to the street entrance.

He watched hands claw the opaque polythene that curtained the gate. Fingers daubed blood on the plastic.

He looked down. His bandaged stump was flecked with blood. Spines pushed through the gauze. He breathed deep. Part sigh, part shuddering sob.

'Are you all right?'

Wade climbed the steps. He gripped the stairwell balustrade for guidance and support.

He listened to ragged fingernails rake plastic.

'Is that them?'

'Yeah,' said Galloway.

'How many?'

'Plenty.'

'They never let up, do they?'

'No. No, they don't.'

'Lupe said there was a bike in the street.'

'She did?'

'Chopped. Chromed out. Big-ass ape hangers. Wish I had my eyes, you know? I'd like to see that Harley. The world has gone to hell, but that bike is still out there, sitting in the alley. Something beautiful. Something that makes sense.'

He bent double. He coughed and retched. He hacked and spat.

'You don't look so good,' said Galloway.

'Getting worse by the hour. Guess I don't have long. Maybe I'll head outside, when the time comes. I'd like to feel the rain on my face one last time, know what I mean?'

'You'd get torn to pieces.'

'Any of those bastards lays a finger on me, I'll fuck them up.'

'Always the rain with you guys.'

'I did some time in Texas. All the guys on The Row, sealed in the same six-by-nine year after year. Some of those guys were running multiple appeals. State. Federal. Any motion to commute their lawyers could dream up. Pretty much a full decade locked down under artificial light. They didn't give a shit about sun. They just wanted to feel rain.'

Galloway unclipped a bunch of keys from his belt one-handed, did it slow and quiet. He selected a cuff key with his teeth. He silently released the handcuffs that clamped the gate closed. He let the cuffs hang loose and open.

'Hell with it,' murmured Galloway. 'We all got to die some-time, right? Just got to pick our terms.'

37

Tombes floated in dark water. He squirmed deep into a crevice between massive concrete slabs.

A half-cut girder. He triggered the plasma arc and touched the cutting head to steel. Metal bubbled, liquefied, ran in rivulets like tears.

Cloke hung back. He watched stuttering flame light from deep within the heart of the rubble pile.

Tombes shut off the arc and withdrew from the fissure. He pulled a chunk of girder clear and threw it aside.

'Can you reach her?' asked Cloke.

'Yeah.'

'Want me to do it?'

'No. It's my job.'

Tombes forced himself deeper into the crevice. He reached Nariko's body. Her face behind the visor: eyes closed as if in a deep sleep.

He unsheathed a knife and began to saw through the fabric of her suit.

'The pistol should be tucked in her weight belt. Can you reach it?'

'No.'

Tombes backed out of the space dragging Nariko's tanks and helmet behind him.

'We're done.'

He shouldered the gear and swam for the surface.

Cloke took a last look inside the fissure. His helmet lamps

lit Nariko's body, half-buried beneath tumbled masonry blocks. Her hair gently wafted in the current. The water around her tinged pink with blood.

He turned away and kicked towards the surface.

The subway car.

They lay diving equipment on the floor beside Ekks. They knelt and inspected the gear.

'She looked peaceful,' said Cloke. 'She looked at rest.'

Tombes ignored him. He checked valves. He checked each tank gauge.

'How much air left in the bottles?' asked Cloke.

'About an hour. Maybe less.'

Cloke got to his feet.

'Get him ready to move. I'll meet you back here in fifteen.'

'Where are you going?' asked Tombes.

'Couple of things I need to do before we leave.'

Cloke returned to the radio carriage. The operator fused to the transmitter, broadcast lights flickering intermittent red and green.

Cloke retuned his Motorola.

'How you doing, son?'

'Please. I don't want to be here any more. It's cold. It's dark. Are you on your way? Will you be here soon?'

'We're coming for you, son. We're almost there. Just hold on. It won't be long. It won't be long now.'

Cloke laid an FDNY shoulder pack on the floor. He unzipped, and took out a cardboard box labelled with brissive warning icons.

DANGER
EXPLOSIVE/EXPLOSIF
Dannex blasting charge Type-E

He pulled back the flaps. Half-pound sausage tubes of ammonium nitrate demo charge wrapped in wax paper.

He carefully picked his way between metallic tendrils snaking across the floor. He crouched beside the radio operator. He lashed a tube of explosive to the table leg with duct tape.

'*I hate it here. It's so dark. So cold.*'

'Hang on, kid. It'll be over soon.'

The subway tunnel. Cloke walked the track, peering into shadows. He was spooked by the silence, spooked by the dark.

A buttressed arch. He mashed explosive against the brickwork.

Tombes unrolled a yellow radiation suit. He dressed Ekks as gently as he could: rolled him in the cot, manoeuvred the rubber suit beneath him, zipped arms and legs. He sealed the gloves and overboots with tape.

Cloke joined him.

'All set?'

'The seals should remain hermetic unless we dive deep. They'll keep out water, but not under pressure.'

Cloke dumped the explosive pack on the floor.

'Laid a couple of charges. Last thing I'll do when we leave this damned place. Bring down the roof.'

'Whatever. I just want to get the hell out of here.'

'You got some kind of detonator?' asked Cloke. 'How do I trip them off?'

Tombes picked up the backpack and unzipped a side-pocket. He took out a plastic box and unclipped the lid. Silver cylinders laid out like cigars.

'Time pencils. Old school, but they work. Each tube holds a little glass capsule full of acid. When the time comes to start the clock, pinch the top of the tube with pliers. The glass will break. Acid will start to corrode a lead wire. When the wire burns through, it releases a spring-loaded percussion cap. Kaboom.'

'All right.'

Tombes held up a time pencil.

'Blue band. Burns for fifteen minutes.'

'How many do I use?'

'One. Two to be sure. Those demo charges are ammonium nitrate, stuff they use for blasting quarries. Pop one charge, and the blast will trigger the rest.'

'How's Ekks?' asked Cloke. 'Any improvement?'

'Holding. Just holding.'

They carefully lifted Ekks and strapped him to the backboard. They lashed cylinders either side of his arms. They put the helmet over his head and sealed the neck with tape.

'Sure this is airtight?' asked Cloke.

'Probably maintain integrity for an hour or so. Long enough to get him to Fenwick.'

The IRT office.

'I don't like it,' said Wade. 'It's chickenshit. Shooting the guy like a sick dog.'

'You've seen what this disease can do.'

'The guy deserves to make his peace. Sure, if Galloway were walking the wing, if he got shanked, I wouldn't give a shit. Probably cheer when I heard the news. But we're not in the joint any more. The man has a right to die on his own terms.'

'We've given him plenty of time, plenty of space. When he turns, it will happen fast. We can't wait for ever.'

'What does Donahue say about this shit?'

'She doesn't give a damn. She just wants to get home.'

'So what do you want from me? I'm blind. If you off the guy, nothing I can do about it.'

'I guess I want your blessing.'

'Looks like Donahue left the phone off the hook. So you're stuck down here with two dead guys and a madman. Do whatever you've got to do.'

Galloway sat on the bench. Blue lips, cold sweat. The stump of his wrist tucked beneath his left armpit. He rocked back and forth.

Lupe wandered from the office. She walked across the ticket hall slow and casual. She sat beside him, kicked back and crossing her legs. She laid the shotgun across her lap.

'So how you doing?'

'Not so great. Painkillers are wearing off. Might need another shot.'

'How's your arm?'

'Minus a hand. How's yours?'

'Let me take a look. Maybe we can redress the wound.'

'Don't worry about it. I'll dig out some fresh bandage later. Patch myself up.'

'Come on. Let me take a look. See what I can do.'

'Forget it.'

Lupe spoke softly:

'Show me your arm.' Edge of menace.

Galloway stopped rocking back and forth. He turned to look at Lupe. He observed the shotgun laid across her lap, barrel trained on his belly.

'Show me your arm,' repeated Lupe.

Galloway slowly held out the stump. Metal spines protruded through bloody gauze.

'Sorry, man.'

'Amputate,' said Galloway. 'Make another cut. Take my arm at the shoulder.'

'No.'

'Please. You'd do the same in my position. You'd fight to your last breath.'

She shook her head.

'When my time comes, I'll look it in the eye. I won't go out snivelling.'

'Bullshit. You're no different from anyone else. You'll cling to life with everything you've got. You'll want every last moment.'

'Don't make this hard on yourself. Don't drag it out.'

'You're my executioner, is that it? Bet you've been dreaming of this moment. Talking everyone round.'

'Swear to God, it's nothing personal. You could bite a cyanide capsule, but you are so far gone there is no guarantee poison would have any effect. Right now the disease, the parasite, is burrowing into your brain. Shot to the head. Only way to be sure. For your sake as well as ours.'

'Fucking bitch. Bet you lay in your bunk fantasising about a moment like this, didn't you? Life-or-death power over a correctional officer. You must have prayed for a riot. You, and every other recidivist thug. Tiers gone to hell, inmates trashing the place, guards at your mercy. Relishing a few snatched hours of anarchy until the takedown squad toss CS and kick their way inside, batons flying. And here it is. Your sweet daydream come true.'

Lupe shook her head.

'I'm just trying to do right.' She got to her feet. She stood in front of Galloway, shotgun at the ready. 'Time to go.'

Galloway shouted across the ticket hall:

'Hey. Hey, Donahue. You're leaving her in charge? This bitch? Fucking barrio trash?'

Donahue sat on the platform steps, staring downwards into the dark. She didn't turn around.

'What the hell happened to you people?' shouted Galloway, addressing the ticket hall. 'Taking orders from some spic gangbanger? Some crack whore? Is she the boss now? Shaking a cup outside Citibank, and now she's calling the shots?'

No reply.

'Come on. She's picking us off, one by one.'

He looked around. Sicknote absorbed in his art.

'Hey,' said Galloway, trying to get his attention. 'Hey, dude. Help me out.'

'You got bit. Sorry, brother.'

Wade leaned against the wall, listening to the conversation.

'Yo, Wade,' called Galloway. Give a guy a break.'

Wade turned away.

Lupe prodded Galloway with the barrel of the gun.

'Make it easy on yourself.'

He slowly got to his feet.

'Here?'

'No.'

Lupe took a step back. She signalled with a wave of the shotgun. The plant room.

Galloway slowly walked across the ticket hall, each step deliberate and heavy, his time left on earth measured in floor tiles.

He reached the plant room door. He pushed it open. Heavy creak. He took a last, despairing look at his companions.

Donahue hadn't moved position. Still sitting with her back to the hall, still turned from the light.

Sicknote was on his knees, scribbling with a pen. He glanced up. Mix of boredom and pity.

Wade groped along the wall to the IRT office.

'Hey,' pleaded Galloway. 'Wade. Please.'

Wade closed the office door. Latch-click.

Galloway's shoulders slumped in defeat. He took a shuddering breath and walked into the plant room.

He was swallowed by shadow.

★

Lupe and Galloway faced each other. The bare bulb overhead threw harsh shadows, turned their faces to grotesque Kabuki masks.

Lupe. Resolute. Deep frown, clenched teeth.

Galloway. Sweat-sheen, panting with fear.

He was mesmerised by the yawning, blacker-than-black cavern mouth of the barrel, inches from his face.

'Want me to turn my back?' asked Galloway. 'Want me to kneel?'

'Makes no difference to me.'

He pushed his hands in his pockets.

'Got a final message for the world?' asked Lupe.

'I'd like to pray.'

Lupe shrugged.

'Our Father, who art in heaven, hallowed be thy name. Thy kingdom come . . .'

He palmed the scalpel.

'. . . on Earth as it is in heaven . . .'

The generator coughed. The light flickered. Lupe glanced upwards at the web-draped ceiling bulb.

Galloway snatched his hand from his pocket. Silver blur. The scalpel blade embedded in Lupe's cheek.

Angry cry. She staggered.

Galloway grabbed one of the generator cables hanging from the wall, and wrenched the clamp from high voltage switch gear.

Sudden darkness.

Lupe pulled the scalpel from her face and threw it aside. Clink and clatter. She raised the shotgun and fired. Blast-roar. Muzzle flare lit the room like a camera flash. Glimpse of Galloway ducking between battery racks, flinching from a high-velocity shower of brick chips as buckshot blew a crater in the wall.

She fumbled for the generator cable. She reattached the

clip. Spark and hum. The bare bulb flickered and glowed steady.

She cranked the shotgun slide. She crept between racks, gun to her shoulder, poised to fire. The room was fogged by a blue haze of stone dust and gun smoke.

'Hey. Galloway.' She wiped trickling blood from her cheek with the back of her hand. 'Step out, dude. No use skulking back there.'

Distant rasp of metal.

'I didn't want it to end this way. It should have been quick and clean.'

She peered into shadows, finger on the trigger.

The air con grate high on the back wall was pulled back. 'Galloway?'

She peered into the narrow conduit. Brickwork receded to darkness. Distant scuffle and pant.

'Is this really what you want?' she bellowed into darkness. 'You want to become a monster? You want to let it win?'

38

Lupe emerged from the plant room. She dabbed blood from her cheek.

'Is it done?' asked Wade.

'No.'

'I heard a shot.'

'He ran. He hid in the pipes. Fuck him. If he wants to endure a living hell, if he wants to be transformed into a sickening mess, then let him. He's not our problem.'

She cleaned her face with antiseptic swabs then pasted a dressing over the wound.

'Are you hurt?' asked Wade, listening to the rustle and rip of sterile wrappers.

'I'm fine.'

'Any word from Cloke or Tombes?'

'Nothing we can do but wait.'

A muffled crash.

'What the hell was that?'

Sicknote stood at the foot of the street exit steps, transfixed, gazing upwards at the entrance gate.

'What's going on, Sick?'

He smiled. He giggled.

Lupe ran to the foot of the stairwell and pushed him aside.

The entrance gate was open. Metal-shriek as infected creatures pushed the Coke machine to one side and stumbled down the steps towards her.

'Holy fuck,' muttered Lupe.

'They're in?' said Wade, panic in his voice. 'Did they get in?'

Lupe shouldered the shotgun and fired. A guy in a pus-streaked Starbucks shirt caught a blast to the chest. For a brief moment Lupe could see clean through his torso: a smouldering, cauterised hole bored through ribs, lungs, shirt fabric and skin.

The guy reeled like he took a gut-punch, but kept coming.

She ran up the steps to meet him. She racked the slide, adjusted her grip, adjusted her aim.

Muzzle-roar. Point-blank skull burst. The headless body toppled backwards and sprawled across the steps. The tight stairwell filled with gun smoke and blood mist.

A blue-haired skater kid, iPod beads fused to his ears.

Lupe racked the slide, took aim and fired. Second head burst, body hurled in a near back flip. Blood and skull fragments dripped from the stairwell ceiling.

Two guys in grey janitor shirts jostled through the entrance gate and stumbled down the steps towards her.

She racked the slide, took aim and pulled the trigger. Click. Empty.

Donahue stood next to her, paralysed with horror.

'Shells,' shouted Lupe. She cuffed Donahue round the head. 'Give me the spare shells.'

Donahue dug cartridges from her pocket.

'Make them count.'

Lupe snatched the shells from her hand and fed them into the breech.

'Grab an axe, a hammer, anything.'

Donahue ran to the equipment pile, pulled a strap and released a clutch of heavy tools.

'Give me something,' shouted Wade. 'Give me something I can swing.'

Donahue ignored him. She grabbed an axe and ran back to the stairs.

Lupe shouldered the gun. She squinted down the barrel sight, waited for a clear and certain shot.

'Come on, fuckers. Come get some.'

Cloke and Tombes lowered the stretcher from the subway carriage and set it on the track. They inspected the oxygen and nitrogen cylinders lashed to the backboard. They checked straps, gas levels and helmet hose.

Ekks lay impassive, face serene behind his visor.

'Let's get him in the hole.'

Tombes squirmed beneath the subway car. He dragged Ekks behind him.

He tied kernmantle rope to the head of the backboard. He looped the rope over a greased axle and slid Ekks into the shaft. It was a tight angle. The head of the backboard scraped against the underside of the coach.

He fed rope hand-over-hand until there was no more slack. He shone a flashlight down the narrow pipe. Concrete ribbed with ladder rungs. Ekks hung far below, suspended by taut rope.

'I'm heading down,' said Tombes. He secured his helmet and equalised suit pressure. His wrist screen flashed brief amber, then green.

He swung his legs into the shaft and began to descend the ladder rungs, flippers swinging from his weight belt.

He paused and looked down. Ekks suspended by rope. Concrete walls shafting downwards into darkness.

'*Looks like this thing drops to the centre of the earth.*'

Cloke stood beside the radio operator.

One last look at the grotesquely transformed figure.

'You've suffered enough, kid. You deserve a long sleep.'

He crouched beside Ivanek. A last inspection of the ammonium nitrate charge strapped to the table leg.

He unhooked the radio clipped to his belt.

'How's it going?'

'*I'm in the water. The shaft is about fifty feet deep.*'

'Okay. I'll set the detonators running. I'm coming down.'

He pinched the pencil timer with pliers, crushing the internal acid vial.

Cloke jumped from the car. He inspected the seals of his suit. He buckled a weight belt. He shouldered the tank harness and checked the gas gauge strapped to his wrist. Flippers hung from his belt, ready to be transferred to his feet when he hit the water.

He took a last look around. Arched shadows. Mausoleum hush.

Something moving in the gloom. He trained his flashlight. An infected soldier, part burned, cut in half at the waist. The creature feebly clawed the air.

'Poor bastard. You been there this whole time? Watching us come and go?'

Cloke lowered the dive helmet and span lock-bolts. Hiss of pressurisation.

He clumsily ducked beneath the subway carriage, squirmed on hands and knees beneath rusted, oil-caked air brakes, leaned sideways as his tanks struck metal.

He swung his legs into the shaft and began his descent.

Last shot. The stairwell fogged with gun smoke and stone dust.

'That's it. I'm out.'

More monstrous creatures headed down the steps. They stumbled over bodies. They slipped on tiles slick with blood and brain tissue. They crawled on hands and knees, eyes fixed on Lupe and Donahue.

'Okay,' murmured Lupe. 'Let's do this shit the hard way.'

She flipped the shotgun and gripped the hot barrel, ready to swing the weapon like a club.

Donahue gripped her fire axe.

A kid in a rot-streaked football shirt. His skin was slashed and peppered with broken glass, like he had been standing near a plate window when the shockwave hit. Lupe felled him with a side-blow to the head. She stood over the kid and pounded his face with the butt of the shotgun until his skull broke, spilling brain.

A girl in a Wendy's uniform. Her name tag said LANA. Metallic growths hung from her mouth like she was vomiting chrome. Donahue swung the axe, punched the blade through the crown of her head in a single, emphatic hammer blow. Sickening bone crunch. Face split in two.

'We have to reach the entrance. We have to close that gate.'

'Too many of them,' said Donahue, backing away. 'Rip us to shreds.'

'We got nowhere to run. We've got to make a stand. Drive them out. We can't let them take the station.'

'Too damn many.' Donahue turned and ran.

Lupe hesitated. She raised the shotgun, adjusted grip, strings of blood dripping from the stock like drool.

Wade groped along the ticket hall wall until he found the stairwell entrance. He held a knife in his hand.

'Get out of here, Lupe,' he shouted. 'Block yourself in one of the rooms. Hide until the chopper arrives.'

'What the hell are you doing?'

'Get out of here. Go on. Get going.'

Wade began to climb the steps. He slipped in blood. He stumbled over sprawled bodies.

'Come on, you fucks,' he screamed, yelling upwards at the street entrance. His voice echoed around the tight space. 'Come on, motherfuckers.'

Four infected creatures headed down the stairs to meet him. They jostled and hissed.

Wade heard them coming. He braced his legs and gripped the knife, ready to strike.

'Okay, fellas. Let's see what you got.'

They seized his arms and shoulders, sank teeth and tore flesh. He roared. He shook his right arm free. He slashed and stabbed.

A bus driver pinned him to the wall. Wade groped, found the creature's face, and drove the knife into its mouth. It gagged and shook itself free, knife still wedged between its jaws.

Wade punched and kicked, battled his way upwards towards the street entrance.

'Come on, you cunts.'

Lupe took a last look as she backed away. Wade at the top of the steps, overwhelmed but still fighting, bloody but exultant.

The water tunnel.

A ferro-concrete channel so vast Cloke couldn't see the full circumference. His twin helmet halogens lit the wall beside him. The rest was cavernous shadow.

A fierce current. Street run-off, burst water mains, and liquid leeched from porous Midtown bedrock. Thousands of tons of water funnelled towards the East River.

A safety wire cinch-anchored to the tunnel wall. A steel cable looped through pitons. A guide-line to enable maintenance crews to snap a carabiner and traverse the passage. Cloke and Tombes gripped the wire, hauled like they were battling a hurricane wind, fought the tide that pressed at their backs, threatened to lift and hurl them into the darkness ahead.

A streaming blizzard of refuse. Leaves, wrappers, newspaper.

A corpse washed by, tumbling in sub-aquatic shadow. A woman in a wedding dress drifting head over heels, satin gown dilating in the current like the skirts of a jellyfish. The spectral cadaver trailed lace like ghost-vapour. It rushed past, and was swallowed by shadow.

'*We are truly down the rabbit hole,*' murmured Tombes.

Cloke dragged the stretcher along the tunnel floor. No sound but the harsh helmet-rasp of his own exertion.

His wrist gauge flashed an amber RMV warning. Heavy oxygen consumption. Raised CO_2.

'*How much further?*' asked Tombes.

'*Look for another inspection shaft. A way up and out.*'

'*We should have found this route earlier. The Captain would still be alive.*'

A distant rumble. A tremor ran through the water.

'*There she blows,*' murmured Cloke.

He pictured the tunnel forty feet above their heads.

Chain detonations. Rock-roar: the tunnel and MTA locomotive obliterated by an avalanche of soil, bricks and fractured cement.

He pictured Nariko's sub-aquatic tomb sealed by a cascade of rubble. Her body enclosed in eternal darkness.

They continued to fight the current as they headed south.

'*How you doing?*' asked Cloke.

'*Fine,*' panted Tombes.

Something massive up ahead. Vast bulk moving among shadows.

They drew closer.

Three huge turbine blades swept the circumference of the tunnel. Slow, stately revolutions. A manganese-bronze cloverleaf, like a ship's screw. Under power, they would have spun at a blur, churning water towards the harbour outfall. The turbine motor was dormant, but the eight-ton blades still gently turned, propelled by relentless water pressure.

A body tumbled past them on the current. A guy in a suit. He hit the edge of a slow-moving blade. His head split in a cloud-burst of blood. He was snatched onwards down the tunnel.

'*How are we going to get past that thing?*' asked Tombes. '*Can we jam it to a standstill?*'

'*With what?*' asked Cloke. '*Gas tanks? We need everything we've got.*'

'*Jesus. We'll get diced.*'

They could feel it. A throb in the water. A subtle, sub-sonic pulse each time the great blades swept past.

'*Just got to time it right,*' said Cloke. '*It's moving slow. A three second interval between strokes. We can duck through, one at a time. I'll go first.*'

He edged closer to the blades. Inches away from blurred metal. He tensed his muscles and settled his breathing. Each sweep felt like a body-blow.

A blade swung past. He closed his eyes and pushed forwards, tensed for a bone-splintering impact.

He opened his eyes. He was through.

'*Go,*' shouted Tombes. '*Don't worry about me. I'll deal with Ekks. Just go. Find us a route up and out of here.*'

A roof vent fifty yards south. Cloke's helmet lamps lit a concrete inspection shaft lined with iron rungs.

'*Tombes. You all right?*'

'*Yeah, I'm through. I'm cool.*'

'*Looks like we got a way out.*'

Cloke gripped rungs and hauled himself up the shaft hand-over-hand.

Lupe's voice:

'*Where are you guys?*'

'*Almost with you,*' said Cloke. '*Had to circumvent a little obstruction.*'

'*They're here. They got inside the station. They're on us.*'

'*We're seconds away. Couple of hundred yards and we'll be at Fenwick.*'

'*I'm heading down to the platform to meet you. We'll have to fight our way to the plant room. Be ready.*'

'*Ten-four.*'

'*Move your asses. We've got a serious fight on our hands.*'

39

Incinerated vehicles. Incessant rain.

Shotgun fire. Reverberations like thunder. Muffled concussions penetrated the skull-socket darkness of vacant windows and storefronts.

HONEYBEE.

A bombed-out boutique. Toppled clothes rails, scattered shoes, denim dusted with broken glass. Half-melted mannequins lay dismembered on the floor. Bald. Blank eyed. Arms and heads angled in a coquettish tease.

Clothing and hangers slowly pushed aside. A Hare Krishna, bald like a mannequin, come to life.

He climbed unsteadily to his feet. Coins fell from the folds of his robes and skittered across the floor.

He stood for a moment, swaying like a drunk.

He headed for the front of the store. His sandaled foot stamped through a dummy's impassive face, shattering it like eggshell.

The Hare Krishna toppled through the storefront window and fell into the street. He lay on the rain-lashed sidewalk and looked around. Transformed vision cut through darkness like infrared. Rubble, buckled automobiles, toppled light poles.

Another distant gunshot.

The Krishna got to his feet and stumbled east.

★

Liberty Street.

The Krishna shuffled between buses, limos and yellow cabs, livery seared down to base metal.

He shambled past a meat truck. Faint lettering: CROWN MEATS sprayed out and DEPT OF HEALTH – DISPOSAL scrawled underneath. The rear doors leaned open. Infected bodies wrapped in sheets and hung from hooks. Still alive. They squirmed like larvae.

'Come on, you fucks.'

A hoarse voice echoed from an alley off Liberty.

'Come on, motherfuckers.'

The Krishna shuffled past the Doric facade of the old Federal Building. Doors boarded and chained.

He entered the alley. An arched gateway. Phantom letters and bolt holes in the stonework: SUBWAY.

A white tiled stairwell heading downwards. A mosaic sign: TO THE TRAINS.

Commotion near the top of the stairs. A big guy, surrounded by skeletal revenants. He thrashed in the confined space: kicked, punched and raged as he was slowly overwhelmed and dragged to the floor.

'Fuck you. Fuck you, motherfuckers. Suck my fucking dick.'

Krishna descended the steps, arms outstretched.

Fresh blood.

Fresh meat.

He shouldered other infected creatures aside and gripped the man's head.

'Fuck you all to hell,' screamed Wade.

The Hare Krishna pressed thumbs into sightless eyes, forced knuckle-deep into brain.

40

Tombes jammed his shoulder against the plant room door and struggled to hold it closed. Shuddering impacts. He braced his legs, strained against the blows. He was still wearing dive gear, still dripping tunnel water. Helmet and tanks dumped on the floor.

His feet lost purchase. Overboots skidded on concrete. The door was slowly pushed ajar.

A guy in bloodied pinstripe began to squirm through the gap.

Cloke threw himself against the door. Tombes kicked at the pinstripe creature, forcing it back into the hall.

Door slam. Sound of scrabbling fingers.

'How many do you reckon?' panted Cloke. 'I counted five.'

'We got to prop this thing.'

Lupe strained to push a heavy iron battery rack towards the door. Metal shriek.

Sicknote watched her work.

'Help me, you dick,' shouted Lupe.

Sicknote put his shoulder against the iron rack and helped shunt it against the door.

They stood back. Pounding fists. Scratching nails. The door shook.

'Guess it will hold,' said Cloke.

He unclipped his weight belt and began to strip out of his drysuit.

Tombes wiped sweat with the back of a gloved hand.

'This is fucked. We can't stay here.'

'You want to head out there, into the hall?' asked Lupe. 'You'd get ripped to pieces in seconds.'

'Sooner or later we'll have to make a break for it. Each hour we wait, more of those bastards gather outside the door. We should hit them now, before the odds get any worse.'

'Any of you guys got a watch?' asked Lupe.

Cloke checked his G-Shock.

'Eleven hours until the chopper arrives.'

'Hey,' said Tombes, looking around. 'Where's Donahue? Anyone seen Donnie?' Dawning horror. 'Christ. She must still be out there.'

Lupe tossed Tombes a radio.

'Donahue, do you copy, over?'

No reply.

'Come in, Donnie. Do you copy, over?'

No reply.

'Talk to me, Donnie.'

Dead channel hiss.

'What happened?' asked Tombes. 'Did anyone see what happened?'

No one spoke. No one met his gaze.

'Come on. Think. Did anyone see her go down?'

Lupe shook her head.

'Too much going on.'

'I was with you,' said Cloke. 'I was dealing with Ekks.'

Tombes took a tentative step towards the door.

'I should go out there,' he said, uncertain, like he wanted someone to talk him out of it. 'I've got to help her.'

The door shook from a fusillade of blows.

'Forget it,' said Cloke. 'She's gone.'

'I have to be sure.'

'I can't let you go out there, man,' said Lupe.

'Who the fuck asked you?'

'Think it through. There's a bunch of those bastards massing in the hall. The door has to stay closed.'

The hammering ceased. Sudden silence.

Cloke slowly approached the door.

'What do you think they are doing out there?'

'Sniffing around, trying to find another way inside,' said Tombes. 'Not much mystery to these roaches.'

'Maybe we should check our pockets,' said Lupe. 'Make an inventory.'

They crouched in a circle and emptied their pockets.

A lock-knife. A bandana. A half bottle of water and a couple of energy bars.

'Wish we had more water,' said Lupe.

'Just got to sit tight,' said Cloke.

'Screw that. We have to reach the radio. If we don't check in, they'll recall the chopper.'

'We'll figure something out.'

'And we can't sit on the roof waiting to get picked up. We'd soak up a shitload of rads. We need to speak to the pilot. We've got to know when he's ready for touchdown.'

'One thing at a time,' said Tombes. 'Better rest a while. Give ourselves space to think.'

Cloke and Tombes stripped out of their suits. They shivered in T-shirts and shorts. Sweat turning to chills. They slapped themselves, rubbed their arms and jumped to get warm. They huddled together with their backs to the wall, and pulled scrap paper over their feet and legs to trap body heat.

Tombes pulled Cloke's weight belt from a nearby pile of dive equipment. He unclipped the Geiger counter. He held the unit in front of his chest. Fierce crackle. He held it beside Cloke. Heavy hiss.

'Guess we were in the water a while,' said Tombes quietly. 'How long before we get sick?'

'The first symptoms will hit pretty soon.'

'What are our chances?'

Cloke shrugged.

'We live or we die. It's out of our hands.'

'What about those iodide pills?' asked Tombes.

'In the hall, with all the other meds.'

'This is going to get bad, right?'

'Yeah.'

Tombes shut off the handset and got to his feet.

'I'm going to check on Ekks.'

Ekks lay at the back of the room. He was still zipped in an NBC suit and strapped to the backboard.

Tombes knelt beside Ekks. He released straps. He flicked open a knife and slit the suit. He pulled the rubberised nylon aside.

'How is he?' asked Cloke.

Tombes lifted an eyelid, checked for dilation. He laid a couple of fingers on the man's carotid.

'Stable, I guess. Good pulse. Good respiration. Wish we could reach the medical gear. The guy could do with more saline. And we have to get some nutrients inside him. Blood sugar must be through the floor.'

Tombes laid scrap paper over Ekks, built up a blanket page by page.

'Should trap a little heat.'

Cloke gestured towards the door.

'Those trauma bags you've got out there. You folks came pretty well equipped, right?'

'Yeah,' said Tombes. 'We respond to pretty much any 911.'

'Have you got some kind of adrenaline shot? Something that can shock him awake?'

'We might have some epinephrine. We keep it for junkies. Once in a while, an unusually pure batch of heroin hits the streets and we get a bunch of OD calls. Always the same. Shitty apartment. Needles on the floor. Sorry-ass kid lying in a pool of piss, respiratory system sedated to a standstill, slowly turning blue. We give them a bump, a little dose of epi, to kick-start their lungs.'

'Could we give Ekks a shot?'

'No. He's pretty frail. Probably kill him stone dead.'

'But there's a chance it could work?'

'Way too risky.'

'He's got no life to lose. He's dying of acute radiation poisoning. Survival isn't an issue. But could we jolt him back to conscious, yeah? Prep him with painkillers and anti-nausea meds, then zap him awake with a shot to the heart. He'd be lucid for a while, right? Long enough to talk. Long enough to tell us what he knows.'

'Forget it. *Do no harm.* That's the oath. My job is to keep people alive.'

'Nariko said you did a couple of years in the marines.'

'I was a kid. I never left the damn base.'

'But what would a soldier do in this situation?'

'You're asking the wrong guy. I've never raised a hand to anyone, not in a schoolyard, not in a bar.'

'These are unusual circumstances. We have to think beyond the old rules.'

'What's right is right.'

'All you got to do is load the hypodermic and give it to me. I'll do the rest. Whatever happens, it will be my responsibility.'

'Yeah. Well, the bags are out in the hall. They might as well be on the moon.'

Lupe sat, back to a wall, eyes closed.

Cloke sat beside her.

'You look strung out,' he said.

'I'm in better shape than you.'

'Nausea? Headache?'

'Forget it. I'm fine.'

'Sorry about Wade.'

'I barely knew the guy,' said Lupe.

'But he saved your life, yeah? Drew off a bunch of infected. Took a lot of courage. Nasty way to die, but he did it for you. He didn't strike me as the heroic type. I guess sometimes people surprise you.'

'He was a rat.'

'Rat?'

'We met at Bellevue. Adjacent cells. Each morning he got led to the shower. Racket used to wake me up. Jangling keys, slamming doors. His escort would march right past my cell. Did you see those tattoos on his arms? All that white power shit?'

'I guess. I didn't pay much attention.'

'First time I saw him, he had a big-ass swastika on his right forearm. It looked fresh. Blacker than black. Couldn't have been more than a few months old. I saw him again a few days later. The swastika was pale grey, like it had been there a decade. A while after that, it faded almost to nothing. You don't have to be a genius to figure it out. He was getting his tattoos lasered off. A session every couple of days. That's why they had him at Bellevue. Witness protection. He wasn't nuts. He wasn't sick. He turned rat. Maybe his biker buddies had a meth lab somewhere. Maybe the Texas angels were running stuff across the border. He traded his hombres to the FBI, set them up for some kind of RICO charge. His get-out-of-jail-free. They transferred him to Bellevue on some bullshit pretext. Psych evaluation, blood tests, anything. Quickest way to get him out of the prison population. Snitches get stitches, right? Couldn't let some Aryan Brother shank his ass then get paraded round the yard on shoulders like a righteous hero. The feds needed a temporary safe house, somewhere to park Wade while they formalised the whole thing with the DA and got him into the witness programme. The Marshals Service arranged the removal of distinguishing tattoos. Bet they were setting him up with a fresh ID, a car, an apartment. A new town, a whole new life.'

'Jeez.'

'They offered me the same deal,' said Lupe. She reflexively touched the tattoo tears etched on her cheek. 'Sat me in an interview room white as heaven. Laid out the whole thing. I could have walked. Picked a new name. Said they would burn me clean with lasers and let me start over somewhere new. They pushed an amnesty document across the table. It was from the DA's office. Big stamp, big signature. I tore it in strips and ate it.'

'Can't say I ever understood that code-of-silence stuff.'

'The first time they put me in a cell with Wade, I spat in his face. He could never look me in the eye, even when he had his sight.'

'He saved your life, though.'

'Maybe he was trying to redeem himself. Cancel the shame.'

'You would be dead, if not for him. Leave it at that.'

An unearthly moan echoed from the air handling system. Long, mournful, unutterably sad.

Lupe and Cloke stood and tentatively approached the grille high on the back wall.

'*Santa Muerte*,' murmured Lupe. She crossed herself. 'What the hell was that?'

41

Galloway crouched in the crumbling brick conduit. He hunched to stop the crown of his head raking mortar.

A faint glimmer of light. If he retraced his steps, if he followed a bend in the pipe, he would find himself back in the plant room.

He pulled bandages from his stump. The wound bristled with spines. Needle-barbs protruding from muscle and bone marrow. Veins and arteries horribly distended.

He didn't want to die alone. He wanted the comfort of people and voices.

Sudden fury.

Rage flaring like a struck match. Clenched teeth, left hand balled into a fist. Tired of being an outsider. Treated with contempt by soldiers back at Ridgeway who saw a correctional officer as some kind of sleazy, low-rent mall cop. Ostracised by a rescue squad that seemed to hold a sneaking admiration for his gang-girl prisoner.

He composed speeches in his head. Things he should have said:

'I got no reason to feel ashamed. I got a flag on my arm, same as you. I swore an oath and did my job. I punched the clock each day and put myself among the meanest, most vicious motherfuckers to ever walk the earth. I did it so you guys could sleep safe in your beds. Fuck yourselves, okay? Army. Fire department. Acting all superior. You can all go to hell.'

Faint noise from the plant room. Distant voices echoed down the conduit.

Lupe:

'Close the damned door. Quick. Close it. Get it shut. Here, use this.'

Cloke:

'Put him down there.'

'Is he alive?'

'Just.'

Tombes:

'Where's Donahue? Did anyone see Donahue? Christ, she must still be out there.'

Galloway touched his face. Needles protruded from his cheek.

He wanted to be back among Lupe, Donahue and Sicknote, even if they despised him, even if they wanted him dead.

He wept metal tears.

42

Donahue ran to the IRT office and slammed the door. Fists pounded the wooden panels.

Heart-hammering panic. She gripped the handle. Her boots squeaked and slid across floor tiles as she struggled to keep it closed. Brief glimpse of hunched skeletal thing wearing a Dunkin' Donuts cap. It gripped the doorframe. It leered.

She threw her shoulder against the door and slammed it closed. Bone crunch. Blood spurt. Severed fingers pattered to the floor.

She slapped deadbolts in position.

Heavy impacts. She grabbed a wooden chair and held it above her head ready to strike.

Gun-crack pop. Sudden darkness. A brief moment of what-the-fuck, then a wave of frustration and anger as she realised she had smashed the single bare bulb that lit the room.

She set down the chair.

She unbuckled her watch. A yellow G-Shock. She used the weak face-light to examine the door. The bolts and hinges looked like they would hold.

She caught her breath. She backed away from the door. Glass crunch. The floor dusted with bulb fragments.

She pulled a bandana from her pocket and wiped sweat from her forehead. A dark stain on the bandana. She touched her face. Blood on her fingertips. She hurriedly explored her scalp and neck, passed the watch-light over her arms and legs looking for bite marks.

Plenty of spray. She had kicked a couple of infected creatures to the ground in the ticket hall, stamped on snarling faces until their skulls shattered and pulped.

No wounds.

She mopped blood from her pant legs and boots.

She walked to the back of the office and slid to the floor. She listened to fists pound the door. The fusillade of blows slowly diminished to silence.

She waited.

She unhooked her radio and whispered into the handset.

'Lupe, do you copy, over?'

No reply.

'Lupe. Anyone. Can you hear me?'

Tombes:

'*Donnie. Holy shit, girl. Are you all right?*'

She turned the volume way down. She crouched over the radio, cupped her hand over the mouth-grille and whispered:

'Just.'

'*Where are you?*'

'I'm in the station office. I've locked the door. Not sure how long it will hold if they make a concerted effort to get inside.'

'*We'll figure something out. Just stay put. Stay out of trouble.*'

'Are you guys okay?'

'*Yeah. Yeah, we're good. We're safe. We're in the plant room.*'

'This is so messed up.'

'*We'll be fine. Just got to keep our heads and think our way out of this mess.*'

'Don't leave me in here, man. You've got to get me out.'

'*We aren't going anywhere without you. You got my word. Is there anything else in there with you? Anything else you can throw against the door?*'

'Not much.'

'*Are they still trying to get in?*'

234

'They were pounding at the door for a while. They've quit. For now.'

'Can you hear them?'

'I can sure as shit smell them. Hold on. I'm going to check.'

'Don't make a sound, for God's sake. Do it quiet as you can.'

Donahue got to her feet and quietly crossed the room.

A peep hole in the door. She wormed dust and grime from the lens with her finger and put her eye to the hole.

She stifled an involuntary gasp. A ghastly, skeletal face, close-up in fish-eye distortion. *Dunkin' Donuts.*

Something in its mouth. It chewed with a ruminative roll of the jaw. A human ear.

It leaned close like it was sniffing the lens.

Donahue kept absolutely still. She slowed her breathing. No sound but the pounding blood-rush of her pulse.

The creature couldn't see her. A one-way spy hole. A bead of black glass. But it pressed against the office door like it could smell the intoxicating scent of fresh meat.

Donahue slowly backed away from the door. Crackle of bulb glass underfoot. She froze. No reaction from the creature outside in the hall. She kept walking.

She crouched in the corner and whispered into the Motorola.

'I can see one of them in the ticket hall. Maybe I could take him.'

'You've got a weapon?'

'I lost my axe. Buried it in some guy's head. Pretty sure I could do some damage with a chair leg. Drive it into his eye.'

'These bastards are dumb, but they're patient. They'll wait us out, be ready to pounce the moment we show our faces. They'll wait a week, a month, a year. They'll never quit.'

'Then we're screwed.'

'Leave it to me, okay? I'll figure a way out of this mess. Get on the radio. Talk to Ridgeway. Tell them to send the

damned chopper. Don't take any shit from those guys. Get a firm ETA.'

'I'm on it.'

Donahue hefted the transmitter and laid it on the floor. She sat cross-legged. She fumbled headphones in the darkness and positioned them on her head.

She flicked on. The power light glowed brilliant green.

She passed the watch-light over the transmitter panel. She tapped needle-dials, checked battery levels, volume and frequency.

She jacked the microphone and pressed Transmit.

'Rescue to Ridgeway, do you copy, over?'

It took fifteen minutes to raise a reply.

The Chief, shouting through whistling static.

'Go ahead, Rescue.'

'This is Donahue.'

'Where's Captain Nariko?'

'Dead, Sir.'

'Say again?'

'The Captain is dead.'

'What about Ekks?'

'We found him.'

'What is his condition?'

'Unconscious. He's sick, heavily irradiated, but he's breathing.'

'Has he spoken? Has he talked?'

'No, sir. Completely unresponsive.'

'What's the status of his team? Are there any other survivors?'

'They're dead.'

'You're sure?'

'They didn't survive the bomb. But we have their papers, their data.'

'Good job, Donahue. Tell your people. Outstanding work. The site is secure?'

'Negative. We're losing ground. We're drawing heavy heat down here. Getting worse by the minute. There are still plenty of infected people among the ruins, messed up but moving. They've sniffed us out, big time. We're pretty much overrun. We need backup, anything you got. Guns, grenades, RPGs. We've got a serious fight on our hands.'

'I'll put a couple of men on the helicopter. They will provide cover fire during extraction. But you must protect Ekks until we can reach you. Everything in your power, yes?'

'We need a ride out of here asap, Sir. We need immediate evac.'

'The helicopter is scouting for a new base. It's out of radio range. We can't reach the pilot.'

'I don't mean to speak out of line, sir, but ten hours from now we'll probably be dead.'

'Problems of our own, Donahue. Hundreds of infected bastards massing outside the perimeter.'

'Don't forget us, Chief. Don't leave us stranded.'

'I'll come myself. And like I said, I'll bring a couple of guys with AR-15s. We'll take care of you.'

'Copy that.'

'Good luck, Donahue. You are in our prayers.'

43

Sicknote stood at the plant room door. He caressed the wood grain. He rested his hand on the panelling and closed his eyes, like he was trying to commune with the creatures milling in the ticket hall.

Tombes crouched by the wall. He watched through half-closed eyes as Sicknote stroked blistered varnish.

'What the hell are you doing?'

Sicknote jumped back.

'Nothing.'

'Then get away from the damned door.'

Sicknote shrugged and gave a dreamy smile. He wandered to the back of the room. He sat beside Ekks and drew patterns in the dust with his finger.

Tombes stood and checked the rack pinning the door closed. He shook it. Heavy iron. Solid. Hadn't moved an inch.

He checked the door. Sturdy. No cracks. Rusted strap hinges holding firm.

Lupe joined him. She yawned and stretched.

'No sound from our guests outside,' she said. 'I guess they're automatons. Just kind of shut down if they don't have an obvious target. Go dormant. Soon as they catch a scent, they perk up and snap into action.'

'They don't sleep. I know that much.'

'Best if we keep our voices down. Don't remind them we are here. Maybe they'll leave us alone. Get bored and head back to the surface.'

'You honestly believe that?' asked Tombes.

'Grasping at straws. We could encourage them to leave, I guess. Maybe cut power to the ticket hall, put out the lights for a while. Let them stumble around in the dark.'

'They like the dark.'

'What's the deal with you and Sicknote?' asked Lupe.

'I don't like the way he keeps heading for the door. Can't take his eyes off it. He's mesmerised. How long has he been off his meds?'

'A while.'

'Look in his eyes,' said Tombes. 'Batshit. Pure madness. He's walking around nice enough, but there are bombs going off in his head. He'll hurt someone, given a chance.'

'Think he wants to open the door? Let those bastards inside?'

'Wouldn't surprise me. Kind of crazy thing he might do. He's going to die. Might want to take the rest of us with him. Like Galloway.'

'You want to tie him up?' asked Lupe. 'Lash him to a water pipe?'

'What else can we do with the guy? They won't let him on the chopper, that's for sure. If he gets back to Ridgeway, the Chief will give the order. And if his men hesitate to pull the trigger, he'll do it himself.'

'He needs a shrink, not a prison cell. Sure as shit deserves to get out of this dungeon.'

'I saw him on TV. He doesn't deserve a damned thing.'

Cloke sat cross-legged in the corner of the room. He thumbed through the battered notebook. He flipped pages patched with tape, studied the dense biro scrawl. He rubbed his eyes. He tried to make sense of letters and symbols.

He lay a crumpled sheet of paper across his knee and began to make notes with the stub of a pencil.

Lupe sat cross-legged beside him.

'So what is it?' She gestured to the notebook. 'The letters. What do they mean?'

'I have no idea. Ekks had this book in his hands when we found him. Gripping it tight. Must be significant. But look at it. Line after line, page after page. What the hell is it? An insanely long equation? Some kind of epic chemical formula? The whole notebook. Letters and little hieroglyphs. Triangles, circles, diamonds. Symbol clusters. Recurring patterns. The slashes seem to indicate word breaks. If I had to make a guess, I would say we are looking at some sort of crude substitution code.'

'Can you crack it?'

'I can try. It's hardly my area of expertise. Shit, I can barely finish a crossword. Haven't got the mindset. Sudoku give me a nose bleed. But if this is a classic substitution code we should be able to discern some obvious patterns. 'E' is the most frequently used letter in the English language. 'O' runs pretty close. Single-letter words will be either 'A' or 'I'. Regular groupings might imply sound-clusters like 'TH' or 'ING'. Nail those recurring symbols, and you could start to turn this gibberish back to actual words.'

'Yeah?'

'Guess I could take a section of text and work out the placement. But Ekks is a smart guy. I doubt he would create such a simple code, something so easy to decipher. It'll be more complicated than that. There will be an additional step. Maybe some kind of weird algorithm. A shifting transposition. A key, that only he can provide.'

'So he's the only one who knows what this shit means?'

'If we had a big-ass computer and the right software we could probably crack the code without his help. Get a couple of chess grandmasters on the case. But we don't have those kind of resources any more. If we can't figure out the code with pen and paper, his research will die with him.'

'But why would he do that?' asked Lupe. 'Encrypt his notes? What was he afraid of?'

Cloke shrugged.

'Maybe he didn't want to be abandoned down here in the tunnels. He wanted to be indispensable. He made sure the documentation was unreadable without his help. A way of ensuring his ass got flown out of here in one piece.'

'The man is a fraud. Hundred bucks says there is no code. Those letters? Those symbols? A sick joke. Page after page of bullshit.'

'We can't be sure.'

'That book is pure voodoo. A prop. An illusion. Might as well be a book of spells and incantations. He has no secret knowledge. He doesn't know anything about this virus. Doctor of Lies. Doctor of Nothing. Happily knife the fucker.'

'The man is an accomplished neurosurgeon. When he turned up at medical conferences he got mobbed like a rock star.'

'Doesn't mean a damn thing.'

'A Saudi prince had a stroke a couple of years back. A young guy. Champion polo player. A maid found him face down on the marble floor of his penthouse bathroom. They summoned Ekks, sent a private jet to ferry him to the Emirates. Ekks declined to leave New York, said he had too many patients in need of care. They offered him millions. The State Department pressured the hospital board. But he still said no. So they loaded that prince on a Gulfstream in Dubai and flew him to Manhattan. They took over an entire floor of Bellevue. Wouldn't trust anyone else to work on their boy.'

'Like I said. The guy's a control freak.'

'You've barely spoken to the man.'

'I've looked into his eyes. One glance. That's all it took. He knew me, and I knew him. I'm a connoisseur of evil. On the streets, in the yard. I've met monsters, and this guy is off the scale. All kinds of horrors crowding his brain. Sure he never acted on his fantasies. Always kept a perfect facade. Smiled and laughed at cocktail parties, turned up at every charity fundraiser with a speech and a big-ass cheque. All round nice guy. But at night, when the lights are out, you can bet demons dance behind his eyes. You think Sicknote is trouble? You think those fucks massing outside the door are a problem? This guy is a hundred times worse.'

44

Lupe sat with her back to the wall. She closed her eyes and leaned her head against the brickwork. Faint snore.

Cloke watched her sleep. A subtle transformation. Her jaw-jutting aggression slowly softened. Hard years melted away and she was a girl once more.

He tore tape and flapped open the plastic bag. Jumbled documents. Photographs, data, suicide notes blotted with tears.

He pulled out a handwritten sheet of paper and started to read.

Harold Donner
Bellevue Dept of Neurosurgery

I killed a man. I, along with my colleagues, participated in murder. We took a healthy person. We infected him, watched him suffer and succumb, then dissected his body. It was an extrajudicial killing. Those of us involved took refuge in circumlocutory language. We called it 'extreme therapeutic measures'. We discussed 'the procedure'. But it was murder, plain and simple. I'm not proud of what I did. I have no doubt it was an absolute betrayal of the Hippocratic Oath.

It had to be done.

We were desperate to find an antidote to this terrible disease. But to fully understand the pathology of the virus, we would need to study its progress from the moment of infection, examine samples of bone marrow and cerebrospinal fluid, watch replicating cells populate a blood-stream and fuse with a central nervous system.

It would cost a life.

A terrible choice. Ekks was adamant each member of our team should play a role. Three doctors, three nurses. We would share responsibility. None of us would shoulder the burden alone.

We could have refused, kept our integrity, gone to our graves morally intact. But that would have been an indulgence.

It was my job to select the test subject.

The day we fled Bellevue hospital, we were accompanied by four prisoners from the Special Management Control Unit. I suspect the orderlies charged with keeping them secure would have happily left them to starve in their cells or get ripped apart by prowlers. But Ekks insisted they travel with us.

Looking back, he already had a plan.

We ran to the 23rd Street Station. We seized a train and rode south to Fenwick Street. We pitched camp.

Ekks outlined his proposal. He wanted to observe the moment of infection, second by second.

Weeks earlier, the Centre for Disease Control had supplied our team with a sample of the virus in its purest form. It arrived under military escort. A white biocontainment box with a strange half-skull symbol on the lid, as if someone hurriedly tried to scribble a warning glyph:

Inside the box was a gloved hand. The glove looked like it had been cut from a cosmonaut pressure suit. White canvas, cooling capillaries, dimpled rubber palm-grip. Splintered bone and dried flesh protruded from the gauntlet. There was a blue anodised lock-ring at the wrist. Cyrillic lettering and part numbers etched into the titanium.

Each outbreak of this disease had been associated with Russian space debris. Months ago, a fuel tank re-entered the atmosphere and crashed to earth in forest north of Spokane. The following weeks saw further starfalls over northern Europe and the Arctic Circle. Each impact was followed by the outbreak of a lethal haemorrhagic pathogen designated Mystery Pathogen 01, aka EmPath.

I asked Ekks about the glove. Was it part of some secret military space programme? Had a Soyuz capsule fallen to earth?

He smiled. He said the gloved hand represented the original, most lethal strain of the virus.

He wanted to observe the virus colonise a human body. He wanted to see it pervade the blood stream, infiltrate tissue, bore into the spinal column and brain stem. Could the initial colonisation be blocked by anti-neoplastic agents? If it were treated like any other malignancy, attacked in the early stages using anti-cancer drugs such as Thioguanine or Methotrexate, could it be stopped?

It was a problem that dogged us during our time sequestered in Bellevue. We had unlimited access to infected subjects snatched off the street. But they were too far gone. Advanced cases. The process of infection, the manner in which the virus first fused with its host, remained a mystery.

Ekks put it to a vote. He wouldn't undertake the procedure unless we gave unanimous consent.

We talked it over. I trusted Ekks. I trusted his judgement. His expertise far exceeded my own. In all the years I have know him, followed his work at Bellevue, he has always acted with the highest integrity. He had been a second father, a guiding hand. So when he sequestered the medical team in one of the subway carriages and laid out his plan, I had no choice but to raise my hand in assent.

It seems ridiculous to spend my last minutes on earth writing this account of our time below ground. We are sealed in a tunnel. Our bodies will never be found. We will lie here for ever, entombed like the pharaohs.

Why should a single death matter? The execution of a recidivist piece of garbage, a valueless fleck of human junk. A man who wasted his entire life, spread misery, achieved nothing. Why care? Every survivor on this continent has witnessed unimaginable slaughter, experienced terrible grief. The world has become an abattoir. New York itself is burning above our heads. The entire city levelled by a nuclear firestorm. Thousands killed. Our team, down here in these tunnels, conspired to take a single life. A trivial deed, by comparison. An insignificant man, a vicious criminal. Is it absurd that this act torments me? That I can't scrub away the disgusting taint of my own complicity?

'Choose,' Ekks told me. 'We will all carry the burden. Like pallbearers, we will each shoulder a fraction of the load. Your duty is to choose. We have four prisoners, four worthless criminals. Decide. Who will be the sacrifice? Who must give his life?'

It haunts me. The moment I stood in front of the captives, pointed a finger and said 'Him'.

Ekks stirred. He shifted his head.

Cloke checked the man's pulse, his breathing.

He leaned close and whispered in his ear.

'Can you hear me? Doctor Ekks? Can you hear me?'

No response.

Cloke poured a capful of water into the man's mouth. Reflex swallow.

'Give me a sign. Blink, or move your fingers, if you can hear my voice.'

No reaction.

Cloke watched him awhile, then resumed reading the sheaf of notes.

The presidential order arrived nine days before the bomb dropped. Our last direct contact with the outside world.

We pleaded for rescue time and again, but help never came. One by one, all radio contacts fell silent. Every army unit that might have conceivably come to our aid had been surrounded, overrun, torn apart.

It added new urgency to our work. The realisation our lives had no value unless we made significant progress in our research.

We were marooned with no hope of fighting our way to safety. Then we received a terse radio message. A chopper would land that afternoon. It had been dispatched from an airfield upstate. It would carry fresh orders.

A brief and perilous touchdown at the junction of Lafayette and Canal. Chief Jefferson and a couple of NYPD SWAT. It must have been a nightmare journey. A quarter-mile dash down the street, ducking between wrecked cars, advancing cover/fire as infected creatures stumbled out of doorways to meet them.

The Fenwick entrance gate was so rusted it took us ten minutes to hammer the padlock loose. Jefferson and his men took position at the mouth of the alley while we worked. They slapped a fresh mag into his rifle and methodically took down a shambling mob of infected headed their way.

We released the gate. Jefferson and his escort ran down the steps to the safety of the station. We sealed the entrance behind them.

The Chief brought a presidential order from the continuity government based at NORAD. As soon as he reached the ticket hall he took the envelope from his jacket pocket and presented it to Doctor Ekks.

Ekks tore open the envelope and read the note.

'You understand the situation?' asked the Chief. 'We haven't got the manpower or equipment to shift your entire team. You folks are stuck here for the duration. It's chaos out there. Anarchy. It's down to you guys now. Continue your work as long as you can.'

247

Ekks nodded.

'I understand.'

'You'll do what needs to be done?'

'Count on it.'

The cops glanced around. They checked out our camp. Six medical staff. Twelve guards. Boxes and bunks. Cold, damp subterranean squalor.

We offered them food. They declined. Their chopper was circling Manhattan. It was a small vehicle, limited fuel capacity. A Bell JetRanger commandeered from a Pittsburgh TV station.

There would be room aboard the helicopter for one additional man.

'Not you, doc. You've got work to do.'

We conferred. Lawson, the youngest member of the 101st platoon, drew the most votes. He shook hands and said goodbye. We gave him letters to pass to our relatives, if they could be found.

We locked the gate after they left, and listened to the sound of distant gunfire as they fought their way back up Lafayette to the chopper.

We were now stranded. Those of us left behind knew there was virtually no hope of rescue.

Ekks showed me the decree. Thick note paper. The presidential seal. An unrecognisable signature. Permission to apply 'extraordinary therapeutic measures' in our search for a cure.

'You must choose,' Ekks told me. 'You must make the selection. One of the prisoners must be sacrificed. You will decide which of them is the ideal experimental subject, the healthiest physical specimen. That is your burden. You must decide who will die.'

We had four captives. Very few medical records. No prison files.

Wade. Judging by his tattoos and blond mullet, he was some kind of biker. He was from Texas. I have no idea how he came to be imprisoned in New York.

Lupe, aka Lucretia, aka Esperansa Guadalupe Villaseñor. She refused to divulge any background information, but her short, violent life was

248

etched in her skin. A map of Honduras on her shoulder. Dead gang brethren inscribed on each bicep. Guns, knives and hypodermics down each forearm.

Marcus Means, aka Sicknote. His skull had been drilled and his thalamus wired with iridium electrodes. A failed attempt to control psychotic episodes using high-frequency electrical impulses. He was lost in nightmares. We had exhausted our supply of anti-schizoid meds and had to quiet his screams with regular doses of Valium. He spent most of each day curled in a foetal ball, staring into space.

Knox. The fourth prisoner. African American. Bright. Articulate. Cooperative.

Time to choose.

I immediately eliminated Means from consideration. His profound mental illness and subsequent brain surgery made him an unsuitable test subject.

Wade was in good physical shape. He was lucid, apparently mentally unimpaired. However, his arms showed signs of long-term intravenous drug use: scarring and collapsed veins. Again, the neurological implications of this drug habit removed him from consideration. A dependence on heroin or methamphetamine would render him an atypical test subject.

Knox and Lupe. Both fit. Both young.

One of them would have to die.

The prisoners were held on the station platform. We had no cells, no containment facilities. Moxon, the orderly charged with guarding the convicts, had drawn chalk squares on the ticket hall floor. The prisoners were confined within the chalk squares. They could sit, lie or pace within the boundaries of their imaginary cell. They could eat from paper plates. They could urinate and defecate in a plastic bucket. They could wash from a basin. But if they stepped beyond the chalk, they would be shot.

I spoke to Lupe first.

I sat cross-legged on the ticket hall floor. She knelt and faced me, the chalk perimeter of her cell between us. She drew a blanket around her shoulders like a shawl.

I'm not sure why Lupe had been sent to Bellevue for psych evaluation. The patient files we rescued from the hospital contained basic medical information. Dosage charts and X-rays. We had no charge sheets or prison documentation. Moxon told me tattoo tears were an emblem of gang-sanctioned assassination. Each tear represented a kill.

I asked Lupe if she was hungry or thirsty. She held out cuffed hands and demanded to be released. I asked if she were cold, if she would like an extra blanket. She looked me in the eye and told me, calm and clear, that I was attempting to use a series of token kindnesses to make myself feel better about holding people captive while the world went to hell, and maybe I should fuck myself.

I shifted position so I could talk to Knox. He sat by the entrance of his cell.

The doorway to each cell was designated by a series of chalk dashes. When the prisoners were escorted to and from their imaginary cells, they were expected to use this demarcated entrance.

Knox sat hugging his knees. He hummed old Motown hits. I gave him a stick of gum.

I liked him. He had been arrested on an assault charge. He told a convoluted story involving mistaken identity and police racism. He was adamant the case should never have seen trial.

He had been transported to Bellevue for treatment to a hip injury following a minor fracas at Sing Sing. A poker game that ended in scattered cards, shoves and recriminations. The prison infirmary had been damaged by a burst water pipe, so he had been sent outside the walls for examination.

I'm not fool enough to think I am a fine judge of character, that I have a deep insight into human nature. But I sympathised with Knox. The pettiest of criminals. No gang tattoos, no track marks. Not a bad man. Not malicious. Just pathetically weak.

Knox or Lupe? Who would you choose?

Lupe deserved to die. Vermin. Irredeemable street trash. A life-long killer. Probably responsible for a dozen deaths, gang rivals shot or knifed in retaliation for near-imperceptible violations of her honour code. Most people would circle her name without hesitation.

250

But what is evil? Is murder part of the normal spectrum of human behaviour? Or is it indicative of illness? If Lupe was a psychopath, incapable of empathy, could that be regarded an actual physical abnormality, rather than simply a mental state? Her anti-social behaviour might be the result of some malformation of the central nervous system. Or it might be the result of post-natal injury. A blow to the head, some form of traumatic encephalopathy. As a doctor, should I regard her as a defective specimen? An imperfect test subject? Was she, on some basic level, less than human?

I handed Ekks the list knowing, as I did so, I had set the death machine in motion.

A folded sheet of paper. Four names. Three crossed in red. A big green tick next to KNOX.

Ekks lay a hand on my shoulder. His solemn, wordless Thank You.

I condemned an innocent person to death. Played my role with cold, clear deliberation.

I did the right thing. I did what needed to be done.

But I'm not the man I used to be. I have become something else. Something ugly. Something broken.

45

Tombes slept, back against the wall.

He swallowed. He choked and convulsed. He woke, and found a thin string of drool hanging from his mouth.

'Christ.'

He took a bandana from his pocket. He dabbed his chin and shirt. He sipped bottled water and rinsed the taste of vomit from his mouth.

He ran fingers across his scalp. Sudden fear his hair might be falling out in clumps.

Sicknote stood by the barricaded door, forehead pressed to the wood panels like he was deep in prayer.

'Told you to keep away from that door.'

Sicknote smiled and backed off.

'You want to go outside, is that it? Want to commune with those bastards in the hall? Embrace the darkness, all that shit? Happy to oblige. Glad to see the back of you.'

Sicknote giggled and walked to the back of the plant room. He sat, rocked, and chewed his nails.

'Stay there. Seriously. Stay put. I got too much to worry about. If you're going to freak out for real, I'll push you out the door. Won't hesitate.'

Lupe sat opposite Tombes.

'It's all right,' said Lupe. 'I'll keep my eyes on him. He won't try anything.'

'If he pulls any shit, I got to take steps. I don't want to hurt the guy. I don't want to hurt anyone. I get it: he's nuts. It's not his fault. But a situation like this, what else can I do?'

'I'll watch the guy, all right? He's my responsibility. If there are problems, I'll deal with it myself.'

Lupe knelt beside Ekks.

She examined his signet ring. A silver snake, eating its own tail. She tried to twist the ring from his finger. His hand slowly balled into a fist.

She studied his face. Silver hair. Wide, Slavic lips.

She leaned close and listened to breath escape his parted lips.

She clapped her hands. He didn't flinch. His eyelids didn't flutter. His jaw didn't clench.

'I doubt he is faking,' said Cloke. 'Nobody is that good an actor.'

'I wouldn't put it past this fuck. He'll wake up when it suits him. Not before. He'll lie there, listening to us talk, map our minds, figure out which strings to pull.'

'You're building this guy up into some sort of satanic manipulator.'

'Damn right.'

Cloke threw the notebook aside. He rubbed his eyes.

'No luck with the code?' asked Lupe.

'I'm not a cipher expert. I haven't got the right sort of mind, the right kind of logic. I've never won a game of chess in my life.'

'I thought you were a scientist.'

'A very average one. Doomed to be mediocre. Some of my college class were effortlessly accomplished. Not me. I had to study night and day. Everything came hard. That's why I hate this damned code. A reminder of my limitations. All the times I sat over a textbook, frustrated and helpless, willing the words to make sense. We need to find a geek. Someone with an aptitude for frequency analysis.'

'We had codes in jail,' said Lupe. 'We used to scribble them on the inside of cigarette packets. Little pencil marks on the foil. They'd change hands in the yard.'

'Contract killings?'

'No. Little stuff. Drug deals, sports bets, love tokens.'

Cloke picked up the notebook and thumbed pages.

'I can't help imagining what it would have been like to be down here, with Ekks, fighting the disease by his side. Dark and desperate hours.'

'You would have died with the rest of them. Blown your brains out in that subway car.'

'I'm a vector specialist. Competent enough in my field. I might have achieved something.'

'You wouldn't have achieved a damn thing,' said Lupe. 'Just an ugly, squalid death.'

Cloke shrugged. He turned his attention back to the notebook.

'We need some kind of key, is that right?' said Lupe. 'Some kind of guide to unlock the text.'

'Yes.'

'He would have to write it down, yeah? It would be complicated. He couldn't keep it in his head.'

'Probably.'

'What would it look like?'

'Most likely some kind of grid or number sequence.'

'Maybe he wrote it on his body. Have you checked him for biro marks? Little tattoos?'

'We gave him a thorough examination. There were no marks.'

'But you frisked him, right? You searched his pockets?'

'It didn't occur to me.'

Lupe leaned over Ekks and patted him down.

A dog tag hung round his neck. A tab of stamped metal with a rubber rim. She broke the ball-chain and examined the tag.

'Feels thick.'

She peeled away the rubber rim. Two tags sandwiched together. A folded scrap of paper the size of a postage stamp between them.

'I'll be damned,' murmured Cloke.

Y	⊔	X	6	N	2	O
◬	H	P	⋏	M	ß	W
S	◇	U	/	E	◭	△
\\	C	4	G	⊡	V	7
S	I	Q	R	8	φ	Z
+	J	D	1	A	→	F
T	O	3	K	9	L	▣

'Is this it? The key to the cipher?'
'Almost certainly.'
'Then get to work.'

Tombes crouched in the corner of the room. He checked his Motorola for charge. The green power light fluttered amber. Low battery.

'Donahue. You there?'

He held the radio close to his ear.

'*Where else would I be?*' Her voice little more than a whisper.

'How you doing?'

'*All right, I guess. Going crazy sitting in the dark. I keep hearing noises, like there's something in the room.*'

'What kind of sounds?'

'*Breathing. Shuffling. Each time I check, there's nothing. Mind playing tricks.*'

'Feeling okay?'

'*Nausea. Got a murderous, fuck-ass headache.*'

'Try not to puke. You could be trapped with the stink for hours. That door still holding?'

'*They stopped pounding the damn thing a while back. Let me check.*'

Brief pause.

'*Yeah. Yeah, she's good. She's holding.*'

'Don't make a sound. Relentless sons of bitches. Patient, like sharks circling a boat. They've got our scent. Blood in the water.'

'*Royal clusterfuck. The whole thing.*'

'I can't talk long. Battery is running low. I've got to conserve power. But you stay safe, you hear? The minute you got a problem, sound off. We'll come running.'

'*Okay.*'

'Take it easy. Try to get some rest, if you can.'

46

David Moxon

Bellevue Dept of Neuroscience

I kept Knox company the night he died.

Ekks insisted the condemned man be extended every consideration. At the very least, he should expect the same privileges as a man on death row. He should be told his fate. He should be given a chance to make his peace with himself, his God. He should be given pen and paper, an opportunity to make a final statement.

I wasn't present when Knox was told he was to be dissected. I heard about it later.

They took him from his chalk-outline cell. He was cuffed and led to the train, told it was part of a routine medical examination. He had endured long days without sunlight. They said they were checking for vitamin D deficiency.

He was isolated in one of the carriages. He was stripped and photographed. They shaved his head. They returned his clothes and chained him to a seat. Then they explained he was marked for death.

Harold Donner, one of the doctors from Bellevue, delivered the news. Knox was to die. He would be deliberately infected, so that Ekks and his team could study the first moments of infection. There would be no anaesthetic, no sedative. Nothing that might interfere with the validity of the results.

Knox screamed and raged. He thrashed, tried to break his cuffs, tried to break the chain that held him tethered to the seat. He begged. He pleaded. He wept.

Donner shook his head. He said he was sorry.

Knox demanded to speak to Ekks. Ekks wouldn't talk to him. Said he was busy.

The procedure was scheduled to begin at midnight.

Knox had twelve hours to prepare himself for death.

My task?

To keep him company during the last hours of his life. Talk. Pray. Fulfil any request within my power. Above all, I was to ensure he did not escape or injure himself. When midnight came, the tie-down team would lead him to the adjacent carriage and strap him to the examination table. Then he would face the needle. A sample of the pathogen would be drawn from biological material supplied by NORAD. It would be injected into his arm.

He sat alone in the carriage. He wore a red prison-issue smock and pants. Bare feet. He was chained to the passenger seat by an ankle shackle. Garbage bags had been taped over the windows so he couldn't see medical personnel carry surgical equipment across the platform to the improvised operating theatre in the adjacent carriage.

Knox had been given a bible. A faux leather king James. It sat unopened beside him.

I set down a tray. His last meal. A couple of luncheon meat sandwiches and a fruit beverage.

'Do you want to pray?' I asked.

'Fuck you.'

'It might help.'

'Help who? You or me?'

'You're not a religious man?'

'Look around you. A billion dead. A billion prayers unanswered. If Jesus didn't break cover to help countless grieving mothers, why the hell would he intercede to save my sorry ass?'

'It might ease your mind. The sound. The old words.'

'God is gone. Packed his bags and left. No forwarding address. Nothing in the sky but infinite dark.'

'I brought a clock.'

258

'To watch my life tick away? How the hell would that help?'

'Anything you want to talk about? You got a few hours left.'

'Seriously. Fuck you.'

'Any messages you want to pass on? I could help you write a letter.'

'Think I'm stupid? Think I don't know how to write my name?'

'No.'

'Read a damn sight more books than your cracker ass. Better educated than half the guys in this sewer.'

'I could fetch pen and paper. Got relatives somewhere? We might be able to get a message to them, somehow.'

'What if I said I had kids? A family out there, worrying about their dad? Would you give a crap?'

'Maybe we should just sit a while.'

'I'm chained to the seat. Ain't got much choice.'

'I can get water. More food, if you need it.'

'Let me ask you something. Ekks. Do you trust him?'

'Barely spoke to the guy. I'm just a turn-key.'

'You've known the man, what, a week? And here you are, colluding in murder.'

'He got us out of Bellevue. The handful that stayed behind? Those assholes convinced tanks and planes were coming to the rescue? Long dead.'

'He saved you folks because you were useful.'

'Those doctors and nurses out there have known him for years.'

'Got a mind of your own, don't you? What do you think of the guy?'

I shrugged.

'I'm sorry it came down to this.'

'What's your name?' asked Knox.

'Moxon. David.'

'They're going to kill me, Dave. They're going to kill me and cut me up. Pull out my spine. Crack open my head.' He tapped his temple. 'This skull. Right here. They'll saw it open and scoop out my brain. My brain, dude. Thoughts, memories, emotions. They're going to take it all away.'

'I'm sorry, man. Sorry you drew the short straw.'

'Do you even know why you're doing this? Any of you?'

259

'A cure.'

'They are going to inject me with the virus. They'll watch me change. Then they'll set the cameras rolling and dissect me like a frog, do it while I'm still alive. How the hell does that help? Thousands of infected roaming the streets. Why would one more make a difference?'

'I'm not a doctor.'

'Even the white coats don't understand why this is necessary. I've heard them whispering outside the window. No one has the balls to stand up to the guy. Too chickenshit. He wants to instigate murder, and everyone falls in line. Makes no damned sense whatsoever. He's going to stick a needle in my arm, watch me die, and somehow that is going to result in some big-ass eureka moment? He's going to kill me, here in this tunnel, and that's going to provoke some world-shaking breakthrough, produce a cure that eluded Nobel Prize winners working in fully-equipped labs? You have to set me loose, kid. Undo these cuffs.'

'Sorry. Can't do it.'

'Give me a paperclip. I'll pick the lock. Tell them I broke free and overpowered you.'

'I'm so sorry. I wish I could help. But I can't.'

'It's not about me, dumbass. It's about you guys. This whole sick cavalcade. One big, deliberate mindfuck. The team in these tunnels, the doctors, nurses and soldiers. They all took an oath to preserve life. Built their lives around it. And they are going to throw it all away.'

'I don't understand.'

'Ekks is a nut. A psychopath. He's laughing at you guys. Laughing his ass off. I don't understand why you can't see it. It's like you're all blind. He acts all paternal and concerned. He smiles, plays The Great Healer. But deep down, any fool can see this is the most fun he's had in his life. The monsters dancing in his head, the dark carnival locked in his skull, finally made it out into the world. All the death and horror out there in the streets? He loves it. He's exultant. Euphoric. Never felt more at home. It's like his dreams leaked out of his ears and took over the world.'

'Have you ever spoken with the man?'

'Ekks? I've watched him real close.'

260

'But have you actually spoken with him? Have you exchanged a single word?'

'I've looked in his eyes. Told me all I need to know.'

'Everyone respects the guy. He's smart. He organised defences back at Bellevue. He rationed food, showed people how to drain water from the pipes. It was his idea to hide here at Fenwick. We'd all be dead a long time ago, if not for him. He saved our asses a dozen times.'

'He saved you so he could kill you. It's not enough to see those infected folks rip you to pieces. Too easy. He's got something better in mind.'

'Like what?'

'We've all become killers. Every one of us. I killed a couple of folks back at the hospital. Patients in gowns. Met them in a corridor. Tried to rip out my throat. I grabbed a fire extinguisher from the wall, did what I had to do. And those 101st grunts. They expended a shitload of ammo during the run from Bellevue to 23rd Street. Hell of a body count. We've all got horror stories, a lifetime of nightmares. But we killed folk who had long since ceased to be themselves, people who were pretty much dead already. Shit, we did them a favour. If they had a voice, if they had a mind, they would have pleaded for a bullet in the brain.

But this is different. This is how Ekks intends to break you. He wants to see his team of ministering angels transformed into a lynch mob. He wants to see them violate every code. Descend to his fucked up level. He's going to rub your noses in the dirt until you admit you are nothing more than pissing, shitting animals, no better than those creeps crawling around the streets outside. He doesn't want to kill me. I'm nothing. A lab rat. A germ in a Petri dish. He's going to push you guys until you destroy yourselves. You have to say No. You have to make a stand.'

'It doesn't make sense. The guy has been a surgeon for years. He's healed thousands of people.'

'Because he enjoys life-or-death power. That's how he gets his rocks off. He likes to drill a person's skull and probe inside their mind.'

'People with strokes, people with Alzheimer's. He isn't some sanatorium butcher dishing out twenty lobotomies a day. He's a world-class neuro-surgeon. He's trying to help.'

'Everyone who got wheeled into that guy's surgical theatre came out changed. Maybe for the better. But they got tweaked. That's the kick. That's the buzz. He's a real-life Doctor Frankenstein. He gowns-up, stands over the operating table and creates something new. The guy is an insect. And this is his time. The Year of the Bug. His moment to reign.'

'Maybe. I don't know. I'm just a guard.'

'You have to save me, David. You have to save yourself.'

47

Galloway scrambled through tight passageways, mapped the warren of pipes.

A network of conduits built in the nineteen twenties, long before the smooth aluminium ducting and monitored flow control of modern ventilation systems. Giant plenum blades in the plant room circulated air through the pipes. Negative pressure drew off stagnant tunnel fumes, replaced fetid vapour with clean air drawn from street vents.

Galloway still had sensation. His hand and feet delivered the texture of brick and abrasive mortar. Yet he was impervious to pain. Rotted skin hung from his arms in strips, exposing muscle threaded with metallic veins.

He knelt, gripped his bicep and ripped away ribbons of loose skin. He felt no pain. He could feel his flesh stretch, peel and tear as if he were shredding paper.

Sometimes he was Galloway. Sometimes he wasn't.

Consciousness came and went like an intermittent radio signal, but his body kept moving. He would sit, staring into darkness. Next moment, he would find himself crouched in an entirely different section of tunnel, exploring a fissure in the brickwork, probing it with his finger. No idea how much time had passed. No idea what instinct had piloted his body during the blackout. Clearly he had moved through the tunnels with deliberation and purpose. But what entity had looked out from behind his eyes? What alien intelligence had displaced his thoughts and memories?

He squatted in the darkness. He could still see. There was no light, but the tunnel around him seemed to dance with a weird bioluminescence as if it were lit from within. He perceived the bark-ripple texture of each brick, and the granular crust of mortar, with the heightened clarity of dreams.

He explored new sensations, a torrential inrush of sense data.

He was not alone.

He could feel something else deep in the tunnel network. A cold intellect, watching, appraising. It sang in the darkness. His body began to respond.

'Who are you?' he murmured, addressing the thing in his head. 'What do you want?'

As if in response, his left arm began to rise. He fought the motion, battled the hijacked limb. He tried to bar the grasping hand with his mutilated right arm and force it down. It was like fighting a hydraulic ram.

He tried to ball his fist, but his fingers overcame the command, reached for his face and began to claw skin. Nails dug into his forehead and tore decayed flesh like it was the putrid, semi-liquefied pulp of a rotten fruit.

He screamed.

Stretch and tear. Epidermis slowly peeled back. He shook his head and blinked away blood as it trickled down the bridge of his nose into his eyes.

A wide strip of skin slowly ripped from his brow, eye socket, cheek and jaw. The glistening musculature of his face fully revealed. Metal-fused bone.

Galloway emitted a guttural howl of revulsion and despair. He spat blood and drool. He tried to pull his head away as the hand clawed his face and gouged skin.

Fingers gripped the back of his neck and peeled off his scalp like a ski mask, exposing the white dome of his skull. The discarded flesh-cap hit the tunnel floor with a slap.

Each ear lobe twisted free, dripping strings of pale cartilage.

A wide slab of tissue torn from his chest, exposing ribs and knitted sinew.

A sleeve of flesh ripped from his arm.

Galloway had lost the battle for ascendancy. He was a passenger in his own head. He watched, helpless, as the methodical excavation continued. Fingers raked and clawed, sloughed dead tissue from his bones as something lean and lethal fought to emerge.

48

Cloke threw the notebook aside.

'No luck?' asked Lupe. 'Thought you could decipher the thing.'

'The key doesn't work. I've transposed letters. But look. More gibberish.'

He held up a scrap of note paper.

HALG CASP LA KLINMOOR FORGUL

'Hovering on the edge of coherence. There must be something I missed. Some additional step.'

'Anagrams?'

'The whole book? Hope not.'

'Ekks is foreign, right?' asked Lupe. 'Naturalised?'

'East European. Ukrainian, I think.'

'No reason the code should be in English.'

'How much water do we have left?' asked Cloke.

'About a pint.'

Lupe passed the nearly empty bottle of mineral water.

Cloke took an appreciative swig and sluiced the water around his mouth. He gestured to the plant room door.

'Prowlers. Do you think they communicate? Their actions seem to be crudely coordinated.'

'You're kidding, right?'

'Think about it. This disease has no use for higher brain function. Once the virus burrows deep into a person's cerebral cortex, their memories, their personality, are wiped away. But what takes their place? Even the most advanced case, skin rotting from the bone, is animated by a crude insect cunning. Whimsical thought, but what if the virus can communicate on some basic level?'

'Say it could talk. What would you ask?'

'Who are you? Where do you come from? What do you want?'

'Speak to Ekks when he wakes. He stared into the heart of darkness. Maybe he'll tell you what he saw.'

Cloke nodded.

He reached inside the data bag, pulled out a fresh sheet of handwritten paper, and began to read.

Sergeant Donovan
101st Airborne

Monday September 23rd

Our third suicide.

Rosa Tracy. A nurse. Pleasant disposition. Liked by all.

She was found hanging in the plant room this morning. She had unclipped the nylon shoulder strap of a holdall and used it as a ligature. Stood on a box and lashed the strap to an overhead pipe. She looped the nylon round her throat, then kicked away the box.

I cut her down. She had been dead for hours. Purple, swollen face. Limbs locked rigid.

I searched her pockets. No note. No explanation.

I wish we had a priest. It seems callous to dump her body in the tunnels without formally commemorating her life. She is not a piece of refuse. She deserves a proper grave.

*

267

A madness has gripped the team.

The two remaining doctors openly inject themselves with opiates and sit in a blissed stupor as if they expect, sooner or later, to be ripped apart and intend to be drugged insensible when it occurs.

Janice, the sole remaining female among our group, seems to have surrendered to a nihilistic sensuality. I am reluctant to be more specific. Her behaviour, and the free availability of narcotics, has destroyed camp discipline.

Ekks could restore order with a glance, a single word. Yet, since the death of Knox, he has been curiously reluctant to establish control. He has spent the past few days alone in his carriage, cross-legged on his cot, transcribing the results of his research.

I visited him yesterday. Knocked on the slide door and entered his carriage.

It was dark. The windows were curtained with garbage bags. I let my vision adjust. Ekks lay on his bunk. His eyes were closed. There was a radio next to the bed hissing static. He wafted his hand back and forth like he was directing music only he could hear.

I stood in the carriage doorway. I told him the camp was going to hell. Food for a couple more days, then we would starve. We needed to get off the island. We needed leadership, some kind of plan.

He didn't move, didn't say a word.

Tuesday September 24th

Ivanek, our young communications officer, heard a brief announcement on the EMS waveband a few hours ago. He has been sat next to the RT for days, listening to a looped broadcast of prayers and hymns. He was half asleep when he heard a woman's voice cut into the transmission. She said the president would address the nation at midnight.

Maybe the address will give us a clear indication of the situation above ground. Perhaps our infantry have regrouped and are preparing to reclaim all major cities. Or perhaps our position is truly hopeless: we are marooned in this troglodytic twilight, without the slightest chance of rescue. In which case I hope firm knowledge of our situation will be enough to galvanise

268

the men. Once they realise their only shot at safety is to walk off this island, battle their way street by street across the bridge and into Brooklyn, maybe they will pull together.

My greatest disappointment these past few days has been Moxon, the guard who accompanied us from Bellevue. I regarded him as an ally. He alone among our number remained sober and focussed. He shaved, while others grew beards. He maintained his uniform while others shambled in sweat-stained lab coats. But he overheard a discussion in which I suggested the remaining prisoners represented an ongoing threat to our safety and should be euthanized. He has threatened to unshackle the prisoners and release them into the tunnels, if we attempt to take any action against them.

So there is nothing to do but watch my companions succumb to orgiastic squalor. I monitor our supplies of food and water and make an hourly inspection of the station gate. And I alone seem to care that Doctor Ekks, the man who embodies the entire purpose of our mission, is currently held captive by an apparent lunatic.

Wednesday September 25th

The standoff continues.

Private Tetsell, one of the least experienced members of our company, has shut himself in the station supervisor's office with Doctor Ekks. He is armed with a shotgun. He has constructed a barricade. We heard furniture moved around, the squeak of chairs pushed against the door, pinning it shut.

He has demanded a helicopter fly him to Philadelphia.

Tetsell is a good man. He's scared, confused, but fundamentally decent. I doubt he will harm Ekks. But I can't be certain. These are extraordinary times. Each day brings fresh horrors. Minds break like porcelain.

We could storm the office, I suppose. We could ram the door until it splits and the furniture stacked behind it falls aside. But the consequences could be catastrophic. It would take many seconds, possibly a full minute, to gain entry to the room. Tetsell might kill himself, or worse, kill Ekks.

269

Our orders were specific. Protect Doctor Ekks. Protect him at all costs. My one and only priority.

Perhaps we could use the ventilation conduits. There are brick tunnels built into the station walls. Maybe a man with a pistol could crawl through the narrow ducts. Maybe he could reach the IRT office, punch out a wall vent and shoot Tetsell dead.

I keep running hostage rescue scenarios. If the world were still intact, our course of action would be clear. We would summon reinforcements, deploy a tac team and have them storm the office. Start a conversation on the radio to distract the guy. Have SWAT kill the lights and simultaneously blow out the hinges with Shok-Lok rounds. An efficient breech-entry. They would kick the door aside, toss a couple of concussion grenades. Tetsell left flash-blind and reeling. SWAT swarming through the doorway equipped with laser sights and night vision helmet rigs. The siege would be concluded in two or three seconds.

But I can't summon a trained takedown team. These elaborate rescue fantasies are a product of impotence and frustration. Tetsell is barricaded behind a heavy door. I have limited men, limited ammunition. Best to avoid a confrontation. I must be patient. Maintain a dialogue. Starve him out.

In the meantime, I have a grim task to perform. Rosa's body is still lying beneath a blanket in the plant room. I suppose I must carry her deep into the tunnels, far enough that we won't breathe the stink of decomposition.

There is a niche in the tunnel wall several hundred yards north near Canal Street. A branch of track aborted during the initial construction of the Liberty Line. It is little more than a cave. A brick arch framing rough walls of schist scarred by chisels and dynamite cartridges.

It is where I laid the remains of Knox, days ago.

I carried a garbage bag full of offal and bone deep into the tunnel. All that was left of him, all that wasn't suspended in jars. No sound but the steady drip of water.

Foolish to travel alone. Plenty of infected stumbling round the passageways.

270

I dumped the bag in the wall niche, doused it in kerosene and set it alight. The tunnel was filled with smoke, meat-stink, the pop and fizz of boiling body fat.

I don't know why I went to such lengths to destroy all trace of Knox. I could have put his carcass out in the alley. Or I could have dumped the bag a few yards into the tunnel near Fenwick and let rats gnaw the marrow from his bones. His death was necessary, legally sanctioned. No reason to feel ashamed.

No one gives a damn about Knox. He was a non-person long before this disease stalked the earth. No one will mourn him, no one will care. There will be no judge, no tribunal. He has been erased. It is as if he never lived.

Cloke folded the notepaper.

'Donavan. Wasn't he the soldier we found floating in the tunnel? That guy turned to rat food?'

'Yeah,' said Lupe. 'Sorry bastard succumbed to infection.'

'How old do you think he was?'

'Young, at a guess. One of those blue-eyed, god-and-country types.'

'Seems the lad walked into the dark rather than become a threat to his companions.'

'Is that what you want to believe?'

'Why not?' said Cloke. 'A good soldier. Took action rather than jeopardise the people around him. Some people do the right thing.'

'You got kids?' asked Lupe. 'Family?'

'No. You?'

She shook her head.

'Times like these, it's good to travel light.'

Cloke stuffed the notepaper back in the bag.

'There's nothing in these letters. Nothing of use. A dozen goodbyes. It seems indecent to read this stuff. Prurient. Eavesdropping on their final hours. Ought to put a match to them all.'

271

'Then you're back where you started,' said Lupe. 'Ekks. You've got to get inside his head, find out what he knows.'

49

Donahue sat in the dark, back to the office wall. She closed her eyes and rested her head against cement. She blanked her mind and tried to sink into hibernation.

She put herself on a wooded hillside. Dappled shade. A trickling stream. Silence and solitude. She lay in long grass and sipped from her canteen.

She expanded the daydream, added detail and backstory.

She had fled the ruins of civilisation and found safety in deep wilderness. She was camped in a forest, far from the horror. A dome tent draped in camouflage netting hidden among trees. Maybe, when noonday heat gave way to evening cool, she would fish from the stream. Lower a hook and line, snag a couple of trout.

Dread crept over her. The hillside dissolved. Summer heat was replaced by bone-chilling cold. Sunlight turned to darkness. The smell of forest pine was supplanted by the stink of mildew and decay.

Back in the IRT office.

She stared into absolute black. Her optic nerves projected fleeting monster shapes.

She couldn't escape a skin-crawling, preternatural sense she was not alone. Something else in the room, inches away, hidden in darkness.

She fumbled her watch and pressed for the face-light. She half expected to see a rotted visage leaning over her, arms outstretched.

Nothing.

She held her wrist and monitored her pulse. She breathed slow, tried to calm her jack-hammer heart.

How much time had passed? It felt like an hour. She checked. Eight minutes.

'Christ.'

She stood. She stretched. Toe touches and back twists.

She crouched and grunted through a dozen half-assed press-ups. She lay on her back and tried a couple of knee-to-elbow crunches. She gave up and lay on cold tiles, fighting a wave of fierce nausea. She suppressed a dust-sneeze.

She heard a soft thump, then the rasp of fingernails dragged across wood.

Something on the other side of the office door. The Dunkin' Donuts guy.

More scratching. The faint creak of body weight pressed against wood.

Donahue got to her feet. She crept across the room, arms outstretched. She felt for the door. She stroked wood and found the peep hole. She put her eye to the lens.

The rotted, skeletal thing staring back at her. Jet black eyes. Blood-matted hair. Skin like ripped parchment.

Donuts sensed her presence. It leaned close to the door. Sniffed the lens, like it caught her scent.

Donuts was suddenly pushed aside. A bald Hare Krishna, mouth smeared with blood, pushed his face to the peep hole.

The infected creatures jostled for position in front of the door. They craned towards the lens, stared back at Donahue in fish-eye distortion.

They leered. They hissed. They began to punch the wood.

Donahue jumped back.

Pounding fist strikes. Again. And again. A determined fusillade of blows. Oak split with a gunshot retort. Donahue heard the splintering rasp of fissures extending through wood grain.

She backed away. The pounding increased as a third pair of hands joined the assault and began to batter the door.

She unclipped her radio.

'Tombes? Can you hear me, over?' She shouted. No point masking her voice. 'Pick up the damned radio.'

'*What's up?*'

'Need some help over here.'

'*What's going on?*'

'Bastards want in. They mean business.'

'*Can you hold them off?*'

'Negative. I need help. Right now.'

'*Throw stuff against the door. Anything you got.*'

'I'm on it.'

'*We're coming, Donnie.*'

50

Lupe grabbed the radio.

'How many?'

'*I don't know. Two. Maybe three. Hammering like crazy.*'

'Is the door secure?'

'*It's started to bow. I can hear it crack each time they hit. It's slowly giving way.*'

'How long can you hold out?'

'*This kind of sustained assault? Minutes. Maybe less. Maybe a lot less.*'

'I'm going out there,' said Tombes. 'Rest of you stay here, okay? Close the door behind me.'

'You'll get killed.'

'Maybe. But I'll lead them a dance before I do.'

'Fuck that shit,' said Lupe. 'They will tear you to pieces.'

'I'm not going to sit on my ass and listen to Donnie get ripped apart.'

'I'll go with you. If we stand back-to-back maybe we can take a bunch of them down.'

'There's another option,' said Cloke.

'Let's hear it.'

Cloke pointed to the jumbled notes in the data bag.

'One of the Bellevue guys took Ekks hostage. Kept him prisoner in the IRT office. Barricaded the door. The officer in charge planned to use air handling conduits to get inside the room and shoot him dead.'

'Did it work?'

'No idea. But that could be the best way to reach Donahue. Crawl through the walls.'

'What about Galloway? He's in there, somewhere.'

'Some of these pipes run for miles. Should be able to avoid him, long as you don't take any detours.'

They pulled paint tins and boxes from the conduit mouth. Tombes tugged the grille until corroded screws sheared and mesh tore loose.

He shone his flashlight into the dark aperture. Crumbling brickwork receded to shadow.

'Worth a shot.'

'Doesn't look too stable,' said Lupe. 'That shit could cave any minute.'

Tombes gripped the lip of the tunnel mouth and hauled himself inside. He twisted round. Lupe passed him a section of rusted pipe.

'Watch yourself. Galloway is in there, somewhere.'

He tucked the pipe into his waistband.

'Catch you later.'

Lupe rehung the grille and stacked boxes against the mesh.

She took out her radio.

'Donahue? Do you copy?'

'*Yeah.*'

'Look around. There's a grille, right? Some kind of vent in the office wall.'

'*There's something high up, blocked with wood.*'

'Can you reach it?'

'*I'm a bit frigging preoccupied right now.*'

'Tombes is on his way. We think he can reach you via the air tunnels. All you have to do is sit tight, okay?'

'*I'm not sure how much longer I can keep them out. The lock is screwed. The door bends every time they hit.*'

'Is there anything else you can use for a barricade?'

'*I've thrown every last thing against the door. I'm holding the damned thing shut. I got my back to the desk.*'

'We'll buy you time.'

Lupe ran to the plant room door.

'Cloke. Get over here. Make some noise.'

Lupe began to punch and kick the door.

'Hey,' she shouted. 'Hey, you fucks. In here. We're in here. Come on. Fresh meat. Come and get it.'

Cloke pummelled the door.

'Hey,' they shouted. 'Hey, in here.'

The door began to shake and rumble as bodies slammed into the wood from the other side.

They stepped back. They listened to the cacophony.

'Guess we drew a few of them off,' said Lupe.

'Sounds like a pretty big crowd,' said Cloke. 'More of the bastards heading down the steps each minute. We should have hit them sooner. A lot sooner.'

'We're smart. They're dumb. We're fast. They're slow. The trick is to keep moving. If you freeze, if you hesitate for a second, they'll converge on your ass, and then you're fucked. Go in hard. Be a whirlwind. Duck and weave.'

'What have we got for weapons?'

'Not much. A couple of sections of pipe. Plenty of stuff in the equipment pile out there in the ticket hall. Rescue gear. Axes, hammers, crowbars. But we have to battle our way through a crowd to reach them. Twenty yards of tough fighting.'

'Got any matches?' asked Cloke.

Lupe dug in her pocket. Galloway's matchbook. Three strikes left.

'What do you have in mind?'

Cloke led her to the back of the room. Stacked boxes. He tore away rotted cardboard. Rusted paint tins.

'Should have thought of this a lot earlier.'

He hefted a tin, wiped grime from the Nu-Enamel label.

'This sludge is oil-based. Thinned with turpentine. It'll burn like phosphorus.'

They stacked tins by the plant room door. Cloke pried lids with his belt buckle. He recoiled from the fierce chemical stink.

Lupe shrugged off her coat and pulled her prison smock over her head. White bra. Big tattoo across her back:

Dios
Patria
Libertad

She bit the sleeve of her prison smock between clenched teeth and tore strips. She pinned each strip beneath a lid to form a wick.

'All right. Let's napalm the bastards.'

Tombes crawled through the narrow pipe. His flashlight lit the brick-lined conduit ahead. Panting breath, and the scuff of boots, reverberated in the confined space.

He was spooked by darkness, and the sinister wind-whisper of the passageways.

A sudden conviction he was not alone. Something else in the tunnel system. He paused, twisted round and shone the flashlight behind him. Nothing. The brick pipe receded to deep darkness.

He turned back, and hit his head on the low brick roof. He winced and checked his scalp for blood.

Lupe's voice:

'*How's it going?*'

'Stinks like someone crawled in here and died.'

'*They probably did.*'

'I found Galloway's boot. He's around here, somewhere.'
'*Watch yourself.*'
'There's a junction. I'm heading right.'
'*How far have you got?*'
'Hard to tell.'
'*We got paint tins. We'll try to set the fuckers on fire, create a distraction.*'
'Hold on. I can see light up ahead.'

Tombes shut off his flashlight and tucked it into his waistband. He crawled forwards. A dust-furred grille in the floor of the conduit. The slats projected lattice light on the tunnel roof.

He took the radio from his pocket and reduced the volume.

'I'm above the ticket hall. I'm looking down. Can't see too well. I count seven infected. Probably more outside my field of vision. They look pretty far gone. Slow. Messed up. I reckon we could take them, if we move fast.'

The pounding stopped. Donahue remained braced against the desk barricade for a full minute, then slowly relaxed.

She wiped sweat from her face. She shook out exhausted limbs.

She shone the watch and inspected the door. The wood surrounding the hinges had started to rip and splinter.

A faint crackle from her radio.

Lupe's voice:

'*Donahue? You there?*'

Donahue crouched in the corner and whispered into the Motorola.

'Yeah. Yeah, I'm here.'

'*How you doing?*'

'The door took a battering. The hinges are tearing loose. Surprised it hasn't caved.'

'*Are they still trying to get inside?*'

'They seemed to have laid off, for now.'

'*We made a ruckus. A bunch of them are outside the plant room, trying to break in. Our door is solid. It should hold.*'

'Okay.'

'*Can you see the vent?*'

'Like I said, there's a couple of chunks of wood screwed high on one of the walls.'

'*Can you shift them?*'

'Hold on.'

A couple of short lengths of wood secured by heavy screws. Donahue reached up, gripped the planks and pulled. She grunted and strained. She lifted her feet off the floor and hung by her arms, tried to wrench the slats from the wall using her full body weight.

'They're screwed directly into the brickwork. Can't shift the damn things. I guess they could be blocking a vent. Hard to tell.'

'*Don't worry about it. Tombes will kick them free from inside once he reaches the office.*'

'All right.'

'*Look, you have to do me a favour. I know it's asking a lot. But I need you to draw these bastards away from the plant room door. We've got paint bombs, Molotov cocktails. We can burn those fuckers to a crisp, but we need them to back away from the door so we can get into the hall and hit them. Can you do that? Can you create a distraction?*'

'You got to time it right. If I make a racket, they'll head my way. The door won't hold out much longer. The moment I start to holler, I'm committed. You've got to get into the hall and take them down. Any delay, and I'm screwed.'

'*We're set. The moment you ring the bell, we'll head into the hall and fry those fuckers.*'

'Let's do it before I change my mind.'

Donahue set the gramophone on the floor. She picked a

random 78, threaded it onto the spindle and set it running. She dropped the needle arm. Pop and crackle.

She braced against the desk.

'Hey,' shouted Donahue. His voice rang loud and metallic in the confined office space. 'Hey. Come on, you bastards. Food's up. Come get me, motherfuckers.'

Benny Goodman. 'King Porter Stomp'. Jazz filled the room. Fists pounded the door.

'Listen,' said Cloke.

Impacts against the plant room door diminished to silence. Faint music.

They gripped the battery rack and hauled it aside. They did it slow, tried to minimise stone-scrape and grit-pop as they dragged the heavy frame across concrete.

'Let's do this.'

Lupe gave Cloke two paint tins.

'Sure it'll burn?'

'Oh yeah. This shit is old school. Flammable as hell. Don't breathe the fumes. They'll strip the lining from your lungs.'

'Okay.'

'You throw. I'll back you up. And, hey. Make them count, all right?'

Cloke held out the tins. Lupe struck a match and lit the wicks. Red cotton smouldered and flared.

She tossed the match and snatched up the section of pipe.

'On three.' She pulled back the deadbolts. 'One, two, three.'

She pulled open the door.

A rotted, infected guy standing directly in front of her. Suit and tie. A ridge of spines across his head like a Mohawk. He grunted and looked up, a grotesque parody of surprise.

'Hi there.'

Lupe caved his forehead with a vicious swing of the pipe. He tottered like a drunk and fell.

They ran into the hall.

A dozen shambling, infected things turned their way.

'Oh fuck.'

Cloke threw the first tin. It hit a garlanded Hare Krishna on the chest. Crimson paint splashed across satin robes and caught alight. Fabric shrivelled and burned with a blue flame, turning the man to a pillar of fire.

A woman in a pus-streaked waitress uniform. Her name tag said DOROTHY. She limped forwards, arms outstretched. Lupe caved her head with a side-swing of the pipe.

'Over there.'

Four rotted creatures battered the IRT door, trying to get inside.

'Burn them.'

Cloke hurled the second tin. It hit the wall above the door. Vapour ignited like a napalm flame-burst, and the four were engulfed in fire.

Lupe and Cloke shielded their faces. They recoiled from searing heat.

A guy ran at Lupe. He was enveloped in flame. She kicked him to the ground. He struggled to his feet. She kicked him again. He sank to his knees, pitched face forwards and lay motionless as he burned.

Lupe ducked back in the plant room and grabbed more tins. She hurled them. Crimson paint dashed against the pillars, ceiling and floor. The paint ignited like gasoline. Fire washed across the hall. Blazing creatures stumbled and flailed. Clothing and hair shrivelling in the flames.

A burning figure staggered towards Cloke, arms outstretched. It waded across the ticket hall, waist-deep in flame, then collapsed as cooked muscle ceased to respond to nerve transmissions.

Cloke and Lupe ran for the plant room, slammed the door and slapped deadbolts back in position.

Shuddering impacts.

They backed away. Black smoke curled from the crack at the foot of the door. They covered their mouths to mask the stench of burning flesh.

Donahue struggled to keep the office door closed. Shoulder to the desk, feet braced against the back wall.

Her radio lay on the floor, out of reach. She could see the LED wink brilliant emerald in the darkness. A faint voice, part-drowned by jazz:

'*Donnie, can you hear me? Donnie, do you copy, over?*'

'Hey,' yelled Donahue, trying to be heard beyond the door. 'Lupe. Anyone. Need some fucking help here.'

The door began to give way. Too dark to see damage, but she could hear oak splinter and split.

More impacts. Orange flame-light. Burning arms punching through the wood, pulling panels aside.

'Help,' yelled Donahue, loud as she could. 'For Christ's sake. Help.'

Sudden crash. A boot kicked out the wall vent.

Dazzling glare. A flashlight beam shafted through the office darkness.

Tombes leaned out of the narrow aperture.

'Give me your hand.'

Donahue ran across the room and grasped Tombes' hand. He hauled her up. She squirmed into the brick-lined conduit.

She twisted around. A last glance back.

The door smashed off its hinges. The desk thrown aside. The gramophone kicked and smashed.

Infected creatures blundered into the office. They burned and flailed, bounced off the walls and set the room alight. Flesh-stink and flame.

'Come on,' said Tombes, beckoning her down the narrow passage. 'Let's go.'

★

Hammering slowed to silence. Lupe pressed her ear to the door. She listened a full minute.

'Anything?' asked Cloke.

'Nothing.'

'Maybe they backed off.'

'Feel the door.'

Cloke put his hand to the door.

'Jeez. Baking hot.'

'I'm going out there,' said Lupe. 'I'm going to take a look.'

'You're sure?'

'I've got to know what's going on.'

Cloke slowly pulled back deadbolts. He held the door handle, flinched as he gripped hot metal.

Lupe gripped the rusted pipe in both hands, ready to strike.

She gave the nod.

Cloke wrenched open the door.

They recoiled from acrid flesh-stink. Lupe waved her hands, tried to clear broiling smoke.

A corpse. A jumble of bone and smouldering rags lying on the tiled floor. The door was carbonised and blistered.

Lupe cupped a hand over her mouth. She pushed the brittle cadaver aside with her foot and edged into the ticket hall.

The hall was dark. The ceiling light was blackened with soot.

Lupe fumbled her way to the equipment pile and tipped out a couple of scorched nylon holdalls. She found a flashlight and switched it on. The beam shafted through smoke.

The hall looked like a battlefield. Bodies littered the floor. Spastic, contorted limbs. Grinning skulls. Seared flesh bubbled and smoked.

'I'm going up top,' said Lupe, gesturing to the street exit

stairs. 'We have to seal the entrance gate before any more of these bastards stumble down here.'

Cloke tossed her a respirator and gloves.

'Don't get careless. Close the gate quick as you can, then get back down here. Every second at the top of those steps is a second too long.'

Cloke returned to the plant room. He knelt beside Ekks. He checked pulse and respiration.

'Still don't like the sound of that chest rattle,' he murmured.

He hung a clear bag of saline from a water pipe above Ekks and ran line to the cannula in his forearm.

'Doctor, can you hear me?'

He leaned over Ekks and gently lifted an eyelid. He shone a penlight. Weak dilation.

'Come on. Give me a sign. Move your fingers.'

No response.

'We need you, Doctor. We have to know. The cure. How close did you get?'

No reply.

'Please. Summon your energy, Doctor. Summon your strength. Talk to me. The cure. Did you succeed?'

No reply.

Cloke sighed and sat back. He glanced at Sicknote. The man was petrified. He was staring past Cloke, shocked rigid by what he saw.

Cloke felt hot, fetid breath on the back of his neck. He slowly turned.

Exposed muscle. Knotted tumours. Bared teeth.

'Jesus,' he murmured. 'Galloway.'

Cloke was lifted clean off his feet. He tried to scream, but a hand clamped round his throat and cut off all sound. His legs danced in the air.

Sicknote watched from the shadows. He squirmed deeper into darkness. He suppressed a terrified giggle.

Cloke fought to release the hand wrapped round his neck. He punched. He strained. He choked as fingers dug into his larynx.

He looked down at the skinless, grinning skull-mask.

He shoved a hand in his pant pocket and retrieved a cyanide cylinder. He struggled to unscrew the cap with his thumb and forefinger.

Galloway slammed Cloke's head against the wall. The cylinder fell to the floor. Brass chimed as it hit cement. The glass ampoule smashed, spilling droplets of amber liquid.

Sicknote squeezed his eyes shut and clamped hands over his ears. He sobbed. He bellowed 'White Christmas' to drown choking screams that reverberated from the plant room walls.

51

Galloway.

No longer human. A grotesque mess of metallic sarcomas and rotting, peeling flesh.

The creature hauled Cloke through the pipe.

It stopped. It listened to voices from the distant plant room. Door slam. Shouts.

Hours ago, Galloway would have understood words, emotions. He would have recognised Tombes and Lupe, understood their anger and fear. But the insect intelligence behind his eyes simply heard human vocalisations at high volume. Alien animal barks.

Shadow and seclusion.

The creature's vision cut through the tunnel darkness. It crouched over the prone man and surveyed every pore, inspected every bead of sweat, every fleck of blood. It caressed Cloke's face and examined fingers wet with tears.

Cloke scrabbled at the tunnel wall. A chunk of brick. He gripped it in his fist and struck out, wild blows flung in total darkness, missing their target. Galloway watched the man flail with detached fascination.

Cloke adjusted his grip, drew back his arm and attempted to deliver a skull-crushing punch. He put all his strength into the blow. Galloway twisted his head to avoid the impact. Cloke's fist slammed into the tunnel wall, breaking fingers.

Cloke lay back and sobbed. Galloway crouched over him, and studied the physiology of fear. Grotesque facial contortion. Eyes wide, pupils dilated with adrenalin. Cloke's mouth pulled down like he was cartoon sad. A howling monkey-jabber of mortal terror.

The creature copied the sound. It emitted a harsh, braying cackle that reverberated in the tight space and echoed deep into the tunnel system.

Cloke thrashed as he was dragged across brickwork. He was drawn further into darkness, further from help. Mortar, sharp as coral, shredded his clothes. Fingers ripped and bloody, abraded to bone as he fought to grip the tunnel walls.

'Stop,' gasped Cloke. 'Think. Remember who you are. You're Galloway. Jim Galloway.'

The monstrous thing paused and turned. It leaned close like it was drinking the scent of fear.

'Kill me,' said Cloke. 'Come on. Kill me now.'

The creature raised a hand.

'Do it. Get it done.'

The hand slammed into Cloke's belly. Talons broke skin. Cloke convulsed. He arched his back and screamed.

'Oh dear Jesus.'

The creature drove a twisting fist into Cloke's gut, tearing muscle, ripping skin. Cloke choked as his diaphragm was compressed, forcing air from his lungs.

'Motherfuck.'

The arm pushed elbow-deep into a slurry of intestines, tearing the wound wide. Cloke's scream turned to a blood-spray gurgle. 'Jesus fucking Christ.'

Galloway leaned over the gaping wound and slowly forced his head inside.

52

Lupe examined the conduit mouth. Blood and strands of fabric hung from torn wire.

She shone her flashlight into the pipe. Brickwork receded to deep darkness.

'Maybe we should go after him,' said Tombes.

'Think he's still alive?'

'Probably not.'

'Why take Cloke?'

'Because he was the healthiest specimen, at a guess. Ekks is half dead and Sicknote has mush for brains.'

Tombes crouched beside Ekks.

'Is he injured?' asked Lupe.

'Doesn't look like it.'

Lupe shone her flashlight into the corner of the room. Sicknote huddled in shadow, rocking back and forth.

Lupe waved a hand in front of his face. She snapped fingers.

'Hey. Sick. Can you hear me?'

She shook his shoulder. No response.

She crouched.

'Dude. What happened to Cloke? Can you tell me what happened?'

Sicknote slowly raised his head and met her gaze. A twisted, sour smile. Then his eyes lost focus like he was looking through and beyond her.

'He's zoned out.'

'Can't we give him something?' asked Donahue. 'A shot to chill him out?'

Lupe shook her head.

'The seizure will pass. Then we can find out what actually happened in here.'

Donahue climbed the steps to the street entrance. She stepped over broken bodies. Bone-chips crackled underfoot. She left boot prints in puddles of coagulating blood.

She pulled on a respirator and adjusted straps. She pulled on gloves.

She checked the gate, rattled the cuff and chain. Secure.

She shone her flashlight into the alley.

Rain had turned to snow. A silent cascade of plump flakes. Asphalt carpeted white. The wrecked motorbike already veiled by a growing drift. The scattered bodies in front of the gate, the frozen screams, clawing hands, sightless eyes, dusted with ice.

The snow was flecked with ash. Particulates from the cinder cloud that still hung over the city like a shroud. Cremated buildings, cremated people. Prevailing winds would already have swept radioactive nucleotides inland, scattering lethal toxins across the Midwest.

She listened to the growling rubble-roar of a distant Midtown mega structure folding in a titanic avalanche of concrete and girders. The iron gate rattled in its frame. Donahue placed a hand on the stairwell wall and felt the tremor slowly subside.

'How's it looking?' called Lupe, from the foot of the stairwell. 'What's it like out there?'

Donahue pulled the polythene curtain back in position. She descended the steps. She took off her respirator and gloves.

'Want to build a snowman?'

'Shit.'

'Turning into a blizzard. Better wrap up warm. This place will get cold as a meat locker soon enough.'

Donahue loaded a hypo with 15mg Diazepam, slapped Sicknote's arm and sunk the needle. His panting breath slowed to steady, gentle inhalations. He closed his eyes and blissed.

A dried trickle of blood down the side of his neck. Donahue gently turned his head and examined the wound.

'Bitten?' asked Lupe.

'No. He's been pulling at the implant behind his ear.'

Lupe contemplated the conduit mouth.

'So. Galloway is back.'

'Or whatever he's become.'

Tombes sorted through the equipment pile. He shook out burned bags. He salvaged clothing and energy bars.

He pulled a scorched tarp aside and wiped soot from a pile of gas cylinders. He checked psi gauges.

Lupe joined him.

'The tanks got pretty roasted. Still intact, though.'

'Yeah.'

'Which is why we didn't get burned to hell. Imagine if this shit ruptured.'

'You shouldn't be out here alone.'

Tombes threw Lupe an FDNY sweatshirt. 'Put it on. This place will be an ice cave in a couple of hours. Get some layers.'

He loaded Lupe's arms with gear. Coats, bottled water, an axe.

'We better fortify the plant room. Turn it into a proper fallback position, in case we get more problems.'

'Are you kidding me? Cloke just got snatched from the damned place.'

'You got a better idea?'

'No.'

'We ought to get a fire going. Generate a little heat.'

Lupe crawled into the conduit, knife in one hand, flashlight in the other.

She crouched and shone her flashlight deep into shadow. The brick pipe receded to a distant junction.

She gripped the knife, tempted to crawl further, find Galloway and drive the blade into his eye.

'Hey,' called Donahue, from the mouth of the pipe. 'Don't go too far.'

Lupe inspected the brickwork. Blood smears.

'Broken fingernails. Looks like Cloke put up a fight.'

She shone her flashlight into the tunnel darkness.

'Cloke?' she shouted. 'Can you hear me?' No response. 'Dude, if you're injured, if you can hear my voice, make some noise.'

Her voice echoed and died.

'He's gone,' said Donahue. 'Come on out. Let's see if we can block this aperture. Do it right this time.'

Lupe backed out of the pipe. She held up ragged, bloody fabric.

'Found a pair of pants.'

'Cloke?'

Lupe examined the fabric. Black polyester.

'No. Galloway, I think. His uniform.'

She threw the bundled rags into the corner.

'Look at this,' said Donahue. She crouched on the floor. A brass case. Flecks of glass. 'Cyanide capsule. I guess Cloke tried to use it.'

'Poor bastard.'

Donahue picked up a couple of empty nail jars and tossed them into the pipe mouth. Broken glass scattered over brickwork.

'That won't stop him,' said Lupe.

'No, but we'll hear him coming.'

Tombes opened a backpack and took out a red plastic case. 'I have something that might help.'

DANGER
EXPLOSIVE/EXPLOSIF

He popped the lid and took out a demo charge.

'How much you got?' asked Lupe.

'Not much. Enough left to blow Galloway to offal.'

He mashed the nub of ammonium nitrate against the side of a small, green oxygen cylinder.

He selected a colour-coded time pencil from a cigar box. Yellow band. He carefully pressed the aluminium tube into the explosive.

'You know how these detonators work, right?' He held up pliers. 'Pinch the tube. Two minute burn. Big fucking bang. Oxygen will create a fierce secondary burn. If Galloway is in the vicinity when she blows, he'll be torn to pieces, and those pieces will be cooked down to the bone.'

He set the bomb and the pliers on a wall ledge.

'Remember. Two minutes. Long enough to get clear. Because you better be on the other side of the hall when she pops. If those explosives are fired in a confined space, they could bring down the roof.'

They held torn mesh over the conduit mouth and lashed it back in place with plastic ties. They stacked boxes against the grille.

'He could punch through easy enough,' said Tombes. 'A pile of boxes won't slow him down. But we'll be waiting. We'll stand guard. If the fucker makes another appearance, we'll shut him down for good.'

★

Sicknote slowly awoke. He looked around. He blinked. No glasses. The plant room was a blur.

Pounding headache. He reflexively reached for the port behind his right ear. He discovered his hands were cuffed and his ankles were lashed with flex.

'What's going on? Why am I tied up?'

'You wigged out,' said Lupe. 'Didn't want you to get hurt.'

'Are you going to let me go?'

'Maybe later. How are you feeling?'

'Like utter shit.'

'That thing in your head. Doesn't seem to help much.'

'I got wires in my brain. I'd tear them out, but the socket is screwed to my skull.'

'Want some Codeine?'

'It won't help.'

'You're sure?'

'The pain will pass in a few minutes. Just got to ride it out.'

Lupe picked his spectacles from the floor and placed them in his hand. He put them on. The left lens was missing.

'Sorry,' said Lupe. 'Guess they broke.'

'Can you blank out the missing lens?' asked Sicknote. 'Tape it over, like an eye patch?'

'If you like.'

'One good eye. I'll see better that way.'

'Tell me what happened to Cloke.'

'Galloway. Must have been watching, listening, lying in wait all the while. Picked his moment, then made the snatch.'

'What did he look like?'

'Pretty far gone. A putrefied mess. Not much left of his face. He looked like those ghouls outside. But stronger, faster. He picked up Cloke with one arm. Threw him around like he didn't weigh a damn thing. Took him into the pipe.'

'So why are you alive? Why not take you? Why not take Ekks?'

Sicknote shrugged.

'Maybe Galloway is toying with us.'

'Average prowler has the brains of a cockroach. They don't play games.'

'Some are pretty smart.'

'They tear people up. That's the height of their ambition.'

'Maybe those guys in the street are just foot soldiers. Drones. Ever think of that? Maybe there is a hierarchy. Creatures we haven't seen yet.'

'Give your imagination a break, all right? Get some rest.'

Lupe stood. She turned to Donahue and Tombes.

'Anytime we leave this room, we go in pairs, okay? From now on nobody moves on their own.'

They nodded.

'No more sleep. And no more pills, Donnie. We need to stay frosty. We have to watch our backs at all times.'

53

Lupe pulled at the plant room door. Jammed. Roof subsidence. The frame had begun to distort, wedging the door closed.

'Son of a bitch.'

Lupe braced a foot against the wall, gripped the handle and strained until the door juddered open with a tortured wood-shriek.

She shone her flashlight round the cavernous darkness of the ticket hall, probed shadows, checked for movement. She clapped a hand over her mouth and nose to mask the stench of incinerated flesh.

'No point going out there again,' said Donahue.

'We better make sure they're all dead.'

Lupe and Donahue advanced into the hall. Lupe carried an axe. Donahue carried a steel pike.

They crossed the ticket hall. Eerie silence. Their flashlights shafted through blue haze. Skeletal bodies. Carbonised limbs. Petrified screams.

Lupe crossed herself.

'Santa Muerte,' she murmured.

Donahue coughed and blinked away tears.

'Damned smoke.'

The walls, pillars and ceiling had been seared by flame. The two-toned white and terracotta tiles burned uniform black.

The bench was charcoal. The wall clock was a fist of melted cogs.

Shattered tiles of the station sign:

Fe   ck eet

Lupe looked up at the leaded glass bowl mounted on the ceiling.

'Guess we killed the lights,' said Donahue.

Lupe lifted the axe and smashed the soot-blackened dome. She shielded her eyes from falling glass. A couple of sodium bulbs still shone within. They cast a weak piss-yellow glow.

'Better than nothing.'

Donahue looked around. One of the central pillars had fractured. Concrete had split and crumbled to powder, exposing a buckled steel column at its core.

'Jeez. Guess heat damage really trashed the place.'

Scattered tiles. Porcelain crunched underfoot like broken glass.

A deep fissure in the roof. Donahue trained the beam of her flashlight and examined the jagged fracture. It ran from the entrance stairwell to the back of the hall.

'The whole building is starting to come apart. It could drop on our heads any minute.'

'Yeah?'

'Stick around much longer, this place will be our tomb.'

Donahue studied the fissure, tensed for gunshot cracks that would signal the roof was about to buckle and collapse.

Lupe began to laugh.

'What's so funny?' asked Donahue.

Lupe walked away, chuckling, shaking her head.

'Seriously, what's so fucking funny?'

★

Crumpled bodies blocked the office doorway. Smoke curled from charcoal flesh. Twisted, interlocked limbs. Grinning skulls. Stench like bacon.

'Help me shift these bodies,' said Lupe.

'Why?'

'We could be down here hours yet. I don't want to look at these bastards. Sure as hell don't want to breathe their stink.'

'Leave it to me,' said Donahue. 'Won't be the first poor souls I bagged and tagged.'

She wrapped a bandana round her mouth and nose.

'Pulled four kids out the ashes once. Gas explosion. A tenement in Queens. Cooked them real good.'

She pulled on leather gloves.

'Propane. Nasty shit. Heavier than air. Pools like liquid.'

She took a deep breath and gripped an arm. Rigor stiff. Flesh tore and leaked pus. She dragged the brittle corpse across the ticket hall and kicked it down the platform steps. It tumbled down the stairway, shedding crisped skin, scattering toes and fingers, and was lost in darkness.

Lupe stood over a second body lying contorted in the office doorway. Hispanic girl, silver crucifix melted to her breast bone. Shrivelled remnants of a maid uniform. The Cedars. A beaux-arts hotel off Wall Street.

Lupe contemplated the corpse like she was staring down at her own doppelgänger. Waitress. Cleaner. Laundry girl. The kind of life Lupe could have led if she swallowed her pride and punched a clock.

She brought down her axe in a hard chop. The blade embedded in the thorax of the charred corpse. She dragged the cadaver across the ticket hall. She tugged the axe free and kicked the body down the platform steps. She heard it tumble. She heard it splash.

★

They retrieved bodies from the entrance stairwell. They dragged them across the ticket hall and pitched them down the platform steps into the flooded tunnel.

'We ought to get out of here,' said Lupe. 'Place is screwed.'

'The Federal roof is the only landing site for half a mile.'

'We could wait across the street. Find a basement.'

'To hell with that,' said Donahue. 'Fenwick Street was padlocked. People forgot it was here. That's why it was a perfect holdout. But every other subterranean space, cellars, underground parking structures, MTA stations, got overrun by refugees. Hundreds of people. Their pets, their bags, their bedding. If we head into any of those sublevels we could find an army of prowlers waiting for us. It would be like kicking an ant nest.'

'What's the time?' asked Lupe.

Donahue checked her watch.

'One. One in the morning.'

'Fucking chopper,' muttered Lupe. 'Scoping the Adirondacks? In the middle of the night? What kind of bullshit is that?'

'Infected folks are warmer than background. Not by much, but they've got a signature. The chopper will buzz Avalanche Lake, overfly the forest a few times. If there is anyone stumbling around between the trees, they'll stand out plainer than day.'

'I don't like it,' said Lupe. 'I don't like sitting here, waiting to be saved. Every instinct tells me to get moving, get the hell out of here.'

'You said it yourself. There's nowhere to go. Just got to survive until dawn.'

'Fuck that shit. Get on the radio. Talk to Ridgeway. Apply some leverage. We've got Ekks, and we've got his papers. How about we put a match to his research? Toast some marshmallows over that notebook? About time we called the shots. If they want their vaccine, their cure, they have to come get it. Right now.'

The office door hung from its hinges. Lupe lifted it aside.

Smoking wreckage. A toppled desk. Smashed chairs. Broken furniture still danced with licks of flame. Varnish bubbled and popped.

Donahue untabbed an extinguisher and trained a jet of carbon smoke. Stuttering gas roar. She swept the hose cone back and forth. A typhoon of fire-suppressant vapour engulfed the debris, leaving the shattered desk and chairs coated in white residue like frost.

She threw the extinguisher aside and began to kick through the wreckage. Carbon fog curled round her feet.

A body huddled in the corner. Black, mummified, rictus grin.

Dunkin' Donuts.

The guy had punched through the door ablaze and careened off the walls, blinded by flame. He set the place alight, turned the room to a furnace. Convulsions gave way to paralysis as cooked muscles and ligaments began to contract, pulling him to the ground, curling him foetal. Finally, the polyester Donuts cap melted to his scalp and mercifully cooked his brain.

Donahue grabbed the cadaver's foot with a gloved hand. Skin crumbled and flaked. She dragged the corpse from the room.

She returned with a DeWalt case and a box of screws. She flipped latches. A power drill.

'Help me shift the desk.'

They shunted the desk beneath the vent. Donahue climbed onto the scorched desktop, a clutch of rock screws held between pursed lips. She bored deep into wood and concrete. She pinned boards over the aperture. The drill sparked and burned out on the last screw.

'I guess it won't take much to bust through that opening. Might slow him down a minute or two.'

'He'll be back,' said Lupe. 'Count on it. That air con network runs for miles, but he won't go far. He'll stay close, wait until we're weak, wait until we are alone. He's probably crouched in that tunnel right now, listening to us talk.'

Donahue picked up the flag pole. The satin stars and stripes reduced to scorched threads hanging from a brass rod. She straightened the pole and propped it in the corner.

'I could read all kinds of symbolism into this shit, but I'm too tired.'

'Got any Dex out there in those bags?' asked Lupe. 'Any kind of boost?'

'Thought you wanted to stay straight.'

'I want an up, not a down.'

Donahue dug in her coat pocket. She rattled a pot of NoDoz and threw it to Lupe.

'Don't eat them all.'

Lupe uncapped and knocked back a fistful of tablets.

Donahue raked through debris with her axe. She lifted the remains of a filing cabinet and pushed it aside. She found the transmitter headphones. She traced the cable hand-over-hand.

The RT lay beneath a toppled chair. She kicked the chair to one side. She crouched and trained her flashlight. She brushed away burned paper. She licked her thumb and rubbed ash from the dials, flicked a toggle switch, hoping to see a green power light.

Dead.

Lupe stood over her and looked down at the charred radio.

'Looks pretty cooked.'

'Fixable?'

'You tell me.'

'I don't know electronics,' said Donahue. 'I just turn the dials.'

Lupe picked up the radio and shook it. Loose components rattled inside.

'Let's get this back to the plant room. Get it open. Take a look at it under light.'

They sat cross-legged on the floor. Lupe turned the heavy transmitter in her hands. She examined the scorched and dented case. Foliage paint burned away, exposing base metal beneath.

She unthreaded screws with a Leatherman. She jammed the knife in the case seam and shucked open the lid.

A mess of cooked components.

'Jeez,' said Lupe. 'Look at it. This thing is toast. Split circuit board. Bunch of wires melted through.'

'But it's old army gear, right?' said Donahue. 'Built for field repair. All we got to do is splice the wires, match colour-to-colour.'

'Forget it. It's totalled. Screwed beyond redemption.'

'We've got serious problems without it.'

'Want me to wave a wand? Expelliarmus? Believe your own eyes. It's trashed.'

Donahue stood and paced. She unhooked a Motorola from her belt.

'We've still got handsets. Ridgeway is beyond reach, but we should be able to talk to the chopper once it's within range.'

'What kind of range?' asked Lupe.

'A mile. Maybe two.'

'If we don't respond to long-range radio transmissions, Ridgeway will assume we are dead. They only have one chopper. They won't risk losing it.'

'They have their orders,' said Donahue. 'The Chief is a

chain-of-command kind of guy. NORAD told him to retrieve Ekks. He'll commit all his resources to get the job done.'

Lupe shook her head.

'We need a plan B. I don't trust people who hide behind uniforms. Never have, never will.'

'The Chief will be here soon,' said Donahue. 'Six hours. Maybe less. Best thing we can do is sit tight and stay alive.'

'Suppose those six hours come and go?' asked Lupe. 'What then? I'm heading out at sunrise. I'm going to hit the streets and head for the shore. You should come with me.'

'There's no way across the river.'

'I'll build a raft, if that's what it takes. Couple of oil drums lashed with rope. Plank for a paddle. About a half mile of water to the Brooklyn shore. I could make it on my own, but it would be easier with your help.'

'The Chief will come. He won't abandon us.'

Lupe shook her head.

'People are people. Scared, stupid, selfish. You know who I trust in this situation? Me. That's who.'

'You're wrong. He'll come. He won't leave us behind.'

54

Tombes kept guard. He sat cross-legged on the floor, axe in his lap, gaze fixed on boxes and tins stacked against the air con grille. He was tensed for the slightest movement: the gentle rasp of crates beginning to shift, the clink of paint tins pushed together. Any sign Galloway was nudging boxes aside in a sly attempt to reach fresh meat.

His head began to nod. Tombes shook himself awake and rubbed his eyes. He got to his feet and paced. He blew his hands and tried to get warm.

Sicknote snored. Mouth open, head thrown back. Each exhalation dwindled to a wheezing chest rattle. He coughed to clear his throat, then spluttered awake as a gulp of vomit splashed down his red state-issue smock.

'Christ,' muttered Tombes.

He picked up the ragged shreds of Galloway's pants. He searched pockets and retrieved cuff keys. He tossed the keys to Sicknote.

'Mop that shit up.'

Sicknote unlocked his shackles. He rubbed his wrists. He pulled the smock over his head. Big belly, thick chest hair. He knelt and sopped a splash of steaming vomit from the floor.

'There's a pile of junk in the hall,' said Tombes. 'Take a look. Most of it got fried, but you might find fresh clothes if you dig around.'

★

The hall was bathed in a steady torrent of chill air from the street entrance. The tiled floor was coated in a treacherous ice-sheen. Roof-rubble glittered as if split bedrock had exposed a mineral seam.

Sicknote stepped over trashed equipment. Melted nylon bags. A steel dive helmet burned black. Plastic hypodermics melted to viscous tar.

He sifted debris. He found a Tunnel Rat shirt. He held it up. Lower half burned away. He threw it aside.

Boot steps. Lupe and Donahue descended the street exit stairs carrying a body wrapped in foil insulation blankets.

'Hold on,' said Donahue. 'Got to rest my arms.'

They lowered the body to the floor. They blew their hands and flexed cold fingers.

They saw Sicknote.

'Thought we had you on a leash,' said Donahue.

Sicknote stood over the corpse.

He lifted the edge of the blanket with his foot. A hand seared to a carbonised claw. He lifted the blanket a little further. Melted sleeve fabric. A trace of red: the remnants of a state-issue smock.

'Damn. Is that Wade?'

'The bits they didn't eat.'

'Poor, poor bastard.'

Lupe glanced at Sicknote's naked belly.

'Aren't you cold? You're turning blue.'

He shrugged.

'We got to get you covered up. You'll freeze to death.'

A couple of holdalls had survived the fire. Lupe unzipped and shook out the bags. Bundled clothes. A fire hat rolled across the floor.

She dressed Sicknote in bunker pants and an FDNY sweatshirt.

'Few burn holes, but it'll trap a little heat.'

'What will you do with Wade?' he asked, as he buttoned pants.

'Put him in the office. We threw the other bodies into the tunnel water, but Wade deserves a little better. Don't want to treat the guy like refuse.'

'How about me? Am I worth a prayer? Or would you toss me like garbage?'

'Yeah. If it comes down to it, I'll say a few words.'

'Thanks.'

'Same goes for me, all right?' said Lupe. 'Don't leave me down here. If anything happens, put me out in the street. I wouldn't want this place to be my grave.'

Sicknote hitched thick yellow braces.

'One nut house to another, my whole life. Drawstrings and elastic. Baby clothes. Can't remember the last time I wore anything with buttons and buckles.'

He pulled on socks and boots. He wrestled into a heavy fire coat and turned up the cuffs. He fastened jacket clasps. He picked up the fire helmet, brushed ash from the brim and set it on his head.

'Must be nice to have a uniform. Actually do something in the world.'

He found a Maglite in the coat pocket. He tested the beam.

'Well. See you around.'

He gave Lupe a mock salute. He headed for the street exit and began to climb the steps.

'Where the hell are you going?' called Lupe from the foot of the stairwell.

Sicknote paused and caught his breath. He leaned against the wall.

He contemplated the entrance gate above him. A night wind stirred the ripped polythene curtain. Snowflakes drifted through the lattice bars.

'I'm insane. Most madmen, the lucky ones, don't know

they are nuts. But I guess that's my curse. I'm batshit, and I know it. There's a real world, a normal world, beyond the voices, beyond the visions, but it's out of reach.' He turned and looked at Lupe. He tapped his fire helmet. 'Truth is, I'm tired. Bone tired. I just want it all to stop.'

He wearily climbed the steps and stood in front of the gate.

'Say that prayer for me. Say it when I'm gone.'

He pulled back the curtain and relished the chill wind that caressed his face.

A cold, white hell. Rubble and wreckage furred with ice.

IT IS FORBIDDEN TO DUMP BODIES.

He pushed a hand through the bars. Snowflakes settled on his palm. He watched them liquefy. A lethal beauty. Exquisite feathered crystals tainted with fallout.

Lupe watched him from the foot of the stairwell.

'Where will you go?'

He shrugged.

'I'll take a walk up Fifth. See how far I get. What do you think the Empire State looks like right now? New York in ruins. You got to be curious. It must be a hell of a sight.'

He took the cuff key from his pocket. He unlocked the gate. He hauled back the lattice. Harsh rust-shriek. He stood in the entrance archway, polished the remaining lens of his spectacles on the sleeve of his fire coat, then looked around.

Spectral silence.

Cotton candy flakes settled on rubble and broken bodies. He shone his flashlight upwards. A vertiginous plane of scorched brick and fire ladders stretching high into the night.

He shivered and turned up his collar.

'Wait,' called Lupe. 'Hold on.'

Sicknote turned around.

'Don't go out there.'

He stared at her.

She held out her hand.

'Come down here. I'll look after you.'

Sicknote hesitated.

'Please. Come on down.'

He pulled the gate closed and descended the steps to the ticket hall.

'There's been too much death,' said Lupe. 'Someone's got to survive this shitstorm. For my sake. Stay.'

55

Tombes carried a chair from the office to the plant room. He swung it over his head and smashed it on the concrete floor. He jammed wood into the rusted fire bucket. Scrunched paper for kindling. He snapped open his Zippo and sparked a fire.

They stood round the bucket and warmed their hands.

'We better shut off the generator,' said Tombes. 'No spare kerosene. If we let the tank run dry, we won't be able to operate the elevator. We've got plenty of flashlights and flares. We'll still have light.'

Lupe shook open a backpack. She emptied the contents on the floor. Cloke's personal stuff. Rolled clothes and a bag of toiletries.

She packed a respirator. She packed NBC gauntlets and a reel of seal tape.

She held up a radiation suit and checked it front and back.

'What you doing?' asked Donahue.

'Bailout bag. Look around you. The building is falling apart. Sooner or later we'll have to hit the streets.'

Lupe climbed the steps to the entrance gate. She set the bag on the floor alongside a rolled NBC suit. Quick inventory: gloves, overboots, sealer tape. She twisted a fresh filter into her respirator. She propped an axe against the wall.

'You shouldn't be out here alone.'

Tombes climbed the steps and joined her. He dumped a backpack and NBC suit on the floor.

'Makes a lot of sense,' he said, gesturing to the backs. 'A fallback plan. That's army thinking. Someone should have sent your ass to West Point.'

'This isn't a fallback plan. I'm leaving soon as dawn breaks. End of story.'

He watched Lupe kneel and tuck a big lock-knife into the side pocket of the backpack alongside a couple of energy bars and a pair of socks.

'Got a canteen?'

'No point,' said Lupe. 'Temperature at street level is sub zero. No point carrying a brick of ice around. Might as well weigh down my pack with cinder blocks.'

'What the hell were you doing in jail, girl? You're smart. You could have been somebody.'

'I am somebody.'

Lupe straightened up.

'I'm not going back to Ridgeway, that's for sure. I'm going to cross the river and get beyond the city.'

'Brooklyn. The streets will be blocked. And there will be plenty of infected running around. Way more than Manhattan.'

'I'll use elevated train track. I'll walk right over their heads. Travel light. Keep moving. That's the trick. Don't let the bastards mass and box you in.'

'Got a street map?'

'I don't need one.'

'Where will you go? After the city.'

'North. Far as I can. Avoid towns and cities. Avoid highways. Travel across open country. See if I can reach Canada before winter kicks in for real. Food won't be a problem. Plenty of pets and livestock running loose. Build a fire every night. Spit some meat.'

They listened to the rising night-wind. The polythene curtain billowed and crackled.

'The night is turning mean,' said Tombes. 'I'd hate to travel in this weather.'

'Might work in my favour. Colder it gets, slower those fuckers move. Easy to outrun. And cold deadens smell. A person could walk right past them.'

'You really want to step out there?'

'Sick of waiting. I'll leave at first light.'

'What are you going to do when you reach the river? Build a raft? Strong currents. Stronger than you think. The strait bumping gloves with water from Long Island Sound. The tides can be pretty nasty. Time it wrong, you could be swept out to sea.'

Lupe held up her Motorola. 'I'll take a radio. Give updates as I move street-to-street. If I run into trouble, you guys will know to take a different route.'

An unearthly sobbing scream echoed from the hall. The sound built slow, peaked, then died away.

'Mother of God.'

They looked down the stairwell to the shadows of the station.

A second juddering howl.

'What the fuck was that?'

Lupe picked up her axe. Tombes unsheathed a knife. They crept down the steps to the hall. They scanned shadows with their flashlights. Scorched dereliction.

'See anything?' asked Tombes.

'If I did, I'd tell you.'

A low, whimpering moan. The sound came from directly above their heads.

They trained their flashlights upwards, examined the dust-furred louvred slat of an air-con vent.

'Must be Galloway. Fucker is in the pipes, trying to spook us out.'

'No,' said Lupe. 'That's not Galloway. Listen.'

A faint, keening whine.

'Cloke. My God, that's Cloke's voice. Mother Mary, he's alive.'

56

Cloke died, time and again.

His chest was ripped open, his body bled dry. His empty heart had fluttered to a standstill. Yet some kind of fusion was taking place. He was melding with Galloway. Their cardiovascular systems were knitted together. Veins and capillaries entwined. Fresh blood filled Cloke's flaccid heart and set it pumping. He jerked back to consciousness.

'Please, I just want it to stop.'

He reached out and scrabbled at the crumbling brickwork, hoping to find a shard he could drive through his eye into his brain.

He gnawed his wrist. He ground his teeth, tried to break skin and tear open an artery. His jaws, his will, were too weak.

He lay on his back. He convulsed as Galloway burrowed beneath his ribs. He lifted his head and slammed it down, tried to knock himself insensible.

'Stop. Please. Just stop.'

The bodies lay conjoined in the tunnel shadows as Galloway pushed deep into Cloke's chest cavity.

'Get out,' whispered Cloke. He fought to regain control of his hands as they began to clench and unclench under alien volition. 'Get the hell out of my mind.'

Galloway shouldered his way into the man's thorax. Ribs peeled back and snapped like twigs. He buried his face deep in gelatinous viscera, opened his mouth wide and inhaled blood and lymph.

He no longer had eyes. Optic nerves swelled and extended from empty sockets like questing tendrils, branching and spreading through muscles and membranes. He assimilated body tissue, drank Cloke dry like a voracious carcinoma. Snaking ganglions punctured Cloke's spinal tract, wormed between vertebrae, fused with his nervous system.

Galloway's mouth was forced jaw-breaking wide as he vomited a knotted root system of metallic fibres. Tumour-strings roped from his nostrils, ears and throat as the relentless colonisation of Cloke's body continued.

Light pierced the darkness. Blurred colours. Muffled sound. A tentative trickle of sense-data.

A collision of memories. First time Cloke kissed a girl. First time Galloway kissed a guy. A fusion of minds.

The Galloway/Cloke hybrid saw through new eyes.

57

Donahue and Tombes pulled boxes aside. Donahue snapped open her knife and cut plastic pull-ties holding the grille in place. They stared into the darkness of the conduit mouth.

'Just for the record, I think this is a retarded idea,' said Lupe.

'I got to find the guy,' said Tombes.

'He's infected. He's beyond help.'

'What if it were you? Want to be left to turn? Dead but not dead? Crawling around the pipes for God knows how long, flesh rotting off your bones?'

'I wouldn't want you to die on my behalf.'

Tombes shrugged off his coat and unzipped his sweatshirt.

He stuffed a couple of paint tins into a backpack. He tucked a clutch of detonators into his waistband. He clipped a radio to his belt.

Lupe hefted the oxygen cylinder lashed with ammonium nitrate.

'You want the bomb?'

'The building is too unstable. Might bring the whole thing down on our heads.' He turned to Donahue. 'Got that rope?'

She threw him a coil of rope. He tied one end round his waist.

'If anything happens, pull me clear. Don't let that ghoul gnaw my bones.'

He wriggled on gloves, gripped the lip of the tunnel, hauled himself up and inside.

'Take this.'

Lupe passed him an iron roof pike.

He switched on his flashlight. He picked his way through broken glass on hands and knees. Rope played out behind him.

He crawled through narrow darkness. Gloves, boots and canvas bunker pants scuffed against rough brickwork.

'I'm at the junction.'

'*Anything?*'

'Few drops of blood.'

'*Which way you headed?*'

'The right hand passage leads to the office. Think I'll head left. See what I can find. Hold on. I can hear something.'

'*Hear what?*'

'Just wait.'

Tombes squirmed along the pipe. An insistent beep. Something winking on the tunnel floor.

Cloke's wristwatch. A black G-Shock with a broken strap. The cracked, blood-spattered countdown flashed 00:00. Time for the team to take their meds.

Tombes shut off the alarm.

'Something up ahead. I got to check it out.'

'*What can you see?*'

'Some sort of chamber. There's a wide-bore pipe running floor to ceiling. Some kind of water main, at a guess. Give me more slack.'

Tombes lowered himself into the chamber. He shone his flashlight round the concrete space.

The back wall was caked with blood and matted hair. Bones embedded in a rippled metallic mess. Ribs. Skulls. Femurs, clavicles and vertebrae.

'Mother of God.'

He touched the crucifix round his neck.

'*What have you found?*'

'I think Galloway has been building himself some kind of nest.'

'*Out of what?*'

'People.'

'*Bail. Get out of there.*'

'I think you're right.'

Tombes shrugged off his backpack. He pulled out a tin of paint and shucked the lid with his knife. He splashed crimson enamel across the wall like he was slopping gasoline.

He pulled a detonator from his waistband. Red tag. Sixty second fuse. He bit the tube and triggered the countdown. He tossed the detonator. It landed at the foot of the wall.

He hauled himself up into the conduit mouth and crawled thirty yards back down the brick pipe. He stopped and looked over his shoulder.

Crack. Thud of ignition. The chamber filled with rippling fire. It was like staring into the open door of a furnace. Flames spat down the tunnel towards Tombes, a fierce plume of dragon breath. Hot air washed over him.

'Take up the rope. I'm heading back.'

He reached the junction. The plant room up ahead. He began to crawl towards the distant disc of light.

A low growl.

Tombes twisted round and shone his flashlight behind him.

Something grotesquely naked blocking the pipe. A distended body, as if two people were trying to occupy the same skin.

'Cloke?'

A bulge at Cloke's shoulder as if a second skull were attempting to force its way up through his neck and wear his face.

The creature hissed.

Tombes bolted down the conduit, scrambled and squirmed towards the plant room.

Urgent drag and scuffle behind him. Cloke on his tail.

'Hey,' shouted Tombes. 'Lupe. Serious fucking problem.'

'I hear it,' shouted Lupe, from the tunnel mouth. 'Keep moving.'

Tombes pulled himself over broken glass. It sliced his gloves, sliced his palms.

'Right behind me,' he shouted, as he threw himself from the conduit mouth into the plant room.

His iron pike clattered to the floor. Lupe snatched it up.

Something monstrous scuttling down the brick conduit to meet her. She braced her legs, raised the pike like a harpoon and stabbed.

Shriek and howl. The creature two yards from the tunnel mouth, spike embedded in its breast bone, face animated by insect hunger.

Lupe and Donahue struggled to hold the monstrous thing at bay. The creature pushed forwards, impaling itself further on the iron spike. Skin stretched and broke as the barbed tip emerged from its back.

Tombes climbed to his feet. He pulled gloves from his hands with his teeth. He pulled a detonator from his waistband, fumbled with blood-slick fingers. He bit down, triggered the sixty-second burn, and threw the timer into the conduit.

He grabbed a tin from a wall-stack and hurled it into the tunnel mouth. The lid popped and white paint splashed the tunnel walls. It dripped from the ceiling. It dripped from Cloke's misshapen body and face. Stink of turpentine.

The creature began to slide itself along the pike.

'Get the bomb,' shouted Lupe.

'Wait,' said Tombes. 'Just hold on.'

Crack of ignition. Paint combusted and filled the tunnel with fire. The creature thrashed and squealed. Lupe and Donahue released the pike and jumped back.

Tombes pulled the remaining detonators from his waistband and hurled them into the tunnel. They fell among the flames and started to cook. Detonations like firecrackers. Flying stone chips.

The hybrid shrieked and retreated down the tunnel. It thrashed and threw itself against the conduit walls as if it were trying to shake off the flames. The pike was still embedded in its chest. The iron rod sparked as it raked brickwork.

The creature turned the distant junction corner and passed out of sight, leaving the conduit littered with scraps of burning, smouldering flesh.

Mewing. Squealing. Inhuman shrieks of rage and pain.

Lupe reattached the conduit grille and stacked boxes against the tunnel mouth.

'You both saw that, right?' she asked. 'Cloke and Galloway. The two of them combined.'

Tombes sat on the plant room floor, back to the wall. Donahue sat beside him. She cleaned blood from his hands and bound them with bandages.

'I'm not going out like that,' said Tombes. 'Absorbed into some kind of giant flesh-monster. Swear to God. Anything but that.'

'It will be back,' said Lupe. 'It won't forget about us.'

'Not by this route. It won't risk getting cooked a second time.'

'Hard to believe it was ever human.'

'I'd like to think there's nothing of Cloke left inside that head.'

58

Donahue sat cross-legged and warmed her hands over the fire.

Sicknote studied her slumped shoulders, tried to work out if she were asleep. He shuffled sideways. He sat next to Ekks.

'How you doing?' he whispered, looking down at the sleeping man. 'The pipes are freezing. Can you hear them? Contracting metal. Creak and groan.'

No reply.

'Come on. You're awake. I've been watching. You've been awake a long while.'

Ekks opened his eyes and stared back at him.

Sicknote held up the notebook.

'You found a cure, didn't you? You nailed it. Everyone else struck out. Biocontainment labs around the world trying to cook up a vaccine. Expert virologists hunched over electron microscopes. You were stuck down here with a couple of scalpels. But you got there. You made the leap.'

Ekks licked parched lips. Sicknote held a bottle of water to his mouth.

'The others think you are a fraud. But they can all go to hell, right? Must be quite a trip. The power to save humanity. In your skull. Makes you the most important guy who ever lived, right? A bigger deal than Napoleon, Lincoln, Hitler. Shit, right now you're bigger than Jesus.'

No reply.

'You want stuff, don't you? You're not going to give up that cure without something in return. Smart guy. Keep them waiting. Keep them guessing. Hold those aces long as you can. Take your own sweet time, then name your price.'

Ekks held out his hands. He mimed pen and paper.

Sicknote looked around. Cloke's jacket. He searched pockets. He found a pencil stub and a crumpled notepad.

Ekks took the pencil. Sicknote held the pad.

Ekks scrawled:

how long have i got?

'Days. Maybe hours. Sorry, man. The bomb was a tactical nuke, some kind of super-radiation warhead. Zapped the whole island in the blink of an eye. Death rays passed through concrete, passed through rock. We both caught a killer dose.'

Ekks closed his eyes.

'You want some meds? These guys are EMTs. They brought a big-ass trauma kit. Uppers, downers, all kinds of shit.'

No reply.

'Hey. You might get lucky. They'll do everything they can to keep you alive. Once they get you back to Ridgeway they'll probably give you transfusions. O neg, right? Nothing fancy? Imagine that. All those cops and army guys lining up, offering the blood in their veins. Shit, they wouldn't lift a finger to save my ass. Wouldn't spit in a cup. But you. You're the big prize. My advice? Keep your mouth shut long as you can. The moment you give them what they need, your life won't be worth a damn.'

Sicknote glanced at Donahue. She gazed into the fire, drowsed on the edge of sleep.

He leaned close to Ekks and whispered in his ear.

'Know what? I can hear the virus. I can hear it, singing in the shadows. See that pipe over there? That grille? It's down there, in the dark. It's calling. You can hear it too, right? You know what I'm talking about. I can feel the pull. It's north of here. Not sure how far. The heart of the city. Must be near the bomb site. Too hot to approach. Too hot for humans.'

Ekks didn't respond.

'You know what I'm saying. I'm not talking about Galloway. I'm not talking about those ragged-ass prowlers out there in the street. There's something else. An intelligence deep within the tunnel system. It's made a home in the lowest sub-levels of the city. It's growing. It's getting stronger. This empty, radioactive world suits it just fine.

It knows we are here. Those sorry fucks in the street. Eyes and ears. Watching us. Relaying our movements like CCTV.

This thing owns the city now, you understand what I'm saying? Manhattan Island. Its domain. Its flesh and bone. It wants us gone. It's sending out antibodies.'

He polished the remaining lens of his spectacles.

'Let me ask you something, doc. I got to know. The virus. Where does it come from? Was it cooked up in a lab? Did it drop from outer space? What's the deal? Come on. You studied this disease a long while. What does it want?'

No reply.

Ekks cocked his head, like he was appraising Sicknote. He waved for a fresh sheet of paper. He raised a weak hand and began to write.

LM741 OPERATIONAL AMPLIFIER.

200 K RESISTOR

220 µF CAPACITOR

15 pF CAPACITOR

47 pF CAPACITOR

10 nF CAPACITOR

20 - 200 pF VARIABLE CAPACITOR.

BOARD
SPEAKER

COIL

ANTENNA

9v BATT.

Sicknote examined the list.

'What do you want me to do with this? I don't know where to get this stuff. Don't even know what it looks like.'

Ekks pointed at the trashed transmitter lying nearby.

'You want the radio?'

Ekks nodded.

Sicknote held the broken radio in his lap.

'This thing is all the way screwed.'

He turned chunks of scorched circuit board in his hands.

'Sorry. I can't fix this shit. I don't know anything about radios. I wouldn't know where to start.'

Ekks pointed at the radio again.

'I don't know what you want from me, doc. I'm not an educated guy. This list might as well be Chinese. I don't know what any of it means. Maybe I should call the others. You want to talk to them? I'll show them the list. They're smart. They can make things work.'

Ekks shook his head. He struggled to raise himself on one elbow. He pointed at Sicknote, summoned his strength and spoke a single word:

'You.'

Sicknote studied the circuit boards. Helpless shrug.

'Why me? I've been locked up my whole life. Seriously. It's been twelve years since I bought something in a store. Never had a phone. Never cooked a meal. I'm a life-long loser. I'm no damn good. Talk to Donahue. Talk to Tombes. They know how to fix machines. I can't help. I wish I could.'

Ekks lay back and closed his eyes.

Sicknote held a sliver of board. Circuit tracery glinted firelight. He adjusted his spectacles and squinted with his good eye.

'Hold on,' he murmured.

He plucked a component from the circuit board. He wiped soot from the surface with a spit-wet finger. A little black chip with silver legs, like a robot cockroach. He held it close, like a jeweller assessing the internal structure of a diamond.

Infinitesimally small letters. A component stamp: LM741.

He checked the list.

'Hey. Hey, I found something.'

Sicknote leaned over Ekks and shook his arm.

'Doc. Wake up. I found one of the things on your list.'

No response.

'Come on. What are we making? What are we trying to build?'

Sicknote was suddenly spooked by the man's pale, gaunt pallor.

'Doc? Hey doc, you okay?'

He checked for breath. A faint whisper of warmth from parted lips.

'Don't worry, doc. I'll get what you need.'

Sicknote got to his feet. He shrugged off his coat and carefully laid it on the floor covering the scattered radio components.

'Hey. Donahue.'

She blinked awake and glanced up.

'You okay?' he asked.

'Yeah.' She rubbed tired eyes. She stretched.

Sicknote pulled a burning chair leg from the fire.

'I'm going to step into the hall. Take a piss.'

'You shouldn't go out there alone.'

'Hell with it. If Galloway shows up I'll torch his ass.'

'Even so.'

'I'll be okay. I get the feeling I'm last on his kill list. Your head will make a better trophy than my sorry hide. I'm barely worth the effort.'

Fierce cold. The walls and vault-spans of the ticket hall sparkled with frost.

Sicknote kicked through ice-furred debris. His breath steamed the air.

Murmur of voices from the street level stairwell. Lupe and Tombes talking near the entrance gate. He couldn't make out words.

He held up the burning chair leg. Flames cast dancing shadows. He glanced around. He couldn't escape the skin-crawling sensation of being watched.

He crouched beside Cloke's equipment trunk. He brushed ice from the latches and lifted the lid.

Radiological gear packed in a foam bed. A couple of spare Geiger handsets. He picked up a handset. He couldn't release the battery compartment, so slammed the unit on the lip of the box, cracked the plastic shell like an egg and extracted a 9v power cell.

Sudden, giddy head rush. That old, dread feeling. Reality melting away.

He gripped the edge of the box.

'No,' he murmured. 'Not again.'

He bit the heel of his palm, ground teeth into flesh, hoped pain would pierce onrushing dementia and anchor him in the present.

'Please, not again.'

He climbed to his feet. He screwed his eyes tight shut.

'I am Michael Means. I am Michael Means.'

He opened his eyes.

Pristine tiles. Dead ceiling lights restored and blazing bright. Fenwick Street at rush hour. 'Silent Night' over the tannoy. Bustle and distant street noise.

Guys in flannel suits shook snow from their umbrellas and queued to drop a nickel fare into the turnstile. Khaki uniforms among the crowd. Duffel bags and bedrolls. GIs headed for embarkation at a liner terminal. Minutes away from a gangplank and a troopship to Europe.

Newsstand, shoeshine, soda fountain. A civil defence fire point: sand buckets and a shovel.

A station announcement echoed from the platform stairwell:

'*Please stand away from the platform edge, especially when trains are entering and leaving the station.*'

'This isn't real,' muttered Sicknote.

He tried to seize a guy in a business suit, grip his collar, his silk necktie, but his hands passed clean through the apparition.

'You're not real,' he shouted. 'None of this is real.'

He stood at the centre of the hall, hands on head. A teeming crowd of ghosts passed through him.

'Get out. All of you. Please. Just get out of my head.'

59

Lupe found Sicknote crouched by a wall. She knelt and snapped fingers in front of his face.

'Poor bastard. Phased out again.'

'You should have let him take that walk,' said Tombes. 'He wanted to die. There was no reason to interfere.'

'Help me get him back in the plant room. He'll freeze to death out here.'

They each took an arm and pulled him to his feet.

They sat Sicknote on the floor next to Ekks. They draped a coat around his shoulders.

'What's this shit?' asked Lupe. She crouched and picked through jumbled radio components. Capacitors, resistors and scraps of circuit board.

'Sicknote put it together,' said Donahue. 'He's been sitting there, talking to himself, messing with wires.'

'What does it do?'

'Nothing.'

Lupe threw the clump of components aside.

'How's Ekks?'

Tombes knelt and checked for dilation.

'Comatose. Dying, slow but sure.'

'How long can he last?'

'I doubt he will wake.'

'We better start monitoring radio traffic,' said Lupe. 'See if we can make contact with the chopper, once it gets within range.'

Donahue sat against the wall, ignoring the conversation, staring at a sheet of paper.

'Something on your mind?' asked Lupe.

'Look at this,' said Donahue. She held out the paper. Lupe took it from her hand.

Orders stamped USAMRIID – CLASSIFIED.

'Where did you get this?'

'Cloke's gear trunk.'

Lupe scanned the text.

'"*You are ordered to locate and rescue Doctor Conrad Ekks of the Bellevue Neurosurgical Department. You are also required to locate and secure any materials, whether in written or digital form, relating to his research. You are further required to locate and retrieve the Vektor artefact.*"'

'What does that mean? That last bit? Vektor?'

'No idea,' said Donahue. 'The guy talked about Ekks so much I'm sick of his name. He never once mentioned any kind of artefact.'

Lupe continued to scan the note.

'"*The artefact is essential to the continuance of the programme.*" The programme?'

Donahue took a sheaf of notes from the data bag.

'Some of the folks on that train wrote a suicide note before they blew their brains out. An account of their last days below ground. Listen to this: '". . . *the Centre for Disease Control supplied our team with a sample of the virus in its purest form. It arrived under military escort. A white biocontainment box with a half-skull symbol on the lid . . .*" Maybe that's what Cloke was looking for.'

'I saw a box,' said Tombes. 'We were in the tunnel. Me and Cloke. We found a pile of burned bodies. He poked around in the ashes. There was a box with a skull on the lid.'

330

'What did Cloke say about it?'

'Nothing.'

'Doesn't matter much at this point,' said Donahue.

'I don't like it,' said Tombes. 'This whole situation. Doesn't smell right.'

'Still think you can rely on these guys to save your ass?' said Lupe.

Deep rumble, rising to a steady thunder roll. The room shook.

'Shit.'

They looked up. Gunshot cracks. Trickle of stone dust. The Federal Building foundations beginning to shift and fracture.

'Christ. Cover your heads.'

The walls continued to tremble. The bucket fire spat embers. Water pipes groaned and sang. The ceiling bulb swung like a pendulum.

'Fuck,' said Tombes. 'The whole lot is going to come down.'

The tremor diminished to silence. They stared at the ceiling for a full minute, braced for a bone-crushing cascade of rubble.

'Is everyone okay?' asked Donahue. 'Anyone hurt?'

'We're cool.'

She opened the door and shone her flashlight into the hall. A cloud of stone dust washed down the street level steps.

'Building collapse. Must have been close. Real close.'

'Has it blocked the entrance stairway?' asked Lupe. 'Can we still reach the alley?'

'I think we're okay. For now.'

Lupe joined her at the doorway. She inspected the ticket hall ceiling. Her flashlight beam traced the deep fissure in the tiled roof.

'Cracks are getting wider. We might have to haul ass in a hurry.'

★

331

Lupe and Donahue crossed the ticket hall. They hugged the walls, kept their eyes fixed on the buckled ceiling for further signs of subsidence.

The IRT office.

Wade's body shrouded by a couple of foil blankets.

'Hey, bro,' murmured Lupe.

They stepped over the corpse and kicked through ashes.

'Give me some light.'

Donahue focused her flashlight beam while Lupe crouched and picked through carbonised debris.

Charred poster tubes. Crisped, blackened paper.

'Nothing. All burned.'

'Help me shift these shelves,' said Donahue, gesturing to a pile of planks. 'Might be something underneath.'

They propped the shelves against the wall. They threw the remains of the phonograph aside.

A section of antique map, brown like parchment, lay on the floor. It had been shielded from the flames.

Lupe spread the ragged section of map on top of the desk.

1939 World Fair Travel Guide. Public transport routes to Flushing.

She flipped open her knife and stabbed Fenwick Street.

'We are here.'

She stood her Maglite next to the knife.

'And Wall Street is here. A short distance. Third of a mile, at most.'

'What of it?'

'The south tunnel mouth is boarded up. I reckon if we bust through those boards and follow that old IRT passage south it will intersect with the modern MTA line near Wall Street.'

'So?'

'What if we retrieved the boat? It's sitting in the north tunnel, near that rockfall. What if we brought it back and headed south? If we reach the MTA network we might be able to travel far as South Ferry before we need to head above ground. We could bypass the streets entirely. Save ourselves a shitload of grief. Reach the shore without setting foot above ground. Then we could use the boat to cross the river.'

'The flood waters are rising. Won't be long before the passageways are completely submerged.'

'There's still enough clearance to navigate.'

'Fenwick Street was a terminal stop. The end of the line. The south tunnel might not connect with anything. It might be a dead end.'

'It's worth a shot.'

'You're asking me to suit up. Put on dive gear, get back in the water and fetch the boat.'

'Yeah.'

'A quarter-mile trip. Another shitload of rads.'

'Up to you, girl. Your call. But if these tunnels carry us south to the river, we're home free. We can cross to the mainland. Shit, we can row up the coast without setting foot on land, put this city well behind us.'

They returned to the plant room.

Donahue sorted through jumbled dive gear, tried to find sufficient intact components to assemble a single functioning dive rig. She laid out a suit and checked front and back for integrity. She found gloves, overboots and flippers. She found a weight belt. She found a helmet and checked the headlamp battery for charge.

Lupe helped strap gas tanks to the back frame.

'How are they looking?' asked Donahue.

Lupe tapped glass and checked psi levels.

'Some of these needles are getting mighty friendly with zero.'

'Fuck it.'

'Hey,' said Lupe, looking round. 'Where the hell is Sicknote?'

'Ought to put that guy on a leash.'

Sicknote stood at the top of the platform steps.

The stairwell danced with ghostlight. Tarnished, broken fixtures unkinked and took on a polished gleam. Shattered bulbs recomposed themselves. Broken filaments fused and glowed incandescent. Mottled wall tiles washed porcelain white.

Phantoms pushed past and through him. Suits and wasp-waist dresses. Slicked hair and bouffants. Attaché cases and crocodile handbags. Edge of the financial district. Commuters, office workers and service staff, instinctively heading down the stairs in racially segregated streams.

Sicknote walked down the steps. He stood in the middle of the stairwell, spread his arms and let the spectral crowd wash through him.

A train pulled up at the station. Decelerating motor hum. Sneeze of air brakes. A silver subway car with old-time port-hole windows.

'*Fenwick Street. This is Fenwick Street.*'

Doors slid back. A fresh stream of commuters filled the platform and jostled their way up the stairwell.

'Why not board the train?' he thought to himself. 'What will happen if I enter the ghost locomotive and take a seat? Where will it take me? What will I find at the end of the line?'

He began to descend the steps.

'*Hey. Hey, Sick.*'

Lupe's voice.

'*What are you doing, dude?*'

Her words echoed down the decades. He heard them above station noise, the clatter of footsteps, babbling voices, the hum of traffic in the street outside.

334

He looked around the stairwell. *Buy War Bonds!* Trilbys, slicked hair, faces knotted with get-there-on-time anxiety.

A couple of girls in the blue blazer/brass button uniform of the Women's Reserve.

All of them watched over by Cary Grant and Joan Fontaine. *Each time they kissed there was the thrill of love . . . and the threat of murder!*

'*Dude, what are you doing?*'

Lupe's voice, stronger, closer.

He searched for her among the jostling crowd, tried to spot her soot-streaked fire coat amongst the sea of grey flannel suits.

'*Look at me, bro.*'

Her voice right by his side.

One by one, the stairwell ceiling lamps died.

The teeming crowd of business men and office girls dissipated like smoke.

Pristine tiles were mottled by a spreading accretion of dust and mould.

Cary Grant faded sepia and flaked to dust.

Sicknote found himself once more in the darkness and dereliction of the platform stairwell, feet at the water's edge.

Lupe stood by his side. She put a hand on his shoulder.

'Fight it,' she said. 'Fight the madness. Be here now, with me.'

He nodded.

'Just breathe. Look at me. Look me in the eye. Breathe deep.'

He instinctively massaged for the implant behind his right ear. He struggled to breathe slow and deep.

'That's it. Better?'

'Yeah.' He smiled. 'Yeah, I'm all right.'

The flood waters erupted. They leaped back. Sicknote lost his glasses. He pawed the step beside him, found the spectacles and jammed them back on his face.

A tumourous, skeletal thing rose from the water and straightened to full height. It waded thigh-deep across the submerged platform towards the stairs.

Lupe and Sicknote scrambled clear. The creature stretched clawed hands. A membranous, translucent lacework of skin hung from bare arms. The rotted thing opened its mouth and vomited filthy tunnel water.

Then it lunged.

60

Lupe pushed Sicknote to one side and swung her axe. The blade embedded in the creature's throat. The creature staggered to maintain balance, head lolling, spinal cord intact. A second axe blow sheered clean through its neck. The head bounced down the steps and splashed in the water. The decapitated corpse toppled backwards and sprawled on the stairs.

Two more infected figures rose from the flood water.

Lupe grabbed Sicknote by the collar and dragged him clear. 'Come on. Let's face them on high ground.'

Donahue ran down the steps to meet them. She gripped an iron pike. She swung at one of the creatures. A glancing blow to the head ripped away its jaw, leaving upper teeth and a lolling tongue.

She gripped the pike like a javelin. She delivered a stab to the chest and pushed the rotted thing into black waters.

Another shuffling figure, arms outstretched. A doorman weighed down by a long braid coat.

Lupe swung her axe. She brought it down hard, missed the guy's head, and lopped an arm. The blade continued its downward trajectory, hit a step and struck sparks.

'Damn,' winced Lupe. Her hands and forearms stung from the impact.

She hefted the axe and swung again. The blade embedded in the doorman's stomach. It lurched backwards, jerking the axe from Lupe's hands.

Lupe and Donahue backed up the steps. Another creature rose from the water. A sanitation worker draped in garbage. Green overalls and hi-viz. It stumbled up the stairs towards them. Lupe delivered a chest-kick that sent it toppling into the flood water. They leaped aside to avoid the toxic splash.

'Tombes,' bellowed Lupe. 'Need some fucking help.'

Tombes fed another couple of chair legs onto the fire.

He crossed the room. He bent and inspected Ekks. The guy lay motionless and sallow. Tombes leaned close and checked for the rise and fall of the man's chest.

Carotid pulse. Weak. Slow.

A distant shout from Lupe.

'*Tombes. Need some fucking help.*'

He snatched up his axe and ran for the door.

Lupe, Donahue and Sicknote scrambled up the stairs. Three infected creatures on their tail, climbing the steps hand-over-hand.

Sudden hiss and fizz. The stairwell lit blood red.

They looked up. Tombes at the top of the stairwell, axe in one hand, flare in the other.

'Here.' He tossed the axe to Lupe. She snatched it out the air.

She braced her legs ready to swing.

'Hey. *Cabron.*'

One of the creatures hissed. Lupe swung the axe and split its head in two.

'Who's next, motherfuckers?'

A broken thing dragged useless legs.

Lupe rotated the axe, swung hard and hammered the spike into the nape of its neck. She jerked the axe free, ripping away scalp, brain and a section of skull.

An eyeless revenant clung to the balustrade. It stumbled

up the steps, left arm clutching the air as it reached for Lupe.

She adjusted position and brought the axe down in a shallow stroke that decapitated the creature with a single blow.

Tombes glanced around for a weapon. A fist-sized chunk of roof rubble lay beside a pillar. Angular enough to crack skulls. He threw down the flare and sprinted across the hall. He skidded to a halt and snatched up the rock.

A splintering crash.

The freight elevator filled with dust and split wood. Something kicking its way through the planked roof.

Some kind of gargantuan, misshapen spider.

Tombes slowly backed away.

The grotesque creature crept from the deep shadow of the elevator and was lit by crimson flare-light. Four legs. Four arms. Bloated torso. Burned flesh.

Cloke's head twisted side to side.

'I knew you'd be back,' murmured Tombes.

A gasp of horror from the stairwell. Donahue and Sicknote standing at the head of the platform steps, transfixed by the monstrous thing crouched in the corner of the hall.

The creature's head swung back and forth. A cold, insectoid intelligence surveyed Tombes, then turned its attention to Donahue and Sicknote.

The creature moved towards Donahue. A powerful, arachnid glide.

'Hey,' yelled Tombes. 'Hey, over here.'

The creature turned its attention back to Tombes.

'What the hell are you doing?' hissed Donahue. 'It'll rip you apart.'

The creature sidled left, then right; a slow dance that pushed Tombes away from the plant room and platform stairwell, and cut off any means of escape.

'Watch it,' shouted Lupe. 'It's boxing you in the corner.'

He nodded.

'Donnie. Lupe. Get ready to run.'

Tombes shrugged off his coat. He tossed the rock hand to hand, assessed it for weight.

'Think you're going to make a meal out of me?' he yelled. 'Sorry to disappoint.'

He turned to one side and pulled back his arm like he had the pitcher's spot.

'I love you, Donnie.'

He hurled the rock. It blurred through the air and struck the creature's flank, tearing flesh.

The deformed thing emitted a high, inhuman howl.

It ran at Tombes. It crossed the ticket hall in a lightning, liquid scuttle.

Tombes turned and sprinted as fast as he could. He ran at the wall. The creature shrieked with rage as, somewhere within its insect mind, it perceived what Tombes was about to do.

Tombes dived headfirst into the station sign.

Fe   ck   eet

His head slammed into the tiles. Skull-shattering impact.

Lupe grabbed Donahue and Sicknote and pushed them towards the plant room.

'We've got to get out of here.'

The creature stood over Tombes. Harsh, braying roar. It grabbed his broken body and swung it back and forth until an arm ripped from a shoulder socket. The cadaver skidded across the tiled floor and came to rest.

Door slam.

The Galloway/Cloke hybrid swung around. Lupe, Donahue and Sicknote shut in the plant room.

The creature loped across the ticket hall and hurled itself against the door.

Lupe and Donahue put their shoulders to the door and tried to hold it closed. Shuddering impacts. Splintering wood.

Lupe shouted to Sicknote:

'Come on, dumb-ass. Get something to prop the door.'

Sicknote backed away in fear.

Rusted strap hinges tore from wood. Tumourous arms punched through the panels.

The door gave way. Broken planks kicked aside.

Lupe and Donahue backed off as the grotesque, melded form ducked beneath the lintel and entered the room.

A bulbous, misshapen head. Two skulls jostling for position behind Cloke's face.

The creature looked around. Jet black eyes. It saw Sicknote and snarled.

Sicknote grabbed an axe. The creature was on him before he had time to swing. He was seized by four arms, lifted clean off his feet. He dropped the axe. He was slammed against the wall.

Donahue snatched the axe from the floor and swung. She put all her strength behind the blow. She buried the blade deep in the creature's back. She hung from the shaft.

A pair of hands reached behind the creature's back and tried to detach the axe blade. Donahue was thrown to the floor.

Engine noise. A sputtering growl.

Lupe revved the stone cutter. She pressed the blade to the creature's waist. Whirling teeth sliced flesh. Shriek and squirm. Blood spray. Bubbling pus and rot-stink.

Bone-crunch as the blade snagged spine. The grotesque thing convulsed and fell to the floor.

Donahue hurled paint cans. The cans hit the wall and

burst open. The wounded creature drenched in white paint. Overpowering turpentine stink.

Lupe kicked over the fire bucket scattering embers. Catastrophic vapour ignition. Fireball. Burn-roar. Lupe and Donahue threw themselves to the floor as flames washed overhead.

The creature lay at the centre of the conflagration, engulfed in fire. Limbs thrashed and cooked. Black smoke. Boiling fat. Popping, spitting flesh.

The monstrous, melded thing contorted and flailed. It ripped itself in half at the waist. The upper torso squirmed away from the flames, trailing ropes of intestine. It gripped water pipes and swung itself up the wall. It snatched at Lupe's head. She ducked the grasping talons and rolled clear.

The Cloke/Galloway hybrid dropped to the floor and crab-scuttled into the hall.

Lupe struck a flare. Crimson fire. She stood in the plant room doorway and peered into the gloom.

'Is he out there?' asked Donahue.

Lupe squinted into shadows. The wrecked roof of the freight elevator. The dark passageway leading to the flooded platform.

'I think he's gone.'

They edged out into the ticket hall.

A crumpled fire coat lying among the rubble. Lupe picked it up. A shamrock patch on the sleeve. *Erin go Bragh.*

Tombes lay beneath the FENWICK sign. Donahue approached his body. She tried not to look at his empty shoulder socket and his shattered head.

She plucked the gold crucifix from his neck and put it in her pocket.

She threw the coat over his upper body. Then she knelt and prayed.

61

A tunnel cave mouth blocked by prop-beams and planks.

Bedrock still bore the scars of drills, picks and dynamite cartridges wielded by nineteenth-century navvies; Irish gangs that descended rope-lashed ladders below ground and bored the subway passage by lamplight.

Schist speckled with coarse flakes of mica. Fissures wept groundwater.

A hobo camp at the back of the cave. A crude bivouac. A shanty built from sticks and blankets. An oil can fire. Crate furniture. Stained bedding. Glass crack stems. Garbage bags and a shopping cart full of cans hoarded for redemption.

The camp was overwhelmed by rising flood water. Inundated shacks slowly listed and collapsed like sandcastles succumbing to an incoming tide. Garbage bags bobbed and bumped.

Three homeless guys curled foetal on a rock shelf. Thick beards and dirt-streaked faces. Laceless army boots. Quilted coats leaked insulation foam. Clothes torn by knotted tumours.

Beside them, on the ledge, was a makeshift griddle made from stacked tunnel bricks and mesh. A pile of bones and torn cycle Lycra. A woman they found lost in the tunnels, bloody and sobbing for help. A woman they raped and bludgeoned with a rock. A woman they cut and ate, cooking up slabs of muscle, salivating over steaks dripping hot fat, unaware she had been bitten and infected.

The ground-tremor of an office collapse somewhere on Broadway. The juddering rumble echoed through the tunnel system like an oncoming

343

train. Trickles of dust and grit from the fractured roof. Flood water shivered and rippled.

One of the homeless guys climbed stiffly to his feet, as if responding to a silent command. He stepped from the ledge and plunged shoulder-deep into black water. He waded towards the cave entrance.

He pressed against the crooked planks. Heightened senses. Somewhere out there, deep within the tunnels, merging with the rush of churning water, he could hear the murmur of voices. An intoxicating scent carried in the air. Blood. Sweat. Fresh meat somewhere south near Fenwick Street.

Fleeting memory. He and his companions hammering planks, driving nails with a chunk of brick, sealing themselves inside the remote cavern.

'Let those motherfuckers fight it out, up there in the world. We'll be all right down here, brother. We can hold out for days. We got food. We got everything we need.'

The skeletal revenant drew back an arm and threw a heavy punch. A fist slammed wood. Blood splash. Broken fingers. A second punch. A third. The fist reduced to a mess of blood and bone. The creature continued to pound the planks and beams. Wood began to splinter and break.

62

Lupe and Donahue sat on the platform steps and gazed into black water.

'I'd go myself,' said Lupe. 'But I know jack shit about scuba. Hell, I can't even swim.'

'First in the door,' murmured Donahue.

Lupe helped Donahue climb into the drysuit.

'Help me get my arms through the harness. All right. Tighten the straps. A little more. That's it, that's good.'

Donahue wriggled gloves. She inspected lock rings.

Lupe bent and picked up the heavy steel helmet. She checked the gas line was firmly screwed in place.

'It's a short swim,' said Lupe. 'Just grab the boat and bring it back.'

Donahue didn't reply. Strength sucked by a sudden wave of sadness. She wiped tears with a gloved hand.

'Hey,' said Lupe.

She slapped Donahue across the cheek.

'Hey, look at me. Look me in the eye, girl. You have to get it together. He would want you to live.'

Donahue nodded.

Lupe slapped her again, shook her shoulder.

'If you die down there, what's the point? What's it all been for?'

'All right.'

Lupe stepped back. She lowered the helmet over Donahue's head and secured hex bolts.

Lupe and Sicknote pitched camp on the platform stairs. They laid Ekks across the steps.

They carried their backpacks to the stairwell and propped them against the wall.

Lupe filled the fire bucket with fresh wood. She uncapped a flare.

'No point saving these, right?'

She struck the flare and jammed it into the bucket. Table legs and chair slats began to burn. The stairwell filled with smoke and crimson flame-light.

A couple of infected corpses lay sprawled at the foot of the stairs. Lupe kicked them into the flood water. The cadavers floated among garbage. Beverage cups and pages of *Sports Illustrated* locked in a thickening crust of ice.

'Versatile bastards,' said Sicknote. 'Who knew they could swim?'

He stood and stretched.

'How long has she been gone?'

Lupe stooped and picked Donahue's G-Shock from a pile of folded clothes.

'Twenty minutes.'

'Freezing down here. Nothing to trap heat.'

'White tiles,' said Lupe. 'I feel cold just looking at them. Makes sense to pitch camp here, though. Better than sitting in the plant room waiting for Galloway to take another bite.'

Lupe warmed her hands over the fire.

'Reckon he's dead?' asked Sicknote. 'Galloway?'

'Doubt it. But he's not half the man he was.'

Sicknote emptied his pockets. Resistors, capacitors, a tuning dial. He cracked his knuckles and began to work on the circuit board.

'So what the hell is this thing?' asked Lupe. 'Trying to repair the radio?'

'I'm following instructions. Ekks showed me what to build.'

Lupe shook her head.

'Voices in your head, dude. Ekks is out for the count. He hasn't told you shit.'

'He woke. He wrote stuff down.'

Sicknote pulled a sheet of paper from his pocket. Lupe held it up, angled so she could read by firelight.

'Dude, this is your handwriting.'

'No.'

'I watched you scrawl all kinds of shit over the walls in Bellevue. Remember the dayroom? All that ketchup? *Hell is coming. We are dust.* You wrote this.'

'No. Ekks woke. He spoke, a little. He asked for pen and paper. I watched him write the list.'

'Look at him. He's comatose. He hasn't moved an inch. Probably never will. You didn't talk to him, dude. Trust me. It was all in your head.'

'I swear. It was his voice.'

'Why would he talk to you? Think it through. You were nothing to him. A lab rat. A chance to test his brain implant. Why didn't he speak to Donahue? Tombes?'

Sicknote looked down at his hands.

'Because he knew I would follow orders.'

He held up the radio components.

'If Ekks has been unconscious this whole time, if he hasn't said a word, then how could I build this? How could I write this list? I don't know the first thing about electronics.' He held up the component sheet. 'Forty-seven pF capacitor. I don't know what the fuck a capacitor does. Doubt I heard the word before today. How could I select these bits and put them in sequence?'

'That pile of junk doesn't do a thing, far as I can tell. Transistors strung on wire. Looks like the kind of tribal jewellery a pygmy would make if they discovered a plane wreck in a jungle clearing. You might as well wear it round your neck.'

Sicknote shook his head.

'I'm sane. Right now, I'm sane. I see the world clear and true. You're wrong about Ekks. He figured something out. He made some kind of big discovery, down here in the dark. It's not a vaccine. It's not a cure. He found something big. And now he's reaching out, trying to make us understand.'

Lupe picked up the notebook and thumbed pages.

'So what has he found?'

'I don't know. But that's why he held on so long. His body is falling apart, but his heart keeps beating. Pure will. There's something he has to tell us, something we need to understand, before he can die.'

63

Donahue hauled herself over the bow skirt and rolled into the boat.

She wiped water from her visor. The floor of the boat was cluttered with dive gear. Spare flippers, spare weights, spare gas.

She found bottled water. She struggled to twist the cap with gloved hands. She split the bottle open with a knife and emptied it over her helmet, arms and chest. She sluiced radioactive flood water from her drysuit and threw the empty bottle aside.

She twisted lock-rings and pulled off her gloves. She unbolted her helmet and lifted it clear. Her breath steamed in the frigid tunnel air.

She released harness clasps and shrugged off her backplate and tanks. She shut off the regulator.

She dumped her weight belt. She unbuckled ankle straps and kicked off her flippers.

She looked around. Impenetrable blackness. Her helmet was still plugged to its nickel hydride battery pack. The lamps still burned. She held up the helmet and surveyed the tunnel.

The flood waters had risen so high her head was inches from the rough brick roof. She could reach up and touch cracked stonework and crumbling mortar.

Too much clutter at the bottom of the boat. She threw stuff over the side. Dive gear. Couple of coats.

She found Nariko's fire hat. Old style, stitched from thick

leather, the kind that got handed down generation to generation, proud emblem of a family's dedication to the service.

She turned it over in her hands, rubbed grime from the captain's shield, buffed it on the sleeve of her drysuit.

She glanced at the rockfall, the curtain of rubble that blocked the north passageway. Somewhere, beneath those tons of concrete and steel, Nariko lay interred.

Donahue pulled the tether line and brought the boat closer to the rubble. The PVC hull abraded concrete. She leaned forwards and placed the hat on a boulder. She adjusted its position, made sure it was sitting straight and proud.

If Nariko had died in the line, if they'd stopped the city traffic, given her the pipes and drums, the helmet would have rested on her coffin at the head of a fire truck convoy.

It belonged close to Nariko.

Donahue unhooked her radio.

'I reached the boat.'

'*You okay?*'

'Yeah. I'm heading back.'

She took position in the centre of the boat. She set her helmet and battery pack on the prow. Twin halogen lamps lit the tunnel ahead.

The boat pushed through a bobbing scrim of garbage. Bottles, sodden newsprint, polystyrene packing chips.

A couple of bodies floating face down. They stank. Rotted and rat-torn. She tried to steer clear. The cadavers bumped against the boat. She pushed them away with an oar.

She was soothed by the tunnel darkness, a mesmeric splash-echo each time she dipped her oar. The place had a funereal beauty. Passageway receding to infinity. Stonework glazed with ice. Rusted roof signals. Fissured brick and dripstone.

Firehouse shift patterns had left her well acquainted with the arid landscape of exhaustion. She understood its bleak,

Arctic terrain. Impaired judgement. Emotional lability. Sudden euphorias: giddy elation followed, minutes later, by black despair.

Detach, she told herself. Crush all emotion. Exhaustion will persuade you to love the womb-like tranquillity of darkness and silence. It will rob you of strength like hypothermia, paralyse you with a smothering wave of peace and wellbeing. You will become entranced by the passageways, their siren beauty. You will sit numb and thoughtless in the boat as the flood waters rise, lulled by dripping water and cool tunnel wind.

Fight it.

Survive.

She threw back her head and roared.

'Fight, motherfucker.' Her voice reverberated from the tunnel walls, alien and shrill. 'Fight, bitch.'

She punched her thigh.

'Yeah.'

Another punch. Invigorating pain, like a shot of caffeine.

'Yeah, that's it.'

She gripped the oar and began to paddle. Strong, muscular strokes. She sang 'Danny Boy'.

Fleeting memory. New Year's Eve. Tombes sitting on the bar at McDonnell's wearing shorts and a fire hat, leading the chorus, beer glass in each hand.

She rowed harder, sang louder.

An arched passageway to her right. A ragged cave mouth blocked by prop-beams and planks. An old work notice nailed to the wood:

**DANGER
DO NOT ENTER
UNSTABLE
KEEP OUT**

351

Donahue turned her dive helmet and trained the halogen lamps on the tunnel entrance. The beam washed across crooked planks and shafted into the darkness beyond.

A raft of garbage had collected behind the planks. Blankets. Plastic drums. Scraps of sheetrock. The remains of a tunnel hobo camp. A refuge built by broken souls fleeing sunlight and city bustle. They had lifted an unchained grate, descended ladders, climbed downwards into darkness and solitude. Permanent midnight. A soothing all-better-now like a mother's embrace.

A splash. A disturbance in the water near the planked cave mouth. Spreading ripples. Donahue focused the light. A skeletal face. An infected creature squirmed between wooden slats. Bone projected through quilted coat fabric. A splintered clavicle.

The putrid revenant pulled itself clear of the planks, hit the water and sank. Waves subsided and the black flood waters settled glassy smooth like onyx.

The creature suddenly broke surface shockingly close and executed a thrashing, spastic breaststroke as it headed for Donahue's boat.

She hesitated. Flight or fight? Row, or confront the weak, dying thing?

Better to fight. She would easily outpace the creature if she rowed for Fenwick, but it would follow her wake. Sooner or later the rotted ghoul would reach the platform steps and emerge from the water. Better to kill it now.

She picked up an oar and snapped it over her knee. Splintering crack. The shaft tipped with jagged fibreglass.

She knelt in the prow of the boat, splintered shaft of the oar held in her hand like a harpoon, ready to strike.

Two more infected creatures wormed between crooked planks, squirmed from the darkness and seclusion of the cave mouth.

Double splash. Spreading ripples. Skeletal creatures thrashing through flood water, heading her way.

'Shit.'

Donahue threw down the makeshift spear and picked up the remaining oar. She began to paddle.

It was a pursuit out of fevered dreams, out of heart-pounding nightmares. She rowed as fast as she could, yet maintained an imperceptible pace. The twin helmet lamps at the front of the boat illuminated the flooded tunnel. Bricks and buttresses passing so slowly it felt like she wasn't moving at all.

She couldn't see the creatures swimming behind her, but she could hear the churn and splash as their arms beat water. The sound echoed from the tunnel walls, loud and intimate.

She glanced back. They were close. They would reach her before she achieved the safety of the station platform.

Something up ahead. The hulk of the old IRT coach sitting on a siding. Warped wooden cladding hanging on an iron frame. Doors hung open. Water almost high as the windows.

Donahue paddled towards the coach. She drifted alongside, and shone headlamps through the vacant windows. Brass fixtures hung from rotted timber. Corroded seat frames protruded from dark water.

She lashed the tether to a window pillar, gripped the frame of a side door, and eased herself into the coach.

She held up the helmet and scanned the dereliction.

Saturated oak panels soft and malleable as cork. Rotted drapes. The wilted blades of ceiling fans.

Waist-deep water. A crisp film of ice fractured as she waded to the front of the coach. Bone-chilling cold.

The planks beneath her feet were soft as carpet. She walked slow, checking each floorboard would take her weight.

She stowed the helmet on an overhead luggage rack, and angled the halogen lights. The flooded coach lit harsh white.

The door at the end of the carriage was jammed. She kicked it. She punched it. Rotted timber fell apart like wet cardboard.

She looked out into the tunnel darkness. She could hear splashes, hands slapping water.

Three creatures swam out of the shadows, thrashing the water with clumsy strokes. They headed inexorably towards her. Bearded vagrants weighed down by winter coats.

She adjusted her grip on the broken oar shaft.

They drew close.

She thought about Tombes. A head full of screaming dissonance. A series of happy memories interrupted by gut-punch trauma:

Summer night. Tombes with his arm round her shoulders as they leaned on a river railing and contemplated the floodlit span of the Verrazano-Narrows Bridge.

Horror-flash:

Tombes lying dead on the ticket hall floor, right arm ripped from his shoulder socket leaving torn muscle and a partial sleeve of flaccid skin.

A midnight promenade along the Wildwood boardwalk. Eating cotton-candy, watching the summer crowd and stately revolutions of the Ferris lights.

Horror-flash:

Smashed skull, spilled brain, tongue lolling in an open mouth.

Donahue rubbed her temples. Sudden wave of nausea. She leaned out the carriage door and puked. She spat to clear the taste.

She leaned against the doorframe.

'Come on, guys.' She could hear the exhaustion in her own voice. 'Party time.'

The first guy reached the carriage. Long, grey beard. Yellow teeth. He gripped the sides of the doorframe, eyes fixed on Donahue. Black eyeballs stared through a curtain of lank hair. He struggled to pull himself up into the carriage, leaning on the submerged coupler for support.

Donahue gripped the lapel of his coat.

'Let me give you a hand.'

She helped the stinking revenant climb into the carriage.

'There you go.'

She drove the splintered oar into the creature's eye socket. The vagrant jerked rigid like he'd had a high-voltage shock. Donahue twisted the shaft deeper into his head. He convulsed a couple of times then toppled backwards, oar still wedged in his head. Donahue tried to maintain a grip, but the smooth fibreglass shaft slipped through her gloved hands.

The vagrant toppled back through the doorway. He floated for a moment. Donahue made a last snatch at the oar shaft. Then his waterlogged coat dragged him down into black.

'Shit.'

She stood in the doorway and looked out into the tunnel darkness.

The other two vagrants were gone.

She froze. She listened for movement. She grabbed her helmet from the luggage rack and began to back down the carriage, sweeping halogen light over smooth waters, tensed for an attack.

Sudden lunge. One of the bearded hobos leaned through a window and grasped for Donahue. She gripped his arm and pulled him further through the window, then swung her steel helmet and delivered a skull-shattering blow. The vagrant slid back through the window and sank.

She edged towards the side door, sweeping her helmet lights around the empty, inundated carriage.

She leaned out the door. She gripped the edge of the boat and pulled it close.

Peripheral movement. She looked up. A rotted vagrant crouched on the carriage roof directly above her head. It leaned forwards, matted hair hanging down, and hissed.

64

Lupe watched the north tunnel mouth. She checked her watch.

'Donnie should be back by now.'

She turned around. Sicknote sat on a stairwell step. Blood ran down his neck and chest.

'What the hell are you doing?' shouted Lupe, vaulting the steps three at a time.

She grabbed Sicknote's wrist and pulled his hand from his ear. Fingers dripped blood. She pushed his head to one side. The implant port hung out of his head, trailing wire.

'Christ.'

'I want it out of my head,' said Sicknote. Woozy smile.

'You'll pull your damn brains out, idiot. I'll fetch a dressing. Sit there. Don't move. Don't touch your head.'

Lupe fetched a first aid kit. She sat beside Sicknote. She brushed blood-matted hair aside and examined the wound.

A small, titanium five-pin socket. Two small screws, threads clogged with blood and bone splinters.

'Jesus. You wrenched this bastard right out your skull.'

Lupe tore the wrapper from a pair of surgical scissors. She snipped iridium wires, thin as hair.

She held up the socket.

'That's the power pack,' said Sicknote. 'Some kind of lithium charge.'

'So what did it do? Zap your brain each time you had one of your visions?'

'It made them worse.'

Sicknote held out his hand. Lupe gave him the implant. He hurled it into the flood water.

She dressed the weeping hole in his skull. She washed her hands with bottled water. She gave him Tylenol.

'How do you feel?'

'Better.'

'Really?'

'I'm not a robot. I don't want to be controlled.'

Lupe checked her watch again.

'Forty minutes since I spoke to Donnie. She ought to be here.'

'She's pretty ill. She might need to stop for a rest. Got any more Tylenol?'

Lupe threw him the pot. He knocked back more pills.

He picked up the tangle of radio components and continued to twist wire. He unscrewed the earpiece of the transmitter headphones and knitted the little speaker to the circuit. He lashed cable round the stairwell's iron balustrade and used it as an antenna.

'Take it easy,' said Lupe. 'You lost a lot of blood.'

'I feel good. Honestly.'

'You're high. Blood loss. In a minute, you'll crash.'

He touched frayed cable to the terminals of a nine-volt battery, and adjusted the tuning dial. He sat with the speaker pressed to his ear, frowning with concentration.

He scratched his scalp.

'I just fixed you up,' said Lupe. 'Don't re-open the wound.'

'My skin. Itching all the time.'

Lupe pointed at the radio.

'You won't reach shit. No power. No range.'

'I'm not trying to talk. I'm trying to listen.'

'Listen to what?'

'The virus.'

Lupe sat beside him. She held the little speaker to her ear.

'Nothing. White noise.'

'Listen harder.'

'There's nothing. It's a dead channel.'

'Can't you hear it? That pulsing sound beneath the static? I've heard it every time anyone used a radio down here. Like a hammer knocking wood.'

'Interference. Lot of iron in these rocks.'

'Listen again. Can you hear it? Each click is different. There are variations. Little changes of tempo.'

She put her ear to the speaker once more.

'It all sounds the same to me. Just noise.'

Sicknote held up the notebook. 'Ekks transcribed the sounds. That's what these letters and symbols represent. Not words. More like musical notation. A precise record of the endless tunnel song.'

'He tuned in to its thoughts? Is that what you're saying?'

'Yeah. That was his big-ass breakthrough. Other labs round the world tried to kill the disease. Nuked it with penicillin and antibiotics. I heard there were a bunch of guys down a missile silo in the Everglades doing all kinds of Frankenstein shit. But Ekks figured out the virus was smart. He tried to communicate. He spoke to the parasite.'

'An actual conversation?'

'Yeah.'

'What did he ask?'

Sicknote shrugged.

'How should I know? Obvious questions, I guess. Who are you? Where are you from? What do you want?'

Lupe picked up the notebook.

'And you think he wrote down answers?'

'That's why the notebook is so precious. It's mankind's first and only communication with this disease.'

'I don't buy it. It's a germ. A bug squirming in a Petri dish.

359

It doesn't have thoughts. It doesn't make plans. You can't talk to it, any more than you can interview syphilis.'

'No,' said Sicknote. 'You're wrong.'

Lupe gestured to the crude radio.

'So you're listening to it right now? Is that what you think? Monitoring its thoughts?'

'Yeah.'

'So what does it say? What's it trying to tell you?'

'It's from somewhere cold and dark. It's travelled a long way. Unimaginable distances. It slept, thousands, millions of years. It dreamed. And now it's awake.'

'Crazy,' said Lupe. 'You're not listening to the radio. You're listening to the voices in your head.'

'It's all true. Swear to God.'

'You don't believe in God. And he sure doesn't believe in a loser like you.'

A warm glow of light from the throat of north tunnel.

Lupe stood at the water's edge.

'Donnie?' Her voice echoed from the tunnel walls. 'Donnie, is that you?'

Faint oar splashes. Donahue paddled into view. She was sweating with effort. The dive helmet propped at the prow projected the weak orange glow of a battery burned dry.

She guided the boat to the foot of the stairwell and threw the tether line. Lupe caught the rope, pulled the boat close, and lashed the line to the stairwell balustrade.

'I brought company,' said Donahue.

Faint splash from the tunnel mouth. Churning water. Lupe trained her flashlight. A rotted skeletal thing. It flailed and thrashed. It nudged plates of ice aside. A vagrant with a long beard and matted hair, trying to stay afloat, fighting the water-logged overcoat that threatened to drag it beneath the surface.

A stack of paint tins on a step. Lupe picked up a tin and loosened the lid. She hurled it towards the creature. The tin hit the water with a cannonball splash. The lid popped loose as it sank. Water surrounding the flailing revenant was filled with shimmering globules of oil. A wide chemical slick shone greasy rainbows.

Lupe pulled a slat from the fire bucket and hurled it spinning into the cavern darkness. The burning shard executed an elegant, flame-fluttering arc, then hit the water.

Ignition.

Blue fire washed across the surface of the flood. Ice fizzed and dissolved. Flames danced high and scorched the tunnel roof.

The creature thrashed and cooked. Burning arms, burning head. Matted beard hair shrivelled to nothing.

The creature fixed its gaze on Lupe and Donahue standing twenty yards away at the water's edge. It strained to reach them from a lake of fire.

Face burned away. No lips, ears or nose. Eyeballs boiled, burst and evaporated.

Convulsions. Slow death. The vagrant sank beneath the surface. Skin crisped and popped as the corpse slowly submerged.

The fire dwindled and died. Blue smoke hung over steaming, fizzing water like swamp gas.

'Any more of these fucks heading our way?' asked Lupe.

'There were three. I killed the others.'

Donahue was bleeding. A gash to the forehead. She released lock rings and pulled off her gloves. Lupe gave her a bandana. She dabbed the wound on her forehead.

'Are you all right?' asked Lupe.

'Yeah.'

'You didn't get bitten, did you?'

'No.'

Donahue sat on a step next to the bucket fire. She rubbed tired eyes.

'Look at me.'

Donahue looked up.

'Swear to me. Tell me that's not a bite.'

'It's not a bite. And by the way, screw you.'

Donahue wearily got to her feet. She unzipped and stripped out of her drysuit. She pasted a dressing over the gash on her forehead. She dressed and pulled on boots.

She pointed at Sicknote, sat on the step listening to the radio apparatus.

'What happened to his head?'

'A little elective brain surgery.'

'What's he doing?'

'Communing with the virus. Let him be.'

A couple of backpacks leaned against the stairwell wall. A couple of rolled NBC suits. Lupe threw them into the boat.

She pointed at crooked planks nailed over the south tunnel entrance.

'Guess we just pull those aside and see how far south we can get.'

'If the water rises any higher we'll drown.'

'This city is dreaming up new ways to kill us every hour. We've got no choice. We got to move out.'

Donahue checked her watch.

'Still a couple of hours before the scheduled pickup.'

Lupe glanced at her watch.

'They're due at seven. At one minute past, we climb in that boat and paddle like motherfuckers, all right? Seven. We don't wait a second longer.'

'I hear something,' said Sicknote. He gestured to the little speaker cone. 'A voice.'

'No shit.'

'Listen.' He held out the speaker. 'A human voice. For real.'

Lupe crouched beside Sicknote and put the speaker to her ear.

'Holy shit. The chopper. It's in range.'

She snatched the Motorola from her waistband. She upped the volume and switched to vox.

'*Rescue Four, this is Air Cav Charlie Charlie Foxtrot, do you copy, over?*'

Donahue grabbed the radio from Lupe's hand.

'This is Rescue Four, good to hear your voice.'

She leaned against the wall, weak with relief.

'*Do you have the objective, over?*'

'Ten-four. We have Ekks.'

'*Rescue, we estimate ten minutes to touchdown, five minutes to reach your location. Prep the doctor. Get him ready to move.*'

'Copy that. Can't wait to get out of here.'

Donahue turned to Lupe.

'See? Told you they wouldn't leave us behind.'

65

Seventy knots. A slow, ten degree bank into headwind.

Byrne twisted in the pilot seat.

'Check it out.'

Chief Jefferson unbuckled his harness. He adjusted headphones.

'What am I looking at?'

Nothing to see but instrumentation reflected in black cockpit glass.

Byrne pointed to a distant orange glow.

'Fire. Miles of it.'

'The city?'

'The refineries. Burn for months. Maybe years.'

Chief turned back to the passenger compartment.

His team:

Craven, chewing gum, cradling a belt-feed SAW.

Bingham, unfolding a stretcher, laying it on the cabin floor. She hung a couple of saline drips from a drip rack.

'The guy will be heavily irradiated,' said Chief, shouting to be heard over rotor roar. 'Don't forget. He's a patient. And he's a valuable asset. But he is also radioactive waste. Don't touch him with bare hands.'

'Yes, sir.'

'Bingham. You all right?'

'I'm fine, sir.'

'You looked spooked.'

'I'm okay.'

The Chief unzipped his radiation suit, reached into a shirt pocket and pulled out a hip flask. He unscrewed the cap and passed it to Bingham.

She took a swig.

Jefferson addressed the pilot.

'Patch me through to Avalanche.'

'Forward Team to Flight One, go ahead, over.'

'How's it looking?'

'Pretty good, sir. We've done a full sweep of the lodge, covered every floor. The building is secure. Open ground on all sides. Hundred yards to the tree-line. Perfect for claymores. One approach road. Good range of vision. The place will make an excellent holdout.'

'Supplies?'

'There's an extensive dry store behind the kitchens. Good inventory.'

'Outstanding.'

'There are a couple of outbuildings near the helipad. We'll check them out at sun-up. Might be some aviation fuel.'

'There's a cabin by the lake, is that correct?'

'Yes, sir. A log chalet.'

'That's where we'll treat Ekks. Move the medical gear to the cabin. See if you can fire up the generator. And check for running water.'

'Sir.'

'He is to be held in isolation, understood? No one goes near him without my permission.'

'Am I to understand Doctor Ekks will be the only arrival? There will be no other patients?'

'He is the sole priority.'

'Ten-four.'

Jefferson pulled the headphone jack from the ceiling socket and threw the headset on the seat beside him.

'What about the fire department guys, sir?' asked Byrne.
Jefferson ignored the question.
'Twenty minutes from target,' shouted Byrne.
'Mask up,' said the Chief. 'Good luck, every one.'

66

The office.

Sicknote sat cross-legged. He pulled back the foil hypo-thermia blanket.

Wade, torn and charred. His face was a charcoal mask. No eyes. Carbon lips curled back revealing brilliant white teeth. His hands were folded across his chest, clenched and curled; muscles and tendons cooked and contracted, twisting his arms into a contorted pugilistic pose.

Sicknote gripped Wade's rigid corpse. He lifted the body a couple of inches. Blood and body fat had boiled away during the fire, depleting the cadaver of half its weight.

He reached into a pant pocket. Crisp fabric tore and flaked. He pulled out the brass cyanide cylinder. He unscrewed the cap and inspected the vial. Intact.

'What are you doing?'

Lupe stood in the doorway.

'You guys are going to ride out of here on that chopper. Guess I'll be staying behind.'

He glanced at Lupe. Melancholy smile.

'I've enjoyed it. These last few days. Isn't that pathetic? Isn't that the saddest thing you ever heard? I've enjoyed the company. My time down here in this shithole has been the happiest I can remember.'

'It'll be all right. We'll look after you.'

'No. I'm dying. And that's okay. I mean, we're all fucked,

right? In the long run. We live out our time, and wonder what it all means.'

'You don't have to die down here in the dark.'

'I'll help you guys get aboard the helicopter. Then I might go outside. Take that walk.'

She put her hand on his shoulder.

'God bless you, Michael.'

He held her hand and fought back tears.

They walked across the rubble-strewn ticket hall to the platform steps.

'Oh Christ.'

They found Donahue crouched over Ekks, delivering rapid chest compressions.

'Help me for God's sake.'

Lupe ran down the steps.

'What happened?'

'He's not breathing.'

'How long?'

'I don't know. I looked at him. His lips were blue.'

She checked his carotid pulse. She checked his breathing.

'Don't you fucking dare.'

More compressions.

'Lungs, right?' said Lupe. That chest rattle. Pneumonia.'

'First aid kit. Quick.'

Lupe tossed Donahue a trauma pack.

Donahue leaned over Ekks and shone a penlight into his mouth.

'Lesions. His airway is swollen shut.'

She tore open a sterile pack and uncapped a scalpel.

'This is going to get messy.'

She probed the man's throat, located his Adam's apple and the cricoids cartilage beneath.

'Here we go.'

The scalpel punctured flesh. Ekks convulsed. Coughing blood-spurt. Donahue pushed a forefinger into the wound and wormed it wider.

'I need some kind of tube.'

Lupe uncapped the pen torch and shook out batteries. She unscrewed the lamp head.

Donahue twisted the metal tube into the neck wound. Whooping, whistling inhalation. Ekks arched his back. His chest began to rise and fall.

'Jesus, that was close,' said Lupe, sitting back.

Donahue watched Ekks breathe. Juddering exhalations, slow and shallow.

She shook her head.

'We've lost him.'

'What?'

'He's slipping away. Nothing we can do.'

'Give him a shot,' said Lupe. 'Adrenalin. Whatever you got.'

'No. He's sinking. For real.'

'You're sure?'

'Yeah.'

They sat beside Ekks and watched his final moments.

Lupe leaned close, as if she wanted to drink his dying breath.

'I know what you are. Hear me, motherfucker? I know what you are.'

One last, shuddering exhalation.

'That's it,' said Donahue. 'We lost him. All for nothing. The whole damn trip.'

67

'*Rescue, this is Flight One. We are on approach. We need your beacon, over.*'

'Ten-four.'

Donahue unzipped a backpack and took out a black cylinder like a Thermos flask. She climbed the street level steps. She pulled on a respirator.

She held back the curtain. Street garbage smothered by a thick carpet of snow. Plump flakes drifted from the night sky.

A CSAR beacon. She thumbed the slide switch to on. She pushed her arm through the gate and threw the strobe into the alley. It bounced and lay in the snow.

The beacon was cupped by an infrared filter. It appeared to be inert, but the chopper pilot, equipped with night vision goggles, would glimpse a brilliant pulse of light as he overflew the ruins of lower Manhattan.

Lupe restarted the generator and returned to the hall.

They rolled Ekks. They slid his arms and legs into a yellow NBC suit. They sealed the chest zip. They pushed his hands into heavy butyl gloves and lashed the cuffs with tape. They strapped an M40 respirator to his face and secured the hood.

'Nice job,' said Donahue. 'By the time they figure out he's dead, we'll already be in the air.'

'If that notebook delivers a cure, they'll name high schools after the sick bastard,' said Lupe.

'He'll deserve it.'

'Easy for you to say. I was next on his kill list.'

'Face it. You're not angry at him. You're angry at yourself, because you know how little you are worth.'

Lupe climbed into an NBC suit. Donahue helped her zip.

'Here's the deal,' said Lupe. 'The elevator is messed up, but it'll work. I'll take the first ride. Soon as they land, I'll head up top and gauge what kind of reception we'll get.'

'No,' said Donahue. 'I'll go.'

'I don't trust him. The guy is a corn pone fascist.'

'Exactly. He'll shoot you on sight. I'll go. Maybe I can talk him round. Persuade him to keep his side of the deal. Fly you out of here and set you free.'

Lupe held out her lock-knife.

'Take a blade.'

'They'll have guns.'

'Take it anyway.'

Lupe tucked the knife into Donahue's belt.

'Hey, hear that?' said Sicknote.

They turned towards the entrance steps and listened. Rising rotor thrum. The JetRanger manoeuvring for touchdown.

'*Flight One to Rescue, do you copy, over?*'

'Go ahead.'

'*Incoming. Prepare for immediate dust-off.*'

'Roger that. Glad to be going home.'

Donahue clipped a fresh filter cartridge into her respirator. She pulled on the mask and adjusted straps. Sicknote helped secure her hood.

Chopper noise reached a crescendo. Change of pitch as it began a controlled descent.

Donahue pictured the landing.

The JetRanger battling a fierce headwind as it hovers over the flat expanse of the Federal roof. The pilot lowers the collective, pulls back the cyclic. Skids settle on bitumen. Rotor downwash kicks up a blizzard. The pilot keeps the engine running, ready for immediate take-off.

The side door is wrenched open and boots hit the ground. NBC suits and heavy respirators. Quick deployment. Cops running for the roof stairs, ducking low beneath blurring blades.

'All set?' asked Lupe.

Donahue gave a mock salute.

'First in the door.'

She stepped into the elevator. Lupe pulled the gate closed.

'Watch your ass,' said Lupe. 'Don't take your eyes off that lizard.'

'It'll be all right.'

Lupe hit Up.

Chief kicked open the stairwell door. He edged into the sixth-floor hallway. He held a Colt auto in gloved hands. A laser sight mounted beneath the barrel. The red needle-beam swept the hallway.

Open doorways. Glimpse of bombed out offices. Toppled chairs and desks. Drifts of paper ruffled by a blizzard wind blowing through vacant windows.

The elevator doors were ajar. He leaned into the shaft and shone his flashlight down into darkness. A dust-furred cable. The splintered roof of the freight elevator six floors below.

He turned back to the roof stairwell and shouted:

'Come on down.'

Craven and Bingham laid the empty stretcher on the hall floor. Bingham fetched a drip stand.

'I'll cannulate both arms and hit him with hypotonic fluid,' said Bingham. 'Best I can do until we get him back to Avalanche. Keep him stable. Then we better try and contact NORAD, see if they can provide specialist help. Bone marrow transplants are beyond my pay grade.'

Chief gestured to Craven.

'Check the rooms.'

Craven gripped the belt-feed SAW strapped to his shoulder. Safety to off. He checked each office. He upturned tables. He kicked open cupboards.

'Hey, boss. Found something.'

A hall stationery cupboard. Bloody handprints on the wall. A woman's shoe.

The Chief crouched beside Craven. He tested blood with a gloved finger. Fresh.

'Prowler. Round here somewhere. Better watch our backs.'

A faint rumble from the elevator shaft. Gears engaged. A concrete counterweight heading down to the basement. The floor indicator needle began to rise.

'Sir,' shouted Bingham. 'We've got company.'

The elevator began its ascent. Lupe watched the brass needle of the floor indicator rise from SUB.

Faint crackle from her radio. She upped volume and held it to her ear. Elevator noise. Donahue must have set her Motorola to transmit.

The floor needle climbed to 6, then stopped.

Donahue stood in the hallway. She was faced by three figures in camo green NBC suits.

'Where's the objective?' asked the Chief.

'Down below.'

'What's his condition?'

'Stable.' She pointed to the SAW. 'Want to point that thing somewhere else?'

Chief gave the nod. Craven angled the weapon at the floor.

'Any other survivors?'

'Just me.'

'Feeling okay?'

'Pretty exhausted.'

Bingham took a Geiger counter from her shoulder bag. She held it close to Donahue and took a reading.

Discreet shake of the head.

The Chief unbuckled his hip holster and drew the Colt. He engaged the laser sight.

'You've done a fine job. It's an inspiration. Way above and beyond the call.' He shucked the pistol slide. 'I'm desperately sorry.'

The Chief took aim.

Donahue pulled back her hood and ripped off her mask. She looked him in the eye.

'Piece of shit.'

The red dot of his laser centred on her forehead.

Gunshot. Clatter. Brief feedback whine.

Lupe stared at the speaker grille of her Motorola. Sicknote opened his mouth like he was about to speak. She mimed hush.

Chief, voice muffled by a respirator:

'*Get Byrne. Tell him to shut off the damn rotor and get in here.*'

Receding footsteps.

A young woman's voice:

'*Sir, there's a green light on that radio. I think it's transmitting.*'

Clunk and rustle. Donahue's radio picked from the floor.

Respirator rasp. Chief, speaking directly into the radio:

'*Who am I talking to?*'

Lupe looked down at her handset. She listened to the him breathe.

'*I know you are listening. Who's down there?*'

Lupe didn't reply.

'*We're on our way. We don't want trouble. We just want Ekks.*

374

Nothing more. Let us have him, and we'll be on our way. We'll leave food, medical supplies, anything you need.'

Lupe shut off the radio.

'Bastards,' she muttered. She stared up at the ceiling, hatred cutting through the building's superstructure like an X-ray as she pictured the Chief and his men standing over Donahue's corpse six storeys above her.

'Motherfucking bastards.'

She clipped her radio on her belt.

She picked up a fist-sized lump of concrete and hurled it at the roof lights, shattering the remaining bulbs.

Sudden darkness. Lupe switched on her flashlight.

She turned to Sicknote.

'Come on. Help me move Ekks.'

Sicknote lost in panic and confusion.

'They killed her. Just shot her.'

Lupe grabbed him by the collar, shook until his eyes regained focus.

'Ekks. The plant room. Now.'

They carried the body to the plant room.

'Back of the room. Come on.'

Lupe covered Ekks with waste paper and cardboard.

'Got a flashlight?' asked Lupe.

'Yeah.'

'Then get out of here. The Chief will search the place. And if he finds us, he'll kill us. Gutshot. Leave us to scream as we bleed out.'

Sicknote shook his head.

'I'm staying with you.'

'Fuck that shit. He wasted Donahue, so he sure as hell won't think twice about popping a cap in your sorry ass. Go down to the platform. Get on that boat and stay out of sight. If anything happens to me, kick through those planks and row far as you can. Get to the shore.'

'We should hand over the notebook. Give him what he wants.'

'No. He thinks we're garbage. Kill us without a thought. But today, he's messing with the wrong motherfucker.'

'Give him the book.'

'I'll let the whole world burn before I bend for a cunt like him.'

'Please.'

'Get out of here. Go on. Go.'

Sicknote sprinted from the plant room. Sudden head-spinning wave of nausea. He stumbled and fell to the floor. He knelt on broken tiles, panting for breath. He touched the surgical dressing taped behind his ear. It was wet with blood.

He looked up. The needle of the floor indicator executing a smooth arc from 6 to SUB.

He coughed and retched. He snatched up his flashlight and struggled to his feet. He ran to the head of the platform stairwell and stumbled down the steps into darkness.

68

The Chief jerked back the elevator gate. He stepped into the ticket hall, pistol raised.

He signalled Advance.

Byrne.

Craven.

Bingham.

They emerged from the elevator, weapons raised, and fanned.

Donahue lay slumped at the back of the elevator, a scorched bullet hole at the centre of her forehead.

The Chief explored the darkness. The brilliant needle-beam of his laser sight swept left and right.

'Give me some light.'

Bingham struck a flare and threw it down.

Compacted pillars and fractured archways. Silence and shadows. Debris and dereliction.

'Keep it tight. Remember: we're not alone down here.'

He crept through the sepulchral gloom. No sound but the rasp of his respirator and the crunch of boots kicking through broken bricks and nuggets of gypsum.

Craven swung his weapon upwards. The barrel light swept across deep fissures in the ceiling. He surveyed the structural damage, the cracked and crumbling concrete that told of the building's imminent collapse.

'Place is coming apart.'

The Chief walked deeper into the hall.

Charred panel ads. A cartoon sunset. '*Camel Cigarettes –*
Pleasure Ahoy!'

The letters of the station sign beneath a smear of dried
blood, matted hair and scraps of scalp:

Fe   ck   eet

'Sir. Got a body.' Craven knelt next to Tombes. He
prodded the dead man's jaw with the barrel of his rifle. 'One
of the firefighters. Looks pretty mauled.'

'Infected?'

'No.'

Bingham took a Geiger handset from her shoulder bag
and took a reading.

'We can take off our masks.'

'You're sure?'

'Tolerable background. But mask up if you go near the
station entrance.'

The Chief pulled back his hood and peeled off his
respirator.

'Christ,' muttered Bingham. 'Dreadful stench.' Her breath
fogged frigid air. 'Cooked meat. Can you smell it? This city
is one giant crematorium.'

'How long are we staying, sir?' asked Byrne. 'This was
supposed to be a quick turn around.'

'I want to be gone as much as you guys,' said Jefferson. 'But
we're not going to piss our pants and run like children.'

He kicked through scattered garbage. He bent and picked
up a scorched scrap of fabric. Remains of a grey T-shirt.

RESCUE 4
FDNY
TUNNEL RATS

'Torched the place. Looks like quite a fight.'

He checked his watch.

'Search every room.'

The IRT office.

Assault entry. Craven kicked the remaining fragments of door aside, and braced to fire. Swift sweep, SAW set full auto. His barrel light washed over charred furniture.

He explored the room. Gramophone records splintered underfoot.

He lifted the corner of a foil blanket with his boot. A cadaver. The part-cremated remains of Wade, charred flesh fused with the remains of his red prison-issue.

Last look around.

'Clear.'

Bingham crossed the ticket hall and stood at the head of the platform stairwell.

Steps sloped downwards into darkness.

She struck a flare. It burned fierce white.

She gripped her pistol and cautiously descended the stairs, flare held above her head. Dark water lapped the foot of the steps. She stood at the water's edge and peered into the cavernous tunnel space.

A couple of infected bodies floating among garbage. They drifted face down, arms outstretched. Ruptured skin. Metallic growths projected from rotted flesh as if their mutated spinal columns had tried to tear free and go squirming in search of a new host.

Bingham shielded her eyes from the flare light and squinted at the floating cadavers. Heads split by axe blows. Spilled brain tissue.

Sicknote was five yards to her left. He crouched in the

dinghy, floating tight against the tunnel wall. He knelt, fist jammed in his mouth, tried not to make a sound.

Bingham unhooked her radio.

'The platform is completely flooded. The tunnel is almost submerged. There's nobody down here.'

She turned and walked back up the stairs.

Sicknote watched white flare light recede as she climbed the stairwell back to the ticket hall. He relaxed, panted with relief, and let the boat drift clear of the wall.

The plant room.

Byrne stood in the doorway. He struck a flare and tossed it inside. It hit the floor. Fizz and smoke. He unslung his rifle and advanced into the room.

Crazy, shifting shadows.

Quick scan of scattered debris. Couple of used hypodermics. A discarded water bottle.

A small portable generator. Cables clamped to wall-mounted switch gear.

The generator was shut down. Byrne bent and put his hand to the compressor. Residual heat. Faint smell of hot metal. The machine had been running minutes before.

He yanked the starter cable. Nothing.

He checked the fuel level. Quarter tank.

He checked the fuse panel. A cavity. Something had been unscrewed and removed.

'Shit,' he muttered.

He got to his feet.

He peered down aisles of web-draped electro-conductive switch gear. He picked up the flare and tossed it further into the room. Tar-coated cables thick as drainpipe. Corroded ironwork.

He took a couple of steps forwards. He squinted into the darkness at the back of the room.

'Hey. Anyone back there?'

Another couple of steps. He shouldered the rifle.

'We just want to talk.'

He reached inside his NBC suit, took a penlight from his breast pocket and peered into shadow.

Crumpled boxes and scattered paper. He stepped forwards, ready to kick through the garbage pile, but was distracted by a grotesque shape at the foot of a nearby wall. Some kind of distended bio-form part-shrouded by a hypothermia blanket.

Byrne crouched and pulled the blanket aside. His barrel light lit a nightmare mess of bone and taut skin. Four legs fused to a distended thorax. Spines and tumourous eruptions. Limbs furred with metallic filaments. Foul meat stink.

'Jesus Christ.' He covered his mouth.

One of the limbs twitched as if it retained a last spark of life.

Byrne scrambled clear and got to his feet.

'Jeez,' he muttered as he backed towards the door. 'Holy Mother Mary.'

Last glance around.

'Clear.'

The street entrance. Jefferson pulled on his respirator and gloves. He tested the handcuff that held the gate closed.

He unsheathed his combat knife and slit the curtain with a swipe of the blade.

He shone his flashlight through the lattice grille into the alley. Steady snowfall had reduced the dumpsters and wrecked bike to a blurred outline.

Figures stumbled through the snow. Three prowlers crusted with snow. The creatures jerked and staggered as if nerve signals were starting to misfire, as if they were about to seize up mid-step and freeze to glass.

They slammed against the entrance lattice. Black eyes. Peeling flesh. Clothes white with frost.

An arm pushed through the bars. Chief let fingers claw an inch from his visor.

He drew his pistol and took aim.

Morning suit and carnation, like the guy had been best man at a wedding, weeks ago, when solemn vows turned to screams as infected burst into the chapel and bit chunks out of the guests.

'Hey, pretty boy.'

The creature snatched at the thin beam of laser light. It hissed. The Chief centred the brilliant red target dot on the back of its mouth.

Gunshot.

The back of the creature's head blew out. It stood for a moment, mouth locked in a frozen yawn, then toppled backwards and sprawled in the snow. Smoke coiled from open jaws like cigarette fumes.

A second infected figure. He took aim.

'How about you? Want some?'

Cashmere overcoat. Spectacles. The red dot hovered on the bridge of the creature's nose. Gunshot. Skull-burst. Wire spectacles cut in two, lenses swinging from each ear. The creature sank to its knees, then fell sideways.

A last revenant. A guy in a black suit. Left arm missing, right arm jammed between the bars.

Lapel badge:

FUTURE MISSIONARY
The Church of
JESUS CHRIST
of Latter-day Saints

'Hey, padre.'

The Chief let the laser sight centre on the creature's

forehead. The dot travelled down the revenant's nose, chin, collar, and centred on its breastbone.

Gunshot.

The creature lay in the snow, smouldering entry wound, spine shattered by the .45 round. It blinked as flakes settled on its face.

The Chief leaned against the cage gate and contemplated the paralysed missionary. 'Where's your soul, padre? Flown to heaven, or is it still locked inside that hunk of meat, waiting for release?'

The creature looked back at him. It lifted its head.

'Must be quite a line at the pearly gates right now. Hell of a queue. And when they're done, when Saint Peter has ticked off the last few names, he'll close those gates for good. Padlock and chain. Because no one else will be coming.'

He took aim at the missionary's forehead. He began to squeeze the trigger.

'There's nothing, is there? That's the truth of it. No Jesus. No angels. Nothing but the dark.'

'Sir?'

Chief shut off the laser and turned around.

Byrne at the foot of the stairwell.

'Sir. We got problems.'

The Chief descended the steps. His boots crackled on frozen blood. He holstered his pistol. He pulled off his respirator and gloves.

'They've disabled the generator, sir,' said Byrne. 'We're trapped. We've got no way back to the roof.'

Jefferson hurried across the ticket hall to the elevator. He jabbed the Up button.

No response.

'They took some kind of fuse, some kind of breaker,' said Byrne.

'Can you fix it?'

'We don't have the tools or the parts.'

'Cunts,' spat Jefferson. 'Motherfucking cunts.'

'They must have done it the moment we arrived,' said Byrne. 'Waited for the elevator to reach a standstill, then pulled the plug.'

'Then they're still close by. Find them. Bring them to me.'

'Sir.'

'About time we straightened a few things out.'

69

Lupe crouched in the conduit. She stuffed the generator fuse into her pocket.

She crawled through the narrow brick pipe. Knees and elbows rubbed raw. She paused and caught her breath. She wiped sweat from her face. She let her head sag and rest on brickwork rough as pumice.

She was sick. She was tired. Focus and fight suddenly overwhelmed by an enervating wave of self-pity.

What would Wade say if he were here, beside her in the tunnel? What hectoring drill-sergeant diatribe would he deliver if he found her ready to lay down and die?

'*Feel it,*' he would say. '*That wave of infantile helplessness. Wallow. Let it happen. Allow yourself a moment of pure snivelling melancholy.*

'*Then pick an enemy.*

'*Hate someone. Nothing galvanises like anger. Pure rocket fuel. Stoke your rage. Despise the Chief. Loathe his rank, the star on his collar, the flag on his sleeve. The walking embodiment of every uniformed, buzz-cut, paramilitary, hide-behind-a-badge asshole that ever demanded you bend and cough.*

'*Compose yourself. Get your shit together.*

'*Now get up and kill him.*'

Lupe lifted her head.

'Come on.' She rubbed her eyes. 'Move your ass, bitch.'

She gathered strength and continued to crawl.

Distant glow. Lattice light. A grille in the conduit floor.

She inched forwards, quiet as she could, and looked down.

She was in the crawlspace above the ticket hall. The Chief was directly beneath her. She looked down on the top of his head. Close enough to hear him clear his throat, close enough to see beads of sweat on his brow.

Chief checked his pistol mag, then holstered the weapon. He took a hip flask from his breast pocket. He threw his head back and swigged, and for an instant Lupe found herself looking directly at his face, his half-closed eyes.

He capped the flask and tucked it back in his pocket.

He cupped his gloved hands and shouted:

'Hello? Hello? I know you can hear me.'

He listened to his voice echo and die.

'You're hiding. I don't blame you. I shot Officer Donahue. That was a mistake. A terrible, idiotic mistake. I'm sorry. I didn't want her to suffer. That's the honest truth. I wanted to save her the pain and degradation of a slow death. It was stupid. I fouled up. What can I say?'

He waited for a reply.

'I have to make decisions. That's my job. I have responsibilities. The men look to me for leadership, protection. I have to make the calls.'

He uncapped his hip flask and took another swig.

'You need help. You've absorbed a massive amount of radiation. More than I anticipated. I swear, I wouldn't have dispatched a rescue team to this hellhole if I fully understood the danger. We have medical gear back at Avalanche Lake. Come with us. You could live.'

Long pause.

'Come on. Talk to me. How do we straighten this out?'

The Chief waited for a reply that didn't come.

He was joined by Byrne.

'We have to get out of here, sir.'

'Not without Ekks. Search the place.'

'We did.'

'Search it again. He's here. You missed him. There can't be many places to hide.'

Lupe looked up from the grille. A preternatural instinct. A sudden, skin-prickle conviction she was being watched from within the tunnel.

She looked beyond the grille, into the conduit darkness. A monstrous, malformed shape blocking the pipe. Galloway/Cloke. Broken, dying.

The hybrid had folded into a small alcove. Water pipes lagged with asbestos. Stopcocks furred with dust. It huddled in the narrow space, arms wrapped across its chest as if it were preparing to pupate, entering a period of deep hibernation that would last until some strange new life-stage cracked the husk of its old, human shell and squirmed free.

Lupe let her eyes adjust.

A monstrous, elephantine head. Fused skulls jostled for position behind Cloke's face. Lips pulled to a wide gash, exposing double rows of teeth and two plump wet tongues.

Bulbous double eyeballs protruding from taut lids, black and featureless like the orbs of a shark.

'Galloway,' she whispered. 'Can you hear me?'

The hybrid had been cut clean in half at the waist. Internal organs ripped from its thorax. Shuddering respirations. Circulatory system bled dry. Twin hearts slowly fluttering to a standstill. Nothing to pump. Ventricles clogged and clotted with stagnant blood.

Dead yet alive. Inert meat animated by impulses sent through the fibrous metallic tendrils which permeated every muscle and nerve. A hijacked corpse still induced to twitch and dance, like severed frog legs pinned to a dissection table and convulsed by electrical stimulation.

'Hey,' hissed Lupe. 'Look at me.'

387

The grotesque head slowly turned. Black eyes glittered in the darkness.

'Galloway. Are you still in there? Can you hear me?'

No reaction.

'It's Lupe. Remember me? Remember the cuffs? The chains?' She reached in her pant pocket. She took out the empty match-book. *Juggs XXX Bar.* She held it up. 'Think back. Me and Wade. We took your smokes. We took your gun.'

The creature began to stir.

'Yeah. That's it. That's right. You remember. Listen. I need one last favour. Do one last thing for me, then you can sleep for ever.'

70

A clatter from the IRT office.

Byrne and Bingham shouldered their rifles and trained them on the door.

Craven swung the SAW and braced his legs.

The Chief drew his Colt and took aim.

Lupe walked from the office, hands raised, red dot of the laser sight centred on her chest.

'Might have known you would survive,' said Chief. 'Fucking roach.' He cocked his pistol. 'I'm going to count to three. Where's Ekks?'

Lupe shrugged.

'If you shoot me, you'll never find him.'

'Yeah, we will. One.'

'You've been here half an hour. That's twenty-eight minutes longer than you intended.'

'It's a small station. We'll rip the place apart. Two.'

'He's all yours. Seriously. I don't want the fuck. I just want to cover my ass.' She gestured to the body slumped at the back of the freight elevator. 'I don't want to end up like Donnie.'

'Lucretia Guadalupe Villaseñor. A puddle of piss. A piece of human excrement. An abortion that wouldn't die.'

'I wear it like armour.'

'Ekks should have vivisected your ass. You. Wade. That poor psychotic bastard. Gutted you all like fish. What happened to Galloway? He was supposed to be tugging your leash.'

'Gone.'

'Guess you put a knife in his back.'

'No.'

'He was a good man.'

'He was nothing.'

'You know what? You are categorical proof there is no god. Billions of righteous dead, and scum like you still drawing breath. Breaks my heart. Truly does. Three.'

Lupe sniffed. Blood trickled from her nose. She wiped her lip clean with the back of her hand.

'You look sick,' said Chief. 'Real sick. Let me give you something for the pain.' He locked his arm and prepared to fire.

'Ekks had a notebook. All his research, all his data.' Lupe gestured to the platform stairwell. 'I've got backup. Marcus Means. Anything happens to me, the notebook goes in the water.'

Bingham edged towards the platform steps.

'Stay where you are,' ordered Lupe.

The Chief opened his mouth like he was about to speak but was silenced by a low, mournful moan that echoed through the ticket hall. Inhuman. Unutterably sad.

'What the hell was that?' muttered Craven.

The soldiers glanced around, tried to locate the source of the noise.

'Sounds close. Sounds like it's in here, with us.'

'Human?' asked Byrne.

'Can't be,' said Bingham. 'Some kind of animal. A dying dog.'

'You checked the rooms, right?' said Chief, glancing round at his men. 'Checked them thoroughly?'

'It's the tunnels,' said Lupe. 'They sing. We've been listening to it all night.'

'Bullshit. That was a living thing.'

'Sure as hell don't want to meet it,' muttered Craven.

The Chief turned to Bingham. He gestured to Lupe.

'Search her.'

Bingham slung her rifle, approached Lupe and began to pat her down.

She searched the pockets of Lupe's bunker pants.

'Got the fuse. We can fire up the elevator.'

She checked Lupe's turnout coat. She checked her collar, groped rolled sleeves.

A knife tucked in an inside pocket. A rescue tool for cutting seatbelts. Bingham flicked open the blade, gave it a cursory inspection and threw the knife aside.

'So what do you want to do with her?'

Sudden cacophonous crash. The hall ceiling vent smashed out. The grille clattered to the floor. An arachnid thing unfolding from the darkness. Suppurating arms roped with metallic tendrils. Jet black eyes. A grossly distended face. Galloway/Cloke, close to death, but impelled to seek rejuvenating flesh.

Craven shrieked as he was lifted clean off his feet, legs pedalling air. A high, animal scream of mortal terror.

Bingham and Byrne ran across the ticket hall. They each grabbed a leg and tried to pull him free.

Chief tried to get a clear shot.

Lupe ran for the plant room.

Craven punched and clawed at the hands wrapped round his neck. The creature began to haul him into the conduit. Fingernails tore flesh. He tried to swing the SAW upwards, but tangled the strap. He pawed his chest, grasping for his bayonet. He stabbed and slashed at the tumourous arms.

He was lifted higher.

'Kill me. Do it, Bingham. Kill me.'

Face-to-face with the monstrous thing. A final scream. The creature tore out his throat and hurled his body aside.

391

Byrne and Bingham shouldered their rifles and fired full auto. Deafening roar. The hall was lit by fluttering muzzle flare. Bullets sparked the metal vent frame. Tungsten rounds blew roof tiles to powder, blew craters in concrete.

The Chief ejected a spent mag and slapped a fresh clip into his pistol. He racked the slide and pumped the trigger. Air full of whirling chips and stone dust.

They jumped back as a large chunk of concrete detached from the fissured ceiling and hit the floor, shattered to powder.

The Galloway/Cloke hybrid crouched among the rubble. It was wreathed in dust and gunsmoke. It looked around and hissed. It edged towards Byrne.

Byrne backed away. He fumbled a fresh mag from a shoulder bag. He fed the clip into his assault rifle and punched it home with the heel of his palm. He cranked the charging handle. Jammed.

'Fuck.' He wrenched the slide, tried to clear the obstruction. 'Fuck, fuck.'

Chief took aim. Dry click. He ejected the spent clip, hurriedly checked nylon mag pouches looped to his belt.

Bingham snatched Lupe's cutting tool from the floor. She ran to Craven's body, sliced through the SAW shoulder strap and hefted the weapon.

The creature ran towards her, crossing the rubble-strewn floor in a smooth scuttle. It hissed.

Bingham braced the SAW and fired from her hip. Muzzle-scream. Cascading brass. Belt feeding through the receiver at seven hundred rounds per minute. She fought to keep the bucking weapon steady.

Chief and Byrne covered their ears. The hall filled with blue smoke.

The hybrid was hurled across the ticket hall. It hit the wall and sank to the floor leaving a bloody smear. It danced and flailed as bullets tore it apart.

The belt ran dry. Bingham threw down the spent weapon. Smoke poured from the barrel and receiver.

'Give me another flare,' shouted Chief.

Bingham struck a flare and threw it on the floor.

The Chief walked across the hall. The hybrid was a pulped mess. It was trying to drag itself towards the street entrance. Broken arms slapped the steps.

He smacked a final clip into his pistol and emptied a single hollow point round into the back of the creature's head.

Chime of a cartridge case hitting the tiled floor.

Abrupt silence.

They stood wreathed in gun smoke and stone dust.

'Should have brought grenades,' murmured Byrne.

Bingham crouched beside Craven. Throat ripped down to the bone. Steaming blood pooled on the floor. His face was locked in a rictus of terror. White, exsanguinated flesh. Sightless eyes.

She put a hand on his shoulder.

'I'll miss you, bro.'

The Chief stood over the body. He trained his pistol. Red dot centred on Craven's left eyeball.

'Leave him,' said Bingham. 'He's dead.'

'Yeah. But sometimes they come back.'

Gunshot.

Bingham shielded her face from blood spray.

'Bag him up,' said Jefferson. 'We'll take him back. He deserves a burial.'

'We've been here forty-five minutes, sir,' said Byrne. He tapped his watch. 'If we wait much longer, the chopper will ice up. We'll be marooned in this fucking city.'

'He's right,' said Bingham. 'We ought to go.'

'Not yet,' said Jefferson.

Chief rolled Craven. He pulled a box magazine from the dead man's backpack.

'I've got a score to settle.'

He picked up the SAW. He fed the belt into the receiver and locked the magazine in place.

'Hey,' he shouted. 'You hear me, Lupe? Come on out. Let's get this done.'

71

Lupe hurriedly rebuilt the plant room door. She grabbed a couple of panel sections and propped them in the frame. She wedged them in position with an iron battery rack.

She could hear shouts and screams from the hall outside. Craven battling the hybrid as it tried to haul him into an overhead vent.

She coughed. She doubled up, then fell to her knees. She puked water.

'Jesus,' she muttered. She wiped her mouth.

She unzipped a trauma pack. Anti-nausea meds. She popped Zofran tablets from a foil strip and knocked them back.

Bottle of Scopolamine. She loaded a hypodermic and injected into her forearm.

Rush of wellbeing. She breathed easy.

She slung the bag over her shoulder.

A protracted roar of gunfire from the hallway. Assault rifles cycling full-auto.

She hurried to the back of the room. She excavated Ekks. She pushed empty boxes aside and pawed through scattered paper.

Her vision suddenly dimmed. White mist descending like a curtain.

'Oh Christ.'

She held her hand in front of her face. Fingers barely discernable through a cataract haze.

'No. Not that.'

She held the wall for support and waited for her head to stop spinning.

She turned the flashlight and shone it into her eyes. The glow of the two-hundred lumen LED barely visible, like distant headlamps glimpsed through fog.

'Anything but that.'

Prolonged machine gun roar. Someone expending a full belt of 5.56mm. Galloway cut down by the SWAT personnel he used to idolise.

She rubbed her eyes. Her vision began to clear.

'Thank God.'

She blinked. She shook her head.

'Come on. That's it.'

She kicked through mounds of garbage. She bent and picked up the bomb. Still intact. Two patties of ammonium nitrate mashed against a small green oxygen cylinder.

She crouched beside Ekks. She lifted his arm and wedged the explosive beneath his hip. She lashed the bomb in place with duct tape, and checked the detonator was pushed firmly into the clay.

Boot steps outside the door. Chief's voice:

'Come on out. Let's get this done.'

Lupe threw herself prone and covered her ears.

Machine gun scream. The crooked panels blocking the doorway blasted to splinters. The room filled with gun smoke and whirling wood chips. High velocity rounds sparking ironwork and embedding in brick.

Sudden silence.

Lupe sat up. Dust sneeze.

She pinched the time pencil with pliers, set the two-minute countdown running. Cupric chloride eating through the striker wire.

'Say hi from me.'

She ran, grabbed the lip of the conduit and hauled herself inside.

A brilliant beam of a laser sight shafted through thick smoke. The Chief toppled the iron rack and entered the room. He checked aisles, checked corners.

He aimed into the conduit. The laser danced over cracked brickwork. A moment of hesitation, like he wanted to climb into the tunnel and pursue Lupe.

'That's right, bitch,' he shouted. 'Crawl away. Die with the rats.'

Bingham:

'We've got Ekks, sir.'

'Then let's get out of here.'

They lifted Ekks and carried him to the hall. They kicked rubble aside and set him down.

The Chief crouched next to the stretcher.

'Can you hear me? Doctor Ekks? You're safe now. We have a helicopter on the roof. We're going to fly you out of here. We have medical personnel on standby. We'll flush your blood, begin the transfusion the moment we land. We'll do everything in our power to save you.'

Chief turned to Bingham and Byrne.

'Mask up. Let's get him up top. Transfer him to the litter and get that drip running.'

Byrne pulled on his respirator and tightened the temple straps. He gripped the foot of the backboard, ready to lift.

Bingham unhitched the respirator from her belt and raised it to her face. She paused. 'Hold on.'

She knelt beside Ekks. She studied the motionless face behind the visor.

'Something's not right.'

She pulled back his hood and peeled away the respirator. White, immobile flesh. She lifted an eyelid.

'He's dead. Been dead a while.'

'Bitch,' spat Chief. He massaged his temples. 'Utter piece of shit.' He took the hip flask from his pocket and drained it dry.

Bingham loosened the collar of the NBC suit. She exposed the tracheotomy wound. 'They tried to keep him alive. Guess it didn't work.'

'Total waste of time,' said Jefferson. 'The whole trip. We're done. Let's go.'

Bingham got to her feet.

'She said something about a notebook.'

'Pure bullshit,' said the Chief. 'Never existed. Come on. We're out of here.'

'What about the body?'

'He's no good to me dead.'

Last glance at Ekks. Something beneath the dead man's arm. Jefferson lifted the arm with the tip of his boot.

'Oh Christ.'

Patties of explosive lashed to the backboard with duct tape.

Jefferson threw the empty flask aside and dropped to his knees.

He tore at the explosive, tried to rip it free. He pawed the slabs of clay, tried to locate the detonator and twist it from the putty.

'Motherfu—'

72

Lupe helped Sicknote climb the platform steps.

Catastrophic blast damage. Smouldering rubble. The palatial elegance of Fenwick Street reduced to a soot-blackened grotto.

'Sure you don't want to come with me?' asked Lupe. 'I could use the company.'

He shook his head.

'Think I might head to the roof. Take in the view.'

Lupe pulled an assault rifle from beneath bricks. She checked it over. Broken stock. Cracked grip. She tested the slide. Functional.

She heaved a chunk of rubble aside. Bingham, chest crushed, sightless eyes matted with grit. Lupe shook out Bingham's shoulder pack. She pocketed a spare rifle magazine. She blew dust from the generator fuse.

'Let's crank up the power.'

They headed for the plant room.

Sicknote stood in the doorway. He leaned against the frame. He coughed and fought back vomit.

'Getting bad, huh?' said Lupe.

'Yeah. How about you?'

'Pretty rough.'

She squatted beside the generator. She screwed the fuse back in place. She wrenched the starter cable and set the machine running.

She put an arm round Sicknote's shoulders and helped him cross the hall.

Her foot hit something hollow, something metal. A crushed hip flask.

The Chief lay beneath a girder. A barely recognisable mess of offal and NBC fabric.

'Fucker.'

Sicknote pointed to the street level stairwell.

'Over there. Something moved.'

Lupe climbed over bricks.

Twisted limbs knotted with metallic tumours.

Galloway.

A blackened hand clenched at the sound of her approach. Weak, spastic movements.

She kicked bricks aside. Cloke's head split open by a bullet. Spilled brain tissue. Black eyes turned towards Lupe. Weak hiss.

'What does it take to kill you bastards?'

She picked up a heavy lump of concrete. She raised the jagged block over her head.

'Cloke, if you're still in there, I'm sorry. This is the best I can do.'

She dropped the rock and pulped the creature's head.

She turned away.

Sicknote was slumped against the ticket hall wall.

'Hear that?' he said. 'Infected. Out in the alley. The gate is fucked. They'll be heading down here in a minute or two. Don't drag it out. Get going.'

Lupe helped him to the freight elevator. He leaned against the back wall.

They looked down at Donahue.

'What a waste.'

Lupe shone her flashlight upwards through the splintered roof of the elevator. The shaft. Sheer, concrete walls. Cable and counterweights.

'Sure you want to do this?'

'Yeah, why not?' He took the notebook from his pocket. He gave it to Lupe. 'Get this to someone who can make sense of it.'

She tucked the notebook in her coat pocket.

'Are you going to be okay up there?'

Sicknote held up a cyanide capsule.

'I'll be all right.'

Lupe stepped out of the elevator and pulled the gate closed. Rust-shriek. Slam.

'Take it easy, brother.'

'See you around.'

Lupe pressed Up. The elevator began its ascent. Rattle and grind. A last smile from Sicknote as he rode out of view.

The brass clock hand of the floor indicator charted the elevator's ascent.

Lupe gripped the bars and watched the wooden platform rise up the shaft.

Distant rumble. Ground tremor. The elevator swung in the shaft.

Grind of stone on stone. Trickles of dust from the hall roof. Lupe hurried to the platform steps. Last look back.

Flame-seared rubble. Blood and splintered bone. An elegant transit hub, now an annex of hell.

To All Trains

Lupe ran down the platform stairs. Thunder crack. A chunk of masonry detached from the roof and smashed across the steps. Lupe danced round the rubble and continued her descent.

She threw herself into the boat. She flicked open her knife, cut the tether and pushed clear.

Gunshot retort. A fissure zagged across the tunnel roof, bringing down a curtain of stone dust.

She grabbed the oar and began to paddle. The prow of the boat split plates of ice.

She drifted closer to the blocked south tunnel entrance. She hefted the assault rifle. She switched on the barrel light and raised the weapon to her shoulder. Planks lit harsh white. She fired, rocked with the recoil, tried to keep a grip on the bucking weapon. Tungsten penetrator rounds punched holes, blew wood chips and splinters.

Floor six.

Sicknote hauled back the elevator gate. A last glance at Donahue. A vague conviction that she deserved better than to be dumped like garbage. He laid her on the elevator floor, arms folded across her chest.

A thin gold chain coiled on the floor. A crucifix. Belonged to Tombes. She must have held it in a gloved hand as she rode the elevator to meet the Chief.

He laid it on her chest.

He crossed the hall and headed for the stairs.

ROOF
No Unauthorised Access

He gripped the balustrade and hauled himself up the steps. Dawn was breaking. He emerged into cold grey light.

Lupe knelt in the boat and prized splintered planks aside.

Another deep tremor sent ripples shivering across the surface of the water.

She created an aperture wide enough to allow the boat to pass. Hurried oar strokes. She ducked beneath jagged wood as the dinghy entered the south tunnel.

She struck a flare. It burned fierce red.

Ancient brickwork. Crumbling mortar. The tunnel roof tight overhead.

Ribbed tunnel buttress stretching ahead into darkness.

She let the current carry her further from Fenwick Street.

Sicknote's voice:

'*Lupe, can you hear me?*'

She unhooked her radio.

'Yeah, I can hear you.'

'*It's beautiful, Lupe. Truly beautiful. The sun is rising. It's topped the horizon. I can see the whole city. Christ, if only you could be here, Lupe. If only you could share this . . .*'

The last reception bar flickered out. The LCD screen flashed:

NO COMMS

Lupe shut off the radio and tossed it into the water.

She picked up the oar and began to row.

The boat was carried on the current, swept deeper into the flooded tunnel system.

Flare light dwindled to a blood-red pinprick as she rode the black tide to the end of the line.

73

Sicknote walked across the wide, flat roof. Boots crunched virgin snow.

Rusted chimney pipes. The remains of a water tower: cedar planks and galvanised steel hoops.

The beige JetRanger parked at the centre of the roof. Empty seats. Headphone coil dangled from an inert switch panel.

He ducked beneath the tail boom and walked to the edge of the parapet.

'Can you hear me, Lupe? I can see the whole city.'

He looked out over broken towers, vertiginous cliffs and canyons. No birds. No traffic. No car horns. Nothing moved. Empty streets, empty avenues. Titanic desolation.

Ruins that would, in time, be reclaimed by vegetation. A slow and beautiful decay. In a couple of thousand years, Manhattan would be woodland one more. Rubble buried beneath forests of hickory, hemlock and pine. Central Park would return to salt marsh. The street grid would be reduced to soft delineations in the forest floor, blurred by leaf mulch and bracken.

Perhaps a handful of landmarks would endure. The marble lions of the Public Library might stand in the humid twilight of an arboreal clearing, draped in vine like a lost Inca temple. A home for salamanders and toads.

The city wiped away. A restored Eden. It would be as if New York never happened, as if the Dutch sailors never came.

A rolling crash like thunder. A partial tower collapse in the far distance. An apartment building on the upper west side. It crumbled like an ice floe. A wave of dust washed down adjoining streets.

Built by giants, smashed by gods.

'*This is it, Lupe. Humanity is finished. Nothing left of us but old analogue TV transmissions radiating out into the cosmos.*

No sound, Lupe. Not even wind. I wish you could hear it. I wish you could be up here right now. Absolute stillness. Absolute quiet. A city of the dead.

'*Can you hear me, Lupe? Are you there?*

'*The silence. My God, the silence.*'

*Five years have passed. Five years in which the plague
has spread across the world leaving only tiny enclaves
of survivors . . .*

OUTPOST

*They took the job to escape the world.
They didn't expect the world to end.*

Kasker Rampart: a derelict refinery platform moored in the
Arctic Ocean. A skeleton crew of fifteen fight boredom and
despair as they wait for a relief ship to take them home.

But the world beyond their frozen wasteland has gone to hell.
Cities lie ravaged by a global pandemic. One by one TV channels
die, replaced by silent wavebands.

The Rampart crew are marooned. They must survive the long
Arctic winter, then make their way home alone. They battle
starvation and hypothermia, unaware that the deadly contagion
that has devastated the world is heading their way . . .

HODDER &
STOUGHTON

Want more?

If you enjoyed this and would like to find out about
similar books we publish, we'd love you to join
our online Sci-Fi, Fantasy and Horror community
Hodderscape.

Follow us on
Twitter @Hodderscape

and visit our Facebook page at
facebook.com/hodderscape

You'll find news, competitions, video content
and general musings, so feel free to comment,
contribute or just keep an eye on what we are
up to. See you there!

HODDERSCAPE

HODDER